DANDELION MEADOWS

DANDELION MEADOWS

BOOK ONE

JENNIFER BECKSTRAND

Six Roses Publishing

Cover design by Hannah Linder Designs

Published by Six Roses Publishing

www.jenniferbeckstrand.com

First Edition: February 2022

Printed in the United States of America

ISBN: 979-8486336805

ASIN: B09HH6MVWC

CHAPTER
ONE

E mma squinted in the early morning light and for a second, couldn't remember where she was. She raised her head just enough to get a good look at her surroundings. They were pink.

She sighed and fell back onto her pillow, which sort of swallowed her head. No surprise since the pillow was upwards of forty years old. She'd used it as a teenager whenever she'd stayed here at Uncle Harvey and Aunt Gwen's house. This pillow probably consisted mostly of dust mites, but Aunt Gwen had never been able to bring herself to throw anything away.

Emma pulled the covers over her head and breathed in the oddly comforting musty smell of old sheets. How long had it been since Uncle Harvey had washed them? It had been six years since Emma last stayed in this room. When Emma left, Uncle Harvey had no doubt laundered the sheets, put them back on the bed, and closed up the room. The sheets had likely been untouched on that bed for the better half of a decade.

Emma cringed. They definitely smelled like old people, but

everything in this house smelled like old people, so it was only to be expected.

She sat up, shivered slightly, and pulled the covers around her chin. Only a crazy person would voluntarily come to Idaho in January when the wind was so cold it made your teeth freeze if you smiled too wide. But it couldn't be helped. Emma had nowhere else to go. Dandelion Meadows, Idaho was her second-to-last hope.

Her last hope was moving in with her parents, but there was no way in a million years she was going to stay in a retirement community in Gilbert, Arizona, even if they did have free non-alcoholic beverages and Sit-and-Be-Fit classes every weekday.

Emma hugged her knees to her chin and gazed around her old room. It looked like it hadn't been touched since she'd last been here. The blush-pink chest of drawers was plastered with pictures of Zac Efron, Orlando Bloom, and the Jonas Brothers, stuck there for all eternity courtesy of Aunt Gwen and a bottle of Mod Podge. The High School Musical curtains matched the High School Musical quilt Aunt Gwen had helped Emma tie when she was thirteen years old. Emma had long since grown out of the décor, but it warmed her heart that Aunt Gwen had been willing to sew High School Musical curtains just to make her niece feel at home.

Emma couldn't stay in bed all day, but the thought of getting out from under her delectably warm—though smelly—covers gave her goose pimples.

Might as well bite the bullet. She'd have to get up sometime.

Emma threw off the covers and ran for her suitcase sitting on the floor against the wall. Shivering violently, she pulled out a ratty pair of sweatpants and an old fleece sweatshirt that her mom used to wear at curling matches. It was about three sizes too big but nice and warm, and Emma wasn't in a position to be picky. She pressed her lips together hopefully and opened the sliding closet door that doubled as a full-length mirror. She squealed in delight. Her old bunny slippers were still in their spot on the shoe rack. Hallelujah! Frostbite would not claim her toes today.

Emma made her High School Musical bed then went to the bathroom, brushed her teeth, and quickly fashioned her hair into a messy bun. There were about five thousand things she needed to do today, not the least of which was to call her parents and try to explain why she was in Dandelion Meadows.

They weren't going to be happy. They'd want to catch the first plane out of Gilbert to Idaho. She'd have to put her foot down about any thought of rescuing their daughter. Emma was twenty-seven years old. If she couldn't solve her own problems, she didn't deserve that expensive MBA she'd just earned. Besides, Mom and Dad were frantically preparing for a curling bonspiel coming up next weekend. Emma wouldn't hear of their missing it just to come to Idaho.

Emma grabbed her phone from the nightstand and padded quickly down the stairs. She didn't get any service upstairs, but on the main floor, she had five bars. Go figure. Hopefully, this wasn't going to be a long-term stay, but if it was, she might have to move downstairs to the master bedroom for the sake of her phone.

As soon as she stepped off the last stair, her phone dinged. Seventeen times. Holy cow! She should have gotten up an hour ago. Who knew what updates from work she had missed? Maybe they wanted her to come back. Maybe they'd decided to fire her. Maybe the SEC, the FBI, and the FTC were all searching for her. *Emma Dustin, wanted fugitive, holes up in a run-down shack in Dandelion Meadows, Idaho.* It would make a great headline but a pretty boring read. The only organization that might be looking for Emma was the AARP, but only because they wanted to recruit her parents.

An exceptionally loud creak came from the family room, and then it sounded like a door closing. This house creaked like an old man's knees and it was as drafty as a tent, but Emma had never known doors to spontaneously close themselves.

Suddenly, a tall man wearing flannel, denim, and a sinister baseball cap came around the corner with a tape measure and a notebook in his hand. He stopped short at the sight of her, and surprise popped all over his face. Emma's heart flipped over, and she lost the ability to breathe. Forgetting that the front door was right behind her and her cellphone was still glued to her hand, Emma lunged at the side table in the front hall and grabbed a handful of thimbles from Aunt Gwen's thimble collection. "Get out!" she yelled, screaming at the top of her lungs and launching thimbles in the robber's direction. "Get out of my house!"

If you can't run away, scare your attacker out of his wits. Make yourself big and loud and menacing. That's what her self-defense coach had taught her. Or maybe that was her Wilderness Ranger leader. She should have paid more attention during the bear lesson. Or maybe she should have gone to Wilderness Ranger meetings more than once in her whole life.

"Ow!" the intruder said, when one of Aunt Gwen's thimbles hit him squarely in the chest. "Stop that!" He dropped the tape measure and held his notebook in front of his face like a shield.

Emma threw all the thimbles she had. Most of them pinged off his notebook, but one of them hit the robber in the thigh, and another ricocheted off the brim of his hat. She'd always had a good aim. He took off his hat and quickly examined it. What kind of robber was that attached to the Denver Broncos?

When she ran out of ammunition, she snatched more thimbles from the table. Aunt Gwen had an extensive collection. "I said get out!" Emma launched another thimble.

The intruder raised his hat like a surrender flag, lowered his notebook, and took two steps back. "Hold on. I'm not going to hurt you."

It was a tactical error on his part. She wound up, threw hard, and beaned him in the head just above his hairline. He gasped in surprise as a trickle of blood crawled down his forehead.

"Emma!" he yelled. "Will you stop for a second?"

He knew her name?

Of course he did. In a town the size of Dandelion Meadows, everybody knew everybody. Even the robbers.

She was just about to let another thimble fly, when the robber grimaced and revealed a very attractive dimple on his cheek.

Oh, crap.

The robber *had* looked kind of familiar. Now that she got a good look, he was very familiar, even though she hadn't seen him for like ten years. Matt Matthews didn't seem like the kind of guy to choose a life of crime. She raised her fist menacingly, as if she was going to launch another thimble any second. "Matt Matthews, I don't know what you think you're doing here, but get out before I give you a matching scar on the other side of your head."

Matt's mouth fell open. "You gave me a scar?"

"I'm calling the police," Emma hissed.

"You could have put out my eye!"

Emma showed Matt the thimbles in her fist. "If you don't

5

want to spend the night in jail, you'd better get out of my house."

Glaring at Emma, Matt set his wounded hat on the side table, pulled a handkerchief out of his pocket, and wiped the blood from his forehead. "It's my house, and *I'm* calling the police."

Emma was faster with her phone because Matt had to fish his out of his back pocket, but then she hesitated because she wasn't sure what number to call. If she dialed 911, would she get connected to a dispatcher in Dallas? Did Dandelion Meadows even have 911 service? If they didn't, she was toast, because she couldn't remember the number for the local sheriff's office.

She took a chance and dialed 911 while she clutched the remainder of the thimbles in her hand and scowled at Matt, just so he wouldn't get any ideas while she was on the phone.

"911. What is your emergency?"

"Are you in Dallas?" Emma said.

"I beg your pardon?"

"My phone has a Dallas area code. Did this call connect to someone in Dallas?"

"No, ma'am. Your call's location is connected to the nearest cell tower. What is your emergency?"

"Oh, that's good to know," Emma said. "I've always wondered how that 911 thing works. I'm glad I'm not talking to someone in Dallas."

Matt glanced up from his phone and smirked. Emma stood up straighter and smoothed a piece of hair from of her face. It had been a legitimate question, and she wasn't going to let Matt the Robber make her feel stupid about it.

"Ma'am, do you have an emergency?" How dare the dispatcher get testy? Weren't they supposed to be trained on how to be patient with distraught callers?

"Yes. Yes. I do have an emergency." She gave Matt a smirk of her own. He wouldn't be so cocky when the sheriff carted him off to jail. "A man broke into my house, and he won't leave."

"He's still there?"

"Yes. I told you, he won't leave. Will you have someone come and arrest him?"

Matt's scowl got deeper as he simultaneously listened to her conversation and talked quietly to someone on his phone. Maybe he'd skipped the police and dialed his attorney. Good. He was going to need one.

"Do you feel that you're in danger, ma'am?" the dispatcher said.

Emma narrowed her eyes and gave Matt the once-over. The blood oozing from his forehead made him look a little intimidating, but he didn't have that crazed look in his eye like those criminals on TV. In fact, his eyes were brown and broody, like a misunderstood hero in a Jane Austen novel. *And* he was wearing a blue flannel shirt. Nothing said "nice boring guy" like flannel.

"Ma'am?" The dispatcher really needed that patience training.

Emma took a step backward. "I'm not in danger, and I still have a whole handful of thimbles if I need them."

"What is your location?" Emma was sort of disappointed the dispatcher didn't want to know about the thimbles. She had successfully fended off an attack with Aunt Gwen's thimble collection. It would make a great story for a self-defense class.

Matt finished his phone call, put his phone back in his pocket, and folded his arms across his wide chest that ten yards of flannel couldn't hide. "Need some help?"

Emma tried for a glare harsh enough to peel the paint off

Uncle Harvey's picket fence, but then she remembered that most of the paint had peeled off the fence already. What right did Matt Matthews have to be so smug? He was wearing flannel, for goodness sake.

"Ma'am? Can you hear me? What is the address?"

An address? "Umm. I'm not sure."

"Can you describe your surroundings? Do you know what city you're in? Do you see any street signs?"

Emma would have looked out the front window, but she didn't want to turn her back on Matt, and the only thing across the road from Uncle Harvey's house was Old Man Kyle's pasture. "I never really knew the address," she said. "All I had to do was tell my ride to drop me off at Harvey Dustin's place and everybody knew where it was. I sent his letters to a P.O. box."

"Ma'am, I want to help you, but I can't unless you help me."

"I know it's on the west side of Dandelion Meadows. It's Harvey Dustin's old house. There used to be a dirt road, but it's been paved sometime in the last six years, and it's blue."

"The road?"

"No, the house." This dispatcher definitely needed more training. Who ever heard of a blue road? "If you're at the Pioneer Hair Museum, you turn north on that main street then drive about three miles, turn left at the big red barn, and go for another two miles or so. You can't miss the blue house."

Matt cocked an eyebrow. "Would you like me to talk to her?"

Emma turned slightly away and pretended not to hear him. Some people just couldn't take the hint that this was a private conversation. She jumped when there was a loud knock on the door behind her. After giving Matt a dark look, she opened the door to a very welcome sight.

Sheriff Hobson stood on her porch with a much younger deputy in tow. The sheriff, who everybody called Hob, had to be at least seventy years old, and he smiled at Emma as if he'd come to pay a social call.

"Ma'am?" The dispatcher was getting testy again.

Emma couldn't be annoyed with the dispatcher. She'd gotten the police here a lot faster than Emma would have expected. "Thank you so much," Emma said into the phone. "That was really quick. Even with my bad directions."

"The police are there?"

"Yes," Emma said. "Thank you so much." She hung up the phone, swung the door wide open, and did her best to point at Matt with her hand full of thimbles. "Come in, sheriff, and arrest this man."

Sheriff Hob's smile got even wider. "Well, bless my soul. If it isn't Emma Dustin."

Emma wasn't really in the mood for pleasantries, but Hob had been one of Uncle Harvey's closest friends. She couldn't just brush off one of the people who had spoken at Uncle Harvey's funeral. "It's good to see you again, Hob."

"You're all grown up," Hob said, stepping into the house. He gave Emma a warm handshake, the two-handed kind that told people you really cared about them. "I'm really sorry about your uncle. He was my favorite fishing buddy."

"Thank you," Emma said. "I miss him terribly."

Hob caught sight of Matt and reached out to shake his hand too. Emma thought it was a little inappropriate to be shaking the hand of an intruder, but maybe Hob was trying to catch Matt off guard so he could cuff him. "Matt Matthews. Making any money on that mine yet?"

Matt grinned. "Enough to pay the bills." He glanced at Emma and back to Hob. "Thanks for coming."

Warmth traveled up Emma's face and clear to the roots of

her hair. It wasn't her 911 call that had summoned the sheriff. It was Matt. Being the outlaw he was, he probably had Hob's number memorized.

Oh, how she hated to be outmaneuvered by someone who wore flannel.

10

CHAPTER

TWO

M att pressed the handkerchief to his head while he paced around Harvey Dustin's family room. If Emma Dustin had given him a scar, he'd never forgive her. He'd probably never forgive her anyway, but a scar would definitely put her near the top of his bad list.

"He appeared from out of nowhere and scared the living daylights out of me," Emma was saying. "A strange man in the house is not something anyone wants to see at eight in the morning. I'm glad I had at least brushed my teeth."

Emma sat on the couch recounting her side of the story to Dallin Hobson, the sheriff's deputy and grandson. Dallin had recently gotten the deputy job, and he looked like he was about twelve years old, with a chubby baby face that had probably never seen the shadow of a whisker. Dallin was writing notes so fast it looked like his pen would explode at any minute. "And then you started throwing thimbles at him?"

Emma nodded. "I thought he was going to attack me. They're my aunt Gwen's thimbles. She's got one from every state in the Union plus Canada and Mexico, so I had plenty to throw." It was plain for everybody to see she had plenty. Thimbles were scattered all over the floor of the family room and into the hall.

"She could have taken my eye out," Matt interjected, just so no one would forget who the victim was here.

"It was either you or me," Emma said, almost as if she'd enjoyed drawing blood.

Hob poked at a thimble on the floor with his cane. "Hawaii. I've never been, but I hear it's beautiful."

Emma looked at Hob. "Oh, it is. The air smells like flowers and ocean. I took a helicopter ride and almost threw up."

"She shouldn't have thrown thimbles at me," Matt said. "I own this house. She's the trespasser."

Emma rolled her eyes. "Oh, right. Like my uncle left the house to you instead of me. Like anybody's going to believe that."

Matt pressed too hard on his head and winced. "Believe it, sister."

Hob pointed to a thimble near Matt's feet. "Can you hand me that? I can't bend over that far."

Matt handed the thimble to Hob.

"Will you look at that," Hob said.

Emma tore her attention away from Deputy Dallin and looked at the thimble in Hob's hand. "Did you find blood?"

"This thimble has a Canadian Mountie on it."

"I love the Canadian Mounties," Emma said, as if she knew each one of them personally. She smiled at Hob. "The cane is new. How did you hurt your leg?"

Hob tapped his cane against his foot. "In the line of duty."

Emma's eyes grew wide. "Did you get shot?"

"Got kicked by a runaway cow. My Shoshone friend in Nampa carved me this cane."

Matt pressed his lips together to keep from laughing—or growling. He wasn't sure what emotion was closer to the surface. This whole mess could be worked out in five minutes if they'd just pay attention to the facts and quit studying Aunt Gwen's thimble collection.

Speed and efficiency had never been Hob's strong points. For that matter, Hob wasn't all that good at police work either. He had been the county sheriff for nearly fifty years, hired when he was impossibly young because nobody else wanted the job.

But really, Hob was the perfect sheriff for a place like Dandelion Meadows. The town was dry so there weren't a lot of drunk-and-disorderly calls, and the worst thing mischievous teenagers did was toilet paper people's houses. The hottest disputes were over water rights, but Hob was friends with just about everybody, and he could usually talk people out of being mad at each other. Hob was more the town therapist than the sheriff, but it could sure be frustrating when someone needed an actual policeman.

And he would be completely useless in a high-speed foot chase.

Why hadn't he retired?

"Can I tell my side of the story now?" Matt said. He had better things to do than listen to Hob's tale of the runaway cow and the broken leg. He'd heard it four times already.

Deputy Dallin gazed at Emma as if she was the key witness in an FBI manhunt. "Do you have anything else you want to say, Emma?"

Matt resisted the urge to roll his eyes. Deputy Dallin was more interested in the witness than the evidence—not that Matt could blame him for being distracted. Emma was a looker. Matt had always thought so. But during the summers when Emma had come to visit her aunt and uncle, she had earned a reputation for being impossibly high maintenance, and Matt had never been in the mood to coddle a princess.

Well...yeah...it had been a decade since he'd seen her, and she looked anything but high maintenance today. Her dirty blond hair was loosely piled on top of her head in a messy bun, but she'd thrown enough thimbles to knock at least half of her hair loose. It sort of spilled down her back and around her face like a waterfall, and individual strands danced in the air whenever she turned her head one way or the other. Her oversized sweatshirt was dark gray, making her eyes seem extra blue, and those bunny slippers lent her a certain vulnerability Matt would be wise to ignore.

The last thing he needed was a vulnerable female, and he'd be skinned before he felt sorry for her. Her uncle had been a crook, and Matt deserved this house.

Emma folded her arms. "Don't you think you have enough evidence to arrest him now?"

"Arrest me? You think they're going to arrest me just because you say so?" Who did she think she was?

"Now, now, Matt," Hob said. "No need to get your knickers in a knot. Nobody's going to get arrested."

It was Emma's turn to be indignant. "But he broke into my house."

Matt shoved his hand in his pocket, pulled out a key, and dangled it in Emma's direction. "I have a key."

She squeaked in surprise. "Where did you get that?" She stood up, strode toward Matt, and tried to snatch the key from his hand. "Sheriff, arrest this man for stealing my uncle's key."

"Now, now, Emma. Nobody is going to get arrested."

Emma tried again to steal Matt's key, but he held it high over his head where she couldn't reach. He had never been so glad to be tall. "Where did you get that key?" she said.

14

"Harvey's attorney gave it to me. Right after he called me and told me Harvey had left me the house."

"That's a lie," Emma said. "Uncle Harvey left the house to me."

"Well, what do you know? Look at this." Hob picked up a frame from the bookshelf and turned it so everyone could see. "This is Harvey and me at Lake Lowell. Look at the size of that fish. Emma, could I take this and make a copy? Nobody believes what a big fish it was."

"Of course you can," Emma said. "But will you make Matt leave first? I'd like to take a shower and clean up the thimbles, and he's a lying snake." She said that last part with a look that could have curdled milk.

Matt wasn't about to let her get away with it. He gave her a dirty look of his own. Unfortunately she didn't flinch. "I am not a lying snake. Harvey left me the house. He owes it to me."

"Uncle Harvey left me the house. I'm his only niece."

Matt had just about had it with Emma Dustin and her delusions. "I don't know what Harvey promised you or what you think you're entitled to, but Harvey left the house to me in his will. You can even ask his lawyer."

Emma straightened to her full height of five feet and a couple of paltry inches. "I will." She looked at her phone, which seemed to be attached to her hand. "Hob, when Johnny confirms that this is indeed my house, will you please arrest Matt for trespassing?"

Dallin's gaze flicked to Matt. "I suppose we could hold him overnight until you get a restraining order."

Hob shook his head while intently studying his photograph. "We're not going to arrest Matt, and there ain't going to be no restraining orders. I've spent forty years trying to stay on Vicki Matthews' good side, and she'd never forgive me if I arrested her son. It's a misunderstanding. That's all." Hob pulled a bulging photo album from the shelf and opened it to the first page. "Would you look at this! More fishing pictures."

Matt ground his teeth together until one of them was sure to crack. "Are you going to call Johnny or not, Emma?"

Emma was looking at her phone as if a hundred hungry children had just appeared on her news feed. She jumped slightly when Matt said her name. "I was looking up the number. Don't get huffy." She scrolled through a few screens. "Does he have a website?"

"Johnny doesn't believe in the internet," Hob said. "You'll have to look it up the old fashion way." He tucked the photo album under his arm, went to one of the kitchen drawers, and pulled out a dog-eared phonebook.

They hadn't quite made it into the twenty-first century here in Dandelion Meadows. Not that Matt minded. He preferred looking at a sunset to his cell phone any day.

"You don't have to do that," Matt said, but nobody paid him any heed. What else was new?

Hob set the phonebook on the counter and leafed through it. "I can't remember if it's under his barbershop or legal services."

Emma furrowed her brow. "How does he survive without a website?"

Hob shrugged. "We used to do it all the time. We'd go visit people or order things from the Sears Catalog."

Matt had nearly reached his breaking point, which had happened maybe only three other times in his life. He usually didn't have much of a temper. "You don't have to look Hob. I've got his number in my contacts."

"Why didn't you say so?" Deputy Dallin jotted something in his notebook, as if adding, "withholding phone information" to Matt's rap sheet.

Matt chose Johnny Cleaver's phone number from his list.

The phone rang only once, like it usually did, as if Johnny sat by his phone all day just waiting for someone to call. "Cleaver's barbershop, legal help, and we'll do your taxes," Johnny said.

Matt watched Emma's face. She seemed confident enough, but she wasn't going to like what Johnny had to say. "Johnny, this is Matt Matthews."

"Howdy-ho, Matt. Do you need a haircut? I raised my prices to a hundred dollars an hour, but that price comes with all the legal advice you want."

"No thanks, Johnny. I don't need a haircut. I wanted to talk to you about Harvey Dustin's will. I just want to confirm that he left me the house."

Emma was suddenly at Matt's side. "No leading the witness. Put him on speaker."

Matt groaned as if he was put out about it, but Emma was right. She needed to hear this from Johnny's mouth. It was the only way she'd believe it. "Johnny," Matt said, "I'm going to put you on speaker. Dallin and Dale Hobson are here. And Emma Dustin."

Matt pushed the speaker button just in time for everyone to hear Johnny's elation over the phone. "Oh, goodness gracious, Emma Dustin. How long has it been? I mean, I saw you at the funeral, but I can't remember how many years before that. Maybe at Gwen's funeral?"

A weak smile formed on Emma's lips, as if she was forcing herself to be cheerful about it. Gwen had been a sweet lady. Everyone was sad when she died. "It's good to hear your voice, Mr. Cleaver."

"Call me Johnny. When anyone over eighteen calls me Mr. Cleaver, I feel old."

Johnny was as much of an institution in Dandelion Meadows as Hob, and Johnny was even older. Near eighty. Nobody had the heart to tell him he was already old.

"You're right, Johnny. You're still a spring chicken," Emma said, glancing at Matt and giving him a full-blown, out-of-this-world smile. He almost dropped the phone. Emma Dustin had the most beautiful smile he'd ever laid eyes on. He wasn't in the mood, but when someone smiled at you like that, you just had to smile back. He smiled so wide, it made his forehead hurt, and just in time, he remembered she'd given him a scar and was trying to steal his house. He'd be an idiot to let that smile get to him. It was fake anyway—at least three thousand dollars' worth of orthodontia, and she probably had her teeth professionally whitened every six months. High maintenance.

Matt hated high maintenance.

She'd probably forgotten that she'd accused him of breaking and entering and had tried to get him arrested. She wouldn't have smiled otherwise.

Matt cleared his throat. "Johnny, we have a little misunderstanding about Harvey Dustin's house, and we thought you might clear it up for us."

"Matt broke in this morning," Emma said. "I was forced to defend myself by throwing thimbles."

High maintenance. Snobby. City girl. "It's my house. I didn't break in."

"Uncle Harvey left the house to me," Emma said. "I've got a letter to prove it."

Matt took four steps away from Emma so he could have the conversation to himself. "So, Johnny, will you please tell Emma what you told me about the house?"

They heard some shuffling of papers on the other end. "Well, about a week ago, I got this envelope from Salt Lake." More shuffling. "Here it is. It's Harvey's last will and testament, handwritten three weeks before he died. It looks like Harvey's handwriting, but I can't be sure. It's kind of shaky. It says he leaves his house and property to Matt Matthews, and there was a key to the house inside, though he shouldn't have sent that through the mail. Don't ever send your valuables through the mail unless you insure them."

Matt eyed Emma pointedly. "So the house is mine."

"Looks that way," Johnny said. "It's notarized and witnessed by a doctor and two nurses at the Huntsman Cancer Institute."

"I don't believe you," Emma said, stalking toward Matt and grabbing his phone before he had a chance to move it out of her reach.

Johnny was shuffling papers again. "I'm afraid it's true, Emma. Legally the house is Matt's."

Emma lost all the color in her face. She handed Matt his phone back without a fight and sank to the nearest object there was to sit on, which was Harvey's rickety coffee table. "But he told me he was leaving the house to me. I have nowhere else to go."

Her reaction sent a twinge of guilt zinging up Matt's spine. He didn't like to see a girl in trouble. "I'm sorry, Emma," he said, doing his best not to feel sorry at all. Emma had no claim on his pity. He needed the money from this house, and Harvey owed it to him.

She stared blankly at the bookshelf. "But I have High School Musical curtains and a bedspread upstairs."

"You can take those with you on your way out," Matt said, not feeling as triumphant as he wanted to. He resisted the urge to growl. Darn it. He had a soft spot for damsels in distress. He liked it better when she was throwing thimbles at him.

"And Orlando Bloom."

Matt wanted her gone. He wasn't going to take the time to ask her to explain Orlando Bloom. "Take him with you too."

"He's attached to the dresser." Emma pressed her lips together, obviously trying very hard not to cry.

"Goodness gracious, Matt," Johnny said. "Hold on a minute."

"Is there a problem?"

"Well, I suppose there is. There's another envelope in Harvey's file I haven't seen before. Unopened. Marian does all the filing and sometimes she forgets to tell me." They could hear Johnny opening the mystery envelope. "Goodness gracious."

Matt's patience finally ran out. "What is it, Johnny?"

"No need to snap at me, young man. I can hear just fine. You're not going to believe this, but I think this is another will from Harvey. This one is typed and it looks like a lawyer in Salt Lake City did it."

Emma came back to life. "What does it say?"

There was a pause on the other end. "I know I'm not flashy, but for Harvey go to some fancy lawyer in Salt Lake City really hurts. It really does. I thought we were better friends than that."

"Maybe he was too sick to make the trip to Dandelion Meadows."

Despite his growing agitation, Matt gave Emma a quick, appreciative nod. It was good of her to try to make Johnny feel better.

"What does it say?" she asked.

"It's dated almost a month before Matt's will, and it leaves the house and property and all worldly possessions to Emma."

Emma made Matt jump when she let out the loudest war whoop Matt had ever heard. She flew into Hob's arms and gave him a big hug. "I knew Uncle Harvey wouldn't forget me. We were very close. I loved him like a father."

Matt frowned as Dallin sidled close to Emma and Hob, inserting himself into a group hug that he hadn't been invited to.

"Could everybody be quiet for a minute?" Matt said, raising his voice so he could be heard over Emma's cries of joy and Hob's congratulations. "This doesn't mean the house is yours. There are two wills. Which one is real, Johnny?"

Hob tapped his cane on the ground. "Howard Hughes had dozens of wills." He drew his brows together. "I hate to tell you this, Emma, but it's usually the most recent will that's the right one."

"Ha!" Matt said. "The house is mine." He immediately regretted it. It was stupid to gloat before all his eggs hatched.

Johnny spoke slowly, as if thinking things over very seriously. "It's true that Matt's will is the most recent, but it's also handwritten, so I'm not sure if a judge would say it's official. Emma's will is older, but it was drawn up by a real lawyer, even if he made a mess of it. Who ever heard of using Comic Sans font on a legal document? You'll need to get a judge to sort this all out."

Matt's heart sank as he pictured all the house money disappearing to pay legal fees.

Emma also deflated like a balloon. "Will I have to hire a lawyer?"

"You should," Johnny said. "I suppose you'll want to hire one of those snotty city lawyers from Boise."

She practically ran to Matt's side and pulled his hand so the phone was close to her mouth. "Will you represent me, Johnny?"

Matt narrowed his eyes. Emma was clever, that was for sure. Johnny was the only attorney in town, and his fees were legendarily cheap. Matt would have to find a lawyer in Boise and pay five hundred dollars an hour for something that should have been settled already.

Matt could practically hear the gratification oozing from Johnny's mouth. "Why of course I'll be your lawyer. But don't say another word. We don't want Matt to know our legal strategy. And don't do anything to hurt your case. Don't try to talk Matt into anything. And for goodness sake, no throwing thimbles. Judges do not like flying objects."

Emma squinted in Matt's direction, as if deciding whether thimble throwing or Harvey's house was more important to her. "I reserve the right to throw things at Matt if he deserves it."

Matt glared in Emma's direction. "If you put out an eye, don't think I won't sue."

"I could get good money for you if she puts out your eye," Johnny said.

Emma got that indignant look on her face and leaned into Matt's phone. "Hey, I thought you were my lawyer."

"That's an entirely different case. I can do Matt's case after I settle yours."

Matt was going to turn into a bear with all the growling he was doing—even though most of it was under his breath. How had it come to this? Matt was the good guy. Why did he have to hire a lawyer? Harvey had stolen his money. If he were still alive, Harvey would be the one who needed a lawyer just to keep him out of jail.

Maybe Matt didn't need a lawyer. Maybe he just needed to call his brother.

A bell tinkled softly on the other end of the phone. "I have to go. Al's here for his haircut. Come by my office this morning, Emma, and we'll talk over your case. Matt, can you still come on Saturday to help us move Cathy's stuff out of the shed?"

Matt shrugged. Weeks ago he'd promised Johnny and Marian he'd help their daughter move. He couldn't go back on his word just because Johnny Cleaver was now Emma's lawyer. Stuff like this happened in a small town all the time. If you held grudges or collected enemies, you wouldn't have many friends. "I'll be there. Eight a.m. sharp."

"Okay. Good luck with the case."

Once again, Emma's jaw dropped. "Hey, Johnny. Don't wish our enemy good luck."

Matt could hear the wide smile in Johnny's voice. "With me as your lawyer, he's gonna need it."

CHAPTER

THREE

Matt hung up the phone and shoved it into his back pocket. Emma folded her arms across her chest, still with her phone tightly clutched in her hand. They stared at each other for a full minute. Matt tried to get Emma to blink first. Emma was like a fence post with eyes.

Except, her shape could in no way be compared to a fence post, unless there was such a thing as a curvy and attractive fence post with blue eyes and a messy bun on the top of her head.

"Well, then," Hob said, poking another thimble with his cane. "I guess that settles that. Dallin and I are headed to the brunch at the museum. Do either of you want to come?"

Emma was righteously indignant. "But...but...you said you'd throw Matt out of my house."

Hob frowned. "I did? I don't remember that."

Matt shot daggers at Emma with his eyes. "You never said it, Hob. But someone needs to go, and since my will is the real will, Emma should leave."

Emma gasped. "My will is the real will, and you have no

right to be here." Emma plopped herself down on the couch as if she were claiming her territory. "I'm not leaving,"

"I'm not leaving either," Matt said, even though he needed to get to work.

Hob handed the photo album and the fish picture to Dallin. "Well, kids, I'm sure you can work this out between yourselves. We don't want to miss brunch. It's waffle day."

He hobbled to the door, and Dallin followed, casting apologetic looks over his shoulder at Emma.

Don't get your hopes up, Dallin. No offense, but Emma is too hot for you.

Okay, it was rude to even think such a thought. Dallin probably had six or seven girls interested in him. Emma just didn't seem like she'd be one of them. Emma was classy—elegant almost. Beautiful and super smart. She didn't even look twice at small town guys.

Matt wiped his hand across his mouth. Why should that thought depress him? He may be a small town boy, but he had a Masters in Geology and an award for being top of his class. A lot of girls thought he was a catch, even if he was wearing a plaid flannel shirt with a big oil stain on the sleeve.

Okay. Never mind. He and Dallin had more in common than Matt wanted to admit. Neither of them was good enough for Emma Dustin—the girl with the thrift-store sweatshirt and the million-dollar smile.

Besides, Matt wasn't the least bit interested in a girl like Emma. Let her find some hedge fund manager in New York City to keep her company.

The front door closed, and the silence between them grew thick.

Emma fingered her phone as if she really wanted to look at it but was reluctant to lose sight of the intruder in her house. "I'm not leaving."

Matt glanced at the clock on the kitchen stove. He couldn't stay much longer. He was meeting with one of the engineers in half an hour. She might change the locks before he got back. But maybe she didn't know that the lock on the window in the laundry room was broken, and it was big enough for him to crawl through. And she wasn't the only one who could change the locks. It wasn't likely things would get out of control before he got back tonight.

"I have to go to work," he said.

"I thought stealing houses was your job."

"That's just a hobby."

She cocked an eyebrow as a smile crept onto her lips. "I guess you need to be going."

"I'll be back," he said. He hoped it sounded like a promise *and* a threat.

The million-dollar smile got wider. "I'm sure you will."

He could practically see the wheels turning in her head. She was going to change the locks. Well, then. He'd let her do it and then crawl through the laundry room window. He wasn't going to let her win, because revenge on Harvey Dustin and his niece was an even better reason to fight for the house.

He picked up his notebook, put on his hat, and scooped his tape measure off the floor where he'd dropped it almost an hour ago. It had made a dent in the wood floor that would have to be fixed before he sold the house. "Goodbye, Emma. I'll be back around seven. Don't wait dinner on me."

"Ha, ha," she said.

"And tell Orlando Bloom I said hi. He was great in *Black Hawk Down*."

Emma snapped her head around to look at him, and what was left of her messy bun disintegrated. Her loose hair fell around her shoulders, and Matt momentarily lost his concentration. He wasn't fond of high-maintenance girls, but he sure had a thing for long hair. "Have a nice life, Matt. I'd like to say that Zac Efron and the Jonas Brothers will be disappointed they didn't meet you, but it would be a lie."

Matt wrenched his gaze from Emma's hair and turned his back on her. There was a crunch under his boot as he headed for the front door. Another thimble had given its life. He didn't even feel bad about it.

Matt stormed down the front steps. There had to be a way to get Emma out of his house without tying the thing up in court for years. First he'd call Levi, then he'd call Mom. Mom knew more about Dandelion Meadows than anybody, and Mom was a fighter. She would do just about anything for her boys, as long as it was honest and ethical and didn't cost too much money.

Matt jumped into his truck, slammed the door, and dialed Levi.

Eight rings later, Levi picked up. "Dude, it's like six in the morning."

"It's eight-thirty. Usually you've run about eight miles by now."

"It's 7:30 California time, and I don't have class until ten. I need my sleep, dude."

Matt loved Levi, but he could sure be spacey sometimes. "If you don't want people to call you, turn off your phone before you go to bed."

Levi grunted and groaned, probably rolling around in his bed or fluffing up his pillow. "I can't turn my phone off. I might miss an important call."

"You don't think I'm an important call?"

"Not really, dude," Levi said.

"Okay, you're my little brother and I used to let you beat me at checkers, but I draw the line at *dude*. Don't call me dude. It's humiliating."

A short pause on Levi's end. "You never let me win at checkers."

"Yes, I did. That one time."

Levi lived in a very old apartment in the bowels of Los Angeles. His bed must have been even older. Matt could hear it creaking loud and clear. "I don't think you called to gloat about being better than me at everything, and I kind of want to go back to sleep. Is there a good reason you called, or did you just want to annoy me?"

Matt turned his truck around and headed toward the main road. "I need some legal advice."

"Dude, I've been in law school for like five months."

"They've taught you something, haven't they?"

"What's your question?"

"Harvey Dustin left me his house in his will," Matt said.

That got Levi's attention. The silence was long. "Why did he do that?"

It was an inevitable question, but the answer was complicated and, Matt could finally admit to himself, pretty embarrassing. "It's a long story, and I know you want to get back to sleep."

"Yes, I do."

"A couple of months ago, Harvey wrote out a will by hand and had it notarized and witnessed by two nurses and a doctor."

"Dude. Right before he died?"

"Yeah. He left me the house."

"I don't get why he left you the house," Levi said.

"It doesn't matter, but don't tell anybody. I haven't even told Mom yet."

An even longer pause. "You better tell Mom"

Matt couldn't agree more. "I'm calling her next." He didn't know what he was going to tell Mom about inheriting Harvey

Dustin's house. *It's a long story* wouldn't fly with Mom. "A month before Harvey wrote my will, he wrote up another will leaving Emma Dustin the house."

"Emma Dustin?"

"Emma was at the house this morning. She says the house is hers, and she won't leave."

"Is she still hot?" Levi said, a little too eagerly.

"Why does that matter?"

"Dude, it always matters."

Matt turned onto the main road and ignored Levi's question. "We don't know which will is legit, and Johnny Cleaver thinks we'll have to go to court to settle it."

"But is she hot?"

Matt growled again. Was no one capable of staying focused this morning? "Yes, she's hot, with a wicked curveball." He fingered the bump on his head. "Now, what do you think about my case?"

"I don't know. You should probably hire a lawyer, but they're expensive."

Matt rolled his eyes. "Why do you think I'm calling you? I'm wondering if I should move into the house. Emma won't leave, and I'm afraid if I don't stay there too, some judge is going to tell me that possession is nine-tenths of the law."

"Nine-tenths what?"

"Possession is nine-tenths of the law. Haven't you ever heard that expression?" Matt said.

"No."

"And you call yourself a lawyer?"

Levi grunted. "I don't call myself a lawyer. That's why I'm in law school."

"Do you think I should move in or not?"

"How much do you want this house?" Levi said.

"Pretty bad."

"Oh." Levi wanted to ask why. Matt could hear it in that one syllable. But to his credit, he didn't mention it. "Dude, if it were me, I'd move in. Stake your claim, ya know? But she's going to make trouble for you, lots of trouble, depending on how bad she wants the house."

"Pretty bad."

"Oh."

"Yeah."

FOUR

ho would have guessed that the cheapest doorknob with a deadbolt cost thirty dollars? It was highway robbery. That's what it was. Did those doorknob companies have no conscience—preying on desperate young women just to make a buck?

The good news was that Emma had only needed to buy two doorknobs, two deadbolts, and a thick wooden dowel. The first doorknob went on the front door, the second one on the door in the master bedroom, and the dowel went at the bottom of the sliding glass door. She'd just see how cocky Matt Matthews was when he was standing on the front porch shivering in a blizzard, unable to get his key to work in the shiny new lock Emma had bought with her new Home Depot credit card.

He'd be glad he was wearing flannel.

Emma found a big bowl in the cupboard, filled it with hot water, and sat down on the sofa to soak her aching hands. The ancient doorknob on the front door had taken half an hour and two layers of skin to remove. Those screws had probably been put in there about the same time women won the right to vote. The knob in the master bedroom hadn't been any easier to remove, and to add insult to injury, her hand had slipped and she'd skewered herself on the rough edge of the door. It took twenty minutes to remove that splinter, which was the size of Rhode Island, and three calls to three different doctors to make sure her tetanus shot was up to date.

But the house was now secure. Of course, she wouldn't put it past Matt to break a window or try to pick the lock. Hmm. Maybe she should have bought the sixty-dollar locks. Or the one that claimed to be "thief proof."

Surely Matt didn't know how to pick a lock. She'd abandoned the idea that he was a professional robber, and lock picking wasn't a skill most guys just picked up along the way. And if he somehow managed to get into the house, there were always her trusty thimbles.

Emma sat cross-legged on the sofa and set the bowl of hot water in her lap. Aside from the day she'd been asked to leave the premises at work, today had been the worst day of her life.

Well...maybe not the worst day. The day her kitty got hit by a car had been a pretty bad day. The day her mom bought her a "training" bra had been humiliating. The day Emma had started her period during math class had been horrible.

Remembering the day Aunt Gwen died still smothered Emma in grief, and Uncle Harvey's passing hadn't been much better. Maybe his death had been easier to deal with because he was in so much pain at the end, and everybody had been expecting it for months.

Okay. Today was not on her top ten list of worst days, but it was definitely somewhere in the twenties. Yesterday she'd taken a very expensive taxi from the airport. This morning she had hoped to drive Uncle Harvey's truck into Boise so she could pay too much for doorknobs, but when she had finally found the keys and tried to start the thing, it hadn't made a sound. Not even the click of a dead battery or the groan of a tired engine. It didn't help that Uncle Harvey's truck was thirty-five years old or that it had been sitting on the side of his house all winter long. It also didn't help that Emma had no winter clothes to speak of. She had draped her High School Musical bedspread over her shoulders just so she could stand to go outside to check the truck.

Emma knew how to charge a battery and she knew where Uncle Harvey's battery charger was, but the hood of the truck was frozen shut and a crowbar seemed a bit extreme. After four or five feeble attempts to pop the hood, she'd gone back into the house and called an Uber driver to take her to Home Depot for doorknobs then to Auto Zone for an engine heater.

She'd try again tomorrow morning with the truck. It was supposed to get above ten degrees. Any more Uber trips and she'd max out her credit cards before the week was over.

Emma hands turned to prunes as she stared at her phone and tried to think about anything but Matt Matthews, the stock market, or document shredders. How did she get herself into these messes?

Her heart did a flip when she heard the front door open. She snapped her head around to look, and water spilled down the front of her nice black yoga pants. Oh, great. Matt walked into the house like he owned the place with a smug smile on his lips and a grocery bag in his arms, still wearing that blue flannel shirt that made him look like a lumberjack—with all those muscles and what not. "That was easier than I thought," he said.

Emma mentally kicked herself. After all the trouble she'd gone to, she had forgotten to actually lock those shiny new doorknobs! This day was definitely moving up on her "Worst Day" list.

She would have stood up and faced Matt with courage and conviction, but her pants were wet, and she wasn't going to try to explain that. So she stayed put while craning her neck to see him behind the sofa, giving him the nastiest look she had ever given anybody—except for Brady Cluff when he'd snapped her bra strap in eighth grade. "This is my house, Matt. Get out, or I'll call the police again."

"If you had wanted to keep me out, you should have locked the door."

"I meant to, but I got distracted because I thought I had to get a tetanus shot. But it turns out I didn't." She held up her wounded finger. "I got a sliver."

"Putting in those new doorknobs?" Matt went into the kitchen and slid his bag onto the kitchen counter.

She bit her bottom lip. "Maybe."

"Serves you right. Although, if you died of lockjaw, I wouldn't have to hire a lawyer."

She narrowed her eyes at him. "You'd like that, wouldn't you?"

"I'd rather not see people die, but I would like you out of my hair."

Emma practically spit at him. "Well, I want you out of *my* hair, and I have a lot more of it."

Matt caught her words as if she'd been throwing them like thimbles. "It's not my fault you gave me a bald spot with that thimble."

"Don't be such a baby. I didn't give you a bald spot. It was already there."

"I don't have any bald spots," he growled, brushing his fingers across his forehead. "But I'm going to have a scar."

"It's your own fault, and if you don't leave now, you're going to get another one." Emma calculated the time it would take her to run from the sofa to the hall table in wet yoga pants to fetch her thimbles. Too long. She'd never be able to catch Matt by surprise like she had this morning.

"I'm not going anywhere."

"If you don't leave, I'll call the police again." Her threat had no visible effect on him. Why would it? They hadn't arrested him this morning. They weren't likely to arrest him tonight. She blew air out from between her lips. "It's not like you don't have anywhere else to go. You were living somewhere else before you showed up this morning."

Matt leaned back against the kitchen counter and crossed his arms over his chest. "It's my house. I have every right to be here. If you don't like it, you can go back to where you came from and let me and Johnny hammer out the ownership details. You were also living somewhere else before you showed up last night."

Emma wasn't about to tell him she had nowhere else to go except her parents' condo, and that it wasn't an option—ever. "I'm not leaving. It will weaken my case if I move out. I'm not stupid. Possession is nine-tenths of the law."

Matt seemed genuinely surprised and a little irritated. "You've heard that saying?"

"Of course."

"My brother Levi is going to law school, and he's never heard it." Matt relinquished his place at the counter and paced in front of the sliding glass door. It seemed he was more than just a *little* irritated.

Emma almost laughed. "That's your whole strategy, isn't it?"

"What strategy?"

"Get me out of the house and stay here yourself. Then you can tell the judge you've been living in the house and you should get it because possession is ninth-tenths of the law. Then you'll bring up some legal jargon about squatters' rights

35

hoping to convince the judge to cut me off." She folded her arms and leaned back on the sofa, pleased that she'd figured out his diabolical plan. "If I stay here, you can't squat."

His lips curled, and he cocked an eyebrow. "I can squat just fine. I have thighs of iron."

She could well believe it. Matt had speed skater thighs. Lumberjack thighs. No doubt he could squat for hours. The tiniest of shivers trickled down Emma's spine. Matt wasn't bad looking for a guy who wore flannel.

He eyed her suspiciously. "You're not as dumb as people think."

Anger bubbled up in Emma's throat. The guy in the flannel shirt was questioning her intelligence? "You think I'm stupid?"

Matt stuffed his hands in his pockets. "I didn't say that." But he'd meant it. That was clear enough from his unapologetic stance and the flippant twist of his lips.

The temptation to stand up and go toe to toe with him almost overpowered her. She glanced down at the wet stain on her yoga pants and stayed put, but she did lift her chin and glare at him. "If I challenged you to chess, Trivial Pursuit, Pictionary, Family Feud, or Jeopardy, I would beat you. Every. Time. Every time, Flannel Boy."

He caught her words with resentment. "What's wrong with flannel? It's a lot more sensible in Idaho than yoga pants and a t-shirt."

He'd noticed the yoga pants. Had he noticed the water stain? She couldn't worry about that now. She had somehow managed to ruffle his feathers, and she was going to press her advantage. "It might be sensible, but nothing screams 'hayseed Idaho farm boy' like flannel and that Denver Broncos baseball cap."

"Hey, don't dis my Broncos."

"And you have the nerve to call me dumb? Did you even

graduate from high school or are you still trying to get that GED? Do you know how to spell GED?"

Well, she *had* wanted to provoke him. It was clear as his face darkened like a storm cloud that he was good and provoked. "I have a Masters degree in Geology from the Colorado School of Mines. Cum laude. Do you know how to spell cum laude? Can you spell Botox, princess? How about fingernail polish?" He slowly pronounced the words as if speaking to an old man with broken hearing aids.

It didn't seem fair to use Botox and fingernail polish as an insult. Emma had never had a Botox injection, and her fingernails were pretty much shot after the doorknob ordeal. She sniffed derisively in his direction. "I think I could make a pretty good attempt at fingernail polish. I also know how to spell mesothelioma. Isn't that a disease miners get? I learned that in my Business and Law class at Northwestern University where I got my Masters in Business Administration, summa cum laude." She batted her eyelashes because she knew it would annoy him. "I believe that's two steps up from cum laude."

He sneered. "And now you're living in a run-down, seventy-year-old house with seventeen garden gnomes and a thimble collection."

"Hey. Aunt Gwen loved those garden gnomes." And the thimble collection had lost three of its members today.

Matt wasn't finished. She must have really upset him with that flannel comment. "I almost forgot Orlando Bloom and Zac Efron."

"And the Jonas Brothers," she said weakly.

"You've really moved up in the world, Emma Dustin. As I remember your words, you were going to leave the manure of Dandelion Springs behind you and never look back. But here you are, plaguing us with your presence once again. What happened? Won't anybody hire you? You come back here because you're broke?"

Tears sprang to Emma's eyes as if they'd been shot from a gun—quickly and without warning. Usually if she could feel crying coming on, she could pinch herself or blink really fast and tamp those tears right back down again. But not this time.

She had a worthless MBA, a pile of student debt, and possible prison time hanging over her head. She hadn't thought she could sink any lower until Matt said that thing about the garden gnomes. But what was wrong with garden gnomes? They were cute and friendly and never pooped on your grass. They certainly shouldn't make her cry—but here she was, sitting in Uncle Harvey's musty family room with tears spurting from her eyes like water from a leaky spigot.

She turned her face from him, but there was no hiding the sniffling. "Go away, Matt, or I'll call the police. I guarantee I can talk Dallin into hauling you down to the station." She hoped it wasn't an empty threat, because as far as she knew, Dandelion Meadows didn't have a police station.

"Hey. Hey, Emma. Hey. Hey," Matt said, each "hey" getting softer and gentler in succession. "Hey. Don't cry." He pulled three tissues from the box on the coffee table, handed them to Emma, and sat next to her.

"I'm not crying," Emma lied. "I have terrible allergies."

He sort of shushed her, as if that would make everything all better. "Look, okay. Just don't cry, okay?"

"Why do you care?"

"I don't like it when girls cry."

If he didn't like it, maybe she'd just keep on doing it. Or maybe not. Some girls used tears to get what they wanted from guys, but that wasn't really Emma's style. She'd much rather win a debate than a crying contest. But there were times it just couldn't be helped. Unfortunately, with her face turned toward the kitchen, she caught sight of Aunt Gwen's cookie jar. It was a black and white milk cow with teats and everything. Emma had inherited a house, a thimble collection, seventeen gnomes, and a cow cookie jar.

She let out a little sob. "I've never used Botox because my lips are already big enough, I got a sliver and my finger really hurts, and it looks like I peed my pants, but I didn't. I was just soaking my hands because they nearly froze when I tried to start the truck plus it took me hours to loosen the screws on those doorknobs. Why do people have to tighten screws so tight? They don't have to be so tight."

Matt grabbed four more tissues and shoved them in her hand. Couldn't he see she already had enough? "It's okay. I didn't think you peed your pants, and Harvey's truck is just cold, that's all. He hasn't been here to drive it."

"I bought an engine heater, but I can't open the hood." It wasn't her fault she didn't have big muscles like *some* people who wore flannel and looked like lumberjacks.

His eyes were full of compassion and pity, with a bit of smug satisfaction at the corners. "Maybe this life is too hard for you. Maybe you should go back to Arizona where they never have to heat their engines."

The thought of "active senior living" made the tears flow even faster. "What did I do to make you hate me?"

Matt frowned and paused a little bit too long. "I don't hate you. I just don't like you very much."

"Why?"

He spread his arms as if it should be obvious. "Because you want to take my house."

"Okay. I guess that makes sense." She blew her nose into her clump of seven tissues. "But what does that have to do with fingernail polish. You said something about fingernail polish."

Matt shrugged. "You've always been high maintenance. I'm not really into high maintenance girls."

The tears dried up faster than they had come. "Because I like to wear makeup and fix my hair?" She'd been right about Matt the first time. He was an idiot. "What did I do? Break your heart thirteen or fourteen years ago? Because I can't remember it, if it actually happened."

Matt scrunched his lips together as if she'd just said something incredibly stupid. She probably had, but for crying out loud, what was his problem? "Emma, you lived with your uncle and aunt every summer for years."

"Seven summers."

"Seven summers. You got cuter every year you came."

"That's very nice of you to say, especially now that I know you don't like fingernail polish." Emma looked down at her hands. Every nail was chipped.

"It's not that I don't like fingernail polish...never mind." He sighed. "Forget I said anything about fingernail polish."

Her feet were starting to fall asleep, and Matt had already seen the water stain, so she stood and took her bowl to the sink, threw away her tissues, and sat down next to Matt again. She felt more powerful not holding a bowl of tepid water on her lap. "I helped Aunt Gwen with all the chores. I did all the things she was too old to do. I didn't use my manicure as an excuse to get out of work, so don't accuse me of any such thing."

"I'm not accusing you. But don't flatter yourself. You didn't break my heart. We barely had anything to do with each other. Summers were busy on the ranch, and I wouldn't have been caught dead at one of the Pioneer Hair Museum stomps. I saw you around town with Torie and Frankie, but everybody knew you were too snooty to give the time of day to one of us cowboys."

Emma hiccupped. Shoot! She always got uncontrollable hiccups after a good cry. "I wasn't interested in country boys. I'm not going to apologize for that. And Calvin Klein jeans were the style in Arizona. A pair of Wranglers would have gotten me shunned at my high school."

"See what I mean? You came across as snooty, like you thought you were too good for us. And anyone could see you were as vain as a peacock."

"Vain? Do you think if I was vain I'd be wearing my hair like this?" She pointed to her ponytail, which had never been a good look for her, but she'd been in such a hurry this morning, she hadn't taken the time to curl her hair. What was the point? There was no one here she wanted to impress.

She frowned. Did that mean she was vain everywhere but Idaho?

No. There was nothing wrong with wanting to look her best, especially when she was hoping to make partner at her financial planning firm. She shouldn't have bothered. She could have worn her hair in a mullet for all the good it did her. Emma ran her fingers through her hair a few times to loosen any tangles. In this cold, dry weather, her hair would probably never be the same again.

"Stop doing that," Matt said.

"Doing what?"

"That thing with your hair. It's distracting."

Emma drew her brows together in confusion. "Because you think it's vain?"

"No. Because it's distracting."

"You're not making any sense, Matt. Are you mad at my teenage self for not swooning over the Flannel Cowboy like every other girl in town?" Another loud hiccup.

Matt went to the sink and brought her back a glass of water. "I'm not mad at you. I just want you out of my house."

"I want you out of my house, and that does not make me high maintenance." Vowing never to cry in front of Matt Matthews again, she dabbed at an errant tear that still sat precariously on her cheek. She needed a backbone of steel if she was going to save her house. She took a drink of water and ran her fingers through her hair again, not caring if Matt found it distracting.

Matt stared at her hair and swallowed hard. "I'm sorry I called you high maintenance. That wasn't very nice."

"You called me dumb too."

"I'm sorry I called you dumb."

She pressed her lips together. "I'm sorry I called you Flannel Boy. It looks like a very warm and comfortable shirt."

Matt stood and retrieved his large grocery bag from the counter. Had he brought food? She might even let him stay a little longer if he'd brought some food. There wasn't anything in the house to eat except what was left of Aunt Gwen's home canning in the cellar: five dozen bottles of peaches labeled *September 1999*, seven dusty bottles of Aunt Gwen's homemade spaghetti sauce, and four jars of currant jelly that Emma had helped Aunt Gwen put up at least ten years ago. Emma hadn't dared eat any home-canned goods, and she'd been so eager to change the locks she'd forgotten to ask the Uber driver to take her to get groceries.

There hadn't been much in Uncle Harvey's cupboards except half a can of coffee, an unopened box of Wheat Thins, and a jar of pickles. Emma had eaten the whole box of Wheat Thins for dinner.

They were stale.

"What's in the bag?" she asked as innocently as she could.

Matt reached in and pulled out a toothbrush. "One flannel shirt, some Wranglers, toiletries, and a change of underwear. It's my overnight bag."

Emma's stomach growled. No dinner for her tonight. No breakfast in the morning. If she couldn't get the truck to start, she'd have to call an Uber if she wanted lunch. Her disappointment tasted like a greasy, empty fast food bag with a little salt sprinkled at the bottom.

Matt wasn't going to see hunger or any sort of weakness in her expression. She took a deep breath and tried to act like a girl who had just eaten a whole cheesecake by herself. "I'm so full," she said.

He lifted an eyebrow.

She felt her face get warm. That wasn't really what she had wanted to say, but hunger had made her punchy.

Wait. His *overnight* bag?

Emma thought she might throw up that entire imaginary cheesecake. Until this moment, she hadn't really considered the possibility that Matt would actually move in. "You...you... can't live here," she stuttered. "I live here."

"I'm staking my claim, Emma. If you don't like it, find somewhere else to live."

How many times must she tell him? "I'm not going anywhere." She snatched the bag from his hand. "And a brown grocery bag is no excuse for luggage."

Matt snatched the grocery bag back and lifted it high in the air. "Possession is nine-tenths of the law, sister. You better hope that lawyer of yours works fast or we might be shacking up together for a long time."

Emma was so mad, she thought her jugular vein might just pop out of her neck. "I don't shack up, and if you dare come near me, don't think I won't throw every thimble in the house at you. Plus the Cutco knives. And those fork things Uncle Harvey used to carve turkeys." She ran to the kitchen, opened the gadget drawer, and pulled out the first thing that looked lethal. It turned out to be the vegetable peeler, but it was good enough. She pointed it in Matt's direction.

With his luggage still in his fist, Matt raised his hands as if Emma was holding a gun on him. "Hold on, Emma. I'm sorry."

"You're sorry?"

"I shouldn't have said that about shacking up. I'm not that kind of guy."

She surprised herself when she realized she believed him. She gripped the vegetable peeler tighter. "Then what exactly are your intentions?"

"I just want what's rightfully mine," he said, lowering his hands.

"Even if it's rightfully mine?"

"It's not."

Emma narrowed her eyes. "How do I know you won't come to my room in the middle of the night and watch me while I sleep, like that creepy vampire in *Twilight*?"

"I promise I won't touch a hair on your head or watch you sleep." He drew a little X across his heart. It was kind of cute and kind of patronizing. "If I don't behave like a perfect gentleman, my mom will have my head on a platter. Literally."

"Oh."

"Until a judge figures this out, we're just going to have to get along." He tucked his grocery bag under his arm. "I get the master bedroom."

"Wait. What if I want the master bedroom?"

Matt shook his head. "I'm not sleeping in the same room as Zac Efron, even if he's making better career decisions these days."

Emma didn't have an argument for that. Her pink bedroom really was a source of comfort for her, even if it smelled like old people. But if her room smelled like old people, Matt's room probably reeked. She'd let him have it. "Okay," she said. "But don't set one foot upstairs, or I'll make you regret it for the rest of your life."

Matt nodded curtly. "Not one foot."

"Okay then," Emma said, cheering up considerably when she realized that she could lock him out of the house tomorrow. And she'd lock her room tonight and drag the Orlando Bloom/Zac Efron chest of drawers in front of the door just in case.

Matt turned and headed toward the master bedroom. "Goodnight, Emma."

"Goodnight, Matt." *I hope the smell keeps you awake all night.*

He turned back. "Emma?"

"Yeah?"

"Don't ever use Botox. You already have really nice lips."

"Oh. Okay. Thanks." Warmth spread through Emma's chest like honey on buttered toast.

But she was still going to lock him out.

CHAPTER
FIVE

Emma smelled the heavenly aroma of coffee and decided she must be dreaming until she opened her eyes to Pink Nirvana and heard her stomach growl like a something at a Monster Truck rally. Not that she'd actually been to a Monster Truck rally, but she was sure it was a place where things growled incessantly.

She sat up with a start, not even minding the wave of cold air that hit her as soon as she emerged from the covers. Coffee! There was coffee downstairs. She didn't even care if it was black, non-latte, foamless, sugarless coffee. She had to have some. She threw on Mom's ratty sweatshirt and those baggy sweatpants and heaved the Orlando Bloom chest of drawers away from her door. The sixty seconds it took her to move the chest of drawers also gave her time to think. If there was coffee, Matt had made it. Was he sitting at the bar eating toast and drinking coffee? Should she make herself more presentable so he'd be motivated to share with her?

If she went down dressed in her Salvation Army-style clothing, maybe he'd feel sorry for her. Maybe he'd pull some eggs and bacon from his overnight bag and cook her a proper breakfast. Wasn't he an Eagle Scout? It could be his good turn for the day.

Emma pushed her chest of drawers back into place against the wall and hesitated. What should she do? Makeup or not? Lip gloss or *au natural*? Sweats or her khakis with the cute stitching on the pockets? Emma didn't feel good about using her looks to manipulate guys. Oh, she liked to look nice and dress up, and it was her dream to own a pair of Jimmy Choos someday, but one of the most important lessons her mom had taught her was that her value didn't come from how she looked.

But right now, she couldn't have cared less about self-esteem, appearances, or Mom's sage advice. The only thing she wanted to know was, would she be more likely to get a cup of coffee with or without her bunny slippers?

She unlocked her bedroom door and looked down at her outfit. It was unattractive but seriously warm, and in January in Idaho, she had to be practical. Besides, the sweatshirt gave her freedom of movement, and she needed the full use of her arms if she had to throw thimbles this morning. Following her nose, she crept down the stairs.

The kitchen was empty—well, except for all the things in the kitchen like the bar stools, but Matt was nowhere to be seen. There was a pot of coffee sitting unguarded in the coffee maker. Either Matt didn't think she'd try to steal it, or he'd left it there on purpose. For her.

That thought would have warmed her heart if the kitchen hadn't been so cold. Besides, there was no toast.

She opened Aunt Gwen's mug cupboard, which contained approximately eighty-seven assorted mugs. One that said, "Virginia is for Lovers," another with the Boston Red Sox logo on it. Another with a bird in a tree that said, "On the first day of

Christmas, my true love gave to me..." Aunt Gwen had trouble throwing anything away.

Because she was feeling nostalgic, Emma chose a coffee mug with Uncle Harvey's face on it. Aunt Gwen loved crafts like that. There was also a mug with Aunt Gwen's face and one with Emma's face buried in the depths of the cupboard. Emma poured herself a cup of coffee and after finding no sugar, drank it straight and black. It wasn't optimal, but then nothing in her life had been optimal for weeks. At least she could warm her hands around Uncle Harvey's face.

She heard the front door open and close. Maybe she should have locked it when she'd come down the stairs, but it didn't seem right to lock Matt out after he'd made her coffee. She'd do it tonight for sure.

Matt appeared around the corner bundled in a thick coat, with chunky gloves on his hands and a Denver Broncos beanie on his head. That guy sure liked his Broncos. He took off his gloves and hat and threw them on the sofa, then unzipped his coat to reveal a red-and-black checkered flannel shirt that really made his teeth look white up against it.

He had a day's growth of whiskers on his face that lent him a dark look and made Emma shiver. She wasn't quite sure why his facial hair made her shiver, except that maybe she'd never seen anyone look quite so handsome while wearing flannel *and* while trying to steal her house.

She held up her mug so Matt had a good look at Uncle Harvey's face. "Thanks for the coffee."

"I made it for me," he said, "but there was a lot left over."

"Do you happen to have toast?"

He cocked an eyebrow, which he seemed to do a lot when he was around her. "No toast. Harvey's cupboards are bare except for a jar of pickles."

"There used to be Wheat Thins too." Emma guiltily took a swig of coffee. Matt never need know who ate those.

"I'm going to pick up some groceries after work. You might want to pick up some for yourself too."

Oh, yes. Well. She didn't expect him to share his groceries with her. He didn't even want her here. She didn't want him here either. Of course, buying groceries would require going outside, trying to start the truck, being unable to pop the hood, then giving up and calling an Uber driver, if she could find one. Buying groceries would take all day, and she ran the risk of getting home after Matt so she wouldn't have a chance to lock him out.

It couldn't be helped. She was starting to feel lightheaded, and if she didn't get a cheeseburger soon, she might be forced to eat her bunny slippers.

Matt took off his coat, got a mug from the cupboard, and poured himself a cup of coffee. His mug said, "IFA Country Store." Boring. But he had made the coffee so she shouldn't find fault with his choice of mugs. He took a sip and grimaced. "It's not very good."

She raised her mug in salute. "I give you an A for effort."

"This isn't my fault. I make great coffee, but Harvey bought the cheap stuff. I couldn't find any sugar." He pointed to the bright yellow canisters on the counter. "The sugar canister has buttons in it."

"Aunt Gwen was afraid the mice would get the sugar if she kept it there. I don't think there's any sugar in the house."

Matt nodded and took another drink. "I started Harvey's truck and left it running so you wouldn't have to jump it again."

Emma was mid-swallow and nearly choked on her coffee. "You did?"

"There's enough gas to get you to a gas station."

49

"Is there enough to get me to a grocery store?"

Matt shook his head. "I wouldn't push your luck."

Emma didn't know what to say. She was so grateful, she thought she might have to give Matt a hug, but Matt was also trying to get rid of her, so it was very likely he had ulterior motives. But she couldn't *not* thank him. He'd saved her hours of standing out in the cold. He might very well have saved her fingers too, because in January in Idaho, frostbite was always a possibility. "Well, Matt. Well, that was...nice of you. Very nice of you." She sighed. It wasn't enough, and she knew it. She set her mug on the counter, went to him, and laid a hand on his arm. "Matt, that is the nicest thing anyone has done for me for months. Maybe years. I'll never be able to express how grateful I am."

He gave her a crooked grin. "You could move out."

She snatched her hand away and gave him the stink eye. "And you could take my truck and run over yourself."

To her surprise, he chuckled. "I shouldn't have said that."

"No, you shouldn't have."

"I do want you to move out, but I really did just want to do something nice for you because you had a bad day yesterday. And because you shouldn't be stuck here all day without a way besides Uber to get places. They charge an arm and a leg to come all the way out here."

"Don't I know it," Emma said. Her day had suddenly gotten a lot better. She could go to the gas station, fill the truck with gas, and get one of those hot dogs that rolled around and around in that cooking contraption, like the ones found in every mini-mart in the world. She started salivating. A chilidog and a Coke for breakfast. And one of those muffins the size of a small child's head.

She'd come home and shower, maybe even shave her legs, and make herself presentable. Then she'd go into town, get some groceries, and stop by Johnny Cleaver's barbershop to see about her case. It was going to be a glorious day.

She eyed Matt and nibbled on her bottom lip. It would be mean to lock him out tonight after he'd fixed the truck. She'd have to wait until tomorrow night, when she was definitely going to do it. The truck only bought him one more night of mercy.

He put his coat back on. "I'm going to work. Don't let that truck idle for much longer, or it'll run out of gas."

"I'll leave right now," she said.

He nudged her arm as she tried to pass him. "You should put on some shoes."

"I can pump gas in bunny slippers."

"Yeah, but if that truck breaks down before you get to the gas station, you'll need to hike out to get help. And it's not a stretch to think that truck will break down."

Emma frowned. She really hoped the truck wouldn't break down. She was crazy for a chilidog. "Okay. I'll get some shoes."

He scrunched his lips together. "Wear a coat."

"I didn't bring a coat."

He did that eyebrow raising thing again. "You don't have a coat?"

"I flew up from Dallas. I don't own a coat."

He gave her a stern look. "Emma, do you want to die out here?"

"That is about the stupidest question I've ever heard."

"You need a coat," he said.

"I'm well aware I need a coat. I didn't have the time or the money to buy a coat." Was he really that oblivious? Girls from Dallas didn't have coats, and they certainly didn't think to buy a coat when they had to flee the state.

"You're going to freeze to death if your truck breaks down."

She didn't know what to tell him. "Let's just pray it doesn't break down."

Matt blew air from between his lips. "Okay, get in the truck. It should be plenty warm by now. I'll follow you to the gas station and back, but then I've got to get to work."

Emma couldn't help but smile. Matt was really a pretty nice guy. He might have just earned himself another night with an unlocked door.

EMMA HEADED into town for the second time, but now her hair was curled, her makeup had been applied, and her lips were a subtle shade of champagne beige. She definitely felt more like herself than she had for days. Matt had rummaged through Uncle Harvey's closets and found a very old, very smelly tan coat that was three sizes too big for Emma, but he had made her take it in the truck in case the truck broke down when he was at work. Thank goodness Emma hadn't needed it yet. It smelled like mold and motor oil.

Uncle Harvey's old Chevy had performed very well all the way to the gas station this morning, even though she heard a strange ping whenever she went faster than twenty miles an hour. Matt had insisted she stay in the truck while he pumped gas for her because she didn't technically have a coat. It was a nice gesture, even if it meant Emma couldn't sneak into the gas station for a chilidog. But Matt had probably saved her from food poisoning. Emma had peered into the window while waiting for Matt to fill her tank, and from the outside, that gas station had looked about as sanitary as a toilet seat. And she hadn't been able to see one napkin dispenser.

Matt had followed her all the way back home, just to make

sure the truck didn't die and Emma didn't freeze. Though, the way things were going, she was more likely to starve.

It was already ten o'clock. Emma had been to the gas station and back, showered, shaved her legs, dressed, and started the truck back up again, and she still hadn't had anything to eat. If she hadn't taken the time to shave her legs, she'd be sinking her teeth into an Egg McMuffin by now—or whatever she could get close to an Egg McMuffin in Dandelion Meadows, Idaho.

Even though the chilidog was calling to her, Emma drove past the gas station and mini-mart and farther into town, such as it was. Dandelion Meadows consisted of approximately a hundred homes spread out over ten square miles. Most homes came with a pasture or some kind of farmland attached. Uncle Harvey had five acres. Old Man Kyle's pasture was about twice that size. Emma used to pick asparagus near the ditch on Mr. Kyle's property. He once told her she could take as much as she wanted as long as she never tried to give him any.

On the outskirts of town, Matt Matthews' family owned the largest property—a two-hundred-acre cattle ranch that didn't have any cattle. Emma didn't think they even kept horses anymore. Rumor had it that Matt's dad had sold all the cows to pay off his debts. Uncle Harvey had said Leland Matthews would have sold the house and the ranch too, but his ex-wife's name was on the deed and she wouldn't allow it.

It was obvious Matt had a perfectly good ranch to live on if he chose. He was just being stubborn or trying to drive Emma crazy, but if he thought she would blink first, he had another thing coming. She'd never lost a staring contest in elementary school.

Maybe she should lock him out tonight after all.

Emma paused at the four-way stop next to the Pioneer Hair Museum waiting to turn left onto Main Street. Or...not Main

Street. The street sign was new. Instead of sitting at the intersection of Main Street and State Road 57, she was at Ktunaxa Street and Sacagawea Road. She'd be in big trouble if she needed to give directions to the emergency dispatcher, because Emma had no idea how to pronounce the street she was about to turn onto.

Who had renamed the streets? Of course, Emma was a big fan of Sacagawea, and she was sure Ktunaxa was a very nice person, but in a place like Dandelion Meadows, where the only thing that changed was the seasons, new street names were downright revolutionary.

No matter how hungry she was, she should see her lawyer first. Her stomach growled in protest as she drove down the road formerly known as Main Street. It had six quaint buildings on the left side and two buildings, a park, and a church on the right. Thank goodness the barbershop was right where it was supposed to be—the last house on the left before the street turned into a dirt road that led to nothing but pastureland and two silos.

Emma jumped out of the truck and ran up Johnny Cleaver's porch steps. Johnny cut hair and practiced law on the first floor, and he and his wife, Marian, lived on the second floor. Emma wasn't sure where Marian did taxes. Maybe in the basement.

Emma tried to open the door, but it wouldn't budge. She knocked urgently. If they didn't let her inside soon, her lip gloss was going to freeze and start flaking off her lips. No answer. Emma wrapped her arms around herself and did a little jig on Johnny's porch to stay warm. She knocked again. Where was Johnny? Didn't he have hair to cut?

A small and completely unnoticeable Post-It note hung to the right of the door. "I'll be back in ten minutes," it said.

Emma growled, ran back to the truck, and cranked up the

heater. Johnny's note was no help at all. Had he just left? If he'd been gone for nine minutes, she didn't want to leave right before he was scheduled to get back. Emma sighed. The truck was toasty. She could scroll through Instagram for a couple of minutes while she waited for her attorney. She pulled out her phone. No service. There was nothing to do to pass the time but check the contents of Uncle Harvey's glove compartment.

Johnny's note was a complete and utter lie because Emma spent thirteen minutes reading the truck owner's manual, but Johnny didn't show up. She glanced around and tapped her steering wheel. How long did she want to wait? Maybe she should go get that chilidog. Maybe she should grab groceries and come back. The way things were going, she should get out of the truck and start looking for a job.

When she put the Chevy in reverse, it made a terrifying noise, but there was nothing to do but drive on. Emma had about decided to go to the Beer Hall to get groceries when she spied the Quirky and Quaint Quilt Shoppe three houses down from the barbershop.

Torie!

They always had sugar cookies and fresh coffee at the quilt shop—at least they used to. It had been over six years, and now she couldn't even pronounce the name of the street, but she'd take her chances. Emma parked around the back of the quilt shop and ran around to the front, which wasn't easy on ice in her yellow high heels.

While she sprinted for the door, she glanced at the park across the street. Something fishy was definitely going on. There was new playground equipment and a beautiful pavilion smack dab in the middle of the park. The new playground equipment consisted of a plastic fort with two levels and a slide, plus a swing set with three swings made of that black rubbery stuff that always got hot in the summer and burned your bottom when you sat on it. The only thing that used to be in the park was a rickety Merry-Go-Round that went very slow unless four people pushed it at once.

That was a lot of change for a place like Dandelion Meadows, even in the short six years Emma had been gone.

The door opened like a dream, and a little bell above her head tinkled a greeting. Emma almost burst into tears. The quilt shop had always felt like a second home to her and not just because there were sugar cookies.

A large Lone Star quilt on frames took up most of the front room, and five women sat around the quilt putting stitches in the fabric. Torie Pyne looked up from her needlework, jumped to her feet, and slid around the quilt to Emma's side. "Emma! You're back."

Emma squealed and jumped up and down, mostly to get the blood circulating. "Torie! It's so good to see you."

Torie threw her arms around Emma and just as quickly pulled away. "You're like an ice cube," Torie turned to her mother who was also sitting at the quilt. "Mom, she's like an ice cube."

Torie's mom, Ardeth, scooted her chair out from under the quilt and extended her arms to Emma. "Well, get on over here by the fire and warm up."

Like most of the businesses on Main, er, Ktunaxa Street, Ardeth's quilt shop was an old pioneer house. Ardeth and her late husband had basically gutted the house, redoing the plumbing, the electricity, the walls. The quilt shop boasted a chunky stone fireplace in the front room and dark wood floors that were so shiny you could see your reflection in them.

"Coffee?" Emma said between chattering teeth.

Ardeth practically ran into the kitchen.

Torie led Emma to the roaring fire and gave her one of the

quilts on sale to drape over her legs. "Do you want something to eat? We've got muffins and deviled eggs."

What? No sugar cookies? Things *had* changed around here. Emma hated deviled eggs, but everything sounded delicious when you were hungry. "Both please."

"And we have sugar cookies," Torie said.

That was more like it. "I'll take everything." She grabbed Torie's wrist. "Except maybe not the deviled eggs. I don't know what I was thinking."

Torie flashed her beautiful white teeth. Emma had always seen Torie as a classic beauty, like one of those old-time movie stars like Audrey Hepburn or Elizabeth Taylor. Or Emma Watson. Torie had great bone structure.

"No deviled eggs," Torie said.

Emma had spent seven summers in Dandelion Meadows and knew just about everyone in town. Marian Cleaver, town CPA and Johnny's wife, sat at the quilt with a needle poised in her fingers, and Betty Frederick, one of Aunt Gwen's dearest and oldest friends, sat next to Marian looking at Emma as if she'd lost her mind. Betty was eighty-five or eighty-six, with a shock of thin white hair and a pair of thick bifocals.

Emma had never seen the other woman sitting at the quilt. She was African-American, maybe in her early forties, wearing a t-shirt that said, "Kiss me. I don't smoke." Her black, curly hair sat wildly atop her head like a mop hit by lightning. It was absolutely glorious. A wide smile stretched across her face as if it was a permanent fixture there. "Where is your coat, girl?" she said. "Only a blamed fool goes without a coat in January."

The woman's face was so friendly and her manner so open, Emma could tell she didn't mean to offend anybody. Emma gave her a sheepish smile. "I left Texas sort of suddenly and came off without my coat. Uncle Harvey's is in the truck if I need it, but you wouldn't want me to bring it in. It stinks."

The woman glanced at Marian. "Uncle Harvey Dustin?"

Marian nodded. "This is his niece, Emma."

"Nice to meet you, Emma. I'm Ladasha Pratt, mayor of Dandelion Meadows."

Emma leaned toward the quilt. "La—what?"

"It sounds like La-*dash*-ah, but it's spelled with an actual dash in the middle. L-A-dash-A. La-a."

"And you're the mayor's wife?" Emma murmured, still trying to figure out how to spell Ladasha and pronounce Ktunaxa.

Ladasha laughed as if Emma had just said something very funny. "I'm the mayor, honey, and I beat my husband out of the job in the last election."

Betty grinned and slapped her knee. "She won seventy-five to twenty-seven. A landslide."

Emma forgot about the pronunciation of Ktunaxa. She could only wrap her brain around one mystery at a time. "LaVerle Pratt was the mayor the last time I was here, but he didn't have a wife back then."

Ladasha's hair fanned up a breeze when she nodded. "Our five year anniversary is in June. He moved me and my son from Mississippi, and I'm still here, so that's proof enough how much I love him. I wouldn't stay through these horrible winters for just any man. My LaVerle is a treasure, even if he doesn't have any sense about how to run a city."

Calling Dandelion Meadows a city was quite a stretch, but Emma didn't argue. Ardeth and Torie had arrived with a mug of hot coffee, a carrot cake muffin, and three sugar cookies. Ladasha could call Dandelion Meadows a metropolis for all Emma cared.

"Ladasha beat LaVerle in the last election," Ardeth said, handing Emma the coffee and taking her place at the quilt again.

Emma didn't mean to pry, but it was a very unusual story. "Is that...did it put a strain on your marriage when you ran against him."

Ladasha wore a pair of hoop earrings the size of canning jar lids. They swung halfway around her head when she shook it. "LaVerle had been mayor for twelve years. It was time to drain the swamp. We never talk about politics at home. It's better that way."

Emma tried to make herself understood with her mouth full of muffin. "It's very exciting to have a woman mayor."

"Dandelion Meadows has never had a black mayor or a woman mayor or a black woman mayor. I'm the first." Her laugh was contagious. Emma nearly choked on her muffin when she laughed too. "As far as I know," Ladasha said, "I'm the only black person in Idaho—except for my son Jamal. He's half black, half Lebanese. It's a very handsome combination."

Betty scrunched her lips together. "You are not the only black person in Idaho. Don't get snooty all of a sudden."

Emma started in hungrily on her sugar cookies. The muffin was already a distant memory. "How long have you been mayor?"

"Three years."

Torie sat next to Emma on the fireplace. "And she's made a lot of changes in town already."

"Like the playground?" Emma said. It wasn't much of a playground, but compared to what they had before, it was definitely an improvement.

Ardeth nodded. "She's been a wonder. It's a miracle she can get anything done with our city council."

Emma wasn't going to argue—again—but Dandelion Meadows wasn't even big enough to be called a town. Calling that group of old men a "city" council was just self-deception.

Torie picked up one of Emma's cookies and stole a bite. "It was her idea to rename the roads."

Emma gave Ladasha a wane smile. Was it really necessary to give the road a name no one could pronounce? "I really like Sacagawea."

Betty nodded vigorously. "Lewis and Clark wouldn't have gotten anywhere without her."

Emma swallowed hard. "And who is Kay-toon-ax-ah?"

Betty looked over her glasses at Ladasha and frowned. "I told you we should have named it Ronald Reagan Parkway. Nobody knows how to pronounce it."

Parkway? More delusions of grandeur.

Ladasha pursed her lips as if she'd just eaten a lemon. "Everybody else knows how to pronounce it, especially after Ktunaxa Awareness Week." She gave Emma a kindly, if slightly irritated, smile. "It's pronounced Toon-ah-hah, and they were a tribe here in Idaho. It's time the Native Americans got their due."

Emma nodded. "Tuna-ah-hah. I should be able to remember that."

Ladasha poked her unthreaded needle into the fabric. "If you'd been here for Ktunaxa Awareness Week, you would have known."

Emma glanced at Torie. "Ktunaxa Awareness Week?" She couldn't help that a cookie crumb fell from between her lips at the same time. It was a consequence of eating greedily and having an intelligent conversation at the same time.

"That's another one of the changes," Torie said. "As soon as Ladasha got sworn into office, she started her awareness campaigns."

Ardeth took Emma's empty mug. "We meet at the Hair Museum every Monday night, and Ladasha gives us a presentation on what we need to be aware of that week. It's a very good presentation. She uses Power Point and everything."

Ladasha smiled wider. "Thank you, Ardeth. I take great pride in my Power Points."

"It's a real talent," Marian said.

Ardeth nodded eagerly and headed toward the kitchen, hopefully to refill Emma's mug. One cup of coffee was not going to be enough. "It's been real educational, that's for sure," Ardeth said on her way out.

"That's a lot of work for you," Emma said, "to do an awareness week every single week."

Ladasha waved away any concern Emma might have. "It never hurts to give ourselves a little education. And I don't always do a Power Point. Sometimes I just use posters, and sometimes I don't even do the presentation. Last week, Matt Matthews gave us a presentation for Back Country Skiing Awareness Week."

Back country skiing? That didn't surprise Emma. Matt wore flannel and cowboy boots. He was practically a mountain man. All he needed was one of those long, creepy beards and a shack out in the woods. For all Emma knew, he did have a shack in the woods. Another reason to lock him out of her house tonight.

Ardeth bustled back into the room with another steaming cup of coffee and handed it to Emma.

"I could kiss you," Emma said, holding the mug under her face and breathing in the heavenly smell. She took a sip. "So what week is it now?"

Torie sort of squished her lips together as if she was trying not to smile too hard. "Old People Awareness Week."

Betty looked up from her quilting. "That was my idea. We old people get discriminated against all the time."

Ladasha patted Betty's hand. "It's called ageism, and it's

unacceptable." She turned to Emma. "This is why we have awareness weeks. To make people aware so they can stop injustice when they see it."

Emma wasn't sure what injustice was associated with back country skiing, but she also hadn't known how to pronounce Ktunaxa. She decided not to ask.

Betty squinted in Emma's direction. "We should have Frostbite Awareness Week. Then maybe Emma wouldn't traipse around town without a coat." She leaned in Emma's direction. "My late husband lost his pinky toe to frostbite. It wasn't pretty. We could find some disgusting pictures on the internet."

Ladasha shook her head. "We can't do it this year. I've got the whole schedule mapped out." She smiled kindly at Emma. "But I'm willing to change the schedule if it would help Emma."

Emma took another swig of coffee. "I'm fully aware of frostbite. I came ill equipped, that's all. It was completely my fault." Well, not bringing a coat was completely her fault. Getting fired or possibly getting fired was not her fault at all.

Her momentary distress must have shown on her face. Torie laid a hand on her leg. "Is everything okay? What happened?"

Emma glanced around the room. "I'll tell you later," she whispered, but anyone with decent hearing could have heard her.

"Now, honey, you might as well tell us." Ladasha shot Betty an accusatory look. "News travels faster than pink eye around here, and if we don't hear it from you, Betty is liable to make up her own story."

"I don't make up stories," Betty said indignantly.

Ladasha grunted with a little indignation of her own. "I seem to remember one about a cow and a raspberry patch."

Betty harrumphed and turned her face away. "I make up a story now and then, but only in an extreme emergency."

"Teancum's prize-winning raspberries is not an emergency."

Betty glared at Ladasha. "It is if they cost eight dollars a pint."

Ladasha looked at Emma. "We want to hear the whole story. No one comes to Idaho in the winter on purpose."

Torie draped her arm around Emma's shoulders. "You don't have to explain, Emma. We understand if you want your privacy." There was no one sweeter or more thoughtful that Torie Pyne. She was Emma dearest Idaho friend. Except for the funerals, Emma hadn't been back to Dandelion Meadows for years, but she and Torie had texted each other almost every day since they were fourteen. But when everything went wrong in Dallas, Emma hadn't had the heart to pick up the phone and call Torie. She'd been too embarrassed.

Did she really want everybody in Dandelion Meadows to know about her humiliation? If it was a humiliation. Everything had happened so fast, Emma wasn't sure herself.

"Where did you say you were from?" Ladasha asked.

"I was—am working in Dallas, but I grew up in Arizona."

Torie smiled. "She came to spend the summer with Harvey and Gwen when she was twelve and stayed every summer here after that for, what was it, Emma? Seven or eight years?"

"My last summer was nine years ago, right before I went to college."

Ladasha eyed her with compassion and curiosity. Emma couldn't figure out a reason for the compassion, unless Ladasha had a low opinion of living in Idaho in general. "What happened to your parents? Did they die?"

Emma gave Ladasha a reassuring smile. "Nothing that dire. My parents were both teachers. During the summer they followed the curling circuit. They went to curling tournaments all over. Sometimes even in Canada. I didn't want to be dragged all over the country, and I quite dislike curling. My dad asked Uncle Harvey if I could stay with him and Aunt Gwen. It was supposed to just be one summer, but we all liked it so much, I kept coming back. My parents got to go curling anytime they wanted, I helped Aunt Gwen with her garden, and I got to spend summers where it wasn't so hot."

Betty pointed her needle in Emma's direction. "You did more than that. Gwen's arthritis made it hard for her to move around. She said you practically ran that household while you were here. You were a real comfort to her, for sure and certain."

Ladasha nodded at Betty. "I'm glad to hear that. We all gotta help each other, cuz nobody's getting out of this thing alive." She fingered one of her hoop earrings. "Maybe we need a Curling Awareness Week."

Emma couldn't figure out how topics were chosen for Ladasha's awareness weeks, but injustice against curlers wasn't really a thing. "That would be nice," she said, because there wasn't really any other useful comment to make.

Ladasha's eyes and smile got wider. "Emma, would you be willing to give the presentation for Curling Awareness Week?"

"Um." Was Curling Awareness Week already on the schedule? Because Ladasha shouldn't mess up her schedule.

Thankfully, Marian had the same thought. "There is no Curling Awareness Week on the calendar, Ladasha."

Ladasha scrunched her lips to one side of her face. "I know, but I hate to pass up the chance to hear from an expert. They say curling is breathtaking if you know the rules."

"I wouldn't exactly call it breathtaking," Emma said. "I mean, my parents love it, and they think it's breathtaking, but it's mostly a lot of sweeping and sliding and yelling at each other." That wasn't exactly fair. Curling was highly technical and took an incredible amount of skill. Emma just wasn't into sports in general, and watching curling made her want to take a nap.

Ladasha reached under the quilt and lifted a purse the size of Delaware onto her lap then pulled out a bright pink binder and leafed through it. "Let's see. Next week is Martin Luther King, Jr. Awareness Week, and nothing will ever replace Martin. But the week after that is Aluminum Awareness Week. I'm willing to move it for curling."

"Burton won't be happy about replacing Aluminum Awareness Week," Betty said. "That was his idea. He's been very concerned about Alzheimer's and anti-perspirant."

Ladasha frowned. "Maybe we can move Aluminum Awareness Week to June instead of Raw Chicken Awareness Week."

Marian shook her head. "Raw Chicken Awareness Week has the potential to save two or three lives a year. We can't skip that."

Ladasha sighed. "Well, as the mayor, I have to make the hard decisions, and I just don't feel we can pass up an opportunity to hear from a curling expert. I'll tell Burton we'll schedule Aluminum Awareness Week first thing next January. Hopefully, that'll appease him."

"But what if Emma isn't comfortable teaching curling awareness?" Torie said. "We have to think of her feelings." Torie was always so thoughtful.

"It's not that I wouldn't want to teach curling awareness," Emma said. "I've just got so many other worries right now, and I don't even know if I'll be here in two weeks." She could be in jail.

Okay, Emma had to stop thinking like that. Such thoughts only sent her into a series of mild panic attacks, and they weren't even real. No matter what happened to her job, she hadn't committed any crimes that she knew of. She definitely wasn't going jail. She really had to start managing her self-talk.

Ladasha closed her binder and set it on top of the stretched-out quilt. "Tell us about your worries, child. You'd rather not let Betty's imagination run wild."

Oh, dear. She shouldn't have reminded them. They had been nicely diverted by Aluminum Awareness Week, and she was starting to feel a sugar headache coming on.

Marian threaded her needle. "For one thing, she's suing the Matthews family."

Betty gasped as if she were having a heart attack. Ardeth wrung her hands together and looked as if she might cry.

Torie's eyes got about as big as monster truck tires. "You're suing the Matthewses?"

Marian nodded, obviously pleased to be the bearer of such shocking news. "Johnny is representing her."

Ladasha drew her brows together. "I hadn't heard that."

Marian poked her needle into the quilt. "It only happened yesterday, and it's all very hush-hush."

Emma's case against Matt Matthews wasn't hush-hush by any means, but Marian seemed to enjoy telling it like that. Who was Emma to ruin her fun?

Ladasha patted her binder as if it contained the secrets to the universe. "I don't like it when my citizens are at odds with each other. What's the trouble?"

Emma squirmed a bit, not because she wasn't happy to tell the story but because everybody was looking at her as if her lip gloss had slipped off her face and taken her lips with it. "I'm not suing anybody. I'm just trying to get what is rightfully mine. Supposedly, Uncle Harvey made up two wills right before he died. In one of the wills, he left the house to me. In the other will, he left the house to Matt Matthews. There's no reason Uncle Harvey would leave the house to Matt. It's all a misunderstanding."

Marian leaned far enough over to pat Emma's hand. "Johnny is the best lawyer in Idaho. He'll get you that house or he wasn't three-time 4H champ in high school."

Emma shrugged. "I don't even know where he is. He was supposed to be back thirteen minutes ago."

Marian frowned. "You mean Johnny? If he don't have any haircuts, he goes to the Hair Museum and hangs out with the boys. You'll find him there, most likely."

Well. He should have mentioned that on his Post-It note. Emma wouldn't have waited. Then again, while perusing the owner's manual, she had learned how to work the radio in the old Chevy. She shouldn't look a gift horse in the mouth.

"So you and Matt both want that old house," Ladasha said. "Can't say as I blame you. It's a nice piece of property. 5.3 acres and two shares of water, but the house could use some work."

After their discussion about Ageism Awareness Week, Emma didn't dare mention that the house also smelled like old people. "I'd like to fix it up a little, but I have to figure out a way to get Matt out first."

If her companions had been surprised before, they looked positively shocked now. "You...he's...he's living in the house?" Torie stuttered.

Ladasha nodded. "He's smart. Squatters rights, you know."

"But." Torie paused. It was plain to see she was thoroughly confused. "But. Where are you living?"

"At the house."

More gasping. Yep. That's just how Emma felt.

"I woke up yesterday morning, and he was there with a notebook and a tape measure." Emma straightened with pride. "I got him with Aunt Gwen's thimbles."

Torie's concern looked to be about a twenty on a scale of one to ten. "You're living in the same house?"

"I've got the upstairs, and he's got the downstairs." She didn't tell them that it was a very temporary arrangement and that she planned to lock Matt out of the house tonight—or tomorrow night at the latest. Gossip traveled fast, and Emma didn't want anyone to give Matt advanced warning.

"Possession is nine-tenths of the law," Marian said. "You're wise to stay put."

Ardeth took Emma's mug. "Another cup, Emma?"

"No thanks. It was lovely. And so were the cookies."

"Why did Harvey leave Matt the house?" Betty said. "Harvey and Leland Matthews were friends, but you don't leave a house to somebody because you and their father hung out at the Hair Museum."

Emma pointed to Betty. "Exactly what I think. Uncle Harvey wouldn't have left Matt the house. The second will is a fake. Or Uncle Harvey wasn't himself and didn't know what he was doing."

Marian nodded. "Johnny will get to the bottom of this or he wasn't 1995 Barber of the Year."

Ladasha had given up on the quilt several minutes ago. She leaned back in her chair and eyed Emma. "So you're in Dandelion Meadows to make sure Matt Matthews doesn't get your house?"

"Not exactly." Emma squirmed again. Did she want the whole town to be privy to her humiliation? "I got an MBA in finance," she finally said. First she'd impress them, then she'd sneak in that part about maybe getting fired and ruining her career.

"Emma's really good at math," Torie said. She always tried to be helpful like that.

Emma *was* really good at math, even though she didn't

especially enjoy it. But people were always impressed with a degree in finance. "When I graduated, I passed the test, got my admin license, and took a job with a financial advisory firm in Dallas."

"She's a financial advisor like her uncle," Ardeth said. "Harvey was always so good with other people's money."

Neither Betty nor Ladasha seemed interested in how good Harvey was with other people's money. "So what happened?" Betty said.

Emma nibbled on her fingernail, a habit she'd given up years ago. Today was just one of those days. "I'm not exactly sure. The advisor called me into his office and accused me of unethical behavior and said there was an SEC investigation and told me to pack my things and get out. Everybody in the whole office heard him yelling."

"But what did he accuse you of?" Torie asked.

"I don't know. I'm always so careful to do everything by the book the way Uncle Harvey did. He told me that his reputation was the most valuable thing he owned. I've tried to follow his example."

"Harvey was a good man," Ardeth said.

Emma looked down at her frosting-tipped fingers. "I don't have any clients yet so I'm not sure what I did wrong. My advisor didn't tell me."

Betty huffed out a breath. "You should have asked."

"I asked," Emma said, "but he kept ranting and raving about betrayal and ethics and the SEC. He was practically foaming at the mouth. I thought it best to just go and then come back later when he'd calmed down. But I'm not even allowed in the building anymore, and he won't take my calls. Then he called my landlady and told her I'd been fired and wouldn't be able to make the rent payments. She kicked me out."

"I'm pretty sure that's illegal," Marian said.

Ladasha slapped her binder. "Darn right, it's illegal. Honey, why didn't you put up a fight?"

"Well, at first I was just so shocked. Then my friend at work told me to just sit tight because there was an investigation and maybe my name would be cleared."

"This is a gross miscarriage of justice, honey. That's what I'm saying."

"The truth is, I can't afford to hire a lawyer, but I have three friends at the firm who are keeping a close eye on things. I wasn't actually fired. The partners are obligated to do an investigation first. I don't know what else to do. Coming to Idaho seemed like a good plan. At least the rent is free."

Marian clicked her tongue. "But now you have a house guest."

Torie gave Emma a hug. "I'm so sorry! Why didn't you tell me?"

Emma melted into Torie's embrace. "I was embarrassed and confused. I didn't want to worry you."

"You're here. That's something good to come out of all this." Torie retrieved the wet wipes from the cut counter and handed one to Emma. She knew Emma so well. Emma loved sugar cookies but hated sticky fingers. "How long do you think you'll be here?"

"I don't know," Emma said. "It could be two weeks. It could be two months. That's why I can't say yes to Curling Awareness Week. I don't even know if I'll be here."

Ladasha wrote something in her binder. "I'm putting you on the schedule. The wheels of justice move very slowly, honey. You'll definitely be here two weeks from now."

Emma's heart sank. She wanted to argue, but Ladasha wasn't wrong. She had no excuses left and no good reason why she shouldn't jump at the chance to do a presentation for

Curling Awareness Week. "I didn't bring my curling stone," Emma said. It was a weak excuse, and she knew it the minute the words came out of her mouth.

"All you need is a Power Point. Or posters. You can use posters." Ladasha shut her binder with a flourish. "We'll plan on you the Monday after the M.L. King holiday. Half an hour to an hour is plenty long. Don't get long-winded or people start to get testy. You'll be magnificent." Ladasha stood, stuffed her binder into her purse-bag, and helped Betty to her feet. "We'll see you next week, Ardeth. The deviled eggs were delicious. I'll remember to add a little horseradish to mine. LaVerle will love it. Jamal will hate it. He is the pickiest eater ever born."

"I've got to go too," Marian said, sticking her needle in the quilt and leaving it there. "I need to get to my spring cleaning before tax season starts."

Ardeth had never been one of those helicopter moms. She gave Emma a wink and ambled back into the kitchen, where she shut the door and turned on the water so she wouldn't be able to hear any private conversations.

"Warm enough?" Torie said. Emma handed Torie the quilt, and Torie hung it back on the wall. Then she giggled, slid next to Emma on the hearth, and took her hands. "Now give me all the details about Matt Matthews. Are you dying?"

"Dying? Why would I be dying?"

"Because he is so good looking. He's got all that thick, dark hair and those eyes and those shoulders, and he's living in the same house. Are you dying?"

Emma ignored the little flutter in her chest. She could admit to herself that Matt was handsome without going all goo-goo eyes over him. She was an independent woman who didn't give in to teenage fantasies anymore. Besides, she would never go crazy over a guy who wore flannel, even if his shirts pulled nicely tight across his chest and revealed his broad shoulders and solid biceps. What did mountain men do to keep in shape besides back country skiing? "I don't care what he looks like."—mostly—"He's trying to steal my house and making a real pest of himself."

"But Emma, he's so handsome, just like all the Matthews boys. Doesn't that interest you at all?"

"Well, I've definitely noticed it, but it's kind of hard to be interested in someone who wants to get rid of me." She raised her eyebrows and scooted closer to Torie. "I gave him a scar."

Torie was horrified. "You did?"

"Don't worry. It won't spoil his good looks. I didn't recognize him, and he startled me so I threw Aunt Gwen's entire thimble collection at him. It really ticked him off when I drew blood."

Torie gasped. "Emma, you shouldn't be proud of it."

"I'm sorry, Torie, but I am. If I'd known he wanted my house, I would have thrown even harder."

"What did he say?"

"We both called the police, and when Hob arrived, we called Johnny. That's when he told us about the two wills. Matt says possession is nine-tenths of the law and refuses to move out, even though I'm sure he has a nice shack somewhere in the mountains."

Torie smiled sympathetically. "That's got to be super uncomfortable. Why don't you stay at our house until you get this mess worked out? Then you wouldn't have to see him every day when you dislike him so much."

Dislike was a very strong word. Emma wanted to get rid of Matt, but she didn't necessarily dislike him. He was nice enough, when he was living in his own house. "I don't know," Emma said. "Is your cousin still living at your house?"

Torie grimaced apologetically. "Yes, and they'll be there for three more months at least."

Torie and her mom were the kindest people on the planet. They took in people who had nowhere else to go, like Torie's cousin who had a couch potato for a husband and four wild kids. Luckily, Emma had somewhere else to go, and she'd rather not wake up with peanut butter smeared on her face or gum in her hair. "I think I'll stay put. Matt needs to learn he can't push people around like this."

"Come on, Emma. You know Matt's not the pushy type."

"Okay, he's not pushy, but I'm going to teach him a lesson about something. I'm not sure what." Emma stood and ran her hand along the fabric on the quilt frames. "Would *you* like to move in with *me*? You deserve more sympathy than I do."

Torie shook her head. "I couldn't leave Mom like that. She needs help with the kids and Lazy Larry."

"Lazy Larry? That's the cousin-in-law?"

"His name's Preston, but the nickname is appropriate, and then we can talk about him without him guessing we're talking about him. He's that oblivious."

"Well, good luck," Emma said.

"You'll need more luck than I will. Matt isn't pushy, but he's persistent." Torie pulled Emma in for a hug and whispered in her ear. "The word is, he's got some financial troubles. He wouldn't hesitate to sell Harvey's house."

Emma pulled away and braced herself to go outside. "Then let the games begin."

She needed the money too, but she wouldn't be selling. Ever.

Matt had no idea.

CHAPTER
SIX

M att parked his truck and grabbed his three bags of groceries from the passenger seat. Harvey's truck was parked by the house, which meant Emma probably wasn't frozen in some ditch on the side of the road next to her broken-down truck. Matt let out the breath he'd been holding all day. He'd rather not feel responsible for Emma's safety, but there it was, whether he'd rather or not.

He tiptoed up the porch steps, not wanting Emma to know he was here until he'd tried the front door. If she'd locked him out, he'd have to crawl in the window, and he rather not be met with a handful of thimbles in the laundry room. He'd have to figure out a way to steal one of Emma's new keys. The suspense of being locked out was too much to handle. Matt was already stressed enough.

He turned the doorknob, and to his surprise, the door opened easily, except for the very loud squeak that accompanied it. He'd have to spray some WD-40 on that so it didn't make such a racket.

Although, maybe it was better that it had a squeak. Then

Emma would know when he came in, and she'd also be alerted if any intruders tried to enter by the front door.

Matt shut the door, and his eyes immediately started to sting. A thin cloud of smoke hung over the entire main floor, and it smelled like charred paper and burnt cheese. Or maybe burnt cooking oil. He didn't have *that* sensitive of a sense of smell. He stepped quickly into the family room. Emma sat on the floor with her back against the fireplace looking at her phone as if Siri had just delivered some very bad news.

Matt set his groceries on the counter. "Is something burning?" he said.

Emma didn't even seem to notice he'd come home, but he discovered the source of the smell in the kitchen sink. A black disc about the size of a dinner plate sat in the sink with a gooey yellow substance oozing from its center. A frying pan sat in the other sink, still smoking and sizzling as if this disaster had only recently happened. Emma had tried to cook something, and it had gone horribly wrong.

Matt quickly opened the sliding glass door just a crack, in hopes the smoke would clear before the house acquired a permanent burn smell. The appraisal would be lower if the house smelled like smoke.

Emma still stared numbly at her phone, but her eyes were red and her skin splotchy. His heart sank. Had she been crying?

"Hey, Emma," Matt said, mentally kicking himself for how "interested" he sounded. If he wanted her to move out, he should at least act a tiny bit hostile that she could have burned down the house. "Bad news?" he prodded. Why did he ask? He didn't want to know, didn't care what Emma Dustin's problems were—probably the trivial kind anyway: *My hairstylist quit. I chipped a fingernail. I ordered a mink coat that won't be here until Wednesday.* "What happened in the kitchen?"

Emma swiped at her face with the back of her hand and sighed like a lonely heifer. "Dinner."

"Dinner?"

"Yes. I'm starving, and my dinner managed to make it into the sink."

"How did that happen?" Matt said.

"I don't cook. I just don't, so deal with it."

"What's it to me if you don't cook?" That was a silly question. If she burned down his house, he'd care very much.

"I tried to make an omelet, but right in the middle I got this very important text, and I sort of forgot to take it off the stove. Before that, Ladasha put me in charge of Curling Awareness Week, and I hate curling."

"I hear there's a lot more to it than people think."

She scrunched her lips to one side of her face. "You don't have to tell me, bub. I have my own curling stone. I *know* curling. I dashed my dad's dreams when I refused to carry on the family curling tradition. And the Beer Hall doesn't carry Totino's Pizza Bites. If I had any doubt before today that I'm in the sticks, I don't now." She stood up and smoothed her hands down a very pretty green top that accentuated the blue of her eyes. Was she purposefully trying to distract him? "Okay," she said.

"Okay?"

"Okay. I'm not saying I want you here or need you here, but it is freezing in this house and I *cannot* start a fire." She gave him a pathetic look. "I'd very much appreciate your help."

She was asking for his help? Matt hadn't expected that from a snooty girl like Emma. Of course, her humility was probably born of desperation. He fixed his gaze on the fireplace. A jumbled stack of paper and wood was crammed into the firebox like an overlarge pile of towels in a front-loading washer. A small pile of matches lay broken and abandoned on the hearth along with a sprinkling of white crystals. Salt?

He wanted to act mad or irritated or put out, but he couldn't help but be amused. One side of his mouth curled involuntarily. "Do you have any matches left?"

Grimacing sheepishly, she reached into her pocket and pulled out a single match. "I kept my head at the last minute." She blinked rapidly. "There was a lot of smoke. My eyes sting, and I think I may have smoke inhalation, but I stopped coughing about five minutes ago so I think I'm okay. But if I'm not okay, I'm perfectly able to drive myself to the hospital."

"I don't think that will be necessary," Matt said.

Emma was visibly upset about something—and it wasn't the fire—but maybe the red eyes were because of the smoke. Maybe she hadn't been crying. Maybe things weren't so bad with her. Maybe Matt didn't have to worry about being gallant after all. He took off his coat and gloves and threw them on the sofa.

"There's a closet behind you," Emma said. "And will you please take off your boots? You're tracking snow onto the wood floors."

She was pretty bossy for someone who wanted him to do her a favor, but he saw the wisdom in removing his boots. The house would sell for more if the floors were in good condition. He also hung up his coat but only because he was feeling sorry for Emma and her terrible cooking skills.

He took the precious match and slid it into his pocket. "Do you want me to teach you how to build a fire?"

She pressed her lips together and nodded. They were really pretty lips, full and curvy with a light coat of some nondescript color of gloss that would taste like strawberries or citrus bliss if he kissed her.

He held his breath and cleared his throat and put that

horrible thought out of his mind. It had been a long day, and he wasn't exactly thinking straight. "Here is your first problem," he said as he wrapped his fingers around the flue damper lever. "You have to open the flue or the fire doesn't have enough air to get started, and there's nowhere for the smoke to go. If the flue's open, the air is drawn up and outside."

Emma frowned. "There was a lot of smoke."

"You need to take everything out of the fireplace. It's overstuffed."

She eyed him doubtfully. "Including the grate?"

"No. Not including the grate."

Emma grabbed a sheet of newspaper from the magazine rack and spread it on the floor. Then she methodically emptied all the wood and paper from the fireplace and stacked it neatly on the newspaper. No wonder she had insisted he hang up his coat.

A neat freak like Emma probably wouldn't trash his house before he sold it. Okay. She could stay for another day or two.

"What's with the salt?" Matt asked.

Emma crinkled her nose, which was about the most irresistible expression he had ever seen. His gut clenched. "I saw it in a movie once. Isn't salt supposed to help the fire burn better?"

He remembered to stop staring at her before she got suspicious. "Nope."

"But I saw it in a movie."

"It's some sort of superstition, like if you spill salt, you're supposed to throw it over your left shoulder."

Emma frowned. "What does that have to do with fire?"

"I have no idea." Matt knelt next to Emma's stack of wood. "Now," he said, "the first thing we need to do is wad up the newspaper loosely and put it on the grate." He walked her through the steps to building a fire and made her do most of the work so she'd know how to do it when he wasn't there.

He couldn't help but watch her hands while she wadded up newspaper. They were graceful hands, on the small side, with short nails and a light pink polish that looked pretty and not high maintenance at all. Their hands touched when they both reached for the same piece of newspaper. The feel of her skin against his made him a little dizzy. This was not good.

Matt stood up, pulled out his phone, and checked his ESPN app for the latest basketball scores, even though it was too early for any scores from tonight's games. But the Nuggets had beat the Jazz last night. That was enough to distract him from the people in the house who were complicating his life.

Matt worked very hard not to growl out loud at his own weakness. This whole thing would be a lot easier if Emma Dustin weren't so pretty. Or so darn cute. Or so vulnerable in her own stubborn way.

Matt had spent the whole day vacillating between anger, curiosity, and downright fascination. He didn't want to be fascinated with Emma Dustin, but it wasn't like he could help it. She had crept into his thoughts and taken up residence there, much like she had done in his house. Matt didn't know which would be harder to extricate, thoughts of Emma or Emma herself.

It was exhausting to be intrigued and mad at the same time. Being mad at Emma was definitely more convenient. Being intrigued was stupid and unreasonable and made him even madder. But when he'd seen her sitting at the kitchen counter this morning with that coffee mug cradled in her hands, his protective instincts had kicked in. It hadn't made any sense. She wasn't some helpless girl lost in the wilderness without supplies or a warm coat.

Okay, she wasn't lost, but she didn't have a coat, and

maybe that was enough to make her seem helpless, even if she wasn't. Because she wasn't. She'd almost killed him with those thimbles, which meant she had a really good arm. She'd be able to defend herself in a dark alley with those fists and a stiff knee to the groin—as long as the guy wasn't too big and maybe if she had a gun.

Matt frowned. She lived in Dallas. Maybe she should carry a gun.

"Are we ready for the match?" Emma said, her chin trembling. She really was cold. At least he could solve that problem.

He pulled the match from his pocket and gave it to her. "Light it as close to the paper as you can, but don't hold it too close or the paper will smother it."

"You should do it. We only have one match, and we don't want to waste it on a rookie."

She was definitely going to mess this up, but Matt had a box of matches in his truck as a backup. Emma need never know unless she had to. Letting her light the fire would give her confidence she could do it next time. "You built this thing. Light it. You'll be fine." Unless raccoons or birds or bats had nested in the chimney, then they'd be in trouble no matter what they did.

Emma took the match as if it were very fragile and retrieved the empty matchbox from the hearth. Leaning very close to the wood, she struck the match and held it against an edge of newspaper. Luckily, the newspaper caught fire, and the whole wad crackled to life. Emma squealed. "I did it!"

Matt grabbed her hand, pulled it toward him, and blew out the match before the fire burned her fingers. Her skin was just as soft as he had imagined. He pulled away as if she'd burned him.

The fire consumed the paper and crept up the smaller kindling above it. Emma watched with unfettered joy, as if she'd never seen a fire before. Well, she'd obviously never *started* a fire before. Soon the flames caught hold of the big logs, and the fire started putting out heat. Emma closed her eyes and sighed, holding her face close to the flame so she could absorb its warmth.

While she wasn't looking, Matt took the opportunity to stare at her. How did she get her eyelashes to curl like that? And what was that lip color? Lit by the firelight, it was the most enticing shade in the world.

Emma slowly leaned backward as the fire got hotter. "You're earning a lot of brownie points, Matt Matthews," she said, with her eyes still closed.

A ribbon of warmth curled up his spine. He cleared his throat, stood up, and went clear to the kitchen before turning around. He didn't want brownie points. He just wanted what was rightfully his. And Emma.

Meaning, Emma out of his life.

He wanted Emma out of his life.

He glanced at his phone to see if there were any other scores he should know about.

Emma wrapped her arms around herself, turned, and sat on the hearth with her back to the fire. "Sometimes when you're really cold, you wonder if you'll ever be warm again, ya know?"

"I don't mind the cold," he said. He frowned. He sounded as if he was choking on his own spit.

She stretched her legs out in front of her, leaned back on her hands, and studied his face as if looking for some sort of button to push. "So. I ruined my dinner."

"You did."

"So."

"So," he said.

"So, did you bring something for dinner in one of those

bags?" She curled and uncurled her toes while she watched him out of the corner of her eye. She had really nice feet, and Matt didn't usually notice such things. She really should wear shoes. Wood floors could be cold.

He shrugged. "I was going to eat a protein bar and call it good."

Matt had never seen someone look so profoundly disappointed over a protein bar. "Have you...have you got anything else in that bag?"

"Nothing for dinner."

She pursed her lips and gave him the once-over, as if deciding whether to be irritated with him or feel sorry for herself. "Do you have an extra protein bar I could eat?"

"They're not very good."

"Why did you buy them?"

Matt huffed out a breath. "Okay. Fine. Get your coat. I'm taking you out. Something tells me you're a lot happier when you've had something to eat."

She tilted her head to one side. "Well, something good to eat that doesn't have fifty grams of protein per serving."

"Let's go then."

Emma wanted to say yes—Matt could see that undernourished look in her eyes—but it was plain she was also doubtful about dining with the enemy. "What about the fire?"

"It's fine. The house will be nice and toasty when we get back."

Emma hesitated. "Where would we go? And don't say McDonalds. The nearest one is in Boise, and I don't have a coat."

"Wear the coat I found you this morning."

She made a face. "Easy for you to say. It smells like wet dog and manure."

"Okay, I'll wear Harvey's coat," Matt said. "You can wear my coat."

"What does it smell like?"

Matt didn't know why every word that came out of Emma's mouth annoyed and amused him at the same time. He pulled his coat from the closet and handed it to her. "You tell me."

Emma buried her face in Matt's coat collar and took a deep breath. He waited. And waited. She inhaled his coat for almost a full minute before she pulled away. "It...it smells really nice."

"It does?" That surprised him a little. His coat couldn't smell like much more than sweat and dirt and maybe the inside of the mining office. Maybe she was just being nice because she was hungry.

She pulled it around her shoulders. "I feel sort of bad that Uncle Harvey's coat stinks. But not bad enough to trade you."

How in the world did Emma manage to look good in a coat that fit her like a sleeping bag? Maybe because it was his coat, and there was something quite attractive about a woman wearing his stuff. It was good he didn't have asthma, because the way she looked would have triggered an episode right there in the kitchen.

Emma went to the front hall and put on her shoes. "I want you to know that just because I'm letting you take me out to dinner doesn't mean I'm going to let you have the house."

Her mentioning the house was like a swift thimble to the head. She thought he was being nice to her to get the house? He gave her his best glare. "And you should know that just because I'm taking you out to dinner doesn't mean I'm ever going to do it again. You need to go back to Dallas and sort out your own life. I'm not going to rescue you whenever you get hungry or your truck breaks down."

She sniffed in his direction. "Nobody asked you to."

"It's why I'm such a nice guy."

Emma grabbed her keys. They'd been sitting on the table next to Gwen's ill-used thimble collection. Matt lifted an eyebrow and made note of their location. Maybe he could steal them when Emma went to bed and have copies made at the Walmart in Boise. It was a half hour drive, but worth it just to see the look on her face when he walked into the house whenever he wanted.

"I'm driving," Matt said, hoping she'd leave her keys on the table for the rest of the night.

"I don't mind driving."

"My truck is thirty years younger than Harvey's and less likely to break down. And it's a Ford."

She cocked an eyebrow. "Oh. You're a truck snob. What makes you think a Ford is less likely to break down than a Chevy?"

He cocked an eyebrow right back at her. "It's built Ford tough."

She laughed so hard she snorted. "That explains it."

"Besides, if either truck breaks down, those heels won't be any good in the snow."

"Don't I know it," Emma said, as if she'd had a recent experience. He wasn't going to ask. Emma set her keys back on the table, just like Matt had hoped she would. Sometimes, he was just too clever for his own good. Matt opened the door for Emma. She glided down the porch steps and then turned around and went back up again.

"What are you doing?"

"I have to get my keys and lock the door."

Matt wasn't going to let his very own key slip away that easily. "Nobody locks their doors in Dandelion Meadows."

She shook her head. "The way things are going in my life,

the truck and my bunny slippers will be gone when we get back. I'm not taking any chances."

Okay. Maybe she'd put her keys back on the table when they got home. He'd have to make sure of it.

"You still haven't told me where we're going," Emma said when she came back outside and locked that shiny new deadbolt.

"The Hair Museum. The gas station usually makes me lose my appetite."

Emma hesitated. "The Hair Museum?" She glanced back at the house. "Do they do takeout?"

Matt opened the truck door for Emma and pretended to be completely shocked. "You don't want to go to the Pioneer Hair Museum? It's the center of everything in Dandelion Meadows. Not only does it have a creepy and astounding display of pioneer hair art, it also has a pretty good restaurant and a room for city council meetings and Awareness Week lectures."

Emma all but growled. "It's just that everybody goes there, and I'm wearing very impractical high heels and a gigantic coat. I look like Smoky the Bear in drag. They're going to laugh at me, or click their tongues."

Matt got in the truck and started it up. "Emma, if nobody laughs at Emmett Wilkins and his toupee made out of lint, nobody is going to laugh at you."

"I wouldn't be so sure."

"What about Cappy Saunders? One night he was eating soup at the museum and a cockroach crawled out of his beard. Lucille Baxter's support hose aren't all that supportive anymore, and Mae Rose's false teeth fall out almost every time she eats. You aren't even on the list of top ten things people will laugh at."

Emma thought about it for a minute. "I suppose you're right. I'm just a little touchy, I guess. I always felt out of place in Idaho but even more so in the winter. I don't do well with cold."

"You don't have to stay," Matt said. "Go back to Texas where it's warmer, and Johnny and I will take care of everything."

"Over my dead body," Emma said, smacking him in the arm. "I'd like to see you try."

"Hey, Johnny's your lawyer. He's not going to stab you in the back."

Emma folded her arms. "You're right, but I'd like to make things easier for him. I have a stronger case if I stay here."

It was too bad for Matt that she thought so, because she was right. It was why neither of them was willing to move out of the house. He never should have underestimated Emma Dustin. Under that high maintenance, shallow, snobby exterior, she was pretty smart. Nobody got an MBA just for being good looking.

Did she have a boyfriend?

Matt jerk his hand on the steering wheel and almost swerved off the road. What did he care if she had a boyfriend? He didn't, unless Romeo showed up in Idaho and wanted to have a sleepover.

Matt scowled. He wouldn't stand for that, no matter how Emma protested.

"Is something wrong?" she said.

Did she mean because of his scowl or because of the swerving? "Let's talk about the boyfriend." *Let's talk about the boyfriend?* Since when had he lost the ability to think before he spoke, and why was he so flustered all of a sudden? He'd already established that he didn't care if she had a boyfriend. He certainly didn't want to talk about the guy.

Emma looked at him as if he was three cards short of a full deck. "What boyfriend?"

Too late to turn back now. "*Your* boyfriend."

She was definitely thinking about jumping out of the truck and running for her life. "I don't have a boyfriend."

Matt swallowed hard and breathed a sigh, but it wasn't a sigh of relief because he didn't really care. "Oh. Okay."

After a long and awkward pause, Emma said, "What about the girlfriend?"

"What do you mean?" He wasn't usually this big of an idiot.

"I mean, do you have a girlfriend?"

If he admitted he didn't have a girlfriend, would she think he was a loser? Probably, but he couldn't pretend to have a girlfriend and then have Emma get suspicious when the girl didn't show up. "No. I don't have a girlfriend."

She smiled, but he couldn't tell if it was a smile of pity for the loser without a girlfriend or a smile of gratification that she'd finally been able to get him to understand the question.

About the time he pulled into the Hair Museum parking lot, Matt seriously started to question his own judgment. It would be all over town in a matter of minutes that Matt and Emma had been seen dining together at the Pioneer Hair Museum. Mayor Pratt would probably post it on the Dandelion Meadows Facebook page. Someone at the restaurant would Tweet about it. The old people who didn't know how to use the computer would call each other on their landlines and spread the gossip. Matt and Emma would be an item before they even ordered dessert. Mom would freak out because "You didn't tell me you had a girlfriend!"

This was the worst idea ever.

Did the Hair Museum do takeout?

SEVEN

E mma was a modern, independent woman. She certainly wasn't going to wait for Matt to be a gentleman and open the truck door for her. The problem was that when she tried to open the door herself, it stuck. She shoved it with all her might, but it didn't budge.

With a guarded expression on his face, Matt came around to her side and opened her door. He had to yank it, so she hadn't been imagining things. "I tried to open it. I really did," she said.

Matt nodded slightly, as if he didn't really care that she was an independent woman and had earnestly tried to open the door for herself. "It must have frozen shut between Harvey's house and here."

"Frozen shut? In what kind of horrible place do car doors freeze shut?"

Matt shrugged and reached out his hand. "It's five below zero."

She wasn't going to repeat her question, but really, in what kind of horrible place did car doors freeze shut? Emma realized he was waiting for her to take his hand. Hah! He'd be waiting a long time. She could get herself out of a truck and into a building, thank you very much. She put one hand in her pocket and braced the other against the dashboard, just so Matt knew exactly what she thought of his chivalry, then put her foot on the pavement.

Unfortunately, she was wearing high heels, and it was five below outside. The parking lot was nothing but a bumpy, crunchy sheet of ice. Her foot slid out from under her, and if Matt hadn't grabbed her arm, she would have fallen backward, smashed her head on the running board, and had permanent brain damage.

As it was, he grabbed her so firmly, he might have dislocated her shoulder. "You okay?" he said.

"Yes. Thanks." He'd been so nice to save her that she decided not to say anything about the shoulder.

"You're going to have to hold onto me," he said, as if he offered his help reluctantly. "Those shoes don't give you any traction."

Much as she wanted to be her own woman, Emma took Matt's arm. If she broke her femur, she'd have to move back to Gilbert so her parents could take care of her. There was only so much she was willing to do for her pride.

The Pioneer Hair Museum was housed in an ancient building some enterprising pioneers had built as a dance hall about a hundred and fifty years ago. You had to go up seven steps just to get to the front door, which was made from a sturdy piece of fir wood. There were large bay windows on either side of the door, but they were covered from the inside.

"Why did they cover the windows like that?" Emma said. She'd always found it fun to look in the windows and see people eating.

"They cover them in the winter to keep the cold out. Wool blankets."

She didn't even blink when Matt opened the heavy museum door for her. Might as well surrender to the inevitable. Matt was good at opening doors, and Emma needed both hands for balance.

The front door opened to a very, very small atrium—about the size of a bathroom. It wasn't really even big enough to be called a foyer, but Aunt Gwen had always referred to it as an atrium, so Emma wasn't going to tick anybody off by calling it anything less.

"Did you know the light in this atrium is made of Italian glass special ordered by the mayor of Dandelion Meadows over a hundred years ago?" Emma said.

Matt shut the outside door. "I kind of don't care."

She pointed to the floor. "The tile mosaic was designed by local artist Matilda Baines. She was awarded the honor of Artist Laureate of Dandelion Meadows for her contributions to the community—the first woman to win."

Matt looked extremely skeptical. "There's no such thing as *Artist Laureate.*"

"I'm only telling you what they told us on the tour."

"The tour?"

"Every summer, Uncle Harvey and Aunt Gwen took me on a tour of the museum. They give tours every Tuesday from four to five."

"I didn't know that. Kind of don't care."

Emma let her mouth fall open. "You grew up here, and you don't even care about your heritage?"

He cracked a smile. "I wouldn't exactly call this my heritage."

"Well, it is. I got a tour every year. I should know."

"Why did you get a tour every year?" Matt said.

90

Emma shook herself out of Matt's coat and shivered. "I'm not sure, except there isn't much to do in Dandelion Meadows. Maybe Uncle Harvey and Aunt Gwen were trying to keep me entertained. Maybe they forgot from one year to the next that they'd already taken me. Maybe they were just extra proud that Dandelion Meadows has its own museum."

Matt stared at the inner door as if he was bracing himself for something very unpleasant to meet him on the other side.

"I'm really hungry," Emma said, just in case he'd forgotten why they were there.

"You're very eager all of a sudden."

"Well, I realized that I don't have to actually wear my coat in the restaurant. I don't think I'll get laughed at."

"But you'll definitely get stared at," he said, tugging open the door.

Emma frowned and smoothed her fingers through her curls. "Why? Do I have egg in my hair?"

"I'm sure you're used to it," he said.

Used to having egg in her hair? Before she could ask what he meant by that, Trudy Howell shuffled up with a stack of menus in her arm and an apron full of pockets around her waist. The town of Dandelion Meadows owned the Pioneer Hair Museum and restaurant, but Trudy's family ran it. Trudy's dad and brother did all the cooking, Trudy worked as the waitress, and Trudy's mom, Lucille, gave tours and did lots of research on how to preserve hair.

"Emma," Trudy said. "You haven't been here for a while."

Emma gave Trudy the biggest, friendliest smile she could stretch her teeth across. "It's so good to see you, Trudy. It's been years."

Trudy pushed her bangs out of her eyes. "Yep. A while."

Trudy's fine, mousy-brown hair fell over her face like a curtain, and she pushed it back again and again so she could see her notepad to take food orders. As a teenager, Emma had wanted to buy Trudy a whole shopping bag full of bobby pins and tell her, *It doesn't have to be this way. You don't have to live like this anymore! Pin your hair back and set yourself free!*

Emma had never had the courage to do it. Who was she to tell Trudy how to wear her hair?

Trudy was in her mid-thirties and the gloomiest person Emma had ever met. She never smiled and certainly never had anything happy to say about anything. Emma always tried to put a little extra cheery sunshine in Trudy's day whenever she saw her. Trudy needed all the sunflowers and butterflies she could get.

Trudy shut one eye and squinted the other one in Matt's direction. "Good to see you're getting out into the world."

Matt's smile was kind, even if Emma could tell he wasn't quite sure what Trudy meant. "I really like your shoes, Trudy. Are they new?"

She shook her head. "I've had these shoes for twelve years. They've been puked on three times. When people spill food on them, I have to take them out back and spray them with the hose."

"Well, they're very practical." Matt turned his smile to Emma and took her coat, which was a very nice gesture unless he was worried Emma was going spill food on it and wanted to get it out of her hands.

Emma didn't like to admit it, but Matt was a pretty nice guy. He'd started her truck for her this morning and been nice to Trudy. Everybody should be nice to poor Trudy.

Trudy shuffled through her menus as if making sure she had enough for the crowd that had just come in. "How many for dinner?"

Matt glanced at Emma. "Uh. Two."

"Okay," Trudy said. "French or English?"

Matt glanced at Emma again as if she might know what Trudy was talking about. "What was the question?"

"My brother Roy just graduated from culinary school. He said we had to print the menu in French to make the place more classy." Trudy looked around the empty restaurant with its red-checkered tablecloths and folding chairs. "I think it's classy enough, don't you?"

Emma pretty much considered herself an expert on "class," and the Pioneer Hair Museum restaurant was not it. But she didn't want to give Trudy any reason to be unhappy. "I like the restaurant just the way it is." Which wasn't necessarily a lie. If someone asked her how she'd change it, she'd have absolutely nothing to say.

Trudy sighed. "We printed the menus in French just like my dumb brother suggested. My folks think he walks on water cuz he graduated from culinary school. I passed the postal workers test, and Mom put a candle in a Twinkie."

Emma nodded encouragingly. "Oh, that's wonderful. Are you a postman too?"

Trudy pursed her lips and smacked them together. "That was six years ago. They're not hiring."

"So you've got menus in French and English?" Matt prodded. He had to be almost as hungry as Emma was.

"We used the French ones for about three days, but no one but Penny De La Croix could read them. Mom got real upset and said Roy's feelings would be hurt, but Dad went ahead and printed a set in English."

"That was smart of you." Emma gazed longingly at the menus in Trudy's hand. Too much longer and she'd have to start eating one. "So, can we have English menus?"

Trudy handed them two menus. "Where do you want to sit?" She motioned toward the seven tables in the restaurant. There wasn't another person in the whole place. "Everybody stayed in tonight," Trudy said. "It's too cold to go out. You'll probably freeze to death out there when you leave."

Emma picked a table away from the windows so they'd be a little warmer. "Your parents couldn't do this without you, Trudy. You're so efficient and tidy."

Tidy? That wasn't exactly the word Emma was looking for, but Trudy sort of smiled anyway. Emma caught a glimpse of metal in Trudy's mouth.

"Oh, my goodness, Trudy. You've got braces."

Trudy scratched at her hairline near her neck. "My mom thinks it will help me get a husband. I told her there's no hope."

"Any man would be lucky to have you," Emma said. "But don't settle." Trudy seemed like one of those women who would give away her life savings to the first guy who paid her any attention. She'd attract a lot more attention if she used a bobby pin or two.

Matt hung Emma's coat—well, Matt's coat—on the coat rack next to the cash register and sat down.

Trudy fiddled with her menus while Matt and Emma got settled at their table. "Our special tonight is pate' fooey graw."

"What is it?" Matt said.

Trudy jerked her head back so her hair flipped out of her face. "It's this weird stuff made out of duck livers. Roy said it's what everybody makes in culinary school. He made a gallon of it yesterday, and nobody's ordered it. I warned him, but nobody ever listens to me. Tonight it's half price, served with toasted French baguette slices."

Matt glanced at Emma. "I think we'd better try some."

Trudy shrugged. "Okay. It's your funeral."

She didn't mean that literally, did she?

"What do you want to drink?"

Emma looked up from her very confusing menu. "Water, please, with lime."

"Roy is saving the limes for the fish tomorrow. We only have lemon juice from a plastic bottle, even though Roy says it's a travesty."

Emma pretended she didn't care that her water would be limeless. "No worries. Just the water then."

"Diet Coke," Matt said. "With lime."

Trudy jotted down Matt's order on her notepad, not saying a word about the lime. Did that mean she was going to bring him one? Did she like him better than she liked Emma? Was she annoyed that Emma had ordered water? Oh, well, Emma wasn't going to make a fuss about it. She could always stick her hands in Matt's drink and steal his lime when he wasn't looking.

Trudy walked into the back room while Matt and Emma studied their menus. Emma couldn't make heads or tails of it. She nudged Matt's leg under the table with her foot.

Matt jumped as if he'd been electrocuted. "For crying out loud, Emma, don't do that."

"I was just trying to get your attention." Emma leaned back and furrowed her brow. "You're pretty high strung for a guy."

He drew his hand across his forehead as if wiping away a headache. "Is there a reason you wanted to get my attention?"

"Have you read this menu? I think she gave us the French ones."

"I thought all you snotty prep school girls knew how to speak French. Isn't that a requirement for all those fabulous vacations you're expecting to take?"

"I went to a regular high school in Gilbert, Arizona and flunked out of Spanish in seventh grade. Maybe you should get to know people before you jump to conclusions about them."

"Maybe I don't really care."

"Maybe I don't care that you don't care, but would you please look at the menu?"

He fell silent and studied his menu for like an eternity. She was just about to nudge his leg again when he said, "It's definitely different."

"I can't understand it. What is *ground steak on a pretzel bun with aged cheddar, Porterhouse tomatoes, and bib lettuce served with a creamy mayonnaise sauce and French cut potatoes*?"

Matt squinted. "Sounds like a cheeseburger and fries."

"A cheeseburger?" Emma read the description again. "Matt, you're a genius."

His lips curled upward. "It's about time you noticed."

"Don't let it go to your head. I've known fire hydrants with more personality."

"And I've known mud puddles with more depth."

Emma expelled an indignant breath in his direction. "At least I don't wear flannel like it's going out of style. Oh, wait. It already went out of style about seventy years ago."

"At least I don't wear high heels in the middle of January," he said.

"Do you wear them in the middle of July?"

He sprouted a reluctant smile. "You might be shallow, but you're quick with the comebacks." He eyed his menu again. "I think you can get anything on the menu you used to be able to get, but they've fancied up the descriptions and added three or four dollars to all the prices."

Emma tried to decipher her choices. "Can I still get those really greasy fish and chips with tartar sauce?"

He turned his menu in her direction and pointed. "It's here under: *Delicacies from the Sea*. Budweiser-battered ocean cod on a bed of cabbage greens with lightly fried potato wedges and sauce *tartare*."

"It sounds three dollars more expensive that way, but the

patrons might starve before they can interpret the menu."
Emma sighed. "I think I'll just have the cheeseburger. The half
pounder. It'll be easier for everybody that way."

"I don't think they have a half pounder."

"Yes, they do. See?" She pointed to the menu. *"8-ounce
option for the hearty appetite."*

Trudy came back with their drinks. Matt's Diet Coke had
three limes floating in it. Emma didn't even get a straw. She
was beginning to suspect some favoritism, though why anyone
would favor Matt Matthews over her was a complete mystery.
Matt might be good looking, but he had no fashion sense, and
he wanted to steal Emma's house. Didn't character matter
anymore?

Trudy pulled out her trusty notebook and held her pencil
at the ready. "So," she said, "how long have you two been
dating? I don't expect it to last past March, but my dad wants
to know."

Matt practically slammed his menu shut, which didn't
really work because it was only two pages long. "We're not
dating."

"You're not?" Trudy said.

"Not at all." He emphasized those three words as if he were
slapping Emma on the wrist with each one of them. "In fact,
we don't even like each other."

Emma didn't know why that stung just a little. Didn't Matt
like her even the tiniest little bit? He didn't have to love her,
but he could at least tell Trudy how he'd helped her build a fire
and followed her to the gas station so she wouldn't freeze to
death. She might not be here long, but she sort of cared what
people in Dandelion Meadows thought of her, and he was
acting as if she was a completely unlikable nightmare of a
person.

Emma folded her arms. Well. She didn't like him either. He

was rude and red-neck and made assumptions about people that weren't even true—like they went to prep school and spoke French. "We're suing each other," Emma said, attempting to prove how much she didn't like him.

Trudy pushed the hair from her face with the end of her pencil. "I know. Johnny told me. I just wondered if you were tricking Matt—making him think you wanted to be his girlfriend."

Emma squeaked in indignation. "I don't want to be his girlfriend. He stole the master bedroom."

"She gave me a scar," Matt said, as if that excused his taking the master bedroom.

"You broke into my house."

Matt glared at her. "It's my house."

Trudy nodded. "Yep. You're not going to make it past March." She tapped her pencil on the notepad. "Now what do you want to eat?"

Matt scowled at Emma while he ordered, but if he hated her that much, would he have ordered the cheeseburger? At least he wasn't likely to steal her fries if he had some of his own.

When Trudy went back into the kitchen, Matt ran his fingers through his hair. "We shouldn't have come."

What had he wanted to do instead? Eat that protein bar? "Why not?"

"We just shouldn't have come."

Emma made sure he wouldn't see any sympathy from her. "It was your idea, not mine."

"I don't know what I was thinking except I wasn't. By tomorrow morning, everybody is going to know we were at the restaurant together. Trudy isn't the only one who's going to assume we're dating."

"But we told her we weren't."

"That doesn't matter," Matt said. "People believe what they want to believe. I saw Trudy poke her head out of the kitchen and snap a picture while we were looking at our menus. She's probably posting it on Instagram right now."

Emma craned her neck to get a good look at the kitchen door. "That must be why the pate' is taking so long."

"When we came in and the restaurant was empty, I was hoping we'd dodged a bullet, but Trudy posts on Instagram three or four times a day. Yesterday she posted four pictures of the new dumpster."

"Why don't you unfollow her?"

Matt threw up his hands. "That's not the point, Emma. Everybody's going to think we're dating."

"Why do you care what other people think? We can go on hating each other in private."

Matt paused as if he was thinking about something very serious. "You're not that easy to hate, Emma."

Warmth traveled up her neck, and she wanted to smile, but there might be some double meaning in what he said, so she kept her mouth shut.

He shifted in his chair. "Of course, you're not that easy to like either."

Emma stifled an indignant gasp and pulled her shoulders back. "What's not to like?"

"Plenty."

Emma ignored his rudeness. "It doesn't matter how we feel about each other. I can't cook, and I've got to eat on a regular basis. You don't want me to starve, do you?"

Matt folded his arms across that wide chest. "I'm not sure."

"Thanks a lot."

"Besides, none of that matters. My mom is going to freak out when she sees Trudy's Instagram post."

"I like your mom," Emma said. "She and Aunt Gwen were great friends."

Matt huffed out a breath. "I called her yesterday and told her about the house."

"What did she say?"

"She warned me to act like a gentleman and then offered to hire a lawyer in Boise to take my case, even though she can't afford it. She was going to call Johnny and lecture him for helping you. She's sure she can talk Sheriff Hob into kicking you out of the house."

Emma didn't know whether to be mad or worried. "That doesn't seem very nice."

"My mom is the nicest person you'll ever meet, but when it comes to one of her boys, she's a mother bear—unless one of us boys has been the cause of the trouble, then she's like a badger. She doesn't let us get away with anything. But this time, she's taking my side. My will is the newest one, so she's sure you're in the wrong."

Emma pressed her lips together. "So why will she freak out when she sees Trudy's Instagram post?"

"Because dating you will weaken my case. She doesn't like it when her boys are stupid." Matt pulled out his phone, pressed a few buttons, and scrolled through the options. "See?" he said, flashing his screen in Emma's direction.

There was indeed a photo of Emma and Matt sitting at this very table staring at their menus. At least Emma had fixed her hair this morning. It was a pretty decent picture, even if Matt was scowling.

"I still don't see what the big deal is," Emma said. "Any judge who sees that photo is going to be impressed that we are trying to get along in a hard situation. If anything, it will soften the judge up. Judge Judy likes it when the people try to work it out before they get on the show."

"Emma, Judge Judy isn't real. You know that, right?"

"Of course she's real. There's no way that show is animated."

Matt swiped his hand across his forehead again. "That's not what I mean."

"What do you mean?"

"Never mind."

Emma didn't ask more questions. Matt had bigger problems in his life if he didn't even believe that Judge Judy was a real person.

Trudy was soon out of the kitchen again carrying a tray with little round pieces of bread and a bowl of a creamy, brown substance that looked sort of like poop. "You spread it on the bread like peanut butter," Trudy said, before disappearing into the kitchen, no doubt plotting to take more pictures: *This is Matt eating duck livers. This is Emma drinking her water. This is Emma stealing Matt's limes. Look at Emma try to eat that burger. Who knew Matt liked ketchup with his fries?*

Matt picked up a piece of bread, dipped his knife into the pate', and spread it thickly on his bread. Smiling, he stuffed the whole thing into his mouth.

"Why in the world did you order pate'?" First Judge Judy and now this. He was definitely not thinking straight.

He chewed and swallowed. "You know why. Because it will make Roy happy, and the Howells won't have to eat pate' for three weeks." He licked his fingers. "Besides, Emma, it's delicious. Try it."

"I don't think so."

"Can you imagine how happy Roy will be to see you on Instagram eating his pate'?"

Emma cringed. "Okay, but only if you give me two of your limes."

Matt smiled as if he found her funny. "Okay. Two limes.

But you have to take at least two bites." He took a spoon, fished two lime wedges from his glass, and dropped them into her water.

She smiled back because that was very nice of him, and she was happy to have limes. With a slight shiver, she spread some pate' on a piece of bread and took a tiny bite. And then another. Maybe it was because she was starving, but it didn't taste all that bad, especially if she didn't think too hard about what it was made of.

She ate six slices of baguette with pate', and Matt had eight. It was turning out to be a pretty good day after all.

Trudy came out of the kitchen with a tray. She set up the tray caddy with one hand and put her tray on it. Trudy might be gloomy, but she was a very competent waitress. Emma had been in the restaurant when every table was full and people were standing at the counter eating their lunch. Trudy handled everything with speed and efficiency.

She set Matt's plate in front of him first and then Emma's. Emma tried not to take it personally. A fat, juicy burger sat atop half a bun with the other half of the bun and the lettuce, tomatoes, and mayo on the side. Trudy pulled a bottle of ketchup from one of her pockets and set it on the table. Closer to Matt. "Roy calls this a deconstructed cheeseburger," Trudy said. "What that means is you have to put it together yourself, but *deconstructed* sounds fancier. He also wanted me to tell you that the hamburger meat is a blend of three different beefs. That's supposed to make it extra good." She rolled her eyes. "He went to chef school for that."

"Thanks, Trudy," Matt said. He grabbed the ketchup and smothered his fries with it.

Emma made a face. "You want some fries with that ketchup?"

"The fries are only a vehicle for the ketchup," he said.

Emma popped a fry in her mouth and moaned softly. "Oh, Matt, you've got to taste these—without ketchup. They are heavenly."

Trudy stuck her head out of the kitchen. "Roy wants you to know they're one-hundred percent Idaho potatoes, double fried and never frozen, with special spices."

Matt picked up a fry dripping with ketchup.

"Try it without ketchup first," Emma said.

He glanced at her and to her amazement, scraped the ketchup off the fry with his spoon before taking a bite. "Wow. Delicious. It's got a little kick to it."

Emma nodded. "I know. It's the most amazing French fry I've ever eaten. This beats a million protein bars." She ate another one and moaned at the sheer pleasure of it.

"Will you stop doing that?" Matt said.

"What?" Had she accidentally nudged his leg again? It couldn't be helped. The table was tiny.

"The moaning thing. Could you not do that?"

Oh, boy. Matt really was high strung. Did he have sensitive ears or something?

She ate another fry—quietly—and then constructed her burger, which was the closest she usually got to preparing her own dinner. "So," she said. "You think your mom is going to freak out about the Instagram photo. What about your dad? Will he care?"

Matt studied his lettuce as if he wasn't sure where to put it. "Mom and Dad got a divorce about six years ago."

"Oh. I'm sorry. I didn't know that."

Matt fell silent and didn't even seem to be trying to figure out how to put his burger together.

Emma didn't know what to say or if she should say anything, especially since Matt wouldn't want comfort from the enemy. Still, divorce hurt. She could show some compassion even if he didn't like her. "I'm really sorry, Matt. That had to be super hard for you. And your brothers."

Matt sat back and stared at the ketchup bottle. "Holt and I were away at school. Clay was okay. He'd just gotten married. It was hardest on Levi and Boone. They were teenagers." He hesitated. "But it was pretty hard on all of us."

"I'm sorry."

"Dad is the best horseman you've ever seen. He could ride better than the guys on the rodeo circuit. He saved Holt's life once when Holt's horse bolted at a snake. He taught us how to work hard. He always said, 'You'll never go hungry if you know how to work.'"

"That's true," Emma said.

"Sometimes he was hard on us, especially Boone, but we never doubted his love for us. He taught us to be men, and I try to make him proud every day."

"Uncle Harvey always thought very highly of him."

Matt's eyes flashed. "I guess he did."

"How is your mom doing?"

He sighed. "She's the one who filed for divorce. I guess she just couldn't deal with it anymore."

"Deal with what?"

"Dad always had trouble managing money. When I was in high school, he tried his first investment in some property in Nevada. But when it went bad, everything at home went south pretty quickly. It was a matter of honor to him to pay his obligations. It always has been. He never made an agreement he didn't feel honor bound to fulfill. First he sold the cattle to make the payments on the Nevada property. He sold the tractor and most of the equipment. Then he sold all the horses except Clay's. That was about the time Mom divorced him."

"Because he was selling all your stuff?"

Matt shrugged. "I don't know. Levi said they yelled at each

other all the time. Dad wanted to sell the ranch, and Mom refused. Maybe Mom got tired of the yelling."

"There isn't an easy explanation for most divorces. It's complicated."

Matt took a drink of Coke. "I was pretty mad at my mom. I thought she'd given up on Dad just when he needed her the most. I barely spoke to her for months, but then I found some maturity. Grandpa always used to say, 'There's no pancake so thin that it doesn't have two sides.' I decided I shouldn't punish my mom when I didn't really know what she'd been feeling. Choosing sides is just an invitation to crushing guilt, and I'm done feeling guilty for something I didn't do."

"It certainly wasn't your fault. Part of each of your parents is inside you. You can't reject either of them without rejecting yourself."

He studied her face as if looking for something important. "That's true." He finally figured out his cheeseburger and stacked the lettuce then the tomato and the pickles. And—no surprise—about a fourth of a cup of ketchup on top of it all. He took a bite and raised his eyebrows. "This is really, really good."

"Yeah," Emma said. "Really good." Surprisingly good. "It's like eating at a five-star restaurant."

"Can you order a cheeseburger at a five-star restaurant?"

Emma grinned. "No. But you can order ground steak on a pretzel bun with aged cheddar, Porterhouse tomatoes, and bib lettuce served with a creamy mayonnaise sauce."

He laughed. "I guess so. Maybe I should have ordered something fancier than a Diet Coke."

"You can't get much fancier than that here in Dandelion Meadows."

Matt raised his glass. "Here's to being a dry town."

Emma picked up her water and clinked her glass with

Matt. "It has its advantages. At least we don't have to pick a designated driver."

Matt took a gulp of his Diet Coke. "Back at the house when you were distraught and delirious, you mentioned Curling Awareness Week."

Emma frowned. "I was not delirious."

"Yes, you were. It was definitely a stream-of-consciousness experience."

"I had just gotten some bad news from Dallas, that's all. I was not delirious. The mayor has asked me to be in charge of Curling Awareness Week. She was so excited about it, she bumped Aluminum Awareness Week off the schedule."

She could tell he was trying not to smile. "I take it you have some curling experience."

"It's not any dumber than Back Country Skiing Awareness Week."

She was trying to get some sort of reaction from him, but she didn't seem to ruffle even one of his feathers. "That's because you've never tried back country skiing. It's the best. I go at least once a week in the winter, and it's really good exercise."

Emma made it clear by her expression that she questioned his sanity. "In this cold?"

"There is no bad weather, only bad clothes."

She cocked an eyebrow. "Is that your motto?"

"An old Norwegian saying. I dress warmly. When it's too cold up here, I go down to Utah. There's a yurt up Logan Canyon where you ski in, sleep overnight, then ski out in the morning. It's amazing."

"Is there a bathroom?"

He shook his head as one side of his mouth curled upward. "It's all done out in nature, baby. But the snow is perfect, and the views are amazing."

The thought of doing her business in the snow was just about enough to make Emma lose her appetite. How did Matt stand it? How could anybody stand it? They were living in modern times when primitive things like going to the bathroom out of doors and eating the bark off trees weren't necessary. But Matt's eyes were lit up like a Christmas tree, and Emma didn't have the heart to make fun of him. It was obvious Matt was passionate about back country skiing.

"So," she said, pretending he hadn't said anything about going to the bathroom in nature, "what activities did you plan for Back Country Skiing Awareness Week?"

Matt scraped ketchup off another fry. "I gave an hour presentation on how to back country ski and the best places to go and the equipment you need. Then we planned a back country skiing trip for the following Saturday, but my brother Holt and I were the only ones to show up. But that's kind of what I expected. Forty-one people attended my presentation, and twenty-six of those were over the age of seventy. The others were my two brothers, my mom, about a dozen teenage girls, and Trudy."

It wasn't hard to guess why a dozen teenage girls showed up to Matt's presentation. He was the kind of guy teenage girls went crazy over, like Zac Efron or Orlando Bloom—rugged good looks and a swoon-worthy smile.

"So I can plan on about forty people at my curling presentation?"

"It depends," Matt said. "Three people showed up for Malaria Awareness Week last year. Practically the whole town showed up for Irrigation Awareness Week. Everybody's pretty testy about water rights."

Emma breathed a sigh of relief. "Nobody gets testy about curling. Maybe nobody will come."

"They'll come, all right, if they know who'll be teaching the class."

What did he mean by that? "So, what should I say?"

"Well, what do you know about curling?"

Emma groaned. "Everything. My parents got to the quarterfinals at the state bonspiel last year. My dad wanted me to be a curler, but I couldn't stand it. They finally gave up on me and sent me to Idaho every summer while they traveled to curling events."

"That's why you came every summer? To avoid the curling circuit?"

"Yep." Emma finished off her French fries. Would Matt give her some of his if she asked?

"I'm surprised your parents didn't have another child," he said. "You know, someone who carried on the curling tradition and made your parents proud?"

Emma glared at him in mock indignation. "I made my parents proud. I never learned French, but I won a math award in eighth grade."

"Good for you."

"My parents married late. Mom had me when she was forty. I was the only child, but why have more when you achieve perfection the first time?"

"Ha, ha."

Emma giggled at his deadpan expression. "They still live in Gilbert, but they moved to a retirement center when I went off to college. They still go curling four times a week."

Matt swirled a fry in a dollop of ketchup on his plate. "So what you're saying is, you know everything there is to know about curling."

"Pretty much. I can tell you the last twenty Olympic gold and silver medalists."

Matt shook his head in mock pity. "Nobody ever remembers the bronze winners." Then he furrowed his brow as if very concerned about something. "This is going to be a very boring presentation."

Emma reached across the table and smacked him in the arm. "Thanks a lot."

He raised his hands in surrender. "I'm kidding. You went to graduate school. You know how to give a good presentation."

"That's true. I once gave a presentation on oil futures. I got an A, and nobody yawned once."

"Is there a way to actually have people do curling in the auditorium?"

Emma dipped one of her fries in the mayonnaise and pointed to a door near the cash register. "And by auditorium, you mean that smallish room over there?"

"Yes. Can you teach them the rules of curling using tennis balls or something?"

Emma finished off the last bite of her enormous cheese-burger. "That's not a bad idea. But it has to be more sophisti-cated than tennis balls."

"You'll figure it out."

He said it in such a nice way, as if he had all the confidence in the world in her presentation abilities. Emma's pulse quick-ened. There was more to Matt than flannel and yurts. And she was kind of starting to not dislike him.

Trudy came back pushing a cart with five slices of dessert on it. "If you want dessert, Roy says to tell you the chocolate is hand grated."

After pate' and a deconstructed cheeseburger, Emma didn't think she could eat another bite, but who knew when her next meal would be? "What have you got?"

"We've got chocolate peanut butter pie made with real German chocolate. Apple and pumpkin pie, piña colada cake, and bread pudding made with French bread. I don't know why

Roy is so obsessed with France. Culinary school was in Omaha."

Maybe Emma could take something home and eat it for breakfast. "I'll have a slice of apple pie to go." Apples were a good breakfast food. Mom made German apple pancakes at home.

"I'll have the peanut butter and chocolate pie," Matt said.

"Okay," Trudy said. "But don't get fat. Nobody would like it if you got fat." She wheeled the cart back into the kitchen.

Emma leaned closer to Matt and whispered, just in case Trudy was listening at the kitchen door. "I think she has a crush on you."

Matt grimaced. "I hope not."

"You don't want a girlfriend?"

"My job's real busy right now. I don't have time for a girlfriend."

Emma smirked. "That's what all guys say until they actually meet someone they want to date."

He shrugged in surrender. "I don't like to be set up, and that's a nice way of saying no thanks."

Emma propped her elbows on the table and laced her fingers together. "So, you're a miner? Have you staked a claim? Are you looking for gold?"

He acted as if she'd just said something incredibly absurd, like 'Gee, Matt, you should think about installing a bathroom in that yurt.' He leaned back in his chair. "What makes you think I'm a miner?"

"Sheriff Hob said something like that the other day."

Matt thought for a minute. "Oh. He asked me how the mining business was going. I'm not a miner. I work for a mining company in Boise. I'm their chief geologist."

"That's nice," was all Emma could think to say. She felt the heat creep up her face. Matt wasn't the only one who made assumptions. Chief geologist sounded a lot more impressive than prospector.

He ate the last fry on his plate. "What do you do when you're not living in other people's houses?"

"Well, first of all, I'm not living in other people's houses. And secondly..." What exactly should she say? *I don't really have a job because I'm being investigated by the SEC and my boss yelled at me and got me kicked out of my apartment.* "I'm a financial planner and advisor."

A frown formed on Matt's lips. "Like your Uncle Harvey."

Trudy came out with a box and a plate of the tallest piece of chocolate pie Emma had ever seen. "Roy says to tell you the cream is hand whipped."

"It looks good," Matt said, for the first time not really giving Trudy his full attention. He seemed unexpectedly upset about something.

Trudy handed Emma her box of apple pie. Emma didn't even have to open it to know it was about a third of the size of Matt's. Life just wasn't fair sometimes. Trudy pulled out her notepad. "Two checks or one?"

"Two," Matt said, which was exactly what Emma expected. They weren't on a date, and she was perfectly capable of paying for her own meal. But he said it so curtly, as if he was mad at Emma all of a sudden.

Trudy jotted down something in her notebook. "I heard you got fired, Emma."

Matt's gaze flashed in Emma's direction.

"I didn't get fired." That was true as far as she knew. "I'm on a leave of absence."

"People can be such jerks sometimes." Trudy set two receipts on the table. "I'll clear these plates away. We want to close early so we'd appreciate it if you ate fast." She ambled away as if nobody wanted to close early.

Matt narrowed his eyes. "You got fired?"

Emma pressed her lips together. "I didn't get fired. I mean, the boss said I was fired, but now they're doing an investigation to see if I really did something wrong."

Matt leaned in as if he was a police officer interrogating a witness. "Did you steal someone's money?"

"Of course not. I don't know what I did. I went in to work one day, and the boss started yelling about betrayal and honesty, and then he ordered me out of the office." Emma picked up her fork and took a taste of Matt's peanut butter and chocolate pie. If he wasn't going to eat it, she would.

His eyes seemed like two glowing shards of hot coal. "I should have guessed. You're just as crooked as your uncle."

Emma nearly choked on her absolutely heavenly piece of peanut butter chocolate pie. "My uncle was the most honest man I know."

Matt's face was a storm cloud. "Do you enjoy cheating people out of their money? Or is that just your retirement plan?"

"What are you talking about? I don't cheat people out of their money. There are laws, not to mention my own personal code of ethics."

"If your code of ethics is anything like your uncle's, you'll probably spend most of your life in prison."

Emma slammed her fork on the table. If he thought she was going to eat any more of his pie, he had another thing coming. "How dare you say such a thing? You don't know anything about me or my uncle. I'm going through a very hard time right now, and you have no right to accuse me of wrongdoing."

He curled his lips sarcastically. "Oh, you poor girl."

Emma's chest tightened with fury. "You don't know

anything, you big oaf. You're just a mountain man with a fancy job title who doesn't even know how to dress himself."

"And you're a selfish, spoiled baby who can't make it in the real world without lying and cheating. You make me sick."

It was like a slap to the face. "Well, you make me want to throw up." Unfortunately, that was the only comeback she could think of, especially when she was boiling mad. How dare he say those things? He knew nothing. Nothing.

Emma jumped to her feet, went to the cash register, and pounded on the little bell that alerted Trudy she had a customer. Even though she was supposedly in a great hurry to close the restaurant, Trudy shuffled slowly out of the kitchen and around to the cash register. Emma pulled a twenty-dollar bill out of her purse. "Keep the change."

"Are you sure?" Trudy said. "That's a six-dollar tip."

Emma forced a smile. "You give great service."

Trudy took her time punching buttons on the ancient cash register, but she finally got the stupid thing open. She pulled six dollars from the till. "Thanks, Emma. I always mostly liked you."

Emma pulled Matt's wonderfully smelling coat from the coat rack and put it on. Every cell in her body revolted at wearing something of his, but her practical side won out. This was no time to freeze to death. She wouldn't give Matt the satisfaction, especially since he'd get the house if she were dead.

She stood with her arms wrapped tightly around herself and watched Matt leisurely eat his pie. He might have been trying to act casual, but he was just as steamed as she was, and he was trying to get under her skin by eating slowly because, darn it all, he was her ride home. Little did he know, she had very thick skin. Why, oh, why hadn't she chosen the protein bar?

He finally finished his pie and wiped his mouth with a napkin, proving that even jerks could have manners. But when he reached for his receipt, his hand bumped Emma's take-out box, and it fell on the floor.

He'd done that on purpose!

Emma pretended not to care that her breakfast was probably a jumbled puddle of apples and crust. Matt would see no weakness from her. From now on, she was a rock. She was solid granite stone.

As a geologist, Matt Matthews would appreciate that *and* seriously regret the day he'd met her.

CHAPTER

EIGHT

Emma pulled into the parking lot of the Quaint and Quirky Quilt Shop. After last night's high heels deba-cle, she'd put on her cross trainers, her sweatpants with yoga pants underneath, and Mom's old sweatshirt that was too big but nice and warm. The cold was not going to conquer her this morning. She had also surrendered to the smell and put on Uncle Harvey's tan, clunky coat. She'd rather be stinky than dead. But just barely.

As an added bonus, she wasn't on the verge of starvation like she had been yesterday. She'd tried her best to keep her pride intact when she'd picked that take-out box off the floor and carried her apple pie home last night. She'd eaten it this morning, and even though it was more like apple pudding than pie, it was a delicious breakfast.

She and Matt had ridden home in silence last night, and he'd stomped off to his room and slammed the door before Emma had even had time to give him back his coat. And that was just the way she liked it. The less Matt Matthews in her life, the better. He'd ruined a perfectly nice evening and a perfectly good apple pie.

Emma's turned off the truck, and her cell phone dinged. "*Quilt Shop at 10:00.*"

The mayor's texts were short and right to the point.

Another text came through. "*I need you for the Dandelion Jelly Festival too.*"

It was the curse of saying yes to anything. Then people thought you had the time to say yes to everything. Well, now that she was unemployed, Emma did have the time. It was a very depressing thought. She needed to get a job. Not only did she need the money, but being employed would get her out of helping with the festival. Maybe. Mayor Pratt seemed the persistent type. Just like Matt Matthews.

Argh! She hated the very thought of his name.

Sort of.

Emma certainly wasn't dressed appropriately for a meeting with the mayor and her Awareness Week committee. No one would be impressed with her fashion sense, but at least she'd be warm. No wonder *some* of the residents of Dandelion Meadows looked like flannel-clad mountain men. It was the only practical attire in this weather—even if she despised his very existence.

She nearly biffed it in the parking lot because the ice was thick, but she was able to catch herself by grabbing the truck's rearview mirror. Luckily, it didn't fall off when she pulled herself upright. Uncle Harvey's truck was as sturdy as they came.

Of course it was. It was a Chevy. Not like Matt's stupid Ford.

What was happening to her? She'd never, ever held any sort of opinion on a truck before. Something was very wrong.

Dodging the thickest ice, she jogged into the quilt shop

because it was still really cold, even with all her gear. The little bell tinkled over the door, and she pulled off her coat the minute she entered the shop. She'd rather not stink up the meeting.

Mayor Ladasha sat at the quilt with Burton Lane and Betty. The Awareness Week committee. Betty and Ladasha were quilting. Burton was cleaning his fingernails with a pocketknife. Torie and Ardeth were nowhere to be seen.

Ladasha looked up from her stitches. "Ah, Emma. We're so glad you could come."

"Me too," Emma said. At least a meeting of the Awareness Week committee had gotten her out of the house. When she'd left this morning, Matt was already parked in front of the TV flipping the channels between some golf tournament and a basketball game. It must have been his version of Saturday morning cartoons.

She hadn't said a word to him, even though he'd propped his feet on the coffee table. She was going to have to give that table an extra coat of wax and hope his boot marks came out.

Ladasha pointed to Burton. "Do you know Burton Lane?"

Emma nodded. Burton and Uncle Harvey used to play poker every Tuesday night. "Good to see you, Burton."

"I suppose," Burton said. "But I'd like an explanation for why Aluminum Awareness Week was bumped for curling."

Ladasha poked her needle in the quilt. "I already told you, Burton. We don't know how long Emma is going to be here. We've got to leverage her talents while we can." Ladasha smiled at Emma. "Have a seat, honey. We always hold our meetings at the quilt shop so we can quilt while we talk."

"I don't quilt," Burton said. "And I don't see the need."

"Idle hands are the devil's playground," Betty said.

Ladasha ran her hands along the fabric. "It's called multitasking, Burton. Doing two things at once. I know for a fact that you sing while you plant potatoes."

Burton closed his pocketknife. "I suppose that is multitasking. Lucille says my singing scares away the birds."

Ladasha reached under the quilt and retrieved a purple binder. "Now, Emma. Here is the Awareness Week procedure book. It will tell you everything you need to know about how to make an effective and interesting presentation."

Emma nearly dropped the binder when Ladasha handed it to her. It was heavy. Was she really supposed to read all this? Maybe she could just pretend to read it. How hard could it be, really? She'd done plenty of presentations in her day, and Matt had assured her she'd do fine.

Emma's heart thumped a couple of irregular beats. Matt had been smiling when he'd told her that. She really liked his smile, even if he was a snake. A slimy, underwater rattlesnake.

"Okay," Emma said. "I've never done a presentation on curling before, but I'll do my best."

Ladasha smiled. "Of course you will. I'm really looking forward to it. I watched curling bloopers on YouTube last night. Hilarious! I'm sure we're going to be very entertained."

Emma's smile faded. She could be informative and interesting, but she wasn't sure if she could make curling entertaining. "I don't know if it will be funny."

"I could have made Aluminum Awareness Week funny," Burton said, giving Ladasha a significant look.

Ladasha fingered her dangly earring. "She'll do fine. Do you have a Mac or a PC, Emma? I need to be sure to have the right hook-ups for your computer."

"A Mac," Emma said. Maybe she wouldn't need to do a PowerPoint presentation. Maybe she could show curling blooper videos for an hour.

Ladasha looked at her phone. "Okay. It's 10:10. This

concludes our Awareness Week committee meeting. Emma, can you stay for the Dandelion Jelly Festival committee meeting? It starts in five minutes."

Burton frowned. "What about the agenda item of rescheduling Aluminum Awareness Week?"

Ladasha opened her binder. "We're booked out until next January. I'll pencil you in for the twenty-seventh."

Burton looked as if he might protest, but before a word came out of his mouth, the bell above the door rang and seven people filed into the shop. It was obvious Ladasha ran a tight ship. Her committee meetings were short, and if all these people arriving at exactly 10:12 was any indication, she expected people to be on time.

Emma knew all but two of the people who came in. Ned and Pamela Goring owned the Beer Hall where they sold groceries but no beer. Pamela was also the pastor of the very small church next to the park. She preached a short sermon every Sunday, and people adored her—mostly because she preached such short sermons. Pamela was no dummy. People tended to put more in the collection plate if they could get out of church early.

Bill Rigby was an old farmer like Burton. He and his wife had raised twelve children and millions of potatoes over the years. Emma had always liked Bill's gravelly voice and the way he could pull random facts about Dandelion Meadows out of the air.

Emma's stomach did a somersault when Clay Matthews and his mother, Vicki, came in. Clay was Matt's older brother —just as brooding, just as tall, and just as handsome as Matt. Emma pressed her lips together. Matt might be handsome, but he had a lot to learn about being nice to people.

Well. Matt *had* been nice to her before he'd been mean. He'd fixed her truck and taken her out for a cheeseburger and taught her how to start a fire. He'd saved her from hitting her head when he could have let her die in the Hair Museum parking lot. He wasn't all bad, even if he had insulted Emma and her uncle and put his feet on the coffee table.

Vicki couldn't have been more than five feet tall. Even Emma was taller than Vicki, and that was saying something. She had to be in her fifties, because Clay was in his thirties, but she looked younger, like an older version of Jennifer Lawrence with a wedge haircut. Her chestnut brown hair was straight and stylish, cut a few inches below her ears and curled slightly under. It was a darling haircut, perfect for the shape of her face. Johnny Cleaver was the only barber in town, but Emma had a hard time imagining that Johnny had done that to Vicki's hair. It was too modern.

Vicki walked into the quilt shop as if she owned it, as if she was a force to be reckoned with. That wasn't necessarily a bad thing, unless you got on Vicki's bad side, and Emma suspected she was very much on Vicki's bad side. Vicki was as formidable as Robert DeNiro in "Raging Bull." She was way more intimidating than Emma's business calculus professor or that one lady who worked at the Texas Department of Motor Vehicles. Vicki had raised five boys. She wasn't a pushover, and she certainly wasn't one to back down from a fight.

Aunt Gwen and Vicki Matthews had been friends, and Vicki had always been sweet to Emma, but now Matt wanted Emma's house, and it was a sure bet Vicki would side with her son.

Vicki hung up her coat and scarf, and Emma's stomach flipped over again. Vicki had dressed for a meeting with the mayor. Her salmon-colored slacks were stunning with the navy cardigan and strand of pearls. Emma looked down at her outfit and thought she might die. She should have risked death and broken bones for Chinos and her lime green pumps. She looked fabulous in her strappy lime green pumps.

Maybe she should take off her sweatpants. A guy at the gym had once told her she looked smoking hot in her yoga pants. But she had a feeling Vicki would not be impressed with "smoking hot."

Escape was Emma's best option. She grabbed her notebook and slinked toward the kitchen door. Unfortunately, Ladasha saw her. "Emma, don't go running off. We need to make assignments."

At the sound of Emma's name, Vicki snapped her head around, like a velociraptor that had just located its prey. Emma clutched her notebook to her chest and backed up against the kitchen door. Vicki swooped in for the kill. "Emma Dustin. How are you?"

"Umm. Fine."

"You're all grown up. I remember sitting on Gwen's porch shelling peas with you and debating which of the Jonas Brothers was better looking."

"Y-yes," Emma stuttered. She hadn't expected Vicki to scowl at her, but she certainly hadn't expected the Jonas Brothers. "How are you, Vicki?"

Vicki smiled as if she was surprised Emma had asked. Maybe they had both assumed the worst. "I've lost ten pounds, gotten a divorce, and had some grandchildren since I last saw you."

"That's nice," Emma said, then mentally smacked herself in the forehead. The weight loss and the grandchildren were nice, but how could she say that getting a divorce was nice?

Vicki's smile widened. "Yes, it is, especially the grand-children."

"How many have you got?"

"Two. Clay got married, had two babies right off, then his

wife left him for a law firm and a hedge fund manager in New York. Clay and the girls live with me now."

"That's nice," Emma said, wishing she could kick herself. How could she say Clay's divorce was nice? It just wasn't her day. No matter what Ladasha said, she was going to go hide in the kitchen. "If you'll excuse me, Vicki, I need to go locate the sugar cookies."

Vicki tilted her head to one side as if to get a better look at Emma. "Is my son being a gentleman?"

"What?"

"I told Matt I'd skin him alive if he didn't act like a gentleman."

"Oh. That. Well." He had taken her coat at the restaurant. He'd let her have some of his limes. Then he'd said some horrible things about Uncle Harvey. She was definitely going to lock Matt out tonight—if she could get him out of the house in the first place.

Vicki's gaze turned intense all of a sudden. "I understand why you think you're entitled to Harvey and Gwen's house. You spent many summers there, but why are you determined to keep it when it is legally Matt's house?"

So much for beating around the bush.

A pressing need for one of Ardeth's sugar cookies nearly overpowered Emma. It would be so easy for her to duck into the kitchen and climb out the window before they even knew she was gone.

Wishing she was wearing her blue and yellow tweed jacket with the gold buttons, Emma squared her shoulders and made herself taller by standing on her tiptoes. Vicki was fearsome, but if Emma had learned anything in grad school, it was to claim her hill and hold her position. The hill was pretty hard to hold on tiptoes. "The legal will leaves me the house. A handwritten note has no validity." That's what Johnny had told her, and it sounded very intelligent.

"The handwritten will was notarized and witnessed. It would hold up in any court of law."

"That's what we're going to find out." With all the confidence she could muster, she raised her chin and pinned Vicki with a cool-as-a-cucumber eye. "Have you even stopped to question why Uncle Harvey would leave the house to Matt and not his niece?"

Vicki didn't even hesitate. "It's obvious to everyone but you, Emma. Except for Gwen's funeral, you hadn't been back to Dandelion Meadows for almost ten years. You practically abandoned your uncle. No wonder he cut you out of his will."

Emma clenched her teeth. That wasn't fair. After high school, she'd started college immediately because she had a scholarship. Then in the summers between semesters, she'd gotten internships in Sacramento and Dallas. Even though she'd been busy, she'd called Uncle Harvey once a week, twice a week after Aunt Gwen died. She'd also handwritten a letter every week because Uncle Harvey liked getting things in the mail. When Uncle Harvey got cancer, she'd flown to Salt Lake six times in three months to visit him—all she'd been able to afford. She'd done everything but come to Idaho, except for his funeral.

Matt wasn't the only one who made unjustified assumptions about her.

She wasn't about to tell Vicki all this. Vicki would accuse her of bragging, or lying, like Matt had last night. Emma blew a strand of hair out of her face. As Uncle Harvey would say, the Matthewses were the raspberry seed in her wisdom tooth. And a downright pain in the neck.

All thoughts of a sugar cookie vanished. Emma was not going to lose this argument. "Despite what you think, I took good care of my uncle. And even if I didn't, why would he leave the house to Matt? They barely knew each other."

For the first time, doubt flashed in Vicki's eyes. "Matt didn't say, but I suspect it's because Leland and Harvey were such good friends."

"Uncle Harvey and Leland were friends, but Uncle Harvey went fishing with Sheriff Hob, played poker with Burton Lane and Bill Rigby, and helped Old Man Kyle sow his field every spring. Leland wasn't more or less special than any of the others. If they were such good friends, why didn't Uncle Harvey leave the house to Leland instead of his son?"

Vicki frowned. "You're right, Emma."

"I'm right?"

"It doesn't make sense. I got so caught up in taking Matt's side that I skipped over that part about why Harvey would leave Matt the house."

"Which he didn't," Emma said.

"Of course he did." Vicki had her doubts, but she was still sure of herself. "It's Matt's house, no matter the reasons, but I suppose it will be settled in court." She pursed her lips. "I'm going to have another talk with Matt. That boy is not going to get away with keeping secrets from his mother." She patted Emma's hand. "Make sure he's a gentleman. If he doesn't treat you well, call me. I'll make sure he behaves himself."

To Emma's relief, Vicki moved away, found a spot at the quilt, and picked up a needle. Emma certainly hoped they didn't expect her to quilt. She couldn't even sew on a button.

The bell tinkled, and Frankie Hiatt blew into the shop with about ten seconds to spare before meeting time.

"Frankie!" Emma squealed.

"Emma!" Frankie charged at Emma, threw her arms around her, and lifted Emma off the floor. Frankie's enthusiasm was boundless.

Frankie and Torie had befriended Emma that very first summer she'd come to Dandelion Meadows. Where Torie was timid and tentative about everything, Frankie was bold and flamboyant, always trying to talk Emma and Torie into things teenagers shouldn't do. She was a year older than Torie and Emma and seemed so wise in the ways of the world.

At fourteen, Frankie had used a leather awl to pierce her belly button and had almost passed out. Nobody but Torie, Frankie, and Emma had known about it, and Frankie had worn a gold hoop in her belly button until her mom discovered it two years later. Frankie had tried to talk Torie and Emma into tattoos, but Torie hadn't dared and Emma thought they were unattractive, so Frankie had gotten one by herself: a paw print on her ankle with the word "Jasper" underneath, in memory of her favorite childhood pet. It was a very appropriate tattoo since Frankie was a veterinarian.

Emma had always been jealous of Frankie's skin. As far as Emma knew, that girl had never had a pimple in her life. And Frankie was definitely a free spirit. She still liked experimenting with all sorts of hair colors. Today her hair was purplish gray and curly. It was a very good look.

Frankie set Emma on her feet. "I'm sorry I didn't get a chance to come by last night. There was a pet emergency."

"It's just as well," Emma said. She had been pretty busy eating cheeseburgers and being mad at Matt.

"Are you on the festival committee too?" Frankie said.

Emma shook her head. "I hope I'm not in town that long, but if you're on the committee, I'll think about it."

Frankie laughed. "It's really pretty fun. We do a parade and a jelly contest and a raffle."

"Oh, I know. I spent seven summers here, remember?"

Frankie took off her coat and draped it over the nearest chair. "How could I forget? The funnest time of my life."

"Ladies," Ladasha said, motioning for Frankie and Emma to sit, "we're two minutes late. Let's go."

Emma sat next to Frankie, which unfortunately was also next to Vicki Matthews, but maybe there'd be too much festival business for any chit-chat on Vicki's part.

Frankie reached over Emma and gave Vicki a hug. This day was just getting better and better. "Love your hair," Frankie gushed.

"Love yours too," Vicki said. "Only someone under thirty can get away with gray."

Hopefully, Frankie wouldn't expect Emma to make nice with Vicki. There was only so much pretending Emma could do in one day.

Ladasha pulled an actual gavel from her purse-bag. How was she going to use that? The quilt would collapse if she hit it. Ladasha turned around and struck her gavel on a blank wooden plaque hanging on the wall. Obviously, she'd done this before. Obviously Ardeth didn't want a hole in her drywall. "Before we talk about the parade, I've added a new feature to our Dandelion Jelly Festival this year."

"You shouldn't add stuff without getting the approval of the committee," Burton said. He was obviously still sore about Aluminum Awareness Week.

Bill Rigby nodded. "The Dandelion Jelly Festival has a rich history. You can't just go changing things without consideration for tradition."

Ladasha pounded the gavel on the plaque, as if quelling a revolt, even though everyone else was sitting quietly in their seats. Ned Goring had already fallen asleep. "I have the floor," Ladasha said. "Please give me your kind attention." She paused until everyone was quiet, which took about one second, since everybody was already quiet. "We have a problem here in

Dandelion Meadows that I think needs to be addressed as part of the festival."

"The Dandelion Jelly Festival is a happy time," Pamela said, "where families gather to share the joy of dandelions and jelly. It is no place for bad news. Can't we address the problem during one of our awareness weeks?"

Ladasha wrapped her fist around her gavel. "No. People will see how important it is if we make it part of the festival."

"What problem are you talking about?" Vicki asked.

"When I got elected, I set out with many goals for our fine city. Plant five new trees, pave the Hair Museum parking lot, and decrease our per capita smoking rate. I've reached all those goals but one. We still have five confirmed cigarette smokers in town, and I want Dandelion Meadows to be the non-smoking capital of Idaho—maybe even the whole country."

"But, Ladasha, LaVerle smokes two packs a day."

Ladasha scrunched her lips to one side of her face. "Exactly. My husband is the worst offender, and I won't stand for it anymore."

Vicki put on her reading glasses and started putting stitches in the quilt. "What do you propose for the Dandelion Jelly Festival?"

"As part of the program, all the smokers have to get up on stage in front of the whole town and pledge to quit smoking."

"What if they don't want to?" was Frankie's obvious question.

"It's called peer pressure," Ladasha said.

"I've got the perfect solution," Bill said. "It's too risky to change the Dandelion Jelly Festival. People won't like it. They're emotionally attached. The jelly festival is in August. What if we have a Stop Smoking Festival in June?"

"That's a whiz-bang idea," said Burton. "We could set up a tent with displays about lung disease."

"Emma's artistic," Vicki said. "She could make a life-size lung out of papier-mâché."

How did Vicki know Emma was artistic? Well, anybody who spent time at Aunt Gwen's house over the years would have seen Emma's drawings plastered all over the walls. Aunt Gwen never threw anything away. "I'm not really a sculptor," Emma murmured.

"We could show videos of lung operations," Burton said. "That would terrify them."

Bill laughed. "They'd all take the pledge after that."

Betty looked up from her quilting. "What if we had a walking parade? The whole town could stroll down the street wearing fancy hats, and the smokers could watch it. That would show them the importance of good lung capacity."

"I think that's called an Easter parade," someone said.

"I'd have to use my cane," Betty added, "even though I have really good lung capacity."

They all waited with bated breath while Ladasha thought about it. Well, not all of them. Clay Matthews acted as if he had about eight other things he'd rather be doing. Ned Goring was asleep, and Frankie was playing a game on her phone. Emma was just hoping no one would give her an assignment.

"I like it," Ladasha said. "If it's a separate festival, people will know how important it is—and I don't want that to take anything away from the Dandelion Jelly Festival. That has always been the jewel of our city."

Bill slapped his knee. "Agreed."

Ladasha stuffed her gavel back into her purse and picked up her needle. She couldn't multitask with a gavel in her hand. "Emma, I was going to ask you to be in charge of the Dandelion Parade."

Bill furrowed his brow, and since he seemed to be dripping

with wrinkles, it was a lot of furrows. "That's a pretty heavy responsibility for a youngster."

Betty and Burton nodded.

"I'm not going to put her in charge of the parade," Ladasha said.

Emma thought she might faint with relief. How nice that they all thought she was too young.

Unfortunately, Ladasha wasn't finished. "I've decided to make you chairman of the Stop Smoking Festival. Your first assignment is to give it a better name than the Stop Smoking Festival. But I like the papier-mâché lung idea."

Emma was glad she wasn't chewing gum because she would have swallowed it. "But...but I'm already giving a presentation for Curling Awareness Week."

Ladasha flashed that really persuasive smile of hers. "You're currently unemployed, and you need something to keep you busy so you don't dwell on your misfortunes. I'd say this is the perfect activity."

How could the Stop Smoking Festival keep her from dwelling on her misfortunes when being in charge was a misfortune all by itself?

"I don't know if that's such a good idea," Burton said. "Remember the dog incident. We can't put a whole festival in the hands of a dog hater."

Really? Did Burton have to bring up the dog? "That was ten years ago. I'm not a dog hater," Emma said. She promptly shut her mouth. If she stayed quiet, Ladasha was bound to change the subject, and everyone would forget about the dog. Hopefully. And she felt sort of bad for telling that little white lie about not being a dog hater. She liked dogs okay, but she hated the hair and the smell and the poop in the yard. Dogs were messy and unpredictable, and Emma didn't like either.

Ladasha rolled her eyes. "That was years ago, Burton,

before I came to town. I'm sure Emma has changed her ways. Haven't you, Emma?"

Emma was torn. How badly did she not want to be in charge of the Stop Smoking Festival? "Um...well...I don't exactly hate dogs, but I don't exactly—"

Frankie put her arm around Emma and squeezed tight. "I volunteer to be her co-chair."

"Wonderful!" Ladasha snatched her gavel out of her purse and smacked the plaque against the wall, making the entire thing official. "Now let's talk about the Dandelion Jelly Festival."

Emma sat through the rest of the meeting like a bump on a log, mostly in a numb stupor and occasionally casting a dirty look in Frankie's direction. What had she been thinking? Emma didn't want to be in charge of the Stop Smoking Festival. She didn't want to be in charge of anything, including making her own dinner tonight.

Then again, the Stop Smoking Festival was so far away. She'd for sure be back in Dallas by then. But it was also true that being in charge of the Stop Smoking Festival would win her some points with the town council, the mayor, and the good citizens of Dandelion Meadows, and it was obvious after that dog comment, she needed more points. Matt Matthews might have made a presentation for Back Country Skiing Awareness Week, but had he ever run his own festival? The town would definitely love her better when every last smoker turned in his cigarettes and signed his name to the papier-mâché lung.

Matt would never see it coming.

To her credit, Ladasha kept the meeting going, making decisions and assignments with lightning speed. Ned and Pamela were put in charge of the parade. Vicki and Clay were given responsibility for obtaining and selling the dandelion jelly and anything else they thought would do well at the festival. Bill got entertainment, and Betty got the title of vice chair. As far as Emma could tell, the vice chair didn't do anything, but Betty was thrilled. It wasn't fair. Emma would have made a very good vice chair.

Ladasha closed the meeting, and the shop cleared by eleven o'clock. Frankie and Emma were the only ones who stayed around. Frankie wanted to talk about the Stop Smoking Festival, and Emma wanted to give Frankie a good scolding.

As soon as the last person left the shop, Ardeth and Torie appeared from the kitchen. Emma's mouth fell open. "You were in there the whole time?"

Ardeth slid an oven mitt off her hand. "We made a batch of cookies and some bread."

"Why didn't you come out and say hello?"

Torie handed Emma a sugar cookie with swirly pink frosting, which went a long way toward soothing her irritation. "We let Ladasha use our shop, but she tends to give assignments to people who attend her meetings."

"And she doesn't even wait for you to say yes." Emma gave Frankie the evil eye. "How could you do that to me?"

Frankie giggled. "Come on, Emma. It'll be fun. Think of all the little kids we can scare into never picking up a cigarette."

Emma rolled her eyes. "That's my goal in life, to scare little children."

"Besides," Frankie said, "One of the cutest guys in Dandelions Meadows is a smoker. I want him to ask me out, but I won't date a smoker. If this festival works, I might get a date out of it."

Emma gasped in mock indignation. "I knew there was an ulterior motive."

Frankie gave Emma a wide grin. "There always is. Besides,

being in charge of a festival in Dandelion Meadows will look good on your resume'."

Emma shook her head. "Nope. It won't." Nobody this side of Horseshoe Bend would take her seriously with something like that on her resume'.

Frankie lost her smile and gave Emma a hug. "I didn't want them chewing on the dog story again. It was forever ago, and you don't deserve it."

"I agree," Torie said. "The dog story should have died years ago."

It should have, but Emma had made her choices. She was willing to live with the consequences. "Speaking of resume's—"

"Were we?"

"Yes, and I need a job. I hate to ask, but can you guys help me?"

Frankie sighed in sympathy. "Torie told me all about what happened at work. I think you should sue."

"The investigators are looking into it. At this point, I wouldn't even know who to sue."

Torie started folding up extra chairs and stacking them against the wall. Frankie and Emma joined in. "What kind of job do you want?" Torie said.

"Honestly, anything. I need to make my student loan payments and eventually buy a plane ticket out of here." And keep herself from starving to death.

Torie took in a quick breath and beamed like a lighthouse. "Emma, it would be so wonderful if you started drawing again. I'd buy one of your pictures."

Emma shook her head. "My artwork isn't going to make me any money. Why do you think I got an MBA?"

"But you love to draw," Torie said. "And you're so good at it."

"That's very nice of you to say." Emma propped another chair against the wall. It was true she liked drawing. A lot more than finance. "But it won't pay the bills. I need cold, hard cash."

Frankie snatched a cookie from Torie's plate. "I wish I could offer you a job, but I'm barely making ends meet myself."

"It takes time to build up a practice." Torie set her cookies on the hearth, picked up the poker, and stirred the fire. "People are already starting to talk about what a good vet you are, even though they think you're too young."

Frankie rolled her eyes. "Only in Dandelion Meadows is twenty-eight too young. The average population is like seventy-five."

Emma pulled out one of the chairs still around the quilt and sat down. "Did you decide to move into that apartment in Boise?"

Frankie smiled wryly. "Well, not exactly."

"Not exactly?" Torie said. "You mean, not at all."

Emma laughed at the look on Torie's face. "What happened?"

Frankie seemed embarrassed yet pleased at the same time. It was a strange combination on her face. "Hey, I'm on a very tight budget." She sat next to Emma. "LaVerle Pratt sold me that old stone house on White Fish Lane."

Emma's mouth fell open, which was not a good look with half a cookie she hadn't swallowed yet. "You bought the Rockwell house?"

Frankie nodded, a slow smile curling her lips.

"The house with all those spooky overhanging trees and broken windows?"

"Well," Frankie said. "There are only three windows in the whole house, but yes, they had to be replaced."

"But...but," Emma stuttered. "That place doesn't even have

indoor plumbing." First Matt and now Frankie. What was it with Idahoans and their bathroom habits?

"LaVerle installed plumbing and electricity before I moved in. The bathroom is the nicest room in the house."

Torie laughed. "And the biggest room in the house."

"It is not," Frankie protested, with a definite tease in her voice.

Emma could well believe it. The Rockwell house had about the same square footage as a well-fitted master bathroom, and if anyone would know, it was Emma. She was an expert on bathrooms in general and the Rockwell house in particular. "But...but, Frankie, the Rockwell house is haunted."

Frankie giggled as if she couldn't contain it any more. "It adds an element of excitement every time I come home from work."

Emma, Frankie, and Torie had sneaked into the Rockwell house plenty of times during Emma's summers in Dandelion Meadows—not that it was super hard to sneak into. The old house had a door that hung permanently ajar and no windows. It was built completely out of stone in the early 1900s and abandoned some time after World War II. The home consisted of two rooms, each about ten feet by ten feet, and an old wood stove that was like Stonehenge or something—immovable and seemingly indestructible.

Once the house had been abandoned, teenagers used to go there to drink or smoke or hang out, basically to get away from their parents. But as legend had it—and this was a Dandelion Meadows legend, so the story never made it big like the Loch Ness Monster or Big Foot—but according to Dandelion Meadows legend, sometime in the early 1980s, Jimmy Nebling and Allison Schmucker sneaked into the house to make out when they heard a horrible moaning coming from the other room. Jimmy swore he saw a specter, the ghost of an old lady dressed in black with white lace at her throat, pacing the back room with a scalp of long brown hair clutched in her fist.

According to Jimmy, the old lady ghost just happened to look like Priscilla Rockwell, the wife of Chester Rockwell, the founder of Dandelion Meadows. No one questioned how Jimmy knew what Chester Rockwell's wife looked like, but it was well known that Chester had long brown hair that his wife periodically cut and turned into hair sculptures. It was one of those weird and creepy things people did back then.

Chester had mysteriously disappeared one winter's night in 1905. After Jimmy and Allison's make-out session and terrifying ordeal, people began to wonder if Priscilla hadn't murdered and scalped her husband and maybe buried him on the property.

Frankie had always been fascinated with the Rockwell house. She had taken Torie and Emma there many times because she liked scaring herself and everyone else. Sometimes Frankie's brothers had tagged along with them. Sometimes they went alone, but they always took Frankie's dog, an unassuming Shih Tzu-poodle mix who would just as soon poop in the yard as bark at anybody. Boone Matthews, Matt's brother, had gone with them a couple of times, one of those times turning out to be a disastrous experience for all of them.

There hadn't been much to do for excitement in Dandelion Meadows in those days. The Rockwell house was about as exciting as it got. Emma decided not to remind Frankie about the many nights they'd run screaming from the Rockwell house. Frankie didn't need more stress in her life.

Frankie was obviously very pleased with her new house. "I'm remodeling it little by little. I've already refinished the wood floor in the main room, and it's really beautiful."

Emma held her tongue, even though she wanted to ask if Frankie had found any bodies under the floorboards.

"I've got a little stove and a sink in there, plus a mini fridge and a couch. It's really quite comfortable, and LaVerle sold the house and property to me for three thousand dollars."

Emma glanced at Torie in disbelief. Three thousand dollars? That was about two months' rent in her place in Texas. "Okay, maybe it's not such a bad deal after all."

"It's ideal, actually. I'm on calls more than I'm home."

"But it's going well?" Emma said. She wanted to ask Frankie if she'd seen any ghosts, but maybe that was too personal a question.

"There's lots of paperwork, but I'm paying my brother Tony to do my accounting."

"Tony? Isn't he like eleven years old?"

Frankie picked up a needle and started on the quilt. She had never been a keen quilter, but she was a vet now. She knew how to make a good stitch. "He's sixteen, but he's really good at math, and he only charges me eight dollars an hour."

"And people are starting to call her," Torie said. "Once word got around that she saved Leonard Passey's cat from a hairball, she's been getting calls from as far away as Nampa."

Frankie seemed genuinely happy. "Let's just hope my car will hold on for another year or so."

"I wish I could offer you a job, Emma," Torie said, looking troubled. "But with my cousin and Lazy Larry living with us, we're stretching dollars as it is."

Emma stood and draped her arm around Torie's shoulders. "I didn't expect either of you to give me a job, but you know Dandelion Meadows better than I do. Is there any place that's hiring?"

"Ask at the Beer Hall. They can always use more baggers."

"How many baggers do they have?"

"None," Torie said.

Yeah. They could probably use more.

Frankie pointed her needle at Torie. "What about the Weed and Feed?"

"Would I have to lift bags of manure?" Emma said.

"I think so," Torie said.

Frankie loved to brainstorm. "What about Johnny Cleaver? He might need a secretary now that Marian will be busy with tax season. Or maybe they'd hire you at the cemetery to keep the snow off the headstones." Frankie put a few more stitches in the quilt. "You could ask Matt Matthews about a job at the mining office. They have trouble attracting good people because nobody wants to live in Boise."

Emma nearly choked on her tongue. "Never mind that."

Frankie looked up from her quilting. "What's wrong with the mining office? I hear they buy chicken wings for the whole team every Friday."

Torie unfolded one of the chairs they'd just folded and pulled it up to the quilt. "Man, Frankie, you *have* been busy. I thought you would have heard the gossip by now."

Emma worked on the quilt while Torie give Frankie all the gory details about Matt trying to steal Emma's house. The only important part she left out was the thimbles. Emma made sure to add that at the end.

Frankie looked as if it was the most outrageous story she'd ever heard. "So Matt Matthews is living there? At your house? With you?"

Emma nodded. "It's the most horrible thing in the world."

Frankie raised an eyebrow. "Maybe not the most horrible thing. It would be worse if he were ugly."

Emma had to agree. Matt was very easy on the eyes, especially when he sat quietly and brooded over something—Emma especially liked the "quiet" part. The minute that guy opened his mouth, his handsome meter hit the floor. "He is handsome, and he got my truck started, but last night he accused me of being a liar and cheating people out of their money—all because I got suspended at work."

Frankie frowned. "Matt's usually pretty levelheaded." She glanced at Emma. "I'm not defending him. Just puzzled."

"I've got to find a job, and I've got to figure out how to get Matt Matthews out of my house."

Frankie gave Emma a sheepish smile. "You could move in with me."

"No, I couldn't. You don't have any room to spare, and there's a dead man under your floor. I hate to admit it, but I'd rather live with Matt."

Frankie shrugged. "Well, he *is* cute. And he's really sweet once you get to know him. If you change your mind, just let me know. You can sleep on an air mattress in the front room."

"That's probably where the body's buried."

By this time, Torie had made five inches worth of stitches. "Oh," she said, looking at Emma and smiling like a cat. "I know the perfect job."

"Does it involve manure or bagging groceries?" Emma said.

"Neither."

"I'm in."

CHAPTER
NINE

Matt sprawled across the couch and turned on the game. Harvey Dustin's house smelled like mildew and every door creaked deafeningly, but sometime in the last three years, Harvey had purchased an enormous big-screen TV with just about every cable channel imaginable. There were some advantages to living here, even if it was temporary.

When Emma had left this morning, Matt had pretended to settle in for a day of watching college basketball on TV, but as soon as she had left, he'd grabbed his tape measure and notepad and gotten to work. He had measured and noted every square foot of the house—3100 square feet, to be exact.

It was bigger than it looked from the outside, and the structure of the house was sound. It was old, but it was also built of stone, immovable and solid. The doors looked like they were original to the house, solid cherrywood that would be beautiful with some sanding and a new coat of varnish. Harvey had refinished the wood floors recently, and they looked really good. Matt could get more money out of this house than he had expected.

He'd spent the rest of the day doing minor repairs around the house to get it ready to sell. He'd fixed the window in the laundry room because he'd been able to swipe Emma's house key and make a copy. He sincerely hoped he wouldn't need the laundry room window as a back up, because no one was getting in that way now. It would be safer for Emma that way.

He had even changed a light bulb and fixed the blinds in Emma's room, not even pausing to notice how tidy her pink High School Musical bedspread looked or to savor the faint scent of citrus that hung in the air. Emma's presence lingered whether she was in the house or not, and Matt found it very irritating. How was he supposed to get anything done while Emma lived here?

He had to admit that some of his distraction was because of his own behavior last night. He'd been a little too hard on Emma. Her uncle might have been a con artist, but that didn't mean Emma was. The trouble at her job wasn't necessarily because she'd done something dishonest. He shouldn't have accused her when he didn't know the full story. He knew better than anyone how unfair it was to blame someone for something one of their relatives had done.

The TV had been on for less than a minute when Emma came through the front door. She hadn't worn her heels today, but he could still hear her amble into the great room and stop behind the couch. He didn't look up, but it was definitely Emma. He could smell her. That citrusy scent was seriously enough to drive any man to distraction.

"What did you do to my kitchen?" she said, the indignation in her voice loud and clear.

Matt glanced into the kitchen and felt just a tiny bit ashamed of himself. He'd made bacon and eggs for breakfast and grilled tuna for lunch and hadn't cleaned up after himself, and he hadn't gotten around to sweeping up the potato chip crumbs on the great room rug. He'd also emptied the mug cupboard because the shelf was wobbling, but he hadn't put any of the mugs back after he'd fixed it. He should have at least done that. But if Emma was irritated, all the better. She'd move out sooner. "Welcome home, dear," Matt said, crossing his hands behind his head and leaning back as if he was settling in for the long winter.

"What have you been doing all day? Or rather, what *haven't* you been doing all day?"

Matt fiddled with the remote because women hated it when men did that. "There were lots of important games today. The NCAA tournament is only six weeks away."

She sighed loudly, probably glaring at him in hopes of searing a hole into the back of his head. "How can you bear to live with yourself?"

"It's pretty easy, actually."

She went into the kitchen and shuffled a few pans on the counter, either trying to find the dish soap or trying to get his attention. She didn't know she had his full attention, even if he wasn't looking at her. "This is a pig sty, and what are all the mugs doing out of the cupboard?"

"I was looking for the one with your face on it." Which was technically true. After pulling out half the mugs and finding one with Gwen's face on it and one with Harvey's, he'd been curious to see if there'd been one of Emma. He'd found it. It was young, teenage Emma, but she had the same eyes.

Emma's pause was barely perceptible, but Matt noticed it. What did she care if he wanted to see her face on a mug? "Are they clean?" she said.

"I didn't use them, except for the one with the hand-painted mouse on it. That's in the sink."

"How thoughtful of you," she said, the sarcasm dripping from her lips. She set about five mugs back in the cupboard before she stopped and turned to him. "I shouldn't be doing this. Get over here and clean up your mess."

"I can't right now. It's a pretty intense game." He hoped she didn't actually look at the TV. The one team was up 75 to 51, and he wasn't even sure who was playing.

Emma marched around the island, grabbed the remote from Matt's hand, and turned off the TV. She was dressed in that gray sweatshirt he liked so much, and her eyes flashed like fireworks. "I'm not cleaning up your mess, Matt Matthews, and if you think I am, you've got another thing coming."

"If you want it cleaned so badly, you're going to have to do it yourself. I'm not missing my game." He snatched the remote away from her and turned the TV back on.

Her irritation was at a boiling point now. "Get out of my house. I will not tolerate a slob."

"This house is mine, and I have every right to mess it up if I want to."

He let down his guard for half a second, and she grabbed the remote from him again. Matt jumped to his feet as she sprinted for the kitchen and turned on the garbage disposal. Holding the remote over the drain, she glared at him. "Clean up your mess, or I'll turn this remote into a pile of dust."

Matt raised his hands as if she were holding a gun on him. "Okay, okay. Don't grind up the remote. We'll both regret it later, and you'd have to pay for a new disposal."

She thought about it for a minute, scrunched her lips to one side of her face, and turned off the disposal. "It gives me no pleasure holding the household appliances hostage, but I refuse to live in squalor."

Matt couldn't really see how a pile of dirty dishes was

squalor. "It's no big deal, Emma. I'm not as tidy as you are, and I'm happy the way I am."

She set the remote on the counter and motioned to the dirty dishes. "I can't live like this."

"And I can't live in a museum where I'm not allowed to touch anything."

"Then move out."

"You move out."

"It's my house."

Matt wasn't going to have this argument again. It went absolutely nowhere. "We just have to stand each other until our lawyers work it out." He wasn't about to tell her he hadn't hired a lawyer. She needed to believe that he had everything under control.

Emma crossed her arms over her chest and huffed out a frustrated breath. "Fine." Without a second's hesitation, she started rifling through the drawers, first the ones in the island, then the ones next to the refrigerator. From the last drawer, she pulled out a giant roll of masking tape and held it in front of his face as if she planned on beating him over the head with it. "We'll divide the house in half. You can do whatever you want in your half, and I'll live in my half."

She strode down the front hall to the door like a woman on a mission. After pressing the end of the tape onto the wood floor, she unrolled it so it divided the hall exactly in half. She took the tape over the couch, cutting it in half, and up the mantel to the bottom of the TV.

"Don't," Matt said. "That sticky stuff will never come off the TV. Besides, we can't watch half a TV."

She pressed her lips together. "But we need a clear dividing line."

"Masking tape is very bad for the floor."

He hated how cute she looked when she was thinking really hard about something. "Maybe we should use yarn."

"Do you have any yarn?" he said.

"No, but I bet Aunt Gwen has a stash somewhere."

"We can't divide the kitchen either. The fridge and the stove are on the same side, and it's impossible to use half a sink."

"I suppose you're right," Emma said, pulling the tape off the floor. "Maybe we don't need tape, just clear divisions. I get the entire upstairs, including the rec room."

"But there's a ping-pong table up there."

Emma had no sympathy for him. "You'll have to go somewhere else to play ping pong."

"Then I get the entire main floor. You'll have to go somewhere else to make dinner."

Emma shook her head. "You said it yourself. We can't divide the kitchen, but I'm willing to let you have the basement."

Matt gave her the stink eye. "There's nothing down there but food storage and about a million spiders."

"You're a geologist. You can start a spider collection."

"That's not what geologists do."

Emma batted her eyes and put extra saccharine in her voice. "I want it to be your own personal space, Matt. A place you can go when the world knocks you down. If you want to paint graffiti on the cement walls, I will not say nay."

"Give me a break."

Emma's smile was cheeky. And irresistible. "It's nothing less than you deserve."

Matt grunted. He wasn't really mad about the upstairs. There really was no reason for him to go up there. He was more of a skier than a ping pong player anyway. "I get the master bedroom and bathroom and the office."

"I want the office."

"Emma, there are four bedrooms upstairs. Convert one of those into an office."

Emma pressed her lips together and nodded. "Fair enough. I get the laundry room on Mondays, Wednesdays, and Fridays, and you get it the other days. I'm giving you an extra day as a gift."

"Thanks a lot," he said sarcastically, even though it was kind of nice that she would be willing to give him an extra day. "What should we do about the TV? There's always a game on."

"I'm binge watching *Gilmore Girls* right now. I'm not giving that up for a stupid basketball game."

"There is no such thing as a stupid basketball game."

"Even you can't really believe that," she said.

"*Even* me?"

"We'll have to make a daily, hourly schedule. It might be complex."

Matt resisted the urge to point out that if she just moved out, they wouldn't have to make a TV schedule. "I'll make a schedule and run it past you for approval."

She thought about it and nodded. "I know you'll make it fair."

Matt studied her face. Why had she said that? She didn't know anything of the kind. It was a really nice gesture, trusting him like that. Or maybe it was just a manipulation to get something else she wanted. "What about the kitchen?"

"I'd like to say 'Every man for himself,'" Emma said, "but I've already seen what that looks like."

"I was gonna clean it up."

Emma narrowed her eyes. "Okay then. Every woman for herself. And you for yourself, but you have to promise to clean up after yourself."

"I'll do my best. Besides, maybe you'll want to go out sometimes."

She suddenly got serious. "I'm never eating at the museum again, and the gas station is out of the question."

Matt cleared his throat. Might as well get it over with. "Hey. I'm sorry about what I said last night. I shouldn't have accused you like that."

"No, you shouldn't have."

"I'm sorry, and I'm really sorry for ruining your pie."

She turned one shade darker. "You didn't exactly ruin it. I had it this morning for breakfast, and it was delicious."

"I'm sure it was. Roy's been to culinary school, you know."

She leaned over and propped her elbows on the counter. "I've had some trouble at work, Matt, and I still don't know all the details, but I'm not a cheat or a liar. You might not believe it, but it's very important to me to be honest."

"I believe you," he said, "and I'm really sorry for hurting your feelings."

She pause for a second then smiled at him and nearly knocked him over. He smiled back and resolved not to scowl for the rest of the evening. Emma was okay, even if she was completely wrong about the house, even if she had a con man uncle who had probably cheated dozens of people out of their money.

"So," he said, "maybe you'll want to try the museum again after all." He'd be eating there a lot. He really didn't like his own cooking, and he couldn't live off protein bars.

"I don't think so," she said. "I'm working there now."

CHAPTER
TEN

Emma pushed the back arrow for the fourth time on the YouTube video. Was this guy even speaking English? She concentrated hard on the screen while the chef mixed butter and salt in one of those cute little white porcelain bowls chefs mix small things in. Emma didn't have a cute little bowl, so she used a blue mug with "Reagan Bush '84" in white letters down the side. There were some great history lessons in Aunt Gwen's mug cupboard.

Emma paused the video and mixed her salt and melted butter together. She was determined to make herself a nice dinner tonight. Lucky Charms weren't going to cut it anymore.

Yesterday, Sunday, had been a simply glorious day, mostly because Matt had been gone all day on some kind of outdoorsy sportsman's trip. He hadn't told her where he was going, but he'd left the house carrying a pair of skis and something that looked suspiciously like an overnight backpack. She hadn't expected Matt was moving out for good, but he hadn't come back last night, and she still held out hope that maybe he'd decide to live in the wild and maybe raise a wolf as a pet.

What really bothered Emma was that she had almost been disappointed when Matt hadn't come home last night. Uncle Harvey's house was big and creaky, and it could get kind of lonely without someone to argue with. Maybe she should get a dog.

Maybe not. A dog would be messier than Matt.

"*Next step, gobbledygook gobbledygook your ham gobbledygook gobbledygook.*" Emma rewound the video. This was going to take forever.

She heard the front door open, and for some unfathomable reason, her heart started pitter-pattering like rain on a tin roof. She hadn't locked Matt out tonight because he was going to be extra cold from all that outdoor air, and she didn't want him to freeze to death on her porch.

Matt came into the great room, peeled off his hat, unzipped his coat, and gave Emma an unexpected smile. She was powerless to do anything but pause her cooking video and stare at him.

"Making dinner?" he said.

"Um."

He suddenly seemed at a loss for words himself. There was a long pause before he pointed to the door to the master bedroom. "I'm going to take a shower."

"Do you speak French?"

He curled one side of his mouth. "I thought you spoke French."

She didn't even roll her eyes. "This guy is showing me how to make chicken cordon bleu, but I think he's speaking French."

Matt took off his coat, tossed it on the couch, and came around to her side of the island. "Let's see." He leaned close so he could get a good look at her phone, and she caught his strong, outdoorsy scent. For a guy who'd spent the last thirty-six hours in the wilderness, he smelled pretty darn good. Emma wasn't especially fond of the outdoors, but it smelled delicious on Matt Matthews. Her heart did that pitter-patter thing again.

She attempted to hold her breath, but she didn't want to pass out facedown into the raw chicken. She'd just have to deal with the heart palpitations. Maybe it would be better after he took a shower, but something told her not to count on it. "It's kind of hard to see the video on my phone, but the SEC has my laptop."

He lost his smile and glanced at her but probably decided not to jump to conclusions and accuse her of being a liar. He pressed the play arrow.

"After this, gobbledygook goggledygook on the side."

Matt made a face. "I have no idea what he just said."

"I don't think this guy is really a chef. He's working with raw chicken on a wooden cutting board. Even I know you shouldn't do that."

"He's hard to understand," Matt said, "but it's pretty straightforward if you watch what he's doing."

Emma pointed to the flattened breasts of chicken on her plastic cutting board. "Yeah. I got this far."

Matt cocked an eyebrow and picked up Uncle Harvey's pipe wrench sitting next to the chicken. "Please don't tell me you used this to pound the chicken."

"Okay, I won't tell you."

Matt groaned. "This is a finely crafted plumbing tool. Your Uncle Harvey is rolling in his grave."

"He'd rather I use his wrench than starve to death."

"I don't think those are necessarily the only choices."

Emma tilted her head to one side. "That's because you didn't see me try to pound the chicken with a smiley face mug."

Matt laughed then gazed at her as if memorizing her face. "Do you want help?"

She ignored the shivers traveling up her spine. "Of course I want help. I'm not even sure how high to preheat the oven."

Matt peeled off the thick forest green sweater he'd been wearing and threw that on the couch too, leaving him in a snug blue Denver Broncos t-shirt that smelled like pine trees and snow.

She shouldn't hold her breath. She'd fall into her chicken if she held her breath.

He washed his hands then picked up her phone and started the video over again. "I think he said to preheat the oven to 350."

Emma glided to the oven. "Check."

They both watched the video for a few seconds. Emma had to practically lean her head on his chest to see the screen. It was uncomfortable and heavenly at the same time.

She was losing her marbles.

Matt pushed PAUSE and cleared his throat. "Okay. Mix the butter and the salt and brush it on the chicken."

"How much butter?"

"I don't know, but I don't think you can ever have too much butter, can you?"

Emma nodded. "That's true." She put a whole stick of butter in Aunt Gwen's FBI mug, melted it in the microwave, and gave it a pinch of salt. "Do I just pour it on?"

Matt showed her the phone. "He's using some sort of brush."

"I don't think Uncle Harvey has one of those. We could use a paintbrush from the toolbox."

"Absolutely not," Matt said. "Gwen would roll over in her grave."

Emma grimaced. "I think she already has. Her thimble collection will never be the same."

"My head will never be the same."

Emma grunted in disbelief. "Your head is just fine."

"It is not. I'm going to have a scar."

She set down her mug of butter and salt. "Let me see."

Matt backed away. "No. I'm not letting you near my hairline ever again."

She backed him into the fridge. "Let me see, you big baby."

He held up his hands in surrender. Emma got on her tippy toes and parted his hair with her fingers and thumb. Matt stiffened like a popsicle at the North Pole and fell silent. It was only when her fingers were stiffly entwined in his hair that she realized how close they were and that Matt was staring faithfully at her lips.

Well, he'd told her she had nice lips. Looking at people's lips was probably one of his hobbies.

If only he wouldn't practice his hobby on her, then she'd be able to concentrate on his head. Her gaze traveled to his mouth, and the urge to kiss him became almost overpowering. It was entirely his fault. If he hadn't gotten her thinking about lips, she would never have thought to look at his.

She was definitely losing her marbles. "You...um..."

"Emma...I..."

His voice sounded like melted butter in an FBI mug, especially when he spoke her name. How was this possible? One minute they were trying to translate French, the next minute they were practically making out against the fridge.

Emma took a deep breath. This absolutely was not happening. Matt might be the hottest mountain man in Idaho, but he wanted to steal her house, and he'd gone to the bathroom in the outdoors in the last twenty-four hours. She ripped her gaze from his very attractive mouth and did a cursory inspection of his forehead. "You can't even see it anymore." She quickly turned her back on him and washed her hands. That chicken wasn't going to make itself.

Matt was as silent as a mailbox, but she didn't dare turn around to see the expression on his face. She looked at her melted butter. "We're going to need that paintbrush."

His voice almost made her jump. "You could use your toothbrush."

"Disgusting."

He came up behind her, reached over her shoulder, and picked up her phone. "Use a spoon and drizzle the butter on top. You don't want to waste a perfectly good paintbrush."

"Okay." Emma did as Matt suggested, and the chicken was soon drenched in butter. Matt directed her to sprinkle the chicken with paprika and then layer it with slices of ham and Swiss cheese.

He showed her the phone again, and they watched as the chef said something in French then rolled the chicken, ham, and cheese into a cylinder. "Now you just roll it up," Matt said, as if it were as easy as that.

"I'm scared," Emma said.

"There's nothing to be scared of."

Emma took a step back. "You do it."

Matt also took a step back. "Me? I don't know how to do it."

Emma clasped her hands together. "Well, it's like rolling up a sleeping bag, and you've had lots more experience than I have."

"It's nothing like rolling up a sleeping bag."

"Of course it is." Matt didn't budge. She'd have to play the damsel in distress card. "Please, Matt. I'm starving."

He didn't seem especially moved by her plight. "This is your dinner."

"If you help me, I'll share."

That got his attention. "And you do the dishes?"

"Don't be unreasonable. We'll both do them. You need the practice."

For whatever reason, that convinced him. He washed his hands again then carefully rolled up the two chicken breasts—just like sleeping bags.

"Matt," Emma said, clapping her hands, "you did better than I ever could have dreamed of."

"I'll take that as a compliment."

"It is one. I promise."

Matt smiled as if he might consider believing her then washed his hands yet again and picked up her phone. "Okay. Let's finish this puppy."

Matt was an outstanding direction giver and surprisingly good at French. He directed her to make an egg mixture, which she drizzled on the chicken cylinders because, again, no brush. She was definitely going to have to buy a cooking brush the next time she went to Boise.

Matt waited until Emma put the chicken in the oven then went to take a shower. They needed something besides chicken cordon bleu for dinner, but Emma hadn't thought that far ahead when she'd gone to the store this afternoon. She opened the fridge and stared into its depths. Sometime in the last four days, Matt had bought a head of lettuce. He probably wouldn't mind if she used it, especially since he was getting half her chicken.

She washed the lettuce and tore it into a bowl. It wasn't much of a salad, but at least it would be something colorful and nutritious on the plate.

Matt came out of the master bedroom. A siren went off in Emma's head, and it wasn't the oven timer. His hair was damp and messy, and the dark scruff on his jaw was the most attractive thing she'd seen all day. And why did he have to wear flannel? Didn't he know how crazy she went over the rugged lumberjack look?

Wait. Her head started spinning. She had never gone crazy over the lumberjack look before. Why was she suddenly wild about it? Maybe it was all this fresh Idaho air. Maybe she'd been holed up in Uncle Harvey's house for too long. Maybe it was the shortage of good looking men in Idaho, although Matt would be considered smoking hot in any state in the union, even Hawaii—plus Guam, Puerto Rico, and all the U.S. Virgin Islands.

While she'd never say it out loud to another living soul, Matt was better looking than Zac Efron. Emma pressed her lips together. It felt like a betrayal to even think such a thing.

The timer rang, and Emma pulled two perfectly lovely chicken cordon bleus out of the oven. She resolved to look on YouTube more often.

"Dinner's ready," she said, because it didn't seem like the right moment for, "I'm thinking of breaking up with Zac Efron."

Aunt Gwen and Uncle Harvey had never owned a kitchen table. When Emma had come to visit, all three of them sat at the bar to eat. She handed Matt a plate and a fork and motioned toward the lettuce. "There's also salad," she said. Maybe he wouldn't notice there was nothing in it but lettuce. Guys tended not to notice little details like that.

A smile inched onto his face. "Any dressing?"

"I'm afraid not."

Matt put a clump of lettuce on his plate, and Emma served him a piece of chicken cordon bleu, being careful not to stare at his lips. No good could come of letting him get to her like that.

He waited for her to make her own plate and didn't take a

bite until she did. Was this what Vicki meant by "being a gentleman"? It was kind of sweet. Old fashioned, but sweet.

The chicken cordon bleu was delicious, just as Emma had hoped it would be.

"This is really good," Matt said. "Thanks for sharing."

"I'm glad you came when you did. I might have pulled out the paintbrush and the electric drill before I was through."

"If you're going to do any more cooking, maybe you should have Roy at the museum give you a few pointers."

Emma furrowed her brow. "I guess I could, but I wouldn't want him to take it the wrong way."

"The wrong way?"

"You know. Like thinking I want to date him. If you're nice to a guy, he thinks you want to date him."

Matt frowned. "Yeah. Better not chance it." He took a bite of lettuce. "How is work, now that you've done it for two days."

Emma put down her fork and fidgeted with her hands. She didn't have to tell Matt everything. It wasn't dishonest to leave out part of the story. "On Saturday, Lucille had me help Trudy at the restaurant. But today she told me Trudy was offended that Lucille thought she needed help, and when Trudy gets offended, she starts spitting in people's drinks."

Matt made a face. "Thanks for the warning. I think I'll take my own water bottle from now on."

"Today I helped Lucille put up her new exhibit. She's collecting pictures and biographies from every citizen of Dandelion Meadows who served in the military."

"That's got to be a pretty short list."

"And hair."

Matt leaned so close, he nearly brushed his shoulder with hers. "What?"

"Since it's a hair museum, Lucille is very attached to the

idea of hair. She wants a lock of hair from every service member in Dandelion Meadows."

"What about the dead ones?"

"That doesn't seem to discourage her. If she can't get original hair, she'll go after the nearest living relative, or rather, she's sending me to go after the nearest living relative."

Matt grimaced. "Oh, crap."

"You said it. I'm the museum's official hair collector. They're thinking of making it a job title. I feel kind of like the tooth fairy, but I don't leave quarters under people's pillows." Emma stifled a shudder. "Next year Lucille wants to make an exhibit of hair from every person in Dandelion Meadows. I think I'd rather haul manure bags at the Feed and Weed." The good news was Emma wouldn't be in Dandelion Meadows next year. With any luck she wouldn't be in Dandelion Meadows next week.

Matt took another bite. "Well, at least she's passionate about her work. That goes a long way to job satisfaction."

"Well, don't get too excited. Lucille will be coming after your hair soon enough."

Matt narrowed his eyes. "Over my dead body."

"I wouldn't put it past her. She sneaks her scissors into funerals."

Matt chuckled. "I hope not."

Matt seemed to really be enjoying his lettuce but maybe it was because he knew she was watching him, worried that he'd like it. It was just lettuce, but she had been the one to carefully prepare it, and she'd take it personally if he didn't clean his plate.

"You did a really good job on this chicken," he said, taking his last bite.

She felt her face get warm. "I just followed your directions.

And you did the rolling. The rolling is the most important part."

He grinned and shook his head. "I wouldn't have been able to roll it if it hadn't been pounded so perfectly flat."

Emma skewered a piece of lettuce and lifted it into the air. "Thank goodness for that pipe wrench."

He looked at his phone. "Hey, let's get those dishes done. We don't want to be late."

"Late for what?"

"Ladasha's Martin Luther King Jr. Awareness Week presentation. She's bringing in a patriotic choir from Boise and serving hush puppies. I never miss it."

Emma drew her brows together. "Do I need a choir for Curling Awareness Week?"

"Last year, Jamal recited the 'I Have a Dream' speech by heart, and Ladasha built a replica of the Lincoln Memorial for him to stand in front of."

"How did she fit it through the museum door?"

"It was about the size of a shoebox. But very detailed," Matt said.

Emma cleared both plates and set them in the sink. "I don't know if I want to go. I'll feel all this pressure to do something spectacular for Curling Awareness Week."

"No offense, Emma, but nobody expects Curling Awareness Week to be anything but a yawner."

She had to agree with that. "It's a sad day when even the presenter thinks it's boring."

Matt surprised her by sticking the plug in the sink and filling it with hot, soapy water. He wasn't as inept around the kitchen as she had first suspected. "Forget about Curling Awareness Week for a minute," he said. "M.L. King Awareness Week is one everybody should attend just to pay tribute to one of the greatest men who ever lived."

For a second, Emma felt ashamed about even considering missing Martin Luther King Jr. Awareness Week, then she tried not to act surprised that a mountain man like Matt even cared about politics or that he was completely sincere in his admiration for Martin Luther King, Jr.

That warm, fuzzy feeling enveloped her again. What was it about Matt Matthews? Emma was at a loss to even describe him. He was "unexpected," like a visit from your grandma or a rainbow on a sunny day or a flower growing in a crack in the sidewalk—not at all what she would have imagined from a guy who was trying to steal her house.

Emma wiped counters while Matt washed the dishes, then they both picked up dishtowels and dried. Emma put the last plate in the cupboard. "Should we ride together? It will save gas."

Matt raised his eyebrow. "As long as we can take my truck."

She looked up at the ceiling as if considering it. "I don't especially want to be seen in a Ford, but I can handle the dirty looks."

"Very funny, considering Harvey's truck looks like you stole it from a junk yard."

"The finest junk yard in Idaho."

Emma grabbed Uncle Harvey's coat from the laundry room. She kept it in there so it wouldn't stink up the whole house. She was either going to have to get used to this coat or scrape up enough money for a new one. It just wasn't practical to freeze to death, even for the sake of fashion, but she couldn't take much more of the humiliation of Uncle Harvey's coat.

Again Matt opened every door for her. If she wasn't careful, she'd find herself getting used to this "gentleman" thing. She slid into the truck and pulled Uncle Harvey's coat more tightly around her neck. Matt slipped in the driver's side and brought his heavenly smell with him. She could barely smell Uncle

Harvey's coat with Matt in the truck. If she wasn't careful, she'd find herself getting used to this Matt thing.

Emma decided to play it safe and cover her face with a tissue. It was the only way to avoid the pleasant smell. She reached into her pocket and pulled out a little plastic bag of hair. It belonged to Teancum Madsen, the only living Vietnam vet in Dandelion Meadows. Emma had collected a lock of his hair this afternoon and then had shared a very nice cup of herbal tea with Teancum and his wife Sini. Sini was from Finland and had lived in the States for almost fifty years, but she still had a charming accent.

Emma smoothed the bag between her fingers. Collecting hair wasn't all that bad a job when herbal tea came with it. "I don't think I'm going to mind working at the museum. If I can just manage to avoid Vicki, I could be perfectly happy there."

Matt tensed as he turned the truck onto the road. "Vicki? You mean my mom."

Emma mentally palmed her forehead. For a minute, she had forgotten where she was and who she was sitting by. She'd been talking to Matt as if he was one of her girlfriends, and she'd gotten distracted by his brown eyes and good smell. She cleared her throat. "Um...what?"

He had that look in his eye. The one he'd had at the restaurant when he accused her of being a liar. "What were you saying about my mom?"

"Nothing."

"Don't say 'nothing.'"

"It doesn't matter," Emma said. She showed the little bag in her hand. "I've already started collecting hair."

"Don't change the subject. What about my mom?"

Torie had mentioned something about Matt being persistent. Torie had no idea. "She volunteers at the museum three days a week."

He glared at her. "You'd better be nice to my mom."

Emma didn't like his tone, as if she'd done something wrong. "Tell her to be nice to me."

"Don't put this on my mom. She's always nice."

Emma shoved the little bag into her pocket. "Put what on your mom? I don't even know what you're talking about."

"There's no reason for you to be mean to my mom, even if you think I'm in the wrong about the house," Matt said.

"I'm not mean to your mom." Was it any use trying to justify herself? "I just try to avoid her, that's all."

"So you're giving her the silent treatment. I should have expected as much."

Emma narrowed her eyes. Matt was so clueless sometimes. "Well, I just love hearing her go on and on about how you deserve the house and how I should move out and go back to Arizona and about what a wonderful son you are and what a horrible niece I was even though I called Uncle Harvey twice a week and wrote him a letter every Sunday. Today she accused me of being an opportunist. I don't even know what that means."

Matt was going way faster than the speed limit. Emma didn't even bat an eyelash. "You have an MBA," he said. "You know stuff she doesn't. I won't have you beating her down with all that education you have."

"Beat her down? Matt, you underestimate your mother. She is way more clever than I am, and twice as sneaky."

"Don't call my mom sneaky."

Emma growled. Matt's accusations were so unfair. Vicki was the one who wouldn't let up, like a bulldog with her teeth clamped around Emma's ankle. "Matt, do you honestly believe you have to come to your mother's defense? She's General George Patton in high heels."

"Was that an insult?"

160

"If the Army boot fits..." She realized too late that any reference to his mother and Army boots would be taken the wrong way.

Matt stepped on the gas. He went all the way up to forty in a thirty mile per hour zone. Emma grabbed door handle. He was going to kill both of them.

Emma tried to keep her voice calm and soothing. "Look, Matt. I wouldn't have applied for the job if I'd known your mom volunteered there. Let's face it. She doesn't like me, and she's very loyal to you. It's a lethal combination." Emma surreptitiously watched the speedometer. It slowed to 38. "I've always admired the mother-bear type. I truly have. But I'd rather not get mauled by a bear. I saw *The Revenant*, and it was gross."

The speedometer inched up to 41. "Don't call my mom a bear."

"It's metaphor, Matt. Even you should know what that is." She sighed. "This would be easier if you didn't purposefully try to misunderstand me."

"This would be easier if you moved out of my house."

"This would be easier if you weren't such a jerk."

Forty-three miles per hour. They were going to die.

CHAPTER

ELEVEN

Matt was living on a roller coaster. One minute he was making dinner with Emma Dustin and actually thinking about kissing her. The next minute, he was seriously considering leaving her by the side of the road.

Matt usually liked roller coasters—the exhilaration of the climb, the wind in your teeth, the death-defying drop that pushed your stomach into your throat. But living in the same house with Emma was not a good kind of roller coaster, and she needed to get off the ride. Sometimes he wanted to push her off. Other times, he felt compelled to hold her close so she wouldn't fall and hurt herself.

Matt growled out loud in the middle of the produce aisle. The problem was that he liked Emma—liked her a lot, even though she'd thrown thimbles at him and insulted his mother and probably committed some sort of federal crime.

Emma was the perfect combination of needy and capable —which didn't make any sense, but that's how Matt saw her.

162

She couldn't build a fire to save her life, but she wasn't afraid to use a pipe wrench to pound a breast of chicken into submission. She hadn't thought to bring a coat to Idaho, but she knew how to install doorknobs and throw thimbles. She'd let her boss walk all over her, but she didn't let Matt get away with anything.

He liked her. He really, really liked her.

And he hated it.

Matt picked up a head of lettuce and smelled it. He'd just have to decide not to like her. She'd insulted his mom, his truck, and his flannel. She'd used his lettuce without asking. And she was related to Harvey Dustin. That was enough to keep her on his bad list for the rest of her life.

He just had to get her and her scent out of the house. Being around Emma was making him go soft. And he couldn't afford to go soft. Literally. Harvey Dustin had taken his life savings.

"Hey, Matt. How does the lettuce smell today?"

Realizing he'd been holding the lettuce to his nose for almost a minute, he tossed it in his basket and turned around. It wasn't a good head of lettuce. He'd have to sneak it back later.

Frankie Hiatt stood next to the tomatoes with an avocado in each hand. She smiled at him as if she found his existence funny. Frankie had been a year ahead of Matt in school, but she had always seemed way older than that, probably because she had done some things in school that seemed like things a college girl would do, like color her hair or pierce her ears about fifty times. Matt had always liked Frankie. She had a heart for the underdog, and she never played the victim, even though her dad had abandoned the family when Frankie was twelve and her mom had been forced to work two jobs just to put food on the table for her six children.

Frankie pointed to the lettuce in Matt's cart. "You look like someone who knows how to pick produce. Do you mind helping me with these tomatoes?"

Matt grinned. "I don't know much about tomatoes. My specialty is lettuce. It will taste the way it smells. If it smells bitter, don't buy it. If the leaves are tightly packed together, it's more likely to be bitter. That's all I got."

"That's pretty good for a geologist."

"You between calls?" he said.

Frankie set the avocados in her cart. "Just finished my last one of the day, but that doesn't mean there won't be an emergency before the night's over. What do you know about celery?"

"As little as possible."

She pushed her cart around so it was facing Matt's. "So. I hear you and Emma Dustin are having a little disagreement."

Frankie and Emma were good friends. It was a sure bet Frankie had heard more than that. "She's trying to take what's rightfully mine."

Frankie just smiled as if Matt were talking about a roomful of puppies and kittens. "She's really cute, don't you think?"

Cute? Of course she was cute, but what did cute have to do with anything? "She doesn't belong here, Frankie. We both know it. She just wants the house for the money."

Frankie crinkled her nose. "And what do you want the house for, Matt?"

Matt hated it when Frankie made sense like that. "That's not really the point."

"Of course it is."

"You know I want to sell it, but I'm entitled to it. It's right there in Harvey's will."

"I would think if anybody is entitled to that house, it's

Emma," Frankie said. "She's practically Gwen and Harvey's only living relative."

"You don't know the whole story." Matt wasn't about to tell her how Harvey had made a fool of him.

"I suppose I don't." She smiled that amused smile again, as if she knew something he didn't. "Now you have to live in that house together until one of you cries uncle."

"Or until the lawyers figure it out."

"That could take a long time," Frankie said.

"Soon enough, she'll get tired of the cold and move back to Dallas." Matt hoped that was true. If the Idaho winter didn't chase her away, she might just decide to stay. Idaho springs were breathtaking.

"It can't be all bad living with Emma. She's fun and chipper and sort of feisty."

Of course she was, but Frankie wouldn't see any chinks in his armor. "She's bossy, and she throws things at people. And she insulted my mom."

Frankie raised an eyebrow. "What did she say?"

"She said Mom is sneaky and wears Army boots. And she called her General George Patton in heels."

Frankie picked up a head of lettuce and smelled it. "That's hardly an insult. You'll be happy to know that your mom is loyal to a fault. She's made it her personal mission to browbeat Emma into giving up on the house."

"My mom doesn't browbeat people," Matt said halfheartedly. Even he knew that wasn't entirely true. Mom liked to get her way, and she'd run over anybody if she thought she was right.

"She most certainly does. Remember when Levi got that speeding ticket and she showed up at Sheriff Hob's house?"

"She took him a plate of cinnamon rolls."

"And then yelled at him for half an hour," Frankie said. "Or the time LaVerle Pratt and the city council voted to pave the road in front of your ranch. Vicki started a dirt road petition then volunteered to be Ladasha's campaign manager. Or how about the time that one girl broke Holt's heart? Your mom drove all the way to Pocatello to toilet paper her house."

Matt felt his face get warm. "Nobody ever proved it was my mom."

"She bought forty rolls of toilet paper at the Beer Hall the day before, Matt. Of course it was your mom. Then there was the time she—"

"Okay, okay. I get it. But that's no excuse for Emma to talk bad about her. My mom isn't hard to get along with as long as you do things her way."

Frankie wasn't convinced. "Whatever."

"This isn't about my mom. It's about Emma trying to steal my house. I'm sure my mom's just trying to make her see reason."

"And what do you think, Matt? Is Emma being unreasonable?"

"Of course she is. It's my house."

Frankie grabbed two tomatoes and put them in her cart without even squeezing them. "Emma doesn't have anywhere else to go."

Matt tried to pretend he didn't care, but Emma seemed to be in more trouble than she was letting on. A lump formed in the pit of his stomach. Emma may have insulted his mother and given him a scar, but he didn't like thinking about her in trouble.

He folded his arms across his chest. Why should he feel sorry for Emma? She'd gotten herself into this. She'd just have to get herself out. "That's her fault, not mine. She's probably guilty of securities fraud or something. If I win the house, she'll only get what she deserves. Even Harvey wanted me to have the house. In the end, he saw her for what she was."

Frankie was still unnervingly calm, as if she was having fun watching Matt dig a deeper and deeper hole for himself. "Emma can't even bring herself to cheat at Monopoly. Do you really believe she'd rip off someone at work?"

"Emma got fired from her job. She's guilty, all right. What other reason could she have for fleeing the state?" He knew it was unfair, but he was mad that Frankie was goading him and mad that she was sort of right and mad that he was honest enough with himself to admit she was sort of right.

"Come on, Matt. Emma's too cute to be a felon."

He was like a runaway train now. There was no stopping his righteous indignation. "You know what kind of person she is? Shallow, stuck-up, self-important."

Frankie never lost that aggravating smile. "That's not the Emma I know. She's pretty. Don't you think she's pretty? She's smart and thoughtful. And honest, like her uncle Harvey."

The mention of Harvey and honesty in the same sentence riled up Matt all the more. "I can't believe you're defending her. She's a crook, plain and simple. And don't you remember how she shot that dog? As an animal lover, you should be offended."

Frankie finally lost her smile and pressed her lips together. Maybe she was sensible enough to see reason after all. "You know that was an accident."

"She shot a gun inside the city limits."

"You should shut up about that."

Matt closed his mouth, more out of surprise than anything else. He'd never seen Frankie get ruffled, but she was definitely upset about something. Maybe she was secretly mad Emma had shot that dog, but Matt had just thrown that out there as an afterthought. Securities fraud seemed a lot more serious than a teenage prank that happened ten years ago.

He gave Frankie a knowing look. "Emma's not as wonderful as you want people to believe, is she?" It almost felt true when he said it out loud like that. Almost.

"You're an idiot, Matt."

That seemed like an overreaction, especially since he'd only told the truth. Besides, he'd been called worse. "Better than a law breaker."

In a flash of shopping carts and arms and hands, Frankie hooked her elbow around his and yanked him away from his cart with surprising force. Frankie had been working out. She dragged him down the back hall and into the storage room where rows and rows of boxes were stacked clear to the ceiling.

"Hey, what about my lettuce?" Matt didn't really care about the lettuce, but he felt the need to lodge some sort of a protest. Frankie couldn't just drag people into the back room whenever she felt like it.

Frankie shut the door and locked it behind her. The good news was that he could just unlock the door and walk out. The bad news was that no one would be able to run in and rescue him if he screamed—not that Matt was a screamer, but it would have been nice to have that option.

Frankie started pacing in the little space between two rows of boxes. "I can't believe I'm doing this. We all pinky swore and wrote our names in blood."

Matt had no idea what she was talking about but figured it was just better to go along. "Blood?"

"The blood was my idea."

He folded his arms. "You may think that surprises me..."

She laid a hand on Matt's arm. "Even though I swore not to tell another living soul, I have a feeling about you and Emma."

"What kind of a feeling?" Nausea? Dread?

"You can't go on believing she's shallow or reckless or dishonest, although she did tell a whopper of a lie once."

Matt nodded. "I believe it."

"Will you shut up for a minute?"

"Hey, you're the one who kidnapped me. I don't have to follow your orders."

Frankie gave him the dirtiest look he'd ever seen from a woman. He decided to shut up. Was there a way to send a distress signal to his mom? "You've got to swear that you'll never tell another soul what I am about to tell you," she said.

"I don't have to swear anything. I don't even want to hear what you have to say. Let me get back to my lettuce."

Frankie ran her fingers through her hair, which was a strange sort of bluish gray. "You're right about that." She twisted one of the earrings in her ear with her thumb and forefinger. "You've got to understand, Matt. I'm doing this for your sake."

She seemed so sincere, he hated to blow her off. Whatever was going on under all that blue hair, Frankie always meant well. And he was kind of curious about this big secret. "I can't promise anything, Frankie, but I'll try to listen with an open mind."

Frankie nodded, and he could see on her face when she made the decision to trust him. "Okay. Do you remember when Emma shot that dog?"

"Yeah. The whole town was furious. She might have gone to juvenile detention if Harvey and Hob hadn't been such good friends."

Frankie smiled wryly. "Hob never had the heart to arrest anybody."

"The teenagers were all very happy about that."

In an instant, Frankie turned deadly serious. "Matt, Emma never shot that dog."

"What do you mean?"

Frankie shoved her hands in her pockets. "You're not going to like this, but I have a feeling..."

"I know. You have a feeling about Emma and me." He had no idea what that meant, unless she was trying to keep him from throwing Emma out of the house as soon as he won the case.

"Me, Emma, and Torie spent a lot of nights at the old Rockwell place, just hanging out or trying to scare each other. It was the most entertaining thing to do in Dandelion Meadows."

"You should have come to my house. We rode horses and castrated bulls."

"Sounds like a party." Frankie relaxed a little. "My brothers sometimes came with us. Sometimes your brothers would come too. Levi came once. Boone two or three times."

"That was nice of you to let them tag along." Those years had been especially hard for Boone. All the sons felt the tension between Mom and Dad, even Levi, who was just a kid. At the age of fourteen, Boone had already been in trouble with the law. Sheriff Hob had never arrested him, but Boone got caught painting graffiti on a building in Boise then vandalizing some trees at the Nampa cemetery. By the time he was fourteen, he'd already been to juvenile detention twice, and Mom and Dad had been fit to be tied.

Frankie tensed again. "Don't tell anybody, Matt, but one night Boone came waltzing into the Rockwell house with a shotgun slung over his shoulder like he belonged in some stupid video game."

Matt frowned. "Whose shotgun?"

"Your dad's. Boone thought he was so cool. Said he was hunting zombies."

Matt wanted to protest that Boone was too smart for that, but at fourteen, Boone was anything but smart. Teenage boys were notoriously stupid, and Boone had been especially reckless. "Sounds like Boone."

"Me, Torie, Emma, and two of my brothers were there. We totally freaked out until he told us it wasn't loaded. Emma and Torie were still freaked out, but I didn't see the harm in it. We heard some shuffling outside the house, and Boone pointed the gun out the window and pulled the trigger. He was as surprised as anybody when the gun actually went off."

"It was loaded?"

"Apparently. We all ran outside and there was Max Hooper's dog lying on the ground, covered in blood and whimpering."

Matt held his breath, dread growing in his chest like mold. Boone had shot Napoleon? "What...what did you do?" he asked, even though he pretty much knew the story from there.

"Emma picked up Napoleon and immediately started for Betty Frederick's house. Cell reception was spotty at the Rockwell place. The rest of us practically chased her out of the woods, she was going that fast. Boone got hysterical. You know how he loves animals. But it wasn't just about the dog. He bawled and carried on about how much trouble he was going to be in if anyone found out he'd been carrying a shotgun and that he'd shot it in the city limits."

Boone had been right to be scared. Not even Hob would have let that one go. Max Hooper was Hob's brother-in-law, and Boone had already had two strikes against him. It would have turned out very badly for Boone.

Would have.

If Emma hadn't...

"Right before Emma knocked on Betty's door, she handed me the dog, snatched the shotgun from Boone, and draped it over her shoulder. She told Boone everything would be okay and asked him to stay quiet. We were all kind of shocked when

Betty answered the door and Emma took the blame for shooting Napoleon. Betty called Harvey, and he drove Emma and Napoleon to the animal hospital in Boise."

And then the whole town exploded with righteous indignation.

Matt had only been seventeen at the time, but he remembered.

Napoleon only had to spend three nights in the animal hospital, and he never walked with so much as a limp after that, but folks were pretty mad. Hob and Harvey were close, which is the only reason Emma didn't get a ticket or a record. She paid for all of Napoleon's veterinary care and apologized to the whole town at a city council meeting.

Max Hooper made the most of it and demanded Emma do a hundred hours of community service on his farm. Emma spent the better part of her summer weeding and thinning sugar beets. She behaved so well and acted so sorry, most people in town had forgiven her by the end of the summer, though they hadn't forgotten about it. Matt hadn't spent a lot of time around Emma, but he'd heard she'd worked more like two hundred hours for Max. Max Hooper bought her a laptop as a going-away gift.

Matt was so astonished, he couldn't speak.

One of the shelves wobbled a little when Frankie leaned against it. "Do you understand what Emma did for your brother?"

Matt nodded dumbly.

"Everybody hated her," Frankie said.

"Not everybody."

"You're right. Not everybody. But she saved Boone from juvie, maybe set him on a better path."

Matt nodded again. From that summer on, Boone had never gotten into trouble with the police.

"The townspeople were pretty hard on Emma, but can you imagine how it would have been for Boone? He wouldn't have stood a chance. People would have labeled him a lost cause. A lot of them would have given up on him or treated him like a delinquent. It was bad enough for Emma. For Boone, it would have been worse."

"Much worse," Matt said.

"Emma promised Boone she'd never tell anybody, but that didn't stop her from having several long talks with him, trying to set him straight. Boone listened to her—maybe like he'd never listened to anyone before—mostly because he knew he owed her big time, but also because Emma was three years older and gorgeous."

Matt's pulse raced. Emma *was* gorgeous, and that wasn't anywhere near her best quality. "But why did she do it? She had no good reason to help Boone."

"You know why, Matt. Emma is a really good person, one of the best. She'd do just about anything to help somebody."

Matt was suddenly very ashamed of himself for every bad thought he'd ever harbored for Emma Dustin. Boone had turned his life around. He'd gone to college when he very well could have gone to prison. And it had been Emma's doing.

Matt's chest felt so heavy, he thought he might sink through the floor. Wow. He'd misjudged her. It didn't even matter if she'd committed securities fraud, she'd helped his brother, and Matt couldn't begin to thank her for that. And maybe that securities fraud thing wasn't what he thought. Like Frankie had said, Emma was too cute to be a felon. He suddenly felt lightheaded.

Frankie folded her arms. "So, will you please not tell anyone?"

Matt took a deep breath and tried to appear more like

himself so Frankie didn't worry about his health. "I might have to pound Boone's face into the ground for being so stupid."

"No, you won't."

"Okay, I won't tell anyone, but only because I feel sorry that you're going prematurely gray."

"Very funny."

He curled one side of his mouth. "Was veterinarian school that stressful?"

Frankie gave him a sour look. "You're the most stressful thing in my life right now."

"I'm honored."

She huffed out a breath. "Now watch. I'll probably get a bladder infection or fall off a cliff for telling you our horrible secret."

Matt held up his hands in surrender. "Your choice, not mine."

"Will that make you feel any better when they find my body scattered along the interstate?"

He nodded. "Yes."

"Well, it had to be done." Frankie's pocket buzzed, and she pulled out her phone. "I have to go. There's a sick hamster in Meridian and this time of day, that's almost a half hour drive."

"You need a siren and one of those flashing lights."

"Don't I know it." She put her phone back in her pocket. "Come on, Chief. You're helping me pick out a head of lettuce before I jet on out of here."

"Take mine," he said. "I'll find another good one."

She smiled. "That's really nice of you, Matt."

She was halfway out the door when Matt half growled, half laughed. "Don't take my lettuce."

Frankie cocked an eyebrow. "Don't?"

"I admit it. I'm still a little irritated at you, but you don't deserve to suffer with a bitter head of lettuce. I'll come help you pick a good one."

She pursed her lips in mock annoyance. "Come on then. Hamsters have a short life span."

He grabbed her arm before she could escape down the hall. "Thanks for telling me, Frankie. I really appreciate it."

She smirked. "Don't say I never did anything for you. I don't regret it, even though I may have brought a curse on myself."

CHAPTER

TWELVE

Emma pulled up to the house, put the truck in park, and let it idle while she bawled her eyes out. It was very unenvironmental of her, but she didn't want to go into the house where Matt might see her cry and she didn't want to freeze to death in the name of cleaner air. The Sierra Club would just have to understand that idling the truck was her best option.

She pulled out her phone and read the text for the fifth time. *There's lots of gossip floating around, but from what I understand, the SEC says you signed clients' names to things they never agreed to and opened fraudulent accounts to get the bonuses. The lawyers are fighting it out, but it doesn't look good. Has the SEC called you yet?*

Oh, yes, the SEC had called. They'd spent the entire twenty minutes accusing her of things she hadn't done and then hadn't believed her when she said she didn't know what they were talking about. To a hammer, everything looked like a nail.

Maybe she should hire a lawyer. Well, besides the one she already had. She needed a high-powered Dallas attorney who wasn't afraid to knock a few heads around. But she certainly couldn't afford one. She was stuck in Idaho with a thirty-five-year-old truck and a twenty-seven-year-old lumberjack who would be happier if she marched into the woods and never came back.

Emma wiped her eyes and turned off the truck. She had to go in sometime, and the hole in the ozone layer wasn't getting any smaller.

The second Emma walked in the door, she knew something was up. The whole house smelled like heaven—that is, if heaven smelled like something hot in the oven. In the sparkling clean kitchen, a bright yellow Post-It note sat next to the crockpot. *"Emma, I threw some stuff in here this morning. I hope you like beef stew."*

Beef stew? She adored it!

Well, maybe she didn't adore it, but compared to Raisin Bran, beef stew sounded like dining at its finest. She lifted the lid and took a sniff. This was definitely what heaven smelled like, with lots of carrots and onions and not a mushroom to be seen.

Emma didn't usually leave for work before Matt did, but this morning she'd needed to catalog some hair samples and get them on Lucille's desk before the museum opened at ten. She had no idea Matt would fix dinner before he went to work.

What was he up to?

For the last two days, Matt had been acting super strange. On Tuesday night he'd come home, opened four cans of Spaghettios, and invited her to eat dinner with him. He'd even made a decent salad as a side dish, with tomatoes, avocados, ranch dressing, and two different kinds of lettuce, and there was burnt almond fudge ice cream for dessert.

Last night, he'd come home with two frozen pizzas and a bottle of root beer. It had been her turn with the TV, so after dinner they'd watched *Gilmore Girls* together. She showed him Season One, Episode One, so he wouldn't be confused, even though she was already well into Season Five. It didn't really matter. She'd seen every season three times—except for Season Six, which she'd seen five times because Logan was her favorite.

They'd watched four episodes before Emma had decided she needed to go to bed or risk dark circles under her eyes. Matt had given her a hand off the couch and then neatly folded the blankets and laid them in the basket.

And now the beef stew. Was he trying to impress her? Kill her with kindness? Fatten her up so she wouldn't fit into her swimsuit this summer?

For two days, he hadn't said a word about the house or how she shouldn't be living there. He hadn't asked about his mother or the SEC. He'd told her a little more about back country skiing and invited her to go with him sometime. He'd helped her brainstorm ideas for her looming Curling Awareness Week presentation.

Emma didn't like it one bit. Matt was being more than a gentleman. He was making himself completely irresistible. Zac Efron was toast. Orlando Bloom didn't interest her. The entire set of Jonas Brothers could have shown up at her door and she wouldn't have even offered them a bowl of beef stew.

Something was horribly wrong.

For one thing, Matt had claimed he couldn't cook.

For another, Emma was beginning to feel weird about Matt, like she couldn't stand him but at the same time wanted to spend every waking moment with him.

Emma looked at her phone. Matt was usually home by now. Maybe he had to work late to make up for the time he'd spent making beef stew. It was an even nicer gesture than she'd originally thought. Emma pressed her lips together and tried to remember that Matt despised her and wanted her out of the house. But that didn't mean she wouldn't eat the stew. She could better ponder Matt's motives on a full stomach.

Emma stood at the counter debating her options. It seemed rude to eat without Matt, but she didn't know what time he'd be home. And if she waited for him, it made it seem like they were a couple or something, and she didn't want him to think she thought they were a couple. She could text him to see when he was coming home, but if he was driving, he'd get in an accident trying to read her text or miss it altogether.

If she called him, he would definitely think she saw them as a couple, and not in a million years did she want him to think that she thought they were a couple, because they weren't. They were as far from a couple as two people could get without being enemies. In fact, by any definition they were enemies. They both wanted the house, and the other person was standing in their way.

Okay. They were enemies. She could call him.

She punched in his number on her phone. Matt answered on the first ring. "Emma?"

"Just to be clear, we're not a...what I mean is..." What was wrong with her? The enemy had made beef stew. The least she could do is see if he wanted to eat with her. "It was very nice of you to make beef stew. Aunt Gwen used to make beef stew, but she used mushrooms. Thanks for not doing mushrooms."

"You're welcome."

"So, I was wondering if you want to eat with me or if I should just dive right in. I mean, I don't want to eat with you, but it would be rude not to wait for the chef. You know what I mean?"

"Not really." There was a hint of amusement in his voice that Emma found quite charming, even though he was her enemy.

"Lucille gave me a loaf of homemade whole wheat bread. It would go well with the stew."

"Sounds great."

"So, when do you think you'll be home?" Emma cringed. She sounded like she was eager to see him, which she wasn't really, even though she'd recently dumped Zac Efron and Orlando. She sounded like she wanted to be a couple.

"Soon," Matt said. That was stupid. *Soon* could be three days from now.

She heard the front door open. Oh. That was pretty soon.

Her chest constricted, and she found herself getting unreasonably breathless when Matt walked into the kitchen. He still had his phone to his ear and a wide grin on his face as if he was happy to see her—ecstatic, really. She couldn't help but return his smile. It was as contagious as laughter.

He hung up on her, and her phone beeped, and she realized she couldn't just stand there staring all day. "I'd better get that bread going."

He really shouldn't stand there staring all day either. "Okay."

Even though he'd shown some signs of tidiness earlier, he threw his coat, hat, and gloves on the couch and didn't remove his boots. He'd made stew for her, so she didn't have the heart to scold him. Instead, she pulled the dense loaf of bread from its plastic bag, found Gwen's bread knife, and cut four thick slices.

"I'll set," Matt said. He washed his hands and pulled two mugs and two glasses from the cupboard. Emma nodded. Mugs seemed appropriate for beef stew.

Emma heated up a frying pan on the stove and retrieved the butter from the cupboard. She slathered one side of each slice of bread with butter and set the slices in the pan. Then she gave the other side of each piece a healthy layer of butter too.

"You want some bread with that butter?" Matt said, putting a spoon on top of the napkin he'd just folded.

"Everything is better with more butter."

Emma carefully tended her bread, making sure it was golden brown on each side. One slice burned on the edges when she looked away and got lost in Matt's eyes, but three out of four wasn't bad.

Matt handed Emma a mug of stew, and they sat down at the counter to eat. She took a bite of potato and almost melted into a puddle on the floor. "Matt, this is delicious."

He grinned. "Don't be too impressed. Mom taught me how to cut vegetables, and they have these little packets at the store with all the seasonings you need. You just pour the whole thing into the slow cooker. It's pretty easy."

"Easy or not, I'm still impressed." There was no way Zac Efron would even attempt beef stew. No wonder she'd broken up with him.

Melted butter dripped from Matt's fingers as he took a bite of bread. "The bread is really good." He looked at her as if she'd found a cure for Alzheimer's. Her pulse sped out of control. Yep, you could never have too much butter.

"Whole wheat bread tends to be dry. Butter perks it right up."

Matt raised his mug so Emma could see the picture on the side. "Did you draw this?"

She felt herself blush, which was a really stupid reaction to a drawing she'd done when she was thirteen. It was a pink-nosed mouse wearing an apron with a wooden spoon in her little paw. One of Aunt Gwen's favorites. "Aunt Gwen used special glue to permanently seal it to the mug. But it's not dishwasher safe."

"I'll hand wash it myself." He said it as if that mug was really important to him. Then he winked. She almost fell off her stool. It was a good strategy on his part. Nothing threw your enemy off balance like a good wink.

Matt took a drink of water as if he hadn't just rocked her world. "How's your Curling Awareness Week presentation coming along?"

"I finished the Power Point presentation on the rules. It's boring, but very informational."

"I had an idea for your presentation that I think might spice it up."

"As long as I don't have to stand on my head, I'll do just about anything."

Matt grinned. "Can you stand on your head?"

"As a matter of fact, I can. I used to do yoga. But standing on your head makes you feel really vulnerable, like someone could just come along and steal your shoes and you wouldn't be able to do a thing about it."

"Does that ever happen?"

"What?"

"Someone tries to steal your shoes while you're standing on your head?" he said.

Emma took another bite of bread and licked the butter from her fingers. "Well, no, mostly because I don't wear shoes while I'm doing yoga. I guess it would be easier for someone to steal my shoes while they're sitting in the little cubby in the locker room."

Matt chuckled. "So are you interested in this thing I have to show you?"

"Of course."

Matt took the last bite of his bread and for some reason, avoided making eye contact. "Okay then. Let's get these dishes done and get over there."

"Get over where?"

"To the ranch. What I want to show you is at the ranch."

It was a good thing Emma had just finished swallowing or she would have choked. "The ranch?"

"I don't think you've ever been."

Of course she'd never been, and she wasn't about to go now. The ranch was deep in enemy territory—especially since Matt's mom was like the queen over there. Or the head of the military.

"Oh. I see." Emma didn't know what to say. If she refused to go outright, Matt would know she was onto his plan, even though she had no idea what his plan was. "Tonight isn't going to work. I've got to paint my nails for my curling presentation." Emma didn't even care if Matt thought she was shallow for painting her nails. She was not going to that ranch.

He studied her face as a smile formed on his lips. "Can you paint when we get back?"

"I've got to do fingernails and toenails. It's a five-step process."

He seemed more amused than suspicious. Good. She had him off balance. "Couldn't you paint fingernails tomorrow?"

"Tomorrow I've got to pick out my outfit."

A slow chuckle rolled from his throat. "Come on, Emma. It's not North Korea. It's the ranch."

She pointed her index finger at the ceiling. "Both enemy territories."

"My mom won't make a peep."

"You can't know that. Your mom is very likely to peep. She hates me."

Matt cleared all the dishes into the sink. "She doesn't hate you, and besides, she won't be there. She's got a meeting for Moustache Awareness Week."

Emma scrunched her lips together. "Why didn't you say so?"

"I realize I should have led with that."

"But what about the rest of your family?" Emma said. "It's not like they're going to welcome me with open arms."

Matt started washing dishes before the sink was full. He was suddenly in a great hurry. "Boone and Levi are off to school."

"I knew that."

"Holt is pretty focused on his own stuff. Honestly, I don't think he even knows I'm living here. Clay doesn't care about any of this. His burdens are pretty heavy without having to worry about me."

Emma thought about it for a minute. "Vicki won't be there, and Clay and Holt are clueless. I'm still a little trepidatious."

"Trepidatious? What kind of word is that?"

"A very good word." Emma picked up a dishtowel. "I'm just wondering why you want me to go to the ranch. Couldn't you bring your great idea here?"

Matt handed her the mouse mug and seemed to purposefully brush his wet thumb across her fingers. "I guess." He stopped washing altogether, dried his hands, folded his arms, and leaned his hip against the counter. "I guess I really want you to see the ranch."

She eyed him doubtfully. "Why?"

"Because...I don't know. I want to show you. I grew up there, and I'd like you to see it." He sighed. "Maybe that's not a good enough reason."

Emma slowly dried the mug in her hand. It *was* a good enough reason. Probably the best reason. The ranch was part of Matt's identity. The fact that he wanted to show it to her meant that maybe he didn't see her as an enemy, or maybe not even as just a friend. A shiver of pleasure traveled up her spine. Should she tell him she was officially finished with Zac Efron?

"Oh...okay," was all she could muster. She turned her back on him and put the mugs in the cupboard. Matt had used the mouse mug. Hers said, "I love my Dallas."

Oh, the irony of her life!

"What do you say?" he said casually, but she could tell her answer was very important to him. More shivers. More light-headedness.

She answered with equal casualness in her voice, even though her spleen was doing the polka with her pancreas. "This had better be a killer presentation idea."

"It is."

MATT DIDN'T KNOW why he was so nervous all of a sudden. Emma was a city girl. She wasn't going to be all that impressed with the ranch. But he wanted to impress her all the same. He gave her a hesitant smile as he turned off the road and onto their property.

The ranch was a thousand times more impressive in the summer time, when the alfalfa grew tall and the rolling hills were covered with wild flowers. It had been even grander when two hundred head of cattle grazed the property, but those days were long gone. Dad had sold every last beef and most of the horses. They still had the land, but the heart of the ranch was gone. In some ways, Dad had been the heart of the ranch, and he wasn't coming back, no matter how badly Matt wanted him to.

Matt pointed to a rise of ground behind the ranch house. "It's almost too dark to see, but in the spring, that hill is covered with dandelions. I think it's where Dandelion Meadows got its name."

"I've always liked dandelions, even though they're just a weed. Uncle Harvey said they were the bees' favorite food."

"This place is swarming with bees in the warm months. Burton Lane and the Moons keep hives."

Emma leaned closer to the windshield. "The house looks bigger this close, which is the most obvious thing I've ever said."

Emma was just as nervous as Matt, though she had no reason to be. His brothers could be intimidating, but they were the nicest guys anyone could meet, and Mom made sure they'd learned their manners. No woman was ever safer than when she was in a house full of Matthews boys. Mom didn't stand for ungentlemanly behavior.

And her definition of "ungentlemanly" was pretty broad.

One time when Matt was sixteen, he'd whistled at Meg Farmer at the Dandelion Jelly Festival. Mom had made him muck out the stables by himself for two weeks.

"It's pretty big," Matt said. "My mom's dad built it in the 1950s. Before that, he and my grandma lived in the little stone house over there. We use it to store feed now, but my mom wants to clear it out and put it on the National Historic Registry."

"How many rooms does the big house have?"

Matt smiled. "Ten bedrooms, but Mom still made us share when we were growing up. She wanted to contain the mess to three rooms."

"I don't blame her."

Matt parked the truck in the circular drive in front of the house. Emma jumped out before he could open the door for her. She was insistent that way. He just wanted to be a gentleman, and she just wanted to be an independent woman. The independent woman won every time, mostly because Matt couldn't make it around the truck fast enough to open the door before she did.

Still, he came around to her side of the truck and took her hand. She instinctively tried to pull away. "I don't want you to slip," he said, which was a lame excuse because unlike the Pioneer Hair Museum, the walks and drives had been cleared of all snow and ice. Clay was meticulous. Even if she'd been wearing high heels, she wouldn't have fallen.

When it came right down to it, he just wanted to hold her hand, to feel that silky skin against his and borrow some of her warmth. Was that so wrong?

Emma raised both eyebrows but didn't question his motives. She let him lead her up the porch steps. The sun was down, but Clay had lit the four gas lanterns on the wrap-around porch. There was plenty of light to see by, which was good because Matt couldn't get enough of Emma.

She wore Harvey's giant coat with a pink beanie and a sky blue scarf. She was smiling, and her eyes sparkled in the flickering gaslight. The urge to kiss her clamped around his throat, and he lost the ability to breathe.

"This porch is so cute," she said, oblivious to the tornado swirling around in his head. She gasped. "Look at the swing!" She dragged him to the porch swing. They sat down, and Emma pushed them back and forth with her feet. She wasn't in danger of slipping on any ice, but she didn't let go of his hand. Matt thought he might faint. "I've always wanted a porch swing where I could sit and do cross stitch or shell peas with my grandma."

He cleared his throat in an attempt to speak. "You...you cross stitch?"

"No. I don't have the patience for it, but I love the idea of it: sitting on the porch after a long day of pioneer chores and doing cross stitch while your husband plays his guitar and sings songs about his days on the old Chisholm trail."

"Right before a swarm of locusts eats your crops."

She gave him a wry smile. "Sounds romantic, doesn't it?"

"Very."

"But not super romantic. I don't know how romance ever bloomed when you had to use an outhouse every day. That kind of thing would kill any sort of budding passion."

Matt laughed. "You are a hopeless city girl."

"Darn right and proud of it." She smiled at him as if she liked him a lot. He wrapped his fingers more tightly around hers and stared into her eyes.

Wow, but she was pretty.

Wow, did he wish he wasn't such a gentlemen.

Fortunately for Matt, a noise from inside the house dragged him back to sanity. It sounded like Clay was playing some sort of game with his girls. There was lots of running and squealing and growling—probably No Bears Are Out Tonight. Mellie and Addy's favorite game.

Emma turned around to look in the window. "Are those your nieces?"

Matt wasn't ready to break whatever connection he'd suddenly felt with Emma. "Why don't we go see the stables first? Then you can come inside and meet the family."

Emma stood up. "I'd like that, but we can't stay too long. Even in Uncle Harvey's coat, I'm freezing."

"Don't worry. The stables are heated."

She formed her lips into an "O." "I'm impressed."

He took her hand again and led her down the porch steps. "You would have been more impressed ten years ago. We had seven horses and a part-time wrangler. Dad sold all but one horse and got rid of the cattle. We have all this land and nothing to show for it. Dad needed the money to pay his debts, and he refused to declare bankruptcy. He's got a real sense of honor."

She nodded. "Uncle Harvey always said so."

Matt ignored the irony of Harvey Dustin having an opinion on Dad's honor. "Mom wouldn't let Dad sell the land, and even though it was painful for Dad that he couldn't pay his debts, I think Mom did the right thing. Money gets made and lost every day, but if you have land, you'll never be poor."

Matt opened the door just wide enough for them to slip into the stable. "We only heat this side now because there's only one horse."

"Oh, look how pretty." Emma immediately gravitated to the stall containing Clay's horse, a beautiful chestnut mare with a white diamond on her nose. Emma patted the horse's neck and put her cheek against the horse's nose. "What's his name?"

"It's Constantinople, but we call her Connie."

Emma frowned and ran her hand down the bridge of Connie's nose. "Sorry I called you a boy. You are most definitely a girl. A very pretty girl."

"She's gentle. Clay's girls ride her all the time."

Emma looked down the row of stalls. "This stable is huge."

"Our ranch used to be a grand place. Every fall, Mom and Dad would host a chuck wagon dinner for the whole town. We had square dancing and a bonfire."

"Matthews is still the most important name in town," Emma said. She was trying to make him feel better, but nothing could soothe the pain of losing everything to the creditors, even if Matt had only been seventeen when it all crashed around their heads. Dad had seemed to age twenty years in a few months. The memory shot a bullet right through Matt's heart.

Emma leaned against the door to Connie's stall. "If the

ranch isn't a ranch anymore, what do Clay and Holt do for a living? Or is that none of my business?"

"Clay builds houses. He got a degree in construction management after the cattle were gone. This is his slow time because it's cruel to ask guys to work in this weather."

"Tell me about it," Emma said. "You'd end up with a crew of nose-less workers."

"Nose-less?"

"They'd all have to get their noses amputated on account of frostbite."

Matt smiled. "Summers are really nice here."

"Oh, for sure. Summers in Arizona are like living in a blast furnace." She tilted her head to one side. "Would you rather freeze to death or die of heat stroke?"

"Are those the only two choices?"

"Yes, if you are trying to decide where to live."

Was she trying to decide where to live? Was she thinking of staying in Idaho? He didn't know whether to feel giddy or despondent. Did he want her to stay or go?

Emma slowly made her way down the row of empty stalls, standing on her tiptoes and looking into each one as if she hoped to discover a horse. "What about Holt? What does he do for a living?"

"He grows alfalfa to sell to other farmers. And he works at the Weed and Feed just to keep some money coming in."

"You mean the Feed and Weed," Emma said.

"No. I mean the Weed and Feed. It says so on his apron."

Emma shook her head. "Nope. It says Feed and Weed on the sign outside the door."

"I don't think so."

She stuck out her hand. "You wanna make a bet?"

"Okay. If it isn't the Weed and Feed, I'll do dishes for a whole week."

"And I'll do dishes if it is."

Matt would have taken that bet any day, just to be able to touch Emma's hand again. "Holt works at the Weed and Feed," he said, emphasizing the words, "but what he really wants to do is bring the ranch back again."

"With cows and stuff?"

"Yes, with cows and stuff. Though I'm not sure what stuff is."

She giggled. "You know, bunnies and goats and chickens. And a windmill. All the things a ranch should have."

"Actually, Holt isn't even sure about the cows. There's an elk ranch in Utah. They give tours."

Emma grimaced. "Do people actually eat elk meat?"

"Some do. I think it stinks to high heaven. He'd do better with a herd of bison, but none of us knows how to raise bison."

"That's what YouTube is for," she said.

Matt cocked a brow. "You think we'll find a bison video?"

"You wanna shake on it?"

Of course he did.

Emma's chin started quivering, and she wrapped her arms around herself.

"You cold?"

She nodded. "I think when you said 'heated,' I expected it to be warm in here."

"Come here." He spread his arms, and she just walked right into his embrace, as if she fit right there beside his heart. Either that or she was just too cold to protest. At this moment, it didn't matter. He'd finally gotten Emma into his arms.

He didn't know how long he'd been hoping for this moment, but when he wrapped his arms around her, he realized it had been a very long time. This was where Emma belonged. This was where he belonged. Couldn't they just stand like this forever?

He rested his chin on top of her head and pulled in a deep breath. She smelled like Harvey's coat and some sort of shampoo designed to drive him wild. She was so close he could hear her teeth chatter and feel her heartbeat against his chest.

Every cell in his body ignited as if doused with gasoline.

Could he still be a gentleman and kiss Emma Dustin like a starving man? At the moment, he kind of didn't care. The good news was that she was looking up at him as if expecting him to do something—like kiss her—so he didn't have to say anything to get her attention. He bent his head and pressed his lips to hers. She caught her breath but didn't try to dodge him. Her mouth was so soft and warm and her lips so full, he never wanted to pull away.

A soft sigh bubbled up from her throat, and she slid her arms around his neck and pulled him closer. He had no objection to that. He crushed her to him and kissed her like a thirsty man on a frosty mug of homemade root beer.

She tasted so good.

He reluctantly pulled away from her. Her eyes were sort of glassy, like someone who'd looked into an eclipse without protective eyewear. "Was that the thing?"

"The thing?"

"The idea you had to spice up my Curling Awareness Week presentation?"

"No."

Still a little dazed, she gave him half a smile. "Well, it would definitely make my Curling Awareness Week more exciting."

Matt thought he might burst. "It would?"

"I suppose if you kissed every woman there, that would liven things up."

"You have to have a special license for one of these." He puckered his lips.

She laughed. "Oh, you do?"

"Besides, Betty Frederick would kill me with her purse if I tried to give her a kiss. She carries a brick in there."

"No, she doesn't," Emma said. "She's got a cute little handgun about the size of a crescent wrench."

"Are you sure?"

"Yep. She showed me the other day."

Matt furrowed his brow in mock concern. "I'm going to help her cross the street more often, just to stay on her good side."

"That would be wise."

Now that he'd had a taste, Matt found Emma's lips irresistible. He laid another kiss on her just because she looked so cute in Harvey's coat. "I don't know what to do with you, Emma."

"You mean my curling presentation?"

"I mean you as a person."

She eyed him doubtfully. "You don't have to do anything with me. I can be in charge of myself."

He couldn't explain what he meant without revealing more than he wanted her to know. And it wasn't even about Boone and the dog, though that had sort of nudged Matt off the cliff. It was the fact that Emma used a pipe wrench to pound chicken and had thrown thimbles at him to defend herself. It was about that ugly, sexy coat and those unattractive, hot sweatpants and the high heels she wore to work every day. It was because she hadn't ever told anybody about the dog, even though everyone in town would have gone a lot easier on her. It was that loopy grin and her quirky sense of humor that made him smile in spite of himself.

Matt wanted that house. He needed that house. But he couldn't stand the thought of Emma not being in the house.

He stood there for so long without saying anything, Emma

started to get suspicious. "When you say you don't know what to do with me, do you mean you don't know whether you should throw me down a mine shaft or bury me on your property?"

He rolled his eyes. "Yes, that's exactly what I'm thinking about."

"You have a very morbid sense of humor."

He'd already strained the bounds of gentlemanly behavior, and if they stood there much longer, he might be tempted to follow where his mind was leading. "Come on," he said. "Let's get you inside where it's truly warm. You can even build a fire, if you want."

She nodded. "I know how."

"Yes, you do."

By the time Emma and Matt got to the house, Emma was able to remember her own name, but she couldn't focus on much of anything else. If Matt was trying to get rid of her, his diabolical plan was beyond her comprehension.

Maybe he didn't hate her. That seemed the only logical explanation for the kiss.

The glorious, romantic, warm kiss.

With that one kiss, Matt had completely spoiled her for regular days.

She was determined not to float off the ground, but she'd have to concentrate very hard to keep her feet planted.

They both stamped their feet on the welcome mat, and Matt opened the front door. She found herself in an entryway with impossibly high ceilings and beautiful dark wood floors. The chandelier above her head was the size of an ottoman, but it wasn't gaudy or tacky like Emma would have expected in an old-timey ranch house like this. Weren't places like this supposed to have chandeliers made out of antlers?

Matt took her coat, and she nearly jumped out of her skin when his hand brushed against her arm, and it wasn't because his fingers felt like sandpaper. Matt's touch was unnerving and divine and altogether too pleasant for a girl who was trying to keep her wits about her.

The entryway opened into a magnificent great room, with not an antler or stuffed animal head in sight. Whoever had decorated preferred overstuffed cabin style furniture with thick, substantial fabrics and neutral colors accented by deep reds and light browns. The room was comfortable and stylish without being stuffy. It was a place where grandchildren could play without being scolded but also where someone who was used to luxury wouldn't feel out of place.

Matt's brother Holt walked into the room from what Emma supposed was the kitchen. "Get a good look. We might have to sell it off to pay the heating bill."

Matt gave his brother a bracing hug. "Things aren't that bad yet. Emma, do you remember Holt?"

Holt was as tall as Matt with the same broad shoulders and a devil-may-care grin on his face. "I remember Emma. She didn't hang out with us very often."

"She didn't hang out with us at all," Matt said, and then he and Holt laughed like it was the funniest joke in the world.

Emma felt her face get warm. What could she say? As a teenager, she had been more concerned about waterproof mascara and Zac Efron. She hadn't been interested in getting to know the Idaho cowboys. The only thing she knew was that they dealt with a lot of manure and horse hair, and she didn't want to have to carry a gallon of hand sanitizer every time she went on a date.

She kind of wished she'd paid more attention, especially

while standing between two of the finest specimens of manhood in the entire Western hemisphere. She immediately repented of thinking cowboys were nothing but smelly, uneducated horse jockeys. Matt had a Masters degree and really nice teeth. He wasn't smelly in the least. And he'd just given her a glorious, amazing kiss. It was a miracle her socks were still on her feet.

Emma turned as another Matthews brother ambled down the stairs to her right. The staircase was itself a work of art, with a sturdy but elegant wrought iron railing and dark wood steps covered with a cream carpet runner.

Clay Matthews was also a work of art, though Emma tried not to stare. The Matthews brothers came in two sizes, tall and broad, and Clay had plenty of both. Clay was quieter than Holt and Matt, but not so quiet that you wondered if he was a serial killer—like the Unabomber.

There was a certain sadness that hovered in the lines around Clay's eyes. Emma had noticed it the other day at the quilt shop. Maybe it was due to his divorce, which Torie described as "horrible," but Emma couldn't begin to know. It was none of her business anyway. She had more than enough to concentrate on with Matt's kissing her. She'd have to let Clay worry about his own problems.

Maybe Clay wasn't so miserable. He got to the bottom of the stairs and smiled as if he was purposefully trying to show off those great teeth. "Matt. You never come around anymore. Some people might think you have more important things to do than visit your family."

"Well," Matt said, "I'm an important guy."

Matt and Clay hugged like they hadn't seen each other for years, and warmth spread clear to Emma's toes. Even her toenails felt hot. Nothing compared to the love of family. If you had a family who loved you, you had everything. The ache of losing Uncle Harvey and Aunt Gwen throbbed right at the base of her throat, where it always did when she thought of them. How lucky she was to have spent seven summers with them before they died. And even though her parents were pretty busy on the bonspiel circuit, they would drop their curling stones in a heartbeat if she needed them.

Matt glanced in her direction. "Is everything okay?"

Emma immediately perked up. *I got lost in a memory* didn't really seem like a good explanation for anything—unless you were one of those quiet Unabomber types. She smiled and reached out her hand to Clay to shake. "Nice to see you again. I heard children in here earlier. Are they in bed?"

"Yeah. Every parent's favorite time of the day." Clay took her hand in both of his to shake it. "I apologize for not coming to your defense the other day at the festival meeting, but if I'd said anything, they would have put *me* in charge of the Smoking Festival. I kept my mouth shut."

Emma laughed. "It's the *Stop* Smoking Festival, and it's going to be stupid. We're doing minimal work on it."

Clay shook his head. "Tell Ladasha it's going to be understated. That's sounds a lot better than stupid."

"Subtle," Holt said. "Subtle sounds even better."

Emma gave Holt a fist bump. "And we're not calling it the Stop Smoking Festival. That's too boring. We're calling it the Cigarette Demolition Festival. What do you think?"

The blank stares were not encouraging.

"Well," Clay said, "that will get everybody's attention."

Holt stuffed his hands in his pockets. "The Kimball boys might show up if they think you're going to blow something up."

Matt nodded enthusiastically. "And they're all smokers."

"Are you going to make a papier-mâché lung?" Clay said.

An even more enthusiastic nod from Holt. "You could blow it up at the end."

Emma heaved a great sigh. "I'll have to make a papier-mâché lung. They asked for it specifically. But I'll wait until it gets warmer and sculpt it outside. A lung that size won't fit in my house."

"My house," Matt said, but there wasn't the usual irritation in his voice. He sounded almost like he was teasing her.

Holt narrowed his eyes. "What is it about this house? You fighting over it or something?"

Matt looked at Emma. "See what I mean?"

Emma grinned. Holt really didn't have a clue. "Uncle Harvey made up two wills. One leaving the house to me and one leaving the house to Matt. Matt's will is the most recent, but my will looks more official. So we both moved in because possession is nine-tenths of the law and *de bonis non administratis* and *habeas corpus* and all that stuff." She wasn't sure what most of that meant, but she'd spent enough time around Johnny to pick up some of the lingo.

Holt leaned over and whispered loudly in Matt's ear. "You were right. She's smart."

Matt thought she was smart? "We're just waiting for the lawyers to figure it out," she said.

Clay eyed Matt. "You got a lawyer?"

Matt's gaze flicked in Emma's direction. "Not exactly."

This was news to Emma. "You don't have a lawyer? Matt, how are we ever going to get this thing worked out if you don't have a lawyer?"

He shrugged. "I was hoping to have a reasonable conversation with the judge."

Holt grinned. "Levi could give you some legal advice."

"I already tried that," Matt said. "Levi is no help."

"But he's in law school."

"That's what I thought," Matt said, "but he didn't even know that thing about possession being nine-tenths of the law. I think law school is just a cover. He's in California on a three-year surfing trip."

Clay didn't flinch. "Probably."

Holt looked at Matt as if he were very confused. "So you guys are in limbo until you get this house thing settled?"

Matt gave Emma a warm smile. So warm, she almost caught fire. "It's not so bad. We've learned how to build a fire and make chicken cordon bleu."

"Matt got my truck started the very first morning," Emma said.

Clay studied Matt's face. "That was nice of him."

"Very nice, especially since it was thirty below outside, and I hadn't brought a coat."

Holt gave her the same look Ladasha had given her—like she was crazy or something. "You didn't bring a coat to Idaho?"

"It's a long story," Emma said.

Holt shrugged. "I have long ears."

Emma giggled. "Your ears are a very normal size for your head. One time I was at one of my dad's bonspiels, and there was a guy on another team who had the longest earlobes I've ever seen. Even though it was rude, I couldn't stop staring. He could have pierced his ears like twenty times and still had room for a tasteful pair of dangly hoops."

All three brothers laughed. Matt and Clay exchanged a look Emma couldn't begin to understand. She was socially savvy enough to know it was "a look." She just didn't know what it meant. Did they think she was witty? Or shallow for talking about people's earlobes? Or maybe they were wondering when she'd leave so they could play video games.

"Our grandpa had really big nostrils," Clay said.

Matt nodded. "And Aunt Gertie had more hair on her chin than Holt does."

"That's not true," Holt protested, sliding his hand across his jaw. "I've got plenty of hair. I just like the clean-shaven look."

Matt nudged Emma with his elbow. "And he only has to shave three times a year."

"It's a very good look on you," Emma said, just in case Holt felt bad about not being able to grow a beard.

Holt narrowed his gaze. "You're pretty clever. I almost didn't notice that you changed the subject about your coat. What's the story?"

Emma sighed in mock forbearance. "All this trouble over a little coat. I came from Dallas, where no one owns a coat, and I didn't have time to buy one before I got here. And then I didn't want to buy one because I didn't think I'd be here that long. Uncle Harvey's coat works perfectly well for the time being."

"It stinks," Matt said.

She cuffed him on the shoulder. "You're the one who insisted I wear it."

Matt stepped out of range of her fist. "It doesn't smell all that good, but it looks pretty cute on you."

Clay's gaze intensified on Matt. "I bet it does."

"Why didn't you have time to buy a coat?" Holt said, apparently not inclined to let the story end there.

"I work for a financial planning firm in Dallas, and something big happened. I sort of get the impression I'm at the center of whatever happened. They fired me, then they unfired me and put me on probation pending an investigation. I came up here because I didn't want to do the active senior living thing with my parents."

Clay smiled sympathetically. "Then Matt invaded your space."

That little gesture was like herbal tea to Emma's heart. Clay, at least, didn't seem to blame Emma for wanting to live in her own house. Vicki was squarely on Matt's side, but after tonight, not even Matt seemed squarely on his own side. Maybe the Matthews boys weren't as hostile as she had feared.

"She threw thimbles at me. Gave me a scar," Matt said.

Clay watched Emma closely while he talked to Matt. "I'm sure you deserved it."

"Oh, he did," Emma said. "He scared the hair right off my legs."

Matt laughed, which was a very good sign. She didn't think she'd heard him laugh about the thimbles before. "She would have killed me. I had to call the police."

Emma gave him the stink eye. "I called the police, and they took my side."

"Hob?" Clay said.

Matt nodded. "He doesn't take sides."

Clay grinned. "Unless Mom gets involved."

Emma scrunched her lips to one side of her face. "It's not so bad. Matt can open really tight jars, and he's pretty good at washing dishes."

Holt's mouth fell open. "He washes dishes? Growing up, he'd always get out of dish duty by pretending he had to go to the bathroom."

"That's not true," Matt said. "I legitimately had to go. You could have waited for me."

Clay motioned to the overstuffed couch. "You just passing through, or would you like to sit a while?"

It was strange, but at that moment, there was nothing Emma would have rather done than stay. The Matthews brothers made her feel like she was home, and that wasn't a feeling to be taken for granted. She glanced at Matt for his agreement. "We can stay, can't we?"

Matt burst into a smile. "If you really want to."

"We could play cards," Holt said. "Poker?"

Clay made a face. "What are you thinking, Holt. No poker."

"I like poker." Uncle Harvey had taught Emma to play, though she hadn't played for at least ten years.

Holt reacted like a little kid at Christmas. "I'll get the cards."

Emma glanced furtively at the deep, overstuffed couch. If she searched between the cushions, she might be able to find some spare change, but not enough for a game of poker. "I didn't bring any money."

"We usually play with M&Ms," Clay said, "but we don't have any."

Holt cleared some magazines off the coffee table. "We've got gumballs."

"They'll roll," Matt said.

Holt was obviously eager to play. He wiped the table with the sleeve of his red flannel shirt. "Mom just bought some Oreos. They make good poker chips."

"We can't," Clay said. "She's making a pie for Curling Awareness Week."

Vicki was making a pie for Emma's presentation? That was nice of her—unless it wasn't. With Vicki, Emma expected an ulterior motive.

Clay gazed up the stairs. "I guess I could steal Addy's stash of Skittles, as long as I replace them."

Holt opened a drawer in the side table and pulled out a deck of cards. "We can use them and put them back. She'll never know."

Emma couldn't allow that. "We'd get our fingerprints and germs all over them. Very unsanitary."

"I've got an idea." Matt went out the door by the stairs and came back with a bag of dried pinto beans. "These have been in our cupboard since the Bush administration. Let's use 'em."

Holt furrowed his brow. "Bush Forty-one or Bush Forty-three?"

"Yes," Matt said.

Holt ducked into another room to the left and came back with a bottle of window cleaner and a sheet of paper towel. He sprayed the coffee table and wiped it off. He was really serious about his poker. Emma pressed her lips together. She didn't have the heart to scold Holt for spraying window cleaner on that beautiful wood table, but it was a pretty good bet he'd get yelled at if Vicki were here.

Emma smiled to herself. Vicki was not here. It really was a very nice evening.

"Let's play at the table in the den," Clay said. "It's smaller, and we can sit right up to it."

Holt held up his paper towel. "*Now* you tell me."

"You did a very nice job on the table." Emma wanted to be encouraging, even though it was kind of not true. You never, *never*, sprayed wood with window cleaner.

They went into the den, which had dark cherrywood paneling and a giant rock fireplace that looked like something right out of the Wild West. It was beautiful but rustic. To Emma's relief, there wasn't one antler or stuffed animal head in the den either. Stuffed heads were most likely to be in the den. If there weren't any in here, there probably weren't any in the house. She was starting to like the Matthewses more and more all the time.

Holt wanted to be the dealer. He obviously loved poker, which meant he was very good at it. Emma didn't like to lose, but at least they were playing for pinto beans. If she won, she wouldn't even know how to cook them.

Holt did indeed turn out to be a very good poker player but

so were Matt and Clay, and Emma had always been able to hold her own. It was the most fun Emma had seen in months. Years maybe. School hadn't been any sort of fun. There weren't very many of them who had actually enjoyed finance. Economics had been the worst. Business calculus had about killed her. Yep. Zero fun in school.

Emma had thought that once she got a steady paycheck, her life would be a lot happier. But being a financial advisor wasn't any more fun than studying to be a financial advisor. There were too many charts and graphs, and Emma wasn't really thrilled with all the detailed work. Uncle Harvey had burst his buttons, and Emma's parents were super proud of her, so that was a little bit of consolation for hating her job so much, but probably not enough to keep her going for another forty years.

Holt whooped like a strange bird when he won the first game, and he had a nice pile of beans to show for it.

Emma heard someone moving around in the great room. "Is one of your girls out of bed, Clay?"

"Probably," Clay said, straightening his cards. "Addy has trouble going to sleep."

"It's good you didn't steal her Skittles."

Clay shuffled the cards, and Emma just about jumped out of her skin when Matt reached under the table and took Emma's hand. But it was jumping out of her skin in a pleasant way, like when you walk into a room and everyone yells "Surprise" or when someone leaves a pie on your doorstep. Matt entwined his fingers with hers and ran his thumb across the back of her hand. She felt it all the way to her shoulder. Could any sensation be more delightful?

Emma's sticky sweet thoughts came crashing to the floor when the door to the study opened and Vicki stepped into the room. Her smile disappeared when her gaze flew to Emma's hand tangled with Matt's. Feeling the instinctive need for self-preservation, Emma pulled her hand away and clamped her arms around her waist. Matt placed both hands on the table, as if to show his mom there was nothing going on.

"Mom," Holt said, picking up his beans one by one. "Emma knows how to play poker, and she's really good."

Vicki took a minute to soak in what she'd seen, then pinned her smile back into place. "I'm glad to know Emma has talents," she said.

It didn't seem that Holt had noticed anything amiss with his mom, but Clay frowned as his gaze flicked between Matt and Emma. "How was the meeting, Mom?"

"Oh, fine. Pamela wants to be like the Rose Parade and make our float completely out of dandelions. There are plenty of dandelions, but they look bad about an hour after you pick them."

"Maybe they could get fake dandelions and reuse them every year."

"Ladasha doesn't want to spend the money," Vicki said. "And nobody wants to spend a thousand hours sticking fake dandelions on the float."

There was always one, and only one, float in the Dandelion Jelly Festival parade. The parade committee spent months working on it. The first summer Emma had spent in Dandelion Meadows, the float had been a giant jar of dandelion jelly. It hadn't really been dandelion jelly, just colored water, and it had sloshed all the way down the parade route. The Beer Hall closed during the parade, and all their workers pushed shopping carts and handed out cheese ball samples. Uncle Harvey had always driven his truck in the parade. It was rusty and made a funny noise, but it was considered a vintage vehicle, so it had always been accepted by the parade committee. The town was usually able to convince a band from one of the Boise high schools to march in the parade, and the county fire-fighters brought their truck and honked the horn for the little kids.

Emma had always adored the Dandelion Jelly Parade.

"Matt," Vicki said, "can I talk to you in the kitchen for a second?"

Matt hesitated before glancing at Emma—as if she didn't know exactly what Vicki wanted to talk to him about. It wasn't because he'd stolen her pinto beans. "Um, sure." Matt followed his mom out of the room.

Clay tried to pretend nothing was wrong. "So, Emma, Matt says your parents like curling."

Holt wasn't quite so tactful. "What was that about?"

"It was nothing, Holt," Clay said, quickly dealing the cards, as if starting another game would make them all forget about Matt and Vicki.

Holt drew his brows together. "It's not nothing. Why doesn't Mom like Emma?"

"Mom likes Emma just fine." Clay said, though why he bothered was anybody's guess. He wouldn't talk Holt or Emma out of being curious.

Emma felt her face get hot. Was she an independent woman, or wasn't she? Was she going to let Vicki walk all over her or was she going to stand up for herself? Did she want to take control of her destiny or not?

What would Matt's brothers think? An independent woman wouldn't care, would she? She stood up. "I'm going to find out."

Holt forced a smile. "What are you going to do?"

Leaving Holt and Clay in the den, Emma walked into the great room and listened for Matt and Vicki. They were in the kitchen, and it sounded like Vicki was doing all the talking. Emma got down on her knees and listened by the kitchen doorknob until she realized that would only work if there was a keyhole. She stood and pressed her ear to the door, but that didn't make much difference either. She finally got down on her stomach and leaned her head close to the little space between the bottom of the door and the floor. That was better. She could hear everything, even if her cheek got dusty.

"Do you want that house or not, Matt? Because you're letting Emma get under your skin. She's smart that way. She'll do anything to get that house, including making you feel sorry for her."

"That's not what's happening, Mom."

"Then why were you holding her hand?"

A long pause. "I like her."

That was nice to hear, even though it wasn't news to Emma. Matt had kissed her, and unless he was the manipulative type, he'd meant it.

"Somebody's got to save you from that girl. You can't see how passive aggressive she is."

"I don't even know what that means, Mom."

Listening at the door wasn't exactly taking control of her destiny, but it was all Emma had the courage to do tonight. Maybe she'd let Vicki have it tomorrow at work. Or maybe she wouldn't. Emma had never "let anybody have it" in her life.

"Look, Matt. I know you have a thing for girls in trouble. I love that you have such a tender heart. But Emma doesn't need that house, and she doesn't deserve it. She's got a great job in Dallas. Not once since Gwen died did she come up to see Harvey. It was like she completely ignored him for six years, and then she expects to get the house. Believe me, Harvey first left the house to her out of guilt, but then he came to his senses and left it to someone who really needed it, someone who could appreciate the gift. Emma saw the opportunity to make a quick buck, and she's milking you for all you're worth. Don't fall for it."

"I know what I'm doing," Matt said.

What did that mean? Maybe Matt *was* the manipulative type. You never saw it coming with the really talented manipulators. Emma wasn't sure, but she'd be wise to be on her guard and not let Matt kiss her again, no matter how much she wanted him to or how good it felt. She puckered her lips. Had Matt enjoyed it as much as she had, or was he just playing some sick game where she got the kisses and he got the house?

Emma heard a slight noise behind her and turned her head to see Clay and Holt standing across the room looking at her as if she'd just taken off all her clothes and starting dancing on the table. Okay. This wasn't exactly a flattering position and listening in on someone else's conversation was breaking all the good manner rules she had ever learned, but she was not about to sit in the den and wonder what Vicki was saying about her.

"Maybe we should get back to poker," Clay said, in his nice, polite way. He didn't mention anything about the fact that Emma's cheek and the floor were getting to know each other very well.

"That's a great idea," Holt shouted. Maybe he thought she couldn't hear well with one ear against the floor.

Emma wasn't about to get up. It was always good to know your enemy's plans. Too late, Emma realized why Holt had been talking so loudly. The talking behind the kitchen door ceased, and before Emma even considered getting to her feet, the door cracked open. Matt poked his head out, looked down, and slowly opened the door, pushing Emma along the floor with it like a human dust mop. Little grains of dirt embedded in her cheek as her face slid across the floor. This little adventure had better not clog her pores or she'd send Matt the dermatology bill. She wisely lifted her head off the floor.

Matt looked down, and his brows crinkled like an accordion. "Lose something?"

Emma rolled onto her back and folded her arms. "My sanity."

"I can see that." He frowned and squatted to get closer to her. "Were you listening?"

"No. I was examining the floor joints. Of course I was listening. What else?" Holding out her hand, she let Matt pull her to her feet. She brushed off her blouse and gave Holt a dirty look. He was the one who had double-crossed her.

"You're not supposed to eavesdrop on other people's conversations," Matt said.

Emma huffed out a breath. "And you're not supposed to talk about other people behind their backs."

"I wasn't talking..."

Vicki poked her head out of the kitchen and nudged Matt aside. "Well, Emma, I'm sure you have better things to do than waste your time playing poker with my boys." She put her arm around Emma in a motherly, bouncer-at-a-nightclub sort of way and led her to the front door. Vicki handed Emma her coat from the coat rack conveniently placed right next to the door. They must have thrown people out of their house a lot and needed quick access to their coats.

Emma put on her coat without giving Vicki any resistance because she was feeling a little lightheaded from standing up so fast.

"Mom," she heard Matt protest, just as Vicki herded Emma over the threshold like a sheep and shut the door decisively behind her. Emma found herself on the porch with seven pinto beans in her pocket and no ride home. Maybe she could steal Clay's horse.

The door swung open as if it had just met with a gust of wind, and Matt stomped onto the porch. He slammed the door behind him as if he blamed it for all his problems.

"You've got no right to be mad at me," Emma said, straightening herself to her full height. Matt still dwarfed her, but it never hurt to attempt to be a little taller.

Matt scrubbed his fingers through his hair. "I'm not mad at you, Emma. I'm irritated that you heard all that."

"Irritated and mad are synonyms."

"My mom was out of line," Matt said. "And she shouldn't have kicked you out. I'm annoyed with her, not you."

"Annoyed and irritated are still synonyms."

Matt growled. "Would you quit with the synonyms and tell me what you're thinking? I don't want you to be mad at me."

Emma brushed away a grain of sand that had lodged in her eyebrow. "I'm not mad. I'm annoyed."

"Synonyms," he said, giving her a cautious smile.

She ignored his lame attempt at humor. "I don't like you and Vicki conspiring to kick me out of the house."

"We're not conspiring. I love my mom, but she's wrong to treat you like this. She's always been ultra loyal to her family."

Emma snatched a piece of lint from her pant leg. "She said I'm passive aggressive."

Matt reached out, took her hand, and laced his fingers with hers. She should have pulled away, but Emma could only resist so much charm for so long. "If by that she means you throw a mean thimble, then she's right." His lips curled upward, and he tilted his head to meet her eye. "How many other people can say that Emma Dustin gave them a scar?"

Emma looked away to keep from smiling. "I didn't give you a scar."

He kissed her on the cheek. She pretended not to notice.

"We're going to work this house thing out, Emma. But my mom is going to be my mom. Can you forgive her for being my mom?"

"She used to like me."

"Don't worry. She'll relax, and you two will end up being the best of friends."

Stranger things had happened, but Emma wasn't going to hold her breath. "Do you think she'd let me borrow her Canada Goose Genuine Coyote Fur trim parka?"

"She has one of those?"

Emma nodded. "It looks really warm. A thousand dollars warm."

Matt's eyes got wide. "You may be best friends someday, but I don't think she'll ever let you borrow that coat."

"It's just as well. I'm probably allergic to fur."

Matt chuckled and drew her into his arms. Was he going to kiss her again? Because if he was, she should wipe the dust off the left side of her lips. He smiled and pulled her closer. "I don't know what to do with you, Emma."

There it was again. "Why don't you kiss me then?"

"That is the best idea I've heard all day." He bent his head and kissed her gently, and Emma really did float off the ground this time. Or maybe he had actually lifted her feet off the porch and was holding her in his arms. However he'd done it, it was the best feeling Emma had ever felt. And if he got a little grit in his mouth, he didn't complain.

He set her on her feet, and they lingered with their arms around each other, his lips hovering within inches of hers. "I'd better get you home," he said.

"You'd better get me off your porch. If your mom sees us, she'll never let me borrow that coat."

He took her hand, and they strolled down the porch steps.

"The answer is four," Emma said.

Matt opened the truck door for her. She didn't even mind. "What was the question?"

"I've given four people scars, not counting you."

CHAPTER

THIRTEEN

Seventy-eight-year-old Bill Rigby was down on his hands and knees, intently studying the concentric circles Emma had taped on the floor of the meeting room. No doubt three younger guys would have to help Bill get off the floor, but for now, he seemed to have forgotten he had two bad hips and a titanium knee. All he seemed to care about was making his next play and beating Iris Markham, Betty Frederick's twelve-year-old great-granddaughter.

"Come on, Bill," someone muttered.

"You can do it."

Ladasha, who had a front row seat to the drama, raised her fist in the air and started chanting. "Go, go, go."

The entire room joined her. It was a pretty good guess this wasn't normal behavior for a curling match, but Emma had given such an enthusiastic presentation, the crowd was definitely fired up. They'd given Iris the same treatment when it had been her turn, so nobody had cause to be offended—at least nobody had cause to be justifiable offended, though Betty

Frederick seemed to do a good job of being offended by just about everything.

Instead of joining in the chanting, Matt folded his arms, leaned back against the wall, and let his gaze fall on Emma. She was standing out of Bill's path, halfway between him and the circles of tape, nibbling on the fluorescent pink fingernail of her index finger. She'd been anxious like that all weekend. But if anybody performed brilliantly under pressure, it was Emma. Matt couldn't have been more smitten. Or more confused.

He was starting to think that if he had to choose between Emma and the house, he'd choose Emma, hands down. But why did he have to choose one or the other. Couldn't he have both? But what if Emma would rather have the house than him? He didn't think he could live with that. He wanted Emma to choose him so badly, he felt the ache of it all the way to his toenails.

"Bill, do you remember the strategy we talked about?" Emma said.

Bill hushed her. "I remember. Don't break my concentration."

Emma took a step back and started in on another fingernail. She was nervous, but she also seemed to be enjoying herself. Matt took a little bit of credit for that. The shuffleboard discs had been his idea.

They had left the ranch last Thursday night without getting what they'd actually gone to get, so Matt had been obliged to go back the next day. Mom stored an ancient shuffleboard in the garage, complete with cues and discs. The shuffleboard discs made perfect non-ice curling stones for Emma's presentation.

Emma had created a stunning PowerPoint, once again reminding Matt that he'd underestimated her brains and her talent. The PowerPoint had animation, graphics, bullet points, and video of an Olympic curling match that had the audience at the Pioneer Hair Museum on the edge of their seats. Even Matt found himself wanting to go curling. All this from a girl who didn't like curling and wasn't even from Idaho.

Emma had also drawn and colored a picture of a cute little baby hedgehog sitting on a curling stone, which she hung on the wall for her presentation. She was talented beyond words.

The meeting room at the Pioneer Hair Museum was packed for Emma's Curling Awareness Week presentation. They had to bring chairs in from the restaurant, and even then, two-dozen spectators had to stand along the walls to watch. It seemed that, at least in Dandelion Meadows, curling had wide appeal. Most of the old-timers were there, lots of middle-aged citizens, and even some of the younger people. All three of the Kimball brothers were there, and Matt had a hunch it wasn't because they were interested in curling. But if Elvon Kimball drooled over Emma much longer, Matt was going to have to kick him out.

"Come on, Bill." Lucille Howell, Emma's boss at the museum, stood a few feet in front of Bill with her broom at the ready. "It's past my bedtime." Lucille was one of Bill's sweepers. There wasn't much for the sweepers to do without ice, but Emma thought it was important everyone learn all the rules and aspects of the game, even if some of them didn't translate well off the ice.

Bill placed his hand on top of the shuffleboard disc, closed one eye, and nudged the disc in the direction of the circles.

"Okay, Lucille and Kyle. Sweep in the direction you want the disc to curl, but don't touch the disc or you get disqualified."

Lucille had obviously swept a few floors in her day, but she did a curling sweep completely wrong. It was a good thing her part didn't matter. Kyle had played hockey in high school, and he scrubbed that broom back and forth across the floor like an expert. He was probably already good enough to join an Olympic curling team.

The chanting got louder as Bill's disc glided across the floor, apparently on a perfect trajectory to knock Iris's disc out of the circle. Unfortunately, Lucille was a thorough sweeper, but not particularly fast. The disc caught up with her and bumped into her broom just as she made a wide sweep in the direction of the chairs. Everyone groaned as the disc slid under the first row.

Emma clapped her hands. "Iris, congratulations. You won!"

Iris hesitated for a split second, almost as if she wondered if it was proper to beat a seventy-eight-year-old man in curling or if it was proper to be happy about it. Then she burst into a grin, raised both fists in the air, and jumped up and down. Matt couldn't help but smile. Iris had a mouth full of braces and a pink bow the size of small airplane on her head. When she jumped up and down, her bow fluttered in the breeze. If she wasn't careful, she'd go airborne.

The entire audience went crazy, as if the high school football team had just won the state championship. Ladasha high-fived everyone she made eye contact with, and her husband, LaVerle, jumped so hard, his comb-over flipped to the wrong side of his head and dangled over his ear like some weird Jedi braid.

"That's the end, everybody," Emma called, trying to make her voice heard above the chaos. "Come see me if you have questions."

Leonard Passey and Alford Jones were standing right in front of Matt. "That was the best Awareness Week presentation I've ever seen," Alford said. "And that includes the time Preston Bowles did a cartwheel."

"I liked Fruit Washing Awareness Week, but this takes a close second."

Landon Kimball and his brother, the drooler, hurried to Bill Rigby and helped him off the floor. Maybe they weren't such bad guys after all—as long as they stayed away from Emma. Of course, the drooler was like four years younger than Emma. She wasn't the type to date a younger guy, was she?

Kyle Strong, the sweeper, handed Emma his broom, but instead of walking away like any normal person should, he hung around and stared at Emma as if she were the sun and he was Mars.

No. Mercury. He was too close to Emma to be Mars. And there was no way he had more questions about curling.

Kyle was tall and blindingly blond, as if he dipped his head in a vat of bleach every morning. He'd been a year ahead of Matt in school and had spent ten months in Africa on some do-gooder agricultural project. What was Emma's opinion on do-gooders? Matt pressed his lips together. If she had an opinion, it was probably favorable. Kyle looked abnormally healthy with really good teeth and the arms of a rock climber.

Matt let out the breath he'd been holding. Emma didn't like outdoorsy types. Matt felt better until he remembered that he himself was the outdoorsy type.

This was not good.

He'd better get over there and save Emma from Kyle's advances.

Mom had a way of sneaking up on people when they least expected it. "It was nice of you to help Emma with her presentation. She did a good job."

"I just let her borrow our shuffleboard discs, Mom. She did the rest."

Mom hooked her elbow around Matt's. She must have sensed that he wasn't entirely paying attention to what she was saying. "She's a very nice girl, but you can't both have the house, and you know it."

Matt really wasn't in the mood for Mom's concern. He had bigger problems on his hands. Kyle was showing Emma his state championship ring and flexing those muscles of his. "Mom, I kind of don't want to talk about this right now."

Mom moved to stand right in front of him, but he was taller so he could still watch Emma over the top of Mom's head. "Matt. Matt, look at me."

He glanced at his mom then back at Emma. "Is that your Canada Goose Coyote coat? Emma really likes it."

"I'm wearing my parka, Matt."

"Oh, it's nice." Drooler boy and his brother had helped Bill to a chair, and now they were also talking to Emma. What were they thinking? They were just kids. At least their presence diverted Emma's attention from Kyle, but it didn't seem to be doing much good. Emma was smiling and laughing and overall being too cute to resist, and Kyle was eating it up like hungry man at an All-You-Can-Eat buffet.

Mom grabbed a handful of Matt's shirt. That got his attention, if only because he'd spent ten minutes ironing it this morning. "Matt, you haven't returned my calls for four days. We need to talk."

Matt sighed and glanced around the room. Most people were still celebrating, some visiting, some putting up chairs and going home. Nobody seemed to be listening in on their conversation. "You did a lot of talking at the ranch, Mom. I know how you feel. We don't need to talk about it again."

"Look, it's obvious you like Emma."

"Mom, I really can't talk right now." Not while Kyle was helping Emma pull the tape off the floor. That was Matt's job. "How about I take you out to lunch tomorrow, and you can ask me everything you want to know but are too afraid to ask."

"I'm not afraid to ask anything," Mom said.

Didn't he know it! "So do you want to have lunch tomorrow or not?"

"Okay. I'll take what I can get." Mom glanced at Emma across the room. "I'd tell you not to go soft on me, but you've always been a softie. That's one of things I love most about you."

"I'm glad you don't think I'm a complete failure."

Mom reached up, pulled his ear so he'd look at her, then gave him the evil eye. "If I thought you were a failure, I would have given up on you a long time ago. I've raised five sons, Matt, and there's not a scrub in the bunch. Don't you ever forget it."

Matt nodded. He should have known better than to try to get to Mom by putting himself down. She didn't ever stand for it.

He definitely should have known better, because now Mom had to reassure him how highly she thought of him. "You're worth three times any other man in this room, except your brothers. I don't think you're any kind of failure, and I don't want you even thinking such a thought again."

"Okay, Mom, I get it, but Emma's a better person than I am. Try to remember that."

"No, she isn't. Emma is nice, but she's only looking out for herself."

Matt put his hands on his mom's shoulders. "Mom, you don't know what you're talking about. Emma did something really nice for our family once that nobody knows about. You shouldn't be so hard on her."

"If nobody knows about it, why do you?"

"I just do, so will you try to be nicer to Emma?"

Mom frowned. "What did she do? Someone left a raspberry pie on our porch once."

"It was way bigger than a raspberry pie, Mom, but if you knew, you'd regret ever saying a bad word about her."

"Why won't you tell me?"

"Because I promised I wouldn't," Matt said.

Mom scrunched her lips together. "If it was something Emma told you about, how do you know she didn't just make up a story to get you to like her?"

Matt pinned Mom with a no-nonsense look. "There you go again, assuming the worst about Emma."

"I'm just being realistic."

"You surprise me, Mom. You always taught us to look for the best in people."

Mom didn't seem sorry. "Unless they're trying to cheat one of my sons."

Four of Dandelion Meadows' older citizens gathered around Emma, but Kyle was still next to her, as if he was her personal assistant or something. "I really don't have time to debate this with you, Mom. We'll do lunch tomorrow." He gave his mom a peck on the cheek and walked away. Hopefully, he hadn't ticked her off, but really, he'd told her about five times that he needed to go. It was fast turning into an emergency situation with Kyle and Emma.

Matt slid between Emma and Teancum Madsen in her little circle of admirers. He would have gone between Emma and Kyle, but they were backed up against the wall, and Matt would have had to practically shove Kyle out of the way. It wasn't quite that big of an emergency yet. Should he put his arm around Emma? Kyle would know what was what, but everyone else in the room might seriously freak out. Matt would keep that as an option in case he needed it.

Emma smiled at him as if she hadn't seen him in weeks. It made Matt's heart pound like a jackhammer in a mineshaft.

"Hey, Kyle," Matt said, just so Kyle knew Matt was on to him.

"Hey, Matt. Holt said you went skiing last week."

That was a low blow. Emma didn't like outdoorsy guys. Well, two could play at this game. "You been rock climbing lately?"

"I can't do much climbing in the winter, but I went to California in December. The Owens River Gorge has some great climbs."

Emma seemed more interested than she should have. "You're a rock climber? That looks so intense. I could never do it. I'm afraid of heights."

Kyle smiled with all those white teeth. "It's not as bad as you might think, if you don't look down."

"How do you go to the bathroom on the face of a rock like that?"

Matt smiled to himself. Emma had bathroom issues. Kyle was, very possibly, toast.

"Hey, Matt," Teancum said. "We were just telling Emma she should be the captain of the curling team."

"What curling team?"

"I used to do some curling in Finland," Sini Madsen said, "but that was fifty years ago. I'd forgotten how exciting it is. We want to start a curling club. There's an ice arena in Boise where we can form a team."

Emma's smile didn't quite reach her eyes. It was obvious she wasn't thrilled about being in a curling club. She'd come to Idaho during her summers to get away from it. "That sounds fun," Emma said, because she was always nice like that. "It would be better to have a local captain, though, because I don't know how much longer I'm going to be here."

In all his excitement of being in Emma's presence, Matt had forgotten that Emma might still have a job in Dallas. If she moved back, would she forget about the house? Worse still, would she forget about him? His heart nearly stopped. Was the only way to keep Emma in Dandelion Meadows to give her the house? But if he ended up financially destitute, would Emma give him the time of day? Not to mention the fact that it wasn't just Matt who was depending on that money. Holt and Clay wanted to bring the ranch back to life. They needed that money as much as Matt did.

Pamela Goring pointed to the hedgehog picture Kyle was so thoughtfully holding for Emma. "My favorite thing about your presentation was the hedgehog. Did you draw that, Emma?"

"I did."

"It is just darling. My granddaughter would love it. Can I buy it from you?"

Emma raised her eyebrows in surprise. "I...I suppose."

"If you don't want to part with it, I completely understand," Pamela said.

"It's not that. I just didn't consider that someone might want it." Emma took the drawing from Kyle and handed it to Pamela. "I hope your granddaughter loves it. No charge."

"Oh, no," Pamela said. "I insist on paying for it." She pulled four twenties from her purse and handed them to Emma. "I'm sure eighty is less than it's worth, but that's all I've got on me."

Emma stared at the money as if she'd never seen a picture of Alexander Hamilton before. "Oh, this is too much."

Pamela studied her newly purchased drawing. "Worth every penny. And I want to commission you to do another one for my grandson. A hundred dollars for a picture of his dog, maybe sitting in the shade of his doghouse. I'll text you a photo."

"That's very nice," Emma said. "Are you...sure?"

"Of course I'm sure. You do excellent work, Emma. Annie

has always wanted a hedgehog, and this is the kind her mom will allow in the house."

Sini tilted her head to look at the picture. "You've got real talent, Emma. You should start an Etsy shop."

"What's an Etsy shop?" Teancum asked.

"It's an online store where people like Emma sell their artwork or jewelry or handicrafts. It's where I got my Darth Vader socks."

Teancum drew his brows together. "You have Darth Vader socks?"

"I only wear them on special occasions," Sini said. "And there aren't very many special occasions in Dandelion Meadows. I'll put them on for the Dandelion Jelly Festival."

Teancum shook his head. "I don't think it's right that your socks have a villain on them. It's like you're glorifying evil."

Sini patted her husband's arm. "He turned good in the end."

"I guess that's true."

Pamela zipped her purse closed. "I'll bring the money by your house tomorrow, Emma."

Teancum pointed back and forth between Emma and Matt. "You two still living together?"

Matt frowned. Did Teancum mean what it sounded like he meant? Were there folks in town who thought Matt and Emma were *living* living together? Of course there were. Gossip wasn't spread unless it was juicy, and "Matt and Emma as housemates" wasn't near as exciting as "Matt and Emma living together." Why hadn't this crossed his mind before? Maybe because when they'd first decided to share the house, that kind of thing was nowhere on Matt's radar.

Of course, it would be the perfect way to get rid of Kyle. If Kyle thought Emma and Matt were dating, he'd for sure back off, because he was a good guy. But Matt would never purposefully do anything to hurt Emma's reputation, and something like this would definitely hurt her reputation. She was an outsider already, she had expensive but impractical taste in footwear, and she had shot Max Hooper's dog—or at least everyone thought she had.

He couldn't let Emma carry this too. As much as he didn't want her to leave him, she needed to get out of that house, for her sake.

Teancum's choice of words didn't seem to bother Emma. She shrugged. "We're still living in the same house until the long arm of the law figures out who it belongs to."

Kyle seemed very interested. "At your uncle's?"

Emma nodded. "I get the upstairs, and Matt has the entire basement."

Teancum scratched his head. "Isn't it unfinished?"

Emma's eyes sparkled playfully. "Matt collects spiders and eats food storage."

Matt smirked. "There's food down there older than you, Teancum."

Teancum laughed. "Gwen never could throw anything away."

The Kimball brothers were back. "Emma, can we help you take anything to your truck?"

"I've got it," Matt said, louder than he needed to. Every single male under the age of thirty-five needed to stay away from Emma. Well, under the age of forty, just to be safe.

The people hovering around Emma said their goodbyes. Kyle took the hint and left peacefully but not before getting Emma's phone number. Matt clenched his teeth. If he could figure out Emma's phone password, he could block Kyle's number and Emma would never have to know. He wouldn't do it, but he sure wanted to. Matt sighed. Sometimes he wished his mom hadn't raised him to have good manners.

Lucille passed them with four brooms in her hand. "We'll see you tomorrow, Emma. That was a really nice presentation. You were so entertaining."

Matt helped Ladasha and LaVerle Pratt and the city council put up chairs. Then Matt swept the floor while Ladasha and LaVerle sat down with Emma to do some sort of Awareness Week evaluation. Ladasha was thorough and serious about her job, but couldn't the evaluation wait a day or two? Emma was beat, and Matt needed to get her home—not that she needed any beauty sleep. She could probably go for weeks without sleeping and still be just as pretty.

Matt didn't mind sweeping. He had some serious thinking to do, and he had to do it before he and Emma went back to Harvey's house tonight.

LaVerle sat in on the evaluation because Ladasha was his ride home. Matt had always liked LaVerle. He was a man of few words and never seemed to have an opinion about anything. That's why Ladasha had defeated him in the mayoral election. For better or worse, she got people lathered up. LaVerle was about as enthusiastic as a bag of Idaho potatoes. Besides that, he was a chain smoker, and his breath smelled like he licked a chimney every morning before work. LaVerle had big, round, 90s glasses and a grand comb over. His hair was so long on one side, it fell to his shoulders when he didn't have it gelled across his head.

Once Matt finished sweeping, he pulled up a chair and sat in on the evaluation. He was Emma's ride home, and he had nothing better to do.

"I'm going to recommend to the city that we upgrade our audio visual system," Ladasha was saying. "Your PowerPoint was spectacular, but only those of us on the first and second rows got the full effect. I have to be honest with you, Emma. I gave you this assignment because I felt you needed a chance to step up. You needed a confidence builder, and I knew this would be just the thing for you. But now I'm worried."

"Worried?" Emma frowned.

"Not exactly worried. More like concerned," Ladasha said.

"Worried and concerned are synonyms," Matt said, winking at Emma. She relaxed into a smile.

Ladasha reached out and patted Emma's knee. "Nothing so serious, honey. The Dandelion Jelly Festival is the jewel of our city, and you did such a fine job on Curling Awareness Week, I don't want the Stop Smoking Festival to overshadow our main summer event."

LaVerle looked over his glasses at his wife. "You're having a Stop Smoking Festival?"

Ladasha huffed out a breath. "To be honest, LaVerle, I'm doing it specifically for you. Kissing you is like kissing a smoke-stack, and I just can't gear up for it anymore. I expect you to take the pledge like everyone else."

"I don't feel right about taking a pledge. That sounds sacri-legious."

Ladasha propped her hand on her hip. "LaVerle, you took the Red Ribbon Week pledge, the Rotary Club pledge, and the Pledge of Allegiance to the flag. Don't give me that horse pucky about being sacrilegious. It won't kill you to take the Stop Smoking Pledge, and you only have to do it once a year—maybe only once if we decide to nix the Stop Smoking Festival next year, which we might if it overshadows the Dandelion Jelly Festival."

Emma laced her fingers together. "Let me put your mind at ease about that. The Cigarette Demolition Festival is going to be subtle and understated."

Matt nodded. "Low key."

Ladasha widened her eyes as if Emma had just given LaVerle a smack on the lips. "That's just what I'm talking about. Cigarette Demolition Festival is a grand title, but people are going to think grand things will be happening there. Are you planning on blowing something up?"

Emma stretched her lips across her teeth. "I was thinking of maybe setting fire to the papier-mâché lung."

Ladasha fell silent as she tapped her finger against her mouth. "I knew it from the first time I met you, honey. You're a creative genius. That's a brilliant idea, and I'm afraid we're going to have to cancel the whole thing."

Emma's features lit up like a package of sparklers on New Year's Eve. "Really? Okay. Thanks so much."

Matt hadn't expected Emma to react with pure joy, but at least she wasn't upset about it.

Ladasha looked confused and a little hurt. "Didn't you want to be in charge of the Stop Smoking Festival? People are usually thrilled to be asked."

Emma was a smart girl. She immediately wiped the smile off her face. "Oh, well, I am...I mean I felt the weight of the great honor you bestowed on me by putting me in charge of the Stop Smoking Festival, but I agree that a separate festival will overshadow the other one. Better to get rid of it."

Ladasha furrowed her brow. "I don't want you to be sad about this, Emma."

Sad was the word furthest from what Emma had to be feeling at this moment.

"Maybe we could still have a Cigarette Demolition booth at the Dandelion Jelly Festival," Ladasha said. "But we'll call it the Stop Smoking booth and give smokers a pamphlet instead of a pledge."

"I'm not reading a smoking pamphlet," LaVerle said.

Ladasha propped her other hand on her other hip. "You read every obituary in the New York Times, our broker's financial reports, and the cereal boxes at breakfast. It won't kill you to read a smoking pamphlet."

"I suppose we could do a booth," Emma said. "And a smaller version of a lung."

Ladasha nodded. "But no blowing anything up. We don't want the parade to feel bad."

Matt almost pointed out that a parade, in and of itself, didn't have feelings, but not blowing up things would be less work for Emma. He kept his mouth shut.

Ladasha stood and folded her chair. "Okay then. No more Stop Smoking Festival. I think we've made the right decision. Will you break the news to Frankie? Gently."

Emma nodded enthusiastically. "I sure will."

"You two go home. It's been a long night. LaVerle and I will lock up. Congratulations on a highly successful Awareness Week."

LaVerle stacked his chair against the wall. "You two still figuring out who owns Harvey's house?"

"Yeah," Matt said, not really eager to talk about it and risk creating bad feelings with Emma.

LaVerle smoothed his hands across his comb over. "Lou Banks says you asked him to come over and give you a painting bid."

Emma frowned at him. "A painting bid?"

Matt hadn't wanted Emma to find out about that, but what did it matter? She should have expected him to think about getting the house ready to sell. "The house will sell better with a new coat of paint."

"You can't change my room. Uncle Harvey painted it specifically for me."

"Emma, nobody wants to buy a house with a pink room."

She folded her arms. "It doesn't matter because I'm not selling the house."

"You won't have anything to say about it if I get the house."

"You can't sell it," LaVerle said.

Oh, great. Everybody had an opinion. "Why not?"

"You just can't." LaVerle nodded at Emma. "You just can't."

Matt got it. He really did. That house had a lot of sentimental value to Emma and obviously to a few other people in town, but he wouldn't allow sentiment to trump good sense. Matt needed that money to replenish his very low bank account, and whether Emma understood or not, Harvey owed it to him. He wouldn't back down from that. But it was nearly 10:00 p.m., Emma was tired, and he wasn't going to argue a moot point, especially since he wasn't a lawyer. "Okay," he said. "A fresh coat of paint would make the whole place smell better, but we can talk about it later."

He helped Emma on with Harvey's coat, and they ventured into the cold, but she wouldn't let him hold her hand. "You've got to promise me you won't paint the pink room, Matt. It reminds me of Uncle Harvey and Aunt Gwen."

"Okay. I won't paint the pink room." But he couldn't promise the new owner wouldn't gut the whole house. He put his arm around her before she could avoid him. "Don't be mad, okay?"

"Of course I'm mad. That house is full of memories."

He risked a kiss on her forehead. "You can make new memories somewhere else."

"Not the same kind of memories."

They walked down the stairs. "I'll tell you what. When the judge rules in my favor, I'll sell the house back to you."

"You know I can't afford to buy it. I'm a hair collection expert at the Pioneer Hair Museum. I'm not exactly raking in the big bucks."

"But you're ambitious."

She snorted softly. "So was Julius Caesar."

"There's always advancement opportunities for those who are ambitious." When they got to the truck, Matt leaned with his back against Emma's door and pulled her into his arms. She felt so good there, and he'd been aching to do it all evening. She didn't resist, but she didn't seem as eager as she had the other night. "I'm sorry I was thinking of painting your pink room," he said. "I didn't know it was that important to you."

"Aunt Gwen and I spent hours looking for the perfect color to match my bedspread."

"It's a really nice bedspread."

She lifted her head to look him in the eye. "How do you know?"

Would he ever learn to keep his mouth shut? "Know what?"

"You sneaked upstairs, didn't you?"

"What makes you think that?"

She cuffed him on the shoulder. "You told me you wouldn't go up there."

"Emma, okay. I wanted to get accurate measurements on all the rooms, and I fixed the light. Didn't you notice I fixed the light?"

She expelled a long breath. "Okay. But don't ever go up there again. Sometimes I hang my bra in the shower."

He frowned in mock disappointment. "I wish I'd seen that."

She cuffed him again. "Whatever."

"Which brings me to something else I wanted to talk to you about."

"My bra brings you to something else you want to talk about?"

"I have an apartment in Boise. It's actually pretty nice, with free coffee and an indoor pool in the clubhouse. I have a lease until the end of April, and I want you to take it."

"Take what?" she said.

"Take the apartment. Go live there."

She gave him a suspicious look, like she thought he'd go home while she wasn't there and paint her bedroom. "What for?"

"I care about you very much, and I don't like what people are saying. I want to protect your honor."

She raised an eyebrow. "My honor?"

A small alarm went off in his head at the look on her face, but he didn't know what to do with it, so he plunged ahead. "Yes, I want to keep your reputation safe, and the only way to do that is to move you into my apartment."

She pressed her lips together. "What about *your* reputation?"

Matt nodded. "If we're not living in the same house, I suppose that will protect my reputation too. I won't have people assuming things about us that aren't true." He got mad just thinking about it. "But I want you to come over all the time. We could still make dinner together every night." He needed Emma like he needed air, but her reputation came first.

"Why don't *you* move back into your apartment, and I'll stay where I am?"

Matt hesitated. That made way more sense, but he could never agree to it. "It's my house."

She stepped back and broke the connection between them. "Are you kidding me?"

"Um, no?" Should he have said yes? Maybe he should have said yes.

He had succeeded in making Emma hopping mad, and he knew this because her nostrils flared and her breath came out of her mouth in great white puffs of steam. It was not altogether beyond the realm of possibility that she would turn into a dragon at any moment. "Matt, are you a pigheaded jerk or just a dumb lumberjack?"

"Which answer will make you less mad?"

She balled her hands into fists, threw her head back, and growled. "For someone who doesn't want to die in his sleep, you sure are stupid. I can see through your little tricks a mile away." She stomped back and forth, either because she was angry or trying to keep her feet from freezing. "I'm sure you're worried sick about my reputation."

"But I am. I don't want you to get hurt."

She got on her tiptoes and went nose to nose with him. "I am not moving out of that house. Period. And don't you come upstairs again or I'll set a booby trap, like Indiana Jones."

"I only went up there once or twice." Maybe once to measure and three times to play ping-pong with Clay. It wasn't fair that she got the ping-pong table. She didn't even appreciate it.

"Don't go up again." She hissed when he tried to open the truck door for her, so he pulled his hand away and quickly jogged around to the driver's side.

She slammed her door. He shut his door with less force, just to prove what a nice guy he was and that he had her best interests at heart. "It was really a nice presentation tonight, Emma. The best I've ever seen. I'm so proud of you."

"Don't talk to me."

Matt made a mental note. In future when he felt the urge to have a serious talk with Emma, it would be wise to wait until they got to the house. The silent treatment made for a long, lonely ride.

CHAPTER
FOURTEEN

S tanding in the gas station mini mart next to the old coffee and the stale Danishes, Emma opened four mustard packets and squeezed them all over her gas station hot dog. She liked mustard quite a bit, and it was one of the few sanitary food items at the gas station because the packets had been packed and sealed by the manufacturer somewhere in Oklahoma. Of course, Emma had no way of knowing if the mustard packet manufacturing plant was sanitary, but she'd take her chances. The mustard covered the day-old taste of the bread and the slightly charred, crunchy texture of the hotdog.

She cleaned her hands as best she could with four napkins and a little water from the soda dispenser, then huddled in the corner near the restrooms and ate her hotdog as quickly as possible. She didn't take the time to savor it, because there was nothing to savor, and if she took too much time, she would think too hard about what she was eating and gag. The hotdog was just to ward off starvation. She didn't need to enjoy it, and she certainly didn't need to think about how many hands had touched that hotdog before she had.

Emma had eaten dinner at the gas station every day for a week because she didn't want to risk making dinner at home where Matt might be lurking, and she refused to eat at Torie's one more time. Not only did she not want to impose on her best friend, but she also refused to be in the same room with Torie's cousin-in-law, who talked with his mouth full, had a disgusting tattoo on his left bicep, and suffered from a permanent head cold. The cold alone wouldn't have made him unpleasant, but every time he sneezed, snot oozed from his nose piercing. It was kind of hard to eat dinner in the company of snot. Last Tuesday night, Emma had suffered through an hour of the cousin-in-law's lecture about how someday the people would rise up and destroy capitalism, as if he had a plan to singlehandedly bring down the entire system. Emma certainly hoped not. Her investment firm still owed her a paycheck.

Never again had Emma accepted Torie's kind invitations to dinner. Eating a hotdog in the gas station was preferable to snot and the demise of capitalism.

She took the last bite of her hotdog and swallowed decisively, longing for a thick, juicy cheeseburger at the Pioneer Hair Museum. But she couldn't go there either. Vicki Matthews was a three-days-a-week, unpleasant presence at the museum, and Trudy Howell didn't like Emma—Trudy had a thing for Matt, and she thought Matt and Emma were a thing.

If only Trudy knew the truth. Emma despised Matt Matthews, and she always would. Still, Trudy didn't know that, and Emma was terrified Trudy would spit in her food or put Ex-Lax in her chocolate pie. It was a sad day when the gas station was Emma's best option for a good meal and a warm place to hang out.

Okay. Emma didn't despise Matt. She liked him. Well, that wasn't exactly true either. She adored him, but he'd really ticked her off this time, and she wasn't going to go easy on him. In fact, the plan was to avoid Matt entirely until one of them got the house and they never had to see each other again. How could she give her heart to a guy who only wanted one thing from her? She'd get hurt, for sure and certain, and she didn't need the heartache in her life right now—not that she ever needed heartache—but now was not a good time for more bad things to happen to her.

She took a deep breath and let it out slowly, concentrating very hard on not tearing up in the middle of the gas station mini mart. Who was she kidding? It was too late to avoid heartache. Matt had already broken her heart. He'd made it very clear the house was more important than she was, and she wasn't about to play second fiddle to five acres of land and a creaky old shack.

She immediately chastised herself for thinking of Uncle Harvey's house as a shack. It was a little rough around the edges and smelled a bit musty, but it was a sturdy house with beautiful wood floors and original doors. Emma loved that house.

She loved it more than she loved Matt—especially now that he'd broken her heart and she was through with him. She'd even bought a deadbolt lock for her bedroom door, with a special key that she hid in the bathroom above the mirror. It might have been overkill, but she was not going to allow Matt to paint her room some boring color like Balanced Beige. And she certainly wasn't going to allow him to set foot in there again to stare at her bedspread or her chest of drawers with Zac Efron's face Mod-Podged on it, especially now that she and Zac might be back on again.

I'm sorry, Zac, for casting you aside for the likes of Matt Matthews. Can you ever forgive me?

Emma threw away her napkins and empty mustard packets and wiped the crumbs from the counter. Time to go home. It was her turn with the TV, and she wasn't going to let Matt cheat her out of it tonight. For a whole week, he'd refused to get out of the great room so she could watch TV by herself. She'd ended up surrendering the TV to him and spending the evenings in her room with the door locked so she wouldn't have to look at Matt or listen to his lame attempts to apologize. She still couldn't get service in her bedroom, so she had spent her free time drawing baby animals for the new Etsy shop Torie had helped her set up online.

In addition to the dog for Pamela Goring's grandson, Emma had drawn a trio of piglets sitting on a porch swing and a baby giraffe poking his head through a window. The day she'd put them online, they'd been purchased. She had a commission for three kittens sitting in teacups and a hamster wearing sunglasses. There had been plenty to keep her busy all alone in her pink room while Matt watched TV on her time downstairs.

But tonight she was taking a break and taking back her power. If Matt wanted to sit and stare at her while she watched TV, she was just going to ignore him—or at least pretend to ignore him. She couldn't really ignore him. Matt was unignorable, if that was even a word. He was so kind and handsome and capable and hot that Emma couldn't keep her eyes off him without trying very hard. But she shouldn't expect too much of herself. If Matt weren't so wonderful and so unignorable, she wouldn't have fallen in love with him in the first place. He'd broken her heart. She just needed to give herself some time. It would get easier, and in a few weeks, she'd never have to try to ignore him again. She'd get the house, and he'd be gone.

For some reason, this thought did not make her feel better.

The drive home was cold, but at least it was short. Matt's truck was parked out in front where he always parked it. Emma's lips curled in spite of herself. He liked to pull it clear off the road so there was no chance of any passing car hitting it, even though cars driving up Uncle Harvey's road were rare. There wasn't much of anything but farmland past the house. Matt loved that Ford, just like Uncle Harvey had adored his Chevy. It was very sweet, in a manly, lumberjack sort of way.

Emma wiped the smile off her face and pulled Uncle Harvey's truck into its usual spot. If she was going to get the great room to herself, she'd had to be forceful and unemotional. Matt would respond to a strong, independent Emma.

Emma marched in the front door, with every intention of kicking Matt out of the great room first thing. She stopped short. From the front hall, she could see the TV. Her heart swelled like a puffer fish. Matt was watching *Gilmore Girls*—the one where Rory graduates and gives that really beautiful speech about her mom.

Emma tiptoed farther down the hall. Was this a trick? Didn't Matt hate *Gilmore Girls*? He knew she was due home at any minute. Was he trying to make her think he was sensitive and stuff?

She wasn't going to fall for that. She folded her arms across her chest. "It's my turn to use the TV tonight."

He turned as if she'd startled him, and there were unmistakable tears in his eyes. Was this for real? Matt stood up quickly and swiped the moisture from his face. "Hey. Did you have a good day?"

"You're watching *Gilmore Girls*."

He grabbed the remote and pushed pause. He didn't turn it off like she would have expected. "Don't make fun of me, okay?"

"I would never make fun of a man who knows how to get in touch with his sensitive side."

"I lost it when Luke started crying. I mean, Rory and her mom have been through a lot."

Emma tried to ignore how adorable Matt looked with mussed hair and a day's growth of whiskers, but she'd forgotten how unignorable Matt really was—especially with tears still in his eyes and that irresistible half smile on his face. It wasn't an act. He really liked Rory's graduation speech. Emma swallowed the giant lump in her throat. "Well, it's a really good episode."

He shoved his hands in the pockets of his well-fitting jeans and studied her face for what seemed like about ten minutes. "I brought you a present."

"You did?"

He grabbed an Amazon box sitting on the counter and handed it to her. "I ordered them a couple of days ago."

She opened the box, peeled back the plastic bubble wrap, and might have squealed just a little. She pulled out two giant yellow coffee mugs with "Luke's" written across the front. "Just like on the show. The right size and everything."

He bloomed into a full-blown smile. How could she resist anything so perfect? "I know you like the show, and your aunt has all those mugs. I thought you'd want to add to the collection."

A space next to her heart about the size of a quarter felt intensely warm all of a sudden. The warmth spread through her chest until she thought she might burst. "They're perfect," she said, her voice cracking in about a million places. It was the most wonderful gift anyone had ever given her, except for maybe the pink bedroom with matching curtains.

Her cheeks stung, and she had to blink about a hundred times a second to keep the tears from pooling in her eyes.

"I brought Chinese takeout. You're going to have a stroke if you eat any more hotdogs."

How did he know about the hotdogs? Did she even care? He'd brought Chinese—heavenly, fattening, greasy Chinese food. She thought she might have died and gone to heaven. Matt took the mugs and set them on the counter. Then he cupped his hands around her upper arms. "Emma, you've been avoiding me all week, and I don't blame you. I keep being stupid, and I'm sorry. I shouldn't have asked you to move out of the house, especially when I don't want you to move. Will you forgive me?"

"Did you get General Tsao's chicken?"

He nodded.

Darn it, Matt Matthews. He'd completely broken down her defenses with a set of coffee mugs and a very sincere apology. Plus, the smell of Chinese food hung in the air like the song of the Sirens, and he'd admitted he was stupid. There was only so much a girl could take before she had to surrender.

Before she could tell him she wasn't mad at him anymore, he drew her into his arms and kissed her, which was very pleasant but also irritating because he hadn't even given her a chance to say something nice to him after all he'd done for her. After about three seconds, she decided to relinquish her irritation and enjoy the kiss. There were so few simple pleasures left in the world.

She snaked her hands around his neck and pressed her lips to his, taking in his absolutely manly scent, which was a mixture of good, strong timber and Old Spice. She loved Old Spice. Zac Efron probably didn't wear Old Spice.

He pulled away, leaving her breathless and a little giddy. "I hope this isn't another stupid thing to say, Emma, but I can't hide it anymore. Don't freak out, but I think I love you."

Okay. He'd told her not to freak out, but she couldn't help

but freak out on the inside. He loved her? Did he already know that she maybe loved him too? This was not what she had expected when she'd walked through the door five minutes ago. How nice not to have to kick Matt out of the great room tonight.

Emma didn't know what to say. There were so many things she wanted to say, but she tended to talk in circles when she was agitated, and no one could understand her train of thought. She wanted Matt to understand.

She slung one arm around his neck and kissed him thoroughly. When she pulled away, she could tell she'd accomplished her goal. She wanted him to feel as off-balance as she did. "First of all, I guess I'm not mad at you anymore."

"I'm glad to hear it."

"Second, in the interest of full disclosure, you should know I already ate, but I'm willing to eat again as long as no hotdogs are involved."

He nodded earnestly. "No hotdogs."

"They'll give you cancer."

He grimaced. "Do you know how many of those things I ate as a Boy Scout?"

"Well, now you are informed, and knowledge is power." She wrapped her arms around his waist, got on her tiptoes, and brushed her mouth across his. He drew in a wobbly breath. "Thirdly—or is this fourthly?" Her head was spinning like one of those rides at the amusement park—a good kind of spin. "Thirdly, I'm going to be a famous artist someday and someone is going to ask me to write my memoirs, so you need to not do any more stupid things or you might show up in my book. I'm thinking of asking J.K. Rowling to ghostwrite it for me."

Matt chuckled. "There's no doubt in my mind you'll be a

famous artist someday. You're that talented. But you should have Tom Clancy write your book. It will be more exciting."

"Tom Clancy's dead," Emma said. "It can't be him."

Matt raised his eyebrows. "Are you sure? I've seen his new books in Walmart."

"He's got a ghostwriter too." Emma took his hand and led him to the couch. "Fourthly or fifthly, we've got to figure out how to live peaceably together in this house, because I think I love you too and I don't want a house to come between us."

His eyebrows went up again. "You...you think you love me?" His smile couldn't have gotten any wider with a crowbar.

"Even though you say stupid things sometimes, and you go to the bathroom outdoors. None of that matters to me. I'll take you just the way you are."

"I only go to the bathroom outdoors when I absolutely have to, and I like *Gilmore Girls*. That has to count for something."

"And you bought me limited edition *Gilmore Girls* mugs."

"I don't think they're limited edition," he said.

"It sounds better if they're limited edition."

"Okay."

Matt leaned back into the sofa, and Emma tucked herself into the space under his arm. It was very nice there. "You started my truck and fixed my light and helped me with my presentation."

"I didn't help much."

Emma scrunched her lips to one side of her face and looked at him with one eye closed. "I'm listing all your good qualities. You shouldn't downplay them. Remember that first night we made dinner together?"

"I wanted to kiss you so bad."

"Yes, well, I had chicken slime all over my hands, and it

wouldn't have been wise to get distracted. We needed our wits about us to translate the recipe from French. But I digress. The night we made chicken cordon bleu was the first time I seriously considered giving up Zac Efron."

"I think I fell in love with you when you started throwing thimbles at me."

Emma laughed in disbelief. "That was like three seconds after we saw each other."

"You're just too cute, and I have a great appreciation for a woman who knows how to defend herself." He laced his fingers with hers. "We need to talk about the house, Emma. One of us is going to be very unhappy about it, but does it have to ruin our relationship?"

Emma didn't want to talk about the house. Not now. Why ruin a perfectly grand evening with a real estate discussion? "The Chinese is getting cold, and even after that hotdog, I'm pretty hungry."

"Emma, we need to talk about this."

She slumped her shoulders. "Can't we pretend the problem doesn't exist, just for tonight?"

Matt squeezed her hand. "It's not going to go away, even if we ignore it."

"That's exactly right," Emma said. "It will still be there in the morning. Come on, Matt. You just told me you love me, and I'm kind of freaking out about it, even though you told me not to. I mean, freaking out in a good way. I just want this feeling to last a few more hours." She picked up the remote. "I've got a papier-mâché lung meeting tomorrow night and a hair collection appointment on Thursday. It's the perfect night to binge watch *Gilmore Girls*. We can get in at least four episodes if we watch while we eat."

A smile grew slowly on his lips. "Who's your favorite, Jesse or Dean?"

"Who's yours?"

"Dean. Jesse's too angsty," he said. "Do you like Jesse better?"

She smiled. "You'll see. There's someone else."

He raised an eyebrow. "I bet we can get in five episodes tonight if we use paper plates so we don't have to do the dishes."

"Paper plates it is." They both leaped to their feet. Emma grabbed some plates and filled her new coffee mugs with ice and Diet Coke. Matt opened the Chinese takeout containers and lined them up on the cupboard. There were seven of them.

"Matt, how many people were you expecting?"

He took her face between his hands and kissed her. She had a feeling it was never going to get old. "I wanted to be sure to get something you liked, just in case you were reluctant to forgive me."

"I was reluctant to forgive you, but a week of hotdogs wore me down. Anything besides hotdogs was a sure bet."

They heard a soft knock on the front door, like someone wanted to get their attention but didn't want to bother them. Matt smiled wryly at Emma. "Maybe we're only destined for four episodes."

"Maybe it's a magazine salesman. I'll get rid of him." Emma jogged down the hall, determined not to miss one extra second with Matt all to herself.

Johnny Cleaver stood on the porch in a Dallas Cowboys beanie and a tattered coat. Even though he was a lawyer, Johnny always looked a little disheveled, as if he'd gotten out of bed ten minutes ago and had forgotten to brush his teeth and comb his hair. "Howdy-ho, Emma. May I come in?"

Emma's heart skipped around in her chest like a drop of water on a hot skillet, and the only reason Emma knew what that looked like was because she'd nearly started a fire years ago trying to fry frozen chicken. Did Johnny have an update on her case? They weren't scheduled in court for weeks. Emma didn't know anyone else who could smile and frown at the same time. Was it good or bad news? Johnny's expression wasn't going to tell her anything.

Johnny stepped into the house and pulled off his beanie. His thin white hair floated out in all directions from his head, brought to life by the miracle of static electricity. He didn't seem to notice that his hair was flying around his head like a halo as he reached into his pocket and produced an envelope. "Emma, I've got another letter."

MATT HAD NEVER BEEN SO happy or so deep in despair. He loved Emma, but it wasn't a stretch to think when he got the house, he'd lose her. Maybe he should just give her the house.

Mom was always warning him about making decisions with his heart instead of his head, but a thousand houses would never make up for losing Emma. Still, other people were counting on him. With the sale of the house, he could get Dad's money back. Then Clay and Holt needed some money to restore the ranch, and Matt couldn't let them down. He'd already let them down once when he'd lost the money in the first place. His family needed that money. Would he be forced to choose between them and Emma?

Emma was right. She'd just told him she loved him. Tonight was the worst time for a conversation about the house. Quite possibly, they could avoid it for weeks and live in ignorant bliss until the judge made a decision. Too bad the conversation wasn't going to get any easier.

Matt arranged the takeout boxes on the island. If it was a salesman at the door, Emma must have been having a hard time getting rid of him. Matt stomped to the front hall, ready to throw the pushy guy out.

Johnny Cleaver stood in the hall, his hair floating and his glasses askew on his face. He wore a thick tie he'd probably purchased in the 70s and those orthopedic shoes popular with the over-eighty crowd. Matt's heart sank through the floor and halfway to China. Had there been a ruling already? Matt hadn't heard anything about it. Hadn't the hearing been scheduled for April?

This couldn't be happening tonight. Not tonight, when Emma still loved him. "Hey, Johnny. Is everything okay?"

Emma turned and gave Matt the most uneasy smile he'd ever seen.

Johnny adjusted his glasses. "I don't know. Has Emma thrown any thimbles lately?" He chuckled, but neither Emma nor Matt had the heart to join him.

"Johnny says there's another letter," Emma said hesitantly. "What is it?"

Johnny unbuttoned his coat. "I don't mind conducting business in the hall, but we'll need more light. Have you got a 60-watt bulb for that overhead fixture?"

Matt expelled a long breath. It must have been an important envelope, or Johnny wouldn't be standing in their hall at 7:00 in the evening. Much as he wanted to put it off until morning, they needed to know what was in that letter. They'd have to invite Johnny in. He'd expect some Chinese food.

Emma glanced at Matt. "You'd better come in the other room, Johnny. All the bulbs in there are at least 60-watt."

Johnny nodded. "Never underestimate the power of good lighting. It increases productivity by thirty percent." He handed his coat and beanie to Emma, who hung them in the closet and led Johnny to the great room.

The TV was still on, suspended on Rory Gilmore's face as

she gave her graduation speech. Maybe they could still get an episode or two in tonight if they were still speaking to each other by the time Johnny left.

"Goodness gracious," Johnny said. "Did I interrupt dinner?"

"Um, we were just going to eat," Emma said, glancing at Matt again. "Would you like some?"

Johnny waved away her offer. "I can't eat anything after six o'clock or my heartburn keeps me up all night. But you two go ahead. You can eat while I talk."

Matt shrugged. Might as well eat now while he still had an appetite. He handed Emma a plate, and she took a little of everything, making sure that none of her food touched any of the other things on her plate. Matt wasn't so persnickety. He piled on the food as if he'd never have the stomach to eat again. Just in case he wouldn't.

Matt sat next to Emma on the couch while Johnny paced back and forth in front of them, his hair waving in the mild breeze fanned up by his movements. "Pull that chair closer," Emma said. "You don't have to stand."

Johnny slid a thick stack of papers from the envelope. "No, thanks. I've been sitting on a plane all day."

Emma smiled politely. "Oh. Were you on vacation?"

For some reason, Johnny had to think about that for a minute. "Not really, although I did get to see where they shot JFK. That was a conspiracy if ever there was one. They never did figure out who was on the grassy knoll."

Matt didn't even know what a grassy knoll was, so the whole conspiracy was lost on him.

Emma perked up. "You were in Dallas?"

"Yeah. The food's good, but everything there is extra fancy, like they're trying too hard. But the people are nice, and the religion is good. I went to three different churches on Sunday, just to see what they were like. All excellent sermons." He unfolded the papers in his hand. "I have to apologize, Emma. As your attorney, I should have given this to you a week ago, but I was out of town, and Marian just files my papers without telling me."

Matt tried not to be annoyed that Johnny hadn't apologized to him. They knew each other better, and Johnny was a close friend of the family. Didn't that count for anything? But Matt was mostly annoyed that Emma had been smart enough to hire Johnny before he had. He was lawyer-less, money-less, and probably about to be girlfriend-less.

"What's in the letter?" Emma acted casual enough, but her hand shook when she raised her fork to her mouth.

Johnny looked at the top paper as if he'd never seen it before. It took him a very long time. "It seems there is a third will."

Emma dropped her fork, and it hit her plate with such force, half her fried rice jumped into the air and landed on the floor. "What?"

Johnny studied the paper for another full minute and nodded. "This one was made by a lawyer in Idaho Falls four days before Harvey died. No doubt some ambulance chaser. The lawyer didn't know Harvey had died until last week. He immediately forwarded a copy of the will to me."

"This is getting stranger and stranger," Emma said.

"Not all that strange when you read Harvey's letter that goes with it. It seems he wanted to give the house to you, Emma, but then something happened. I'm not sure what it was, but he felt like he should give the house to Matt."

Matt turned his face from Emma. He knew exactly what had happened. Harvey had known he was dying and had suddenly developed a conscience.

"Harvey made that will leaving the house to Matt, but then

he wasn't sure how legal that would be, so he hired an Idaho lawyer to draw up a will that would be legal in Idaho." Johnny frowned and adjusted his glasses. "He should have called me. I'm not one of those fancy lawyers, but I was one of his oldest and dearest friends."

It was obvious Emma was incredibly upset, but she set her plate on the couch, stood up, and gave Johnny a big hug. "Uncle Harvey loved you and trusted you more than anybody, but maybe he wasn't thinking straight or maybe he didn't want to burden you with all the arrangements."

Johnny nodded thoughtfully. "He was always thoughtful that way."

"You know he would have had you do his will if he hadn't been so concerned about your feelings."

Matt pressed his lips together. This was why he loved Emma. Her concern for others was astounding. Boone, Johnny, Lucille, even his own mother, were all beneficiaries of Emma's kindness.

Matt hated to bring it up, but he'd rather not prolong the inevitable. "What does the new will say?"

Johnny looked at his papers again. "Harvey says he was torn about who to leave the house to, and he asks your forgiveness, but he finally decided to leave it to both of you."

Matt felt as if someone had just smacked him in the head with a two by four. Harvey had left the house to both of them?

Emma frowned. "What?"

"He's left half of everything to you, Emma, and half to Matt." Johnny ran his finger down the page. "He only asks that you never sell the house or the property. I guess he wants to keep it in the family, and maybe he thought Emma could buy Matt's half."

"Can I...can I see it?" Emma said.

Johnny handed her the stack of papers, and she read as if she'd never read anything so interesting in her life.

Matt tried valiantly to gather his scattered wits from the floor. "Is it legally binding, Johnny?"

"What? The will? As far as I can tell, the ambulance chaser did a good job."

"No," Matt said. "The part about not selling the property. Is it legally binding?"

Johnny took off his glasses and wiped them on his shirt. "Not that I can see. Harvey didn't want the property sold, but there's nothing in the will prohibiting it."

Matt's heart started doing somersaults.

This was what they'd been looking for—the most logical, fairest solution to their problem. Harvey's property had a sturdy house and five acres. They could get a good price for it and split the money. It wouldn't make Matt or his dad completely whole, but it was more than he could have hoped for, especially a few months ago when he thought he'd lost everything. Emma would be happy too. Half of the profit from Harvey's property was a good chunk of change.

Emma stood very still, her watery eyes glued to Harvey's letter.

Matt frowned. Wasn't she as thrilled as he was? "Are you okay?"

"He had such beautiful handwriting. You could just feel the affection on the paper."

"I'm sorry about your uncle," Johnny said. "He was a good man."

"One of the best."

While Matt couldn't agree that Harvey was "one of the best," he was not unmindful of what Harvey had done for him. Even though Harvey had fraudulently taken his money, in the end he'd tried to make it right.

Johnny slid his glasses into his shirt pocket. "It's late, so I'll let you get back to your dinner. The sooner you eat, the less heartburn you'll have in the middle of the night. Come by the barbershop tomorrow, and we can get all the legal details hammered out. Marian can talk to you about estate taxes. It's not going to be pretty. The government gets you coming and going."

Emma wiped her eyes and gave Johnny another hug. "Thank you for coming over. This saves us the trouble of a court battle."

Yes. Matt didn't want any more battles with Emma. From now on, there'd be nothing but love and harmony between them. And he still had his appetite.

Emma walked Johnny to the door while Matt filled his plate with more Chinese. It was lukewarm, but still better than a gas station hotdog.

Emma ambled back into the great room and sank into the sofa, not taking her eyes from Harvey's letter. Matt sat next to her with his plate of food. She looked so unhappy that all he wanted to do was give her a big hug, but he couldn't hug her while balancing a plate full of Chinese food. He'd have to eat fast. "I'm sorry. I know this isn't what you wanted."

She sniffled quietly. "He says I was like a daughter to him. I should have gone to visit him in the hospital one more time. It was all so sudden, you know? And Dallas is so far from Salt Lake. I couldn't afford to fly every weekend."

"You called and wrote letters. He knew you loved him."

"I guess so." She seemed to remember the plate of food she'd set on the sofa several minutes ago. She picked it up and took a halfhearted bite of Kung Pao chicken. "I guess we should talk about the house now."

"We can wait until tomorrow if you'd rather watch *Gilmore Girls*."

She gave him a wane smile. "I've seen every episode at least three times. I already know how it ends."

"Maybe we'd better talk," he said.

"Maybe we should."

She didn't seem enthusiastic about Harvey's latest will. Matt shoveled some fried rice into his mouth, just in case their talk got intense and he didn't get to finish his food. But surely once she saw how this was beneficial for both of them, she'd be happy. He set his plate next to him on the sofa and took Emma's hand. "I'm sorry you're disappointed, Emma. I know you need that money as badly as I do, but I think this is the best possible outcome. We both get some of the money. That's better than none."

Emma smoothed her hair out of her eyes. She had really nice eyes. "I know what you're trying to say, but I don't think you understand."

Matt reached out and tucked a strand of her hair behind her ear. She had nice ears. "Emma, a few minutes ago I told you I love you. Do you believe it?"

She smiled. "Yes."

"I was ready to give you the house because I didn't want it to come between us. You are more important to me than any house."

Her smile got bigger. "I am?"

"Yes. Of course."

"When you asked me to move out..."

"I know," he said. "That was dumb, and I'm sure you saw it as a ploy to get the house. It wasn't."

"I know."

He turned his body so he was fully facing her and took both her hands. "Emma, I wanted to give you the house, but there are other people counting on me. I love you, but I can't let them down either."

251

"What do you mean?"

"Mom's parents left the Larkspur Ranch to her when they died. I don't think Dad cared at the time, but when their marriage went bad, it was a sore spot that his name wasn't on the deed. Dad wanted to sell part of the ranch to pay our debts, but Mom refused. So Dad sold everything else that wasn't bolted down, including all the equipment, the cattle, and the horses."

"Except Clay's," Emma said.

"Except Clay's because Clay had paid his own money for Connie." He gently squeezed Emma's hands. "Mom had the ranch put in the five brothers' names years ago—maybe to protect it in the divorce."

Emma drew her brows together. "But that left her without a home."

"She'll always have a home. She knows that. And as far as I'm concerned, she is still the owner of the Larkspur. Me and my brothers want to bring it back."

"Bring what back?"

"The ranch. We want to buy a herd of cattle, or maybe bison, and start ranching again. I mean, it's mostly Clay and Holt who want to ranch. I don't want to quit my day job, but I'd like to help them get things off the ground. Right now, we can barely afford to pay the property taxes."

"And for that, you need money."

Matt nodded. "That's what you do for family." He decided not to mention his dad. Emma need never know what Harvey had done to both of them.

She pressed her lips together. "We both would do a lot for family."

"Emma, the house has always come between us, but now we can split the profits and be done with it. Then we might have a chance for a normal relationship where I pick you up from your apartment and we go on a date and we don't argue about who gets the house and you don't put a deadbolt on your bedroom door because you're afraid I'll paint it."

"How did you know I have a deadbolt on my bedroom door?"

The answer to that question was another argument waiting to happen. It was best to go for a diversion. "That's what I'm talking about. We would never have another disagreement about the house if we sold it. We could just be with each other without being suspicious of ulterior motives. You wouldn't have to keep a thimble in your coat pocket."

One side of her lips curled upward. "You never know when you'll need an emergency thimble." She narrowed her eyes. "How did you know about the thimble in my pocket?"

Matt cleared his throat. Weeks ago, he'd rifled through her pockets so he could steal her house key and make a copy. Better not to mention that. "See what I mean? This is the kind of thing we would never argue about if we had a normal relationship."

"I don't know," she said. "I might still have a primal need to throw a thimble at you."

He pointed to the spot on his head where she'd dinged him. "You gave me a scar."

"I did not. But that doesn't mean I won't try in the future."

He rubbed his head and smiled. "Okay. I can't say I haven't been warned."

Emma laughed and shook her head. "I like the thought of a normal relationship, but if we sell the house, I'll have nowhere to go."

He hesitated. The real solution was one he'd already suggested, but the first time he'd brought it up, she'd cut him off at the knees. If she lived at his apartment, he could move into the ranch house until a better situation presented itself. "I know you need the money, Emma, but don't you think it's better if we both get half instead of one of us getting none?"

"Matt," she said, pulling her hand from his. "I agree with just about everything you've said, except the part about the scar, but it's not about the money. I guess I've been hedging, and it's not fair to you. The truth is I can't sell Uncle Harvey's house."

Her words fell between them like a two-ton stone. "Of course you can. We sign the papers, and you get half."

"I can't sell it, Matt. Uncle Harvey specifically asked me not to."

"Harvey's dead. He's not going to know one way or the other."

The lines bunched up on Emma's forehead. "Every time I went to visit Uncle Harvey in the hospital, there were two things he always said to me. 'I love you,' and 'Promise me you won't sell the house.' It was like an obsession with him. I'm sorry, Matt, but I can't sell."

"Then buy my half."

Emma sighed. "We've already talked about this. I can't afford to buy a coat. I certainly can't afford to buy your half of the house."

Matt's frustration grew with Emma's stubborn insistence. "Maybe Harvey wasn't thinking straight. Why would he leave you the house if you couldn't benefit financially from it?"

"I don't know. Maybe he knew I was the only person who wouldn't betray him and sell it when he died."

"Betrayal is a pretty strong word to be using on a dead guy, Emma. I love your sense of loyalty. I love everything about you, but I can't imagine Harvey would ask you to hold on to the house when you need the money so badly."

Emma shrugged. "I've had a place to stay for the last four weeks. Uncle Harvey's gift hasn't been useless to me."

Was there any way to make her see reason? "You said you love me. Won't you do this because I need the money?"

Confusion and hurt traveled across her features. "I do love you, but I made a promise to Harvey a long time ago."

He shouldn't have pulled the You-Don't-Love-Me card. It felt like emotional blackmail. Matt's chest tightened. Harvey was still ruining his life from the grave. "You're being unreasonable."

Emma pulled her shoulders back and lifted her chin. It was one of her signals that he'd pushed one too many of her buttons. "I am the closest relative Uncle Harvey and Aunt Gwen had. They rescued me every summer so I wouldn't get sucked into the bonspiel circuit. Aunt Gwen made me a bedspread and put my artwork on her mugs. I helped her bottle fruit and make fudge for sick neighbors. I thinned peaches with Uncle Harvey and picked so many cherry tomatoes, I thought I was seeing spots. We did all of those things here in this house. We were family here."

Matt huffed out a long breath. "Those are wonderful memories, Emma. You don't have to keep the house to keep the memories."

She studied him like she might study a patch of mold on her shower curtain. "I don't get it. It's obvious why Uncle Harvey left me the house, but why would he even think about you?"

It was Matt's turn to hedge. Emma was the last person he wanted to tell about his stupidity. And as angry as he was at Harvey, Matt didn't want the truth to hurt Emma. "I'm a nice guy."

"So are dozens of other men in Dandelion Meadows. Why you?"

Matt picked up his plate and pretended to be very interested in cold Chinese food. "He and my dad were friends. Maybe he wanted to help save the ranch."

Emma frowned, her gaze never leaving his face. "I don't think so."

Matt stuffed a forkful of Char Shu fried rice into this mouth. "It makes sense to me."

Emma took the drastic measure of prying Matt's fork and plate from his fingers. She stood and set his dishes on the counter, dampened a paper towel, and threw it to him.

"What?" he said. "Do I have sauce on my face?"

"What aren't you telling me?"

Matt swiped the paper towel down his cheek to give him a chance to think. She was on to him, and she wasn't easily distracted. "It doesn't matter why Harvey left half the house to me. I does me no good if I can't sell it."

Emma tended to be snippy when she was mad. She leaned with her back against the counter. "Then why not just give it to me. You don't deserve it."

"Don't deserve it?" Matt came out of his seat. "You think I don't deserve it?"

"Uncle Harvey was a nice guy, but he wouldn't give you a house just to be nice."

Matt had lost his temper more in the last four weeks than he had in his entire life. Emma could do that to a guy. But this time was different. He was mad, to be sure, but Emma's blind trust of her undeserving uncle was too much to bear. Something inside him snapped. "You're so naïve, Emma, and I'm tired of it. Harvey was not a nice guy. He was a crook who suddenly got a conscience right before he died." He was yelling by the time he finished.

Emma reacted as if she'd been slapped. "That's not true."

"Oh, it's true, princess." Matt spit the words out of his mouth. Somebody had to set Emma straight about her uncle, and he was the only one who could do it. The truth would be embarrassing for him and painful for her, but it was time Emma climbed out of the fairy-dust-and-daisy-chain life she'd been living and came into the real world. "Do you want to know how much money Harvey stole from me?"

"He didn't."

"One hundred thousand dollars," Matt said. "My entire life savings plus a small inheritance I got from my grandma. He stole another hundred thousand from my dad."

Emma caught his words with utter disbelief. "Matt, I don't know what happened to your money, but my uncle had more integrity than anyone I know. He never would have done that."

"Oh, he did, and I've got the documentation to prove it." He didn't want to hurt Emma, but he took a perverse sense of satisfaction at the look on her face. It was probably a lot like the look he had when he realized his money was gone.

"I don't believe you," she said, softly this time, as if maybe she was considering it but didn't want to say it too loud for fear it was true.

She wasn't going to be completely convinced until she saw it with her own eyes. Well then, he'd show her. Matt marched into his bedroom and retrieved his laptop from the nightstand. Every shred of proof he needed was on this computer. Emma was a finance major. She'd have no trouble deciphering financial documents and bank statements. It would be the work of ten minutes to convince her.

He picked up his computer and felt the weight of it in his hand. Emma loved Harvey fiercely, and Matt was about to ruin every beautiful memory she had of him. Did he really want to cause her such pain?

No.

But he had no choice. If he wanted to convince her, she had to see everything. Harvey's duplicity was not Matt's fault. He had to keep reminding himself of that. Matt was just the messenger, and he was about to give Emma a dose of reality. It would be painful, but she'd thank him later.

And she'd likely agree to sell the house.

Matt brushed that thought aside. That wasn't why he wanted to show her. He needed validation and maybe a little justification. Emma could handle it. The truth was always better than ignorance.

Still, he didn't feel quite right as he sat down on the couch and turned on his computer. Emma folded her arms and stared at him from the kitchen, but her curiosity got the better of her, and she sat down next to him, close enough to see his computer screen but not close enough to touch. He couldn't begrudge her distance. She was mad at him. Once she knew the truth, she wouldn't be so cold.

He had a separate file labeled LPC Properties, which held every piece of documentation he'd ever collected from Harvey, his dad, and the bank. He clicked on the very first file. "Can you see, Emma?"

She responded by scooting a few inches farther away from him. "I have 20/10 vision."

Okay. No use trying to butter her up. "Last October, my dad came to me with a proposal from Harvey. He said he had a great REIT opportunity, but we had to act fast. REIT stands for Real Estate Investment—"

"I have an MBA in Finance, Matt. I know what a REIT is."

She was understandably testy. Just get this over as quickly as possible. He clicked on the next document, which explained the REIT and the company behind it. "The initial investment was $200,000. Neither Dad or I had that much, so Dad offered to put in half. I met with Harvey three or four times, and he was pretty excited about it." Of course he'd been excited about it. It was $200,000 of free money. But Emma could figure that out for herself.

"What was the rate of return? How long were you committed for?"

Matt clicked on another document. "Here are all the numbers."

Probably without knowing it, Emma scooted closer and seemed to absorb the numbers on the page. "It looks like a sound investment. Relatively low risk but high return."

"Believe me, I looked over the numbers a dozen times. I signed the papers, put the money in my checking account, and gave Harvey authorization to transfer the money. It never made it."

"What do you mean?"

"The money never made it into the investment. I checked a week later, and it had disappeared."

"It doesn't happen that way," Emma said, sliding right next to him and scrolling through documents on his computer.

"It's not supposed to happen that way. The best I can figure is that Harvey just cleared the money from my account and took it for himself. My dad and I lost it all."

Emma found the bank record of the transfer. "What did Uncle Harvey say?"

"He was in the hospital in Salt Lake City before we even knew what had happened. I drove down there and confronted him. Had to talk my way around three nurses and a doctor. He said the money should have gone through, told me to wait a few days. I came back to Idaho and waited another week, but the guys at the brokerage said they never got my money. They never got my dad's money either. My dad drove to Salt Lake, but Harvey refused to see him. I went down there again a couple of weeks before he died."

"We just missed each other," Emma murmured, her gaze still fixed on that bank statement.

"He had refused to see my dad, so I expected he'd do the same to me. But they let me go up to his room." Matt would never forget that day at the hospital. He'd been so furious about his money, but the sight of Harvey wasting away had softened Matt up. Harvey had barely been able to speak, and he coughed violently with almost every breath he took. No one, no matter how dishonest or corrupt, should have to go through cancer. But Matt didn't have to tell Emma that. She knew. She'd seen Harvey near the end.

Emma pressed her lips into a hard line. "I hope you didn't say anything to upset him."

Matt didn't expect the ache of guilt that crawled into his chest. "I was angry, Emma. Two hundred thousand dollars was gone. I didn't behave like Mother Teresa, if that's what you want to know."

She scooted away from him and folded her hands in her lap. "I see."

"To his credit, he apologized."

Emma furrowed her brow. "What did he say?"

"He said, 'I'm real sorry about what happened to your money. When I get out of here, we're going to make it right.' We both knew he wasn't ever going to make it out of the hospital, but he felt bad about cheating me. I guess the fear of death will do that to a guy. He promised he was going to make it right. That's why he left me the house. I've had an appraiser come. I should be able to get enough from my half to pay my dad back."

"And you get nothing?"

"My dad's living in a trailer in Reno. He needs it more than I do. Or my brothers. And I wouldn't have had to make that choice if your uncle hadn't done this."

Her eyes flashed like they always did when she was about to call him a jerk or chastise him for being a lumberjack. "I don't believe it."

His anger subsided. Now he and Emma could move on. Emma knew the truth. Now he just needed to gently and lovingly help her accept it. He tried to take her hand. She recoiled as if he'd tried to trim her fingernails. "I know you feel really bad right now, Emma, but it's going to be okay. I promise."

"I'm sorry you lost all that money, Matt, but Uncle Harvey would not have done that. I don't believe it."

Matt's neck muscles tightened. "Don't be dense, Emma. He apologized. He admitted to stealing my money."

"He might have apologized, but he didn't admit to stealing your money."

"He said he'd make it right when he got back to Idaho."

Emma jabbed her finger in his direction. "He didn't steal your money."

His anger wound up again. "Emma, you are purposefully ignoring the facts. Harvey defrauded me and my dad. Just because you don't want it to be true doesn't mean it's not true."

"And just because you want to blame Uncle Harvey doesn't mean he's to blame."

Matt couldn't believe how stubborn she was. "Then why did he leave me the house, Emma? Think about it. Can't you just be reasonable enough to think about it?"

"You just want to make me feel guilty so I'll agree to sell the house. I won't do it."

"That's not why I told you," he said, scrubbing his fingers through his hair.

"I'm not selling."

"Can't we talk about it?"

"We just did." She turned her back on him, rummaged through the cupboard for a coffee mug, and poured herself some milk. "The TV's all yours," she said. "I'm going to bed."

Matt tried not to be concerned that she hadn't used the new *Gilmore Girls* mug he'd bought her, especially since he'd gotten a glimpse of the mug she had picked. It said, "It's been lovely, but I have to scream now."

It had probably been a completely random choice.

FIFTEEN

Emma and Frankie sat at the ping-pong table eating the street tacos Frankie had brought for dinner. Thank goodness for the Boise food truck business. Emma was done with hotdogs, and she was done with eating in her own kitchen. Matt was there too often, and she was done with Matt in general.

How dare he accuse her uncle like that?

How arrogant was he to think he could show her a few bank statements and convince her that the uncle she loved with all her heart was a cheat. Had Matt purposefully done it to get her to sell the house? To hurt her feelings? To prove what a trusting idiot she was?

Whatever the reason, she'd never trust him again. Or speak to him. This would prove difficult since he still lived here and he wasn't going to let the issue go so easily.

And then there was that stupid little mosquito of an idea buzzing at the back of her brain. She'd seen the bank statements. Was there the slightest possibility Matt was right? Was it disloyal to her uncle to even consider the evidence Matt had shown her? It was pretty compelling evidence, and she'd brushed it off because of her faith in Uncle Harvey. But had she put her trust in a fake memory?

Was she angry or mortified?

Either way, she could never face Matt again.

Frankie glanced across the net to Emma's small pile of artwork. She pointed to the one Emma had been working on before dinner. "That's so cute. I love ladybugs."

"Me too," Emma said, without much enthusiasm, even though she had nothing against ladybugs. In fact, she adored ladybugs. They were such a friendly insect, and as an added bonus, they ate aphids off rosebushes.

Frankie took a bite of her Thai peanut taco. "Is it for someone on Etsy?"

"A teacher in Colorado wants a lark bunting for her classroom. I thought a ladybug crawling on a nearby leaf would be cute."

"That is cute, but wouldn't the bird eat the ladybug?" Frankie said.

Emma stood and strolled to the other side of the table. She picked up her lark bunting picture and studied it. "Hmmm. I didn't think about that. Maybe I should get rid of the ladybug."

Frankie grinned. "I was just teasing. I don't think anybody expects realism from your drawings. Your lark bunting is wearing a bonnet."

Emma nodded, feeling better but not much. She slumped back into her chair. "In my world, birds and ladybugs are friends. They invite each other to tea parties and belong to the same book clubs. It's such a nice world."

Frankie patted Emma on the shoulder. "Animals are always more reliable than people."

"And trustworthy," Emma said, feeling the pain of it right at the base of her throat.

Frankie patted Emma's hand. "Matt's a great guy, Emma, even if he's wrong about your uncle. Everybody makes mistakes."

"Do you mean Matt or Uncle Harvey?"

"I don't know what to think, Emma. Your uncle Harvey was a good man, but Matt has no reason to lie. Harvey did leave him half the house."

Emma nodded "Maybe I made a fool of myself with Matt, but I just can't believe Uncle Harvey would do such a thing. I knew Harvey. He was a second father to me. He wouldn't do this. I know how unfair it is to be unjustly accused of something. That's exactly what's happening to me in Dallas at my firm"

The sound of a loud cheer traveled up from the main floor. Matt and two of his brothers were watching a basketball game. Until three days ago, his brothers hadn't ever come to the house. After Emma and Matt's big blowup, Matt must have needed them for support—just like Emma needed Frankie. That, or he felt more entitled to the space now that he officially owned half of it.

Luckily, Matt knew better than to set one foot upstairs. The second floor was Emma's sanctuary, and Matt wasn't allowed in her territory. His brothers also knew to steer clear. Holt had tried to climb the stairs tonight to say hello to Emma, and Frankie had hissed at him like a cat.

Frankie finished off her taco. "There's a reason Harvey left Matt half the house."

Emma closed her eyes. She didn't want to believe the most logical reason. Maybe he'd done it because he felt sorry for Matt.

Frankie sighed, stood up, and put on her coat, a nice, sturdy parka with a lined hood. A horse could walk all over that thing, and it would never show the wear. "You should talk to Matt. What would it hurt to sell the house and take half the money?"

"Because it would be a silent admission that Uncle Harvey did something wrong. I'm not about to concede that."

Frankie wrapped her scarf around her neck. "It's just as well. I don't think you could sell this house. It's five acres, but nobody wants to live in Dandelion Meadows."

Emma lifted her eyebrows in mock surprise. "Nobody wants to live in Dandelion Meadows? I'll have you know, we have a hair museum, a mediocre gas station mini-mart, and the best Dandelion Jelly Festival this side of the Mississippi. Not to mention, we're about to become the non-smoking capital of the world. No amount of money can buy that kind of prestige."

Frankie gave Emma one of her looks, like she was about to scold her. "You need to talk to him, Emma."

"I can't face him. If he's trying to destroy Uncle Harvey's good name to get me to sell, I never want to see him again."

"That isn't Matt, and you know it."

Emma felt that ache in her throat again. "If I'm wrong, I still can't face him. I'd be too embarrassed. He can gloat from a distance."

Frankie intensified her look. Scolding times two. "Matt isn't the type to gloat."

"He sure is, and with all that's gone wrong in my life, I'm just not up to dealing with it right now."

Frankie threw her hands up. "Talk to him or don't talk to him, but you should know he's going crazy being banished from your life like this. You come home and run upstairs and won't let him explain himself. He's miserable, Emma. Even if he wrongly accused Harvey, it's not malicious. Can't you forgive him?"

Emma's voice cracked like an ice cube against the pavement. "I don't know."

Frankie came to rest like one of those Fourth of July spinners the neighborhood boys used to light in the middle of the street. She put her arms around Emma. "I'm sorry. You know I'm on your side. It's just that I really like Matt, and he's miserable, and I had a feeling about you two."

"I can't ignore the fact that Matt attacked Uncle Harvey." Emma drew in a deep breath. "I've seen Uncle Harvey at some of the worst times in his life, like when Aunt Gwen died. He comforted other people at the funeral. He had all the flowers sent to the veteran's hospital in Boise. He stayed and helped the janitor clean up the church after the graveside service and the luncheon. He was not a selfish man." Emma sat up straight and nibbled on one of her fingernails. "I don't care what kind of documentation Matt has, Uncle Harvey did not steal that money. I've never been more sure of anything in my life."

"What are you going to do?"

Emma grimaced and laid a hand on Frankie's wrist. "I need you to do me a huge favor."

"What is it?"

"I need you to steal Matt's computer."

Emma just about turned back at the entrance to the Larkspur Ranch. Asking Vicki Matthews for help seemed about as appealing as a root canal or a tax accounting final. But she had to clear Uncle Harvey's good name, and unfortunately, Vicki Matthews was the only person who could help her do it.

It was 4:00 p.m. Vicki left the museum at 3:30 sharp every Wednesday, so Emma was pretty sure she'd be home. Hopefully. Emma didn't think she was up to making this trip more than once, and there was always the danger of running into Matt. He usually didn't get off work until five or six. Chances were very good he wouldn't be at the ranch this time of day.

Emma huffed out a breath and rang the doorbell. It chimed like a bell tower. No wonder so many people in town thought the Matthewses were self-important. The jury was still out on whether Emma felt the same way.

Vicki answered the door, and Emma took an involuntary step back. She was kind of hoping for a more friendly face like Holt or even Clay, but it didn't really matter. Vicki was the one she'd come to see. Might as well get it over with.

True to form, Vicki didn't wait for Emma to explain herself. Vicki always thought what she had to say was more important anyway. "I appreciate how you've cut Matt off. He's unhappy, but he couldn't think straight when it came to you and the house."

Emma tucked her coat around her chin. She was completely accustomed to the smell now. "Can I ask you something?"

"Matt finally told me what Harvey did to him. I told you there was a good reason for Harvey to leave Matt the house."

Emma wasn't going to argue. She needed Vicki on her side, or she at least needed Vicki to believe her. Badly. "I need your help."

Vicki closed her mouth and drew her brows together. "Matt deserves the house, and you should quit dragging your feet and agree to sell it. I've hired an attorney in Boise to look into it."

Emma didn't even bat an eye. Maybe Vicki would change her tune. Maybe she wouldn't. "Did Matt tell you he went in on that bad investment with his dad?"

"It wasn't a bad investment. Just a bad advisor."

Do not argue. Do not get defensive. "Matt and Leland each agreed to put in $100,000."

The brows inched closer. "Matt didn't mention that."

"Leland set the whole thing up between Uncle Harvey and Matt."

Vicki pressed her lips together. "You're telling me Leland was involved in this?"

"From the start."

"And all the money has disappeared?"

Emma nodded. "Every last penny. I've done some research."

Vicki stood as still as stone, staring at Emma, a fire burning behind her eyes. "Every last penny?"

Emma took a deep breath. "I need your help."

"You sure do, sweetheart."

"Are you up for a road trip?" Emma said.

Vicki folded her arms across her chest and leaned against the doorjamb. "I hear Reno is lovely this time of year."

CHAPTER
SIXTEEN

"Road trip with Vicki Matthews" were not words Emma thought she'd ever put together in a sentence, but there they were.

And not in a million years would Emma have guessed that a road trip with Vicki Matthews would be so much fun. But here they were.

Vicki had picked Emma up on Friday morning in her old Honda Pilot. It wasn't exactly a newer model, but it was quite a bit younger than Uncle Harvey's pickup and more likely to get them to Reno in one piece. Emma didn't know why she had expected Vicki to drive something else, like a Lexus or a Tesla, but the Honda was practical and very unintimidating to a girl who'd lost her job and was in self-imposed exile on the second floor of Uncle Harvey's house. At least she had Zac Efron, Orlando Bloom, and the Jonas Brothers to keep her company.

It was six and a half hours to Reno, and Vicki was able to drive too fast and talk at the same time. They spent an hour going over Emma's research on Matt's money and LPC Properties, and Emma couldn't help but be impressed with Vicki's knowledge of REITs, LLCs, and investments in general. Not to mention, Vicki talked enough about Matt to make the discussion especially interesting for Emma.

After the money talk died down, Vicki and Emma traded stories about Harvey and Gwen and then about Clay and Holt and, occasionally, Matt. Emma soon discovered that Matt was her favorite subject, which was good because Matt was one of Vicki's favorite subjects too.

They got on the subject of sexual harassment in the workplace—Vicki was against it—and what had happened at Emma's job. Vicki was against that too. In fact, Vicki was so indignant about how Emma had been treated in Dallas, Emma might have thought she was Vicki's own daughter instead of her sworn enemy.

Okay. That wasn't fair. Emma was not Vicki's sworn enemy as far as she knew. Vicki had given Emma a lot of grief about Matt, but who didn't admire loyalty to family members? And Vicki had come on the road trip. You wouldn't go on a road trip with your enemy, would you? Not unless you were planning on leaving her at the gas station in Winnemucca and driving away.

Leland Matthews lived on the outskirts of Reno in a relatively nice trailer park with a sign and a white picket fence out front and decorative rocks instead of grass in every yard. Vicki hadn't used Siri, so she'd obviously been here before.

She pulled her Honda next to a trailer with a nice awning over the door. It was cold, but there wasn't any snow on the ground so Emma could see that fake plastic grass surrounding the perimeter. The place looked friendly enough, but a thread of trepidation crawled up Emma's spine even so. She'd met Leland the first summer she'd come to Dandelion Meadows. He'd wandered in and out of events at Uncle Harvey and Aunt Gwen's house, much like a few dozen other friends of Gwen and Harvey's. Emma had paid about as much attention to Leland as she had to anybody. She had been disinterested at best.

Leland was handsome and charming, just like his sons. He was also a liar and a thief, but he was Matt's father. Emma didn't know how she felt about that.

Vicki turned off the car and exhaled an irritated breath. "I'd tell you to prepare yourself, but nothing can prepare you for this."

"Has he...has he changed that much?"

Vicki smirked. "He's just gotten bigger."

"Fat?"

"No. He was always charming and larger than life. It's why I fell in love with him. Now he's louder, more charming, and larger than the universe." She glanced at Emma. "But don't worry. He's insufferable but mostly harmless. You'll like him. Everybody likes him—in small doses."

Emma followed Vicki up the four steps to the covered patio and the sliding glass door. Vertical blinds covered the door from the inside. Emma was glad. If there had been no blinds, she would have been tempted to peek into Leland's house, which would have been extremely rude.

Vicki knocked on the sliding glass door as if she was a member of the SWAT team and they were about to raid the house. She glanced at Emma and nodded curtly. "Just remember, Leland's a snake charmer. He'll try to distract and divert. Don't let him get to you."

"I'll try not to."

Vicki smirked. "I guess it doesn't matter. That's why you brought me."

Yep. Emma might cave under all that Matthews charm, but Vicki wouldn't. She was a battle-worn veteran, and she never backed down from a fight.

The vertical blinds rustled slightly, as if they'd been teased by a passing wind. A set of fingers with hot pink fingernail polish curled around one of the blinds and pulled it back. A blonde with matching lipstick and fingernails and impossibly long eyelashes stood and stared at them from behind the glass. She wore a form-fitting black dress with a strand of pink sparkly beads around her neck.

"We need to talk to Leland Matthews," Vicki said, loudly enough that the Barbie doll behind the glass could hear them.

Of course, Emma had nothing against Barbies. She had played with them for hours when she was a little girl. And, okay, there might have been two or three special-edition Barbies still sitting on her dresser at home. But Emma had come to accept that she couldn't actually look like a Barbie without extensive plastic surgery and a lifetime of starvation.

The woman on the other side of the door must eat like a rabbit. And there was no way those breasts were real. On the up side, Emma loved her outfit. It was pink and whimsical and sexy all at the same time.

The woman—who couldn't have been much older than Emma—shuffled the blinds around until she found the cord to open them. Then she unlocked the door and opened it about three inches. "I'm so sorry," she said. "We're not interested. We already have a church."

Vicki pasted a no-nonsense smile on her face and folded her arms. This was her I'm-barely-putting-up-with-you pose. Emma had seen it several times. "I'm glad to hear it. We all need a little religion."

The woman gave Vicki a half smile, like she wanted to be polite and wasn't quite sure how to get rid of the religious nuts on the patio. "Yes, well, we were about to leave. Good luck in your missionary efforts."

Vicki stuck her hand in the door and slid it open farther.

"We're not here to convert anyone, though I don't doubt it's sorely needed. We're here to see Leland."

The woman pressed her lips together, no doubt frustrated that Vicki wasn't taking the hint. "He doesn't need a church. He's a Methodist."

Vicki's smile got wider and more fake. "Actually, he's a Lutheran, or used to be. I doubt he finds much religion now except at a casino."

"Yes," the blonde said, bursting into a smile, glad she'd finally gotten Vicki to understand. "That's where we're going right now."

"I'm sure you are," Vicki said, "but I'm afraid we're going to have to delay you for just a few minutes. We need to talk to Leland."

The woman suddenly seemed to realize that Emma and Vicki might not be missionaries. "Why do you want to talk to Leland?"

Vicki didn't lose her smile. "What's your name?"

The blonde tilted her head to one side. "Hazel. Retro's really in right now."

Emma nodded. "Is that your real name, or did you change it? I mean, retro wasn't in when you were born."

Hazel shrugged. "I changed it. Guys like retro, ya know."

"I get what you mean. I used to date a guy who would only drink Coke from those old-fashioned bottles."

Hazel rolled her eyes. "Yeah. Guys and their obsessions. I mean, a car is a car, ya know. Who cares if it's a Camaro or a Mustang?"

Emma smiled. "My uncle loved his Chevy truck. He wouldn't have been caught dead in a Ford." Emma swallowed hard. She missed Uncle Harvey. She missed Matt teasing her about Harvey's truck. She missed teasing Matt about his truck. She hoped he hadn't taken it personally. Matt's Ford was really nice too. He'd kissed her in that Ford the night he'd taken her to the ranch.

Fords were really very nice trucks.

Hazel laughed. "My dad had a Dodge. He polished it every Saturday."

Vicki cleared her throat. She was getting testy and impatient, but there was no reason not to be nice to Hazel. She was a person too, even if she was living with Leland Matthews and her eyelashes looked like giant spider legs. Everybody made mistakes.

Emma tucked her laptop under one arm and slid her other hand into her pocket. Somebody had told her that hands in pockets made you seem less threatening. "Hazel, this is Vicki, and I'm Emma."

"Emma's a retro name," Hazel said.

Emma smiled. "Thanks. My mom has a thing for Jane Austen. Anyway, we really need to talk to Leland. My uncle died a few months ago, and Leland was a friend of his."

Hazel drew her brows together. "Oh. I'm so sorry. How did he die?"

"Cancer."

"That sucks."

"Yes, it does."

Hazel stepped back and motioned for Emma and Vicki to come in. Vicki glanced at Emma and raised an eyebrow. Emma smiled back. She was proving to be somewhat useful on this trip after all. There was more than one way to skin a cat.

Well, there was never any call for skinning a cat. It was just an expression.

Hazel smoothed her hair behind her ear. "I'll go see what's keeping Leland. Sometimes he parks on the toilet for twenty minutes."

"Don't I know it," Vicki said.

Emma grimaced. "Does he struggle with constipation?"

Vicki cracked a smile. "God does have a sense of humor."

Emma laughed. Who knew Vicki was going to be this entertaining?

After a few minutes, Leland Matthews strolled down the hall with Hazel following. He wore an impeccable black tuxedo and a black bow tie. His shoes were the shiny patent leather kind you could see yourself in, like a mirror. He and Hazel weren't just going out. They were going *out*.

Leland was as tall as Clay and as broad as Matt. He had to be in his late fifties, but there was an undeniable vitality to him that made him seem a decade younger. Emma was glad she had Vicki with her. She hadn't seen Leland in ten years. She'd forgotten how much he looked like Matt. There was no way she could be completely objective, even knowing what he'd done to Uncle Harvey.

Leland strutted into the room like he owned it, which he probably did, so that wasn't much of an observation. Emma caught the slight twitch of his eyelid when he saw Vicki standing in his living room, but he hid whatever his true feelings were on seeing his ex-wife and gave her a gloriously wide smile. "Vicki," he said, quickly crossing the room, wrapping his hands around her upper arms, and giving her a peck on the cheek.

Vicki didn't react negatively or positively. She just stood there and let him kiss her. Maybe she didn't want to tick him off. Maybe it took too much energy to get annoyed about it. Maybe she didn't really care one way or the other. She'd probably made peace with her feelings about her ex-husband.

Leland went to Hazel and snaked his arm around her shoulders. "Hazel, this is my ex-wife, Vicki."

Hazel stiffened, gave Vicki an artificial smile, and

awkwardly patted the lapel of Leland's tux. "Well, don't try to steal him back. I'm not letting him go."

One side of Vicki's mouth curled upward, and she propped her hand on her hip. "Oh, honey, I wouldn't take him back if you threw in a million dollars and a crock pot."

Leland never lost that smile, but he hissed through his teeth. "Ouch, Vicki. You still know how to throw a punch."

Vicki acted as if she really couldn't care less what Leland had to say. She folded her arms and looked at Hazel. "Hazel, we have something private we need to discuss with Leland. Do you mind waiting in the other room?"

Hazel stuck out her bottom lip. "Leland and I don't keep secrets from each other."

Vicki turned to Leland for confirmation. "I doubt you want her to hear this."

Leland hid his uncertainty behind a smile. "Anything you say to me, you can say to Hazel." What else could he do? You didn't ask the girl you were sleeping with to step into another room.

Vicki shrugged. "It's your funeral."

Leland seemed a bit uncomfortable with Vicki's reply, but he'd drawn his line in the sand, and Hazel was firmly attached to his arm. There was no turning back now. He motioned to the couch. "Please, sit down." He walked Hazel to her very own chair. Maybe he hoped putting some distance between them would keep Hazel off balance. Emma glanced at Hazel one more time. Hazel had brains, though she probably didn't realize it herself. She'd understand was what going on.

All the worse for Leland.

Leland seemed to notice Emma for the first time. "And who is this pretty young lady?"

Emma tried not to blush. Pretty was just a word. Anybody

could toss it around. It didn't necessarily mean anything. "I guess you don't remember me. It's been a few years."

Leland sidled closer and took Emma's hand in his warm fingers. "It would be a crime to forget a face like yours."

Leland stood between Emma and Hazel, so Emma couldn't know how Hazel reacted to her boyfriend flirting with another girl. But Emma knew how she would feel if Matt flirted with someone else. She pulled her hand from Leland's grasp. "I'm Emma Dustin, Harvey's niece. I used to stay with Harvey and Gwen every summer."

There was a slight hesitation in Leland's smile. Emma would have missed it if she hadn't been watching him so closely. "Good old Harvey. He was a great friend." He tried to take Emma's hand again. Emma wrapped both arms around her computer. "I'm sorry for your loss," he said, putting his hands behind his back.

"Me too," Emma said. Did it matter if she believed him or not? She sat down and pulled her computer from its case. "I'm settling Harvey's accounts, and I've found some inconsistencies. I have some evidence I want to show you."

Leland's eyes flickered with just a hint of panic. He froze in place, like one of those poor creatures in *The Chronicles of Narnia* who gets breathed on by the White Witch.

Emma smiled to herself. *Evidence* was a good word. It implied that a crime had taken place and that someone was investigating it.

Leland's lips curled into a painful smile. "Hazel, do you mind waiting in the bedroom."

"Of course I mind." Hazel stood up and hooked her elbow around Leland's arm in case he'd forgotten who his girlfriend was. "We're a team, remember?" She formed her mouth into an attractive pout.

Leland was truly stuck. Who could reject that kind of loyalty?

Vicki actually looked sympathetic. "Have you given him any money, Hazel?"

Hazel reacted as if Vicki had just kicked her dog. "Of course not. Leland doesn't need my money."

"Good. A smart girl like you would never let Leland manipulate you into giving him money." Vicki pinned her icy gaze on Leland. "And Leland has enough decency to refrain from preying on trusting young women. Don't you, Leland?"

Leland frowned, swallowed hard, and sank into the nearest chair.

It was obvious Leland would have asked Hazel for money given the opportunity, but it wasn't likely she had enough to bother with. Maybe he hadn't been able to find a wealthy older woman. Yet.

Hazel sat back down and reached over to pat Leland's leg. She smiled and nodded and made her earrings tinkle. "Leland's working on a deal with the biggest builder in Nevada."

Leland seemed to perk up a little. "They want to build a new casino on the water's edge at Lake Tahoe. I'm arranging the deal. It could mean millions." There was that Matthews charm Emma knew too well.

Vicki didn't seem impressed. "Sounds fabulous."

More earring tinkling from Hazel. "They're going to build one of those swimming pools that looks like it just floats off into the sky. On the fortieth floor."

Vicki nodded politely. "Interesting, since nothing as high as forty floors is allowed at Lake Tahoe." Emma was absolutely in awe of Vicki's calm demeanor. She was like a tiger stalking her prey. Patient and deadly.

Leland got up and poured himself a drink of something

that looked pretty strong. He chuckled as if Vicki had made a joke, but his laughter came about thirty seconds too late. "The architects work out all those details with the planning commission. I don't concern myself with the small stuff."

Vicki gave Leland her I'm-barely-putting-up-with-you sigh. "Well, Emma, we're being very rude keeping Leland and Hazel from their date at the casino. Why don't you show Leland what you've discovered? Then we can get this resolved and be on our way."

Leland seemed to recover some of his composure. He sat up straight and acted as if there was nothing he'd rather do than take a look at all this incriminating evidence.

Emma opened her computer and clicked on the "Uncle Harvey Finances" file. She turned the computer so Leland could clearly see the screen and hit the space bar, bringing up her first PowerPoint slide. A PowerPoint presentation might have been overkill, but she had wanted to be prepared and organized. She'd done dozens of PowerPoint presentations in graduate school. They were as natural as breathing and made her feel especially confident. They also had the added benefit of helping her keep her temper in check. It was easier to be dispassionate while scrolling through PowerPoint slides.

"In October of last year, you approached my uncle Harvey about finding a REIT investment. You asked your son Matt to invest with you." Emma hit the space bar and a photo of Matt came on the screen. It was a totally unnecessary graphic, but he was just so darn handsome, Emma hadn't been able to resist putting it in there.

"I like that picture," Vicki said.

Emma smiled. "Me too. Thanks for sending it to me."

"He wears his hair a little shorter than he used to," Vicki said.

Yep. Emma loved it like that. She forwarded to the next

slide. "The two of you signed all the papers, and Uncle Harvey made arrangements to have the money withdrawn from your accounts." Emma forwarded the slide to the bank statement she had stolen from Matt's computer. She'd studied this thing so many times, she had it memorized.

Leland wiped some beads of sweat from his upper lip. "Harvey withdrew the money but kept it for himself." He pointed to the date on Emma's screen. "You can see that from the statement right there. The money never made it into the REIT." He actually had the gall to give Emma a look of pity. "I'm sorry, Emma. I know how much you respected Harvey."

Emma resisted the urge to glare at him. "I still do."

Hazel's mouth fell open. "Emma's uncle stole your money? That's terrible."

"I want you to know, I hold no ill will for Harvey in my heart. He must have gotten scared. His medical bills were piling up."

Emma bit down on her tongue to keep herself from lashing out at Leland Matthews. Instead of clawing at his face, she calmly pressed the spacebar and advanced the slide. Leland's quaint and sad little story was about to crumble like a pillar of sand. Emma pointed to a number on the screen. She didn't make a habit of touching her computer screen, but this was important enough to leave a few fingerprints. "Matt had given permission for LPC Properties to withdraw a hundred thousand dollars from his account, but the withdrawal came from LPC Property Management, LLC. Somebody at the bank missed that big time. It was very clever. Devious, but clever. Matt didn't even notice what had happened."

Emma glanced at Leland. His hand was tightly clenched around his glass, and his knuckles were white. Sweat trickled down the side of his face, and his cheeks were a bright, crimson red. That tuxedo must feel like an oven right about now. Leland pulled at his collar. "Yes. It was clever of Harvey to redirect the money that way."

Emma pressed the spacebar and ignored the anger bubbling inside her. She was going to get through this, then she could beat Leland senseless with her computer if she wanted. But she'd never really do it. She'd paid too much for this laptop. "Uncle Harvey was very clever, but he was never devious. That's what compelled me to do some research in the first place. I knew Uncle Harvey wouldn't have cheated Matt out of his savings."

"He needed to pay his medical bills. He would have done anything to get that money." In a show of fake outrage, Leland slammed his glass on the small table next to his chair. "Harvey cheated me, and he cheated my son." Leland may have been sweating, but he wasn't going down without a fight.

Little did he know that Emma had a brilliant attack plan. She pressed the space bar. "LPC Property Management, LLC is a limited liability corporation chartered in October of last year in Nevada. The sole owner and manager of the LLC is..." She paused for dramatic effect, even though everyone in the room but Hazel knew the answer. "Leland Matthews." She pointed to her screen again, leaving another fingerprint. "You see, Leland, you waited until you knew the name of the company offering the REIT, then set up an LLC with a very similar name so no one would notice it was you. You pulled that money out of Matt's account, and he was none the wiser."

"That's not true," Leland said. He pinned his gaze on Vicki. "I would never do that to our son."

Vicki folded her arms. "I lived with you for thirty years, Leland. You're charming, intelligent, and narcissistic. I don't believe a single word you say."

Leland narrowed his eyes. "Don't psychoanalyze me."

"I'm not finished yet," Emma said, feeling more powerful

than she ever had before. She'd spent hours on this research. Leland was going to hear every last bit of incriminating evidence. "You thought you'd gotten away with it when Harvey was admitted to the hospital. It was so easy to blame a dying man."

"This is absurd," Leland said. "Harvey was my friend."

Emma nodded. "It is absurd, as is your use of the word *absurd*. I'll ignore your archaic word choice for the moment, but I'm not going to pretend that you were Harvey's friend. Uncle Harvey discovered what you'd done when Matt called him frantic about his investment. Harvey called you on it. You went to the hospital to see him."

"I went to the hospital to get my money back."

Emma showed him another slide. It was picture of one of the nurses at the hospital. Leland had no idea how thorough Emma had been. "You told Matt that Uncle Harvey refused to see you, but according to this nurse, you and Harvey were in his room with the door closed for almost two hours."

Leland scowled. "She can't tell you that. It's doctor-patient privilege."

"She's not a doctor, and visitors aren't one of those things you have to keep confidential like blood pressure and urine samples. Besides, Uncle Harvey gave permission to the doctors to talk to me about his medical condition."

"It's still not right," Leland said. "Any judge would agree I've got a pretty good case."

Vicki sank back into the couch as if they were talking about the weather. "I wouldn't advise suing over this, Leland. Lawyers are expensive, and you'll get slaughtered."

Hazel fingered the necklace at her throat. "I don't understand what's going on."

"Harvey, being the good guy he was, tried to talk you into giving the money back," Emma said.

Leland shot to his feet. "I couldn't give it back. I'd already spent it on...the Lake Tahoe project."

"Sit down, Leland," Vicki said coolly. "We both know there is no Lake Tahoe project."

Hazel frowned. "Yes, there is. They're going to sign the papers any day now."

Vicki stood, took both of Hazel's hands, and pulled her to sit next to Emma and herself on the couch. Her voice was surprisingly mild when she said, "Hazel, I don't blame you for believing everything Leland tells you. I fell into that trap myself. I want you to know that our marriage was very, very good for many years. He was charming and kind and very good to me. We had five sons. Did he tell you he has five sons?"

Hazel looked slightly in shock, as if Vicki's kindness surprised her. Emma couldn't fault her reaction. Emma was sort of surprised herself. "He's very proud of all his sons," Hazel said.

Vicki nodded. "And they are very proud of him. I've made certain to never say anything negative to my sons about their father. I've tried to protect them from the truth. It's the only thing I have left to give them."

Emma's heart swelled to twice its size. Vicki wasn't cold-hearted or spiteful. She was strong and feisty and loyal to a fault, trying to protect her family the only way she knew how. Emma suddenly wanted to be just like her when she grew up.

Vicki squeezed Hazel's hand. "You need the truth about Leland before you get in any deeper."

"She knows me well enough already," Leland said. "We all have faults. She loves me anyway."

Hazel's gaze flicked in Leland's direction. "Yes," she said doubtfully, "I love him no matter what."

"Believe it or not, I understand," Vicki said. "I love Leland too, but I couldn't let him hurt my family anymore. I had to cut him loose. You see, a few years ago, Leland got caught up in gambling. He cleared out our bank account and then started selling everything. The ranch was in my name, and I refused to let him sell it. I finally asked for a divorce. I didn't want him to drag my boys down with him. I had to protect their future."

Emma pressed her lips together. "That's what happened with Uncle Harvey. He took the blame for losing Matt's money because he wanted to protect Matt. He didn't want Matt knowing what kind of a man his father really is."

"But...he's a good man," Hazel said.

Emma didn't want to hurt Hazel's feelings, but she couldn't let that misconception go unchallenged. "No, he isn't, not in the ways that really count." Not like Uncle Harvey, who was willing to leave Matt the house rather than tell him the truth about his father. Leland was Matt's father, but he could never hope to measure up to his son. Emma frowned at Leland. "Matt went to visit Uncle Harvey in the hospital, and Uncle Harvey promised Matt he'd make it right. He was still planning on trying to get the money back from you."

Vicki studied Leland's face. "But no one can recover the money, can they? It's gone."

Leland bowed his head and massaged his forehead as if the money would appear if he just rubbed hard enough. "I was going to pay Matt back. I really was. I had a sure thing on a horse. I was going to pay it all back with hefty interest."

"Making you look like the hero," Emma said. And Uncle Harvey would still be the crook.

Vicki leaned forward and propped her chin in her elbow. "It's gone, isn't it, Leland?"

He covered his face with his hands. "All but five thousand dollars."

Hazel furrowed her brow. "There is no Lake Tahoe deal?"

"No deal," Vicki said.

Hazel took in a sharp breath. "But."

Sometimes there were no words.

Vicki turned her attention to Leland. "How much have you got?"

He looked up at her. "What?"

"How much of the money have you got here at the trailer? I'm taking it back to Matt."

"Nothing. It's in a high yield CD. I can't pull it out without a penalty," he said.

Vicki stood and laid a firm hand on Leland's shoulder. "Give it to me."

"I can't. I said it's in a CD."

Vicki got a hard, icy look in her eye. "Give me every penny, Leland, or I'll take this trailer apart until I find it."

"He said he didn't have it." Hazel obviously didn't believe it herself.

Leland stood and trudged down the hall, his shoulders slumped and his steps slow—not quite the man who had greeted them fifteen minutes ago. Hazel nibbled at her pink fingernails until she managed to rip one of them off. "I really shouldn't keep them this long. They make it harder to serve food."

Emma closed her computer and gave Hazel a sympathetic smile. Hazel's world had just come crashing down on her. She needed a little sympathy. "You're a waitress?"

Hazel nodded. "That's how Leland and I met. We've been together six months." She took a deep, shuddering breath. "He threw a lot of cash around. I didn't know he'd stolen it."

"You couldn't have known," Emma said.

Vicki kept her gaze down the hall. "Leland's fun. He knows how to show a girl a good time."

Hazel took the drastic measure of peeling her eyelashes off, maybe in preparation for a good cry. "I can probably get my old place in Sparks back. And I have a girlfriend with an extra bed a couple of blocks from here."

Emma patted her hand. "If you get desperate, you can always come stay with me in Idaho."

Hazel scrunched her lips to one side of her face. "Are you kidding? It's like sixteen below up there. And I refuse to use an outhouse."

Vicki rolled her eyes. "Hazel, we have indoor plumbing."

"You do?"

"And big screen TVs and the Internet," Emma said.

Hazel thought about that for a minute. "I still don't want to come, but thanks for the offer."

Vicki started opening drawers in the kitchen and rifling through them. "Do you have a stick of gum, Hazel?"

"I don't think so. Gum is bad for your teeth."

Vicki seemed determined to find a piece of gum, even though it was bad for her teeth. She zeroed in on a cookbook propped against the refrigerator and paged through it, but it wasn't likely she'd find any gum in there. Or maybe it was. "Here we go," Vicki said, pulling something from between two of the pages. She slammed the cookbook shut and waved the gum over her head in triumph. Only, it wasn't gum. It was a handful of hundred-dollar bills.

Emma's eyes nearly popped out of her head. "You found some money?"

"Leland can't follow a recipe, and I'm guessing Hazel doesn't do a lot of cooking."

"We always go out," Hazel said.

"So why does Leland keep a cookbook around if not to stash money in?"

Emma smiled. "A very good deduction."

Vicki quickly counted her booty. "Two thousand dollars,

give or take. It's a drop in the bucket, but a drop is all we're going to get." She quickly stuffed the money into her purse.

Leland shuffled back down the hall. He was still in his immaculate tux, but the look on his face was nothing but pathetic. He held a small stack of bills. "This is all I got, Vicki."

"How much?" she said, not at all inclined to believe him.

"One thousand dollars. Really, Vicki, it's all I've got."

"You said you had five thousand."

"I overestimated," Leland said.

Vicki sighed and held out her hand. "Okay then. I'll take it."

"I need it, Vicki."

"It's Matt's money."

"Rent is due next week," Leland said, "and I have to buy groceries."

Vicki shook her head as if she truly pitied him. "I suppose you'll have to get a job, Leland. Hazel could find you something at the restaurant."

Hazel made a face. "They like me at the restaurant. I can't in good conscience recommend you. They don't like to hire liars."

Leland reached out his arms to Hazel. "Hazel, baby. Come on. I love you. I made a mistake. Won't you forgive me?"

Hazel held up her hand to stop Leland from coming any closer. "You stole a hundred thousand dollars from your own son. That's not a mistake. That's fraud, and quite frankly, despicable to the core." Her glare could have started Leland's cookbook on fire. "And I'm not a baby."

"Of course you aren't," he said.

"Don't try to butter me up. My mom warned me, and look. I've turned into a stereotypical bimbo." She poked her finger repeatedly into Leland's chest. Luckily for him, it was the one with no sharp fingernail attached. "I can't believe I let you do this to me."

"You're not a bimbo," Emma said.

Hazel let out an unladylike grunt. "Yes, I am, and I did it with my eyes wide open. But no more." She started that poking thing again. Leland stepped back. "I'm going to law school so I can sue dishonest jerks like you."

Emma slid her computer back into its case. "You're not a bimbo, Hazel. You know what *stereotypical* means. You want to go to law school. You have really good fashion sense."

Hazel stopped poking and turned to Emma. "You think I have good fashion sense? I used to help my sisters pick out outfits for school." She glared at Leland. "I have good fashion sense, and I'm not a bimbo. And we're through, Leland. I can't live with a guy I can't trust."

Leland pressed his hand over the spot where Hazel had poked him. "How can you be so shallow? You used me. You only stayed with me because I had money and took you to the fancy parties. Now you want to abandon me in my time of need?"

Hazel raised an eyebrow. "I guess I did use you. There's nothing more attractive than a man with money, even one old enough to be my father. I made a mistake."

Leland's mouth fell open in indignation. "I'm not that old."

"You're ancient," Hazel said. She glanced at Vicki. "No offense."

Vicki smiled wryly. "None taken. You'll be my age soon enough."

Hazel lifted her chin. "Your money made you more attractive than you are, Leland, but I'd rather have a poor, honest thirty-year-old than a rich sugar daddy who uses his own son for money." She clapped her hand over her mouth. "Oh, no. We've been living off stolen money."

"You couldn't have known," Emma said. "You're an innocent victim."

Leland lost all composure. "She's not innocent. She's a bimbo, and she used me."

In one simultaneous motion, Emma, Hazel, and Vicki turned and glared at Leland. Vicki looked like a cobra about to strike—not that Emma had ever seen a cobra about to strike, but it had to be at least as terrifying as the look Vicki was giving Leland. "If I were you, Leland, I'd stop talking right now."

Leland pointed to Hazel. "But she—"

Vicki hissed—it was definitely snake-like. "Not another word." She put her arm around Hazel. "Do you want us to stay while you pack?"

"Yes. That would be very nice." Hazel waltzed down the hall, pausing long enough to give Leland the evil eye before she disappeared.

Vicki regarded Leland like she might look at a rat in her pantry. "Now, Leland. I have something to say to you, and you need to listen very carefully."

"Haven't you done enough to ruin my life?"

Vicki folded her arms. "Not yet. Here's the deal, Leland. You will not take one more penny from my boys. You will not borrow a quarter for the vending machine. You will not let them pay for dinner. You will not call in the middle of the night and ask for gas money."

Emma raised her eyebrow. "He did that?"

Vicki tilted her head to one side. "You will not invite my boys to join you in any investment deals or ask them for a loan. Do you understand?" She moved in for the kill like a lioness or a very ticked-off cobra. "Because if I get wind of you messing with any of my boys again, I will sit them down and tell them what a skunk their father really is. I'll tell them you're addicted to gambling and have a thing for girls half your age. Then I will call the police and have you arrested for not paying alimony for six years. Do you understand?"

Leland folded his arms across his chest, but it wasn't a gesture of strength or defiance. He looked completely defeated. Emma might have heard him whimper. "Vicki, I need at least a thousand to live off until I can find a job. You don't want me to starve, do you?"

Vicki got nose to nose with her ex-husband. "Do you understand, Leland?"

He exhaled an immense amount of air from his lungs. "I understand, but you don't have to be so mean about it."

Vicki marched around the bar and started opening kitchen cupboards and pulling things out. There was lots of alcohol but also a loaf of bread, a giant tub of peanut butter, and bottle of green olives. "You'll survive until you find a job. Mahatma Gandhi went for weeks without eating."

"You're cruel, Vicki. I regret ever marrying you."

Vicki cocked an eyebrow. "Finally something we can agree on."

With a giant duffle bag over her shoulder, Hazel wheeled two large suitcases into the living room.

"Is that everything?" Vicki asked.

Hazel nodded. "Yeah. I left a lot of my stuff at my friend's house."

"Do you need a ride somewhere?"

Hazel shook her head. "My friend will be here any minute. She's just down the street." Emma relieved Hazel of the duffle bag. Hazel rolled her suitcases to the door. "Leland," she said, "I won't say it hasn't been fun. But there comes a time when a man has to admit he needs help." She slid the door open and strutted out of the house with her head held high.

It's too bad Hazel lived in Reno. Emma would totally borrow that dress.

And the earrings.

Vicki and Emma followed Hazel without a backward glance. They helped Hazel load her stuff into her friend's car and watched her drive away. With nothing left to accomplish, they climbed into Vicki's Honda. "Will he be okay? I mean, I don't like what he did to Uncle Harvey and Matt, but is he going to be homeless in a week?"

"Oh, I'm guessing he still has four or five thousand dollars stashed in that trailer somewhere."

Emma's jaw fell to the floor. "Four or five thousand?"

"He wouldn't willingly give up more than he thought he could get away with. I knew he wasn't going to part with it all. That's why I went searching. Isn't he going to be surprised when he finds the empty cookbook."

"Oh, my. He'll be mad!"

Vicki laughed. "Makes it all the more sweet, doesn't it?"

Emma should have felt bad about it but took a perverse sense of satisfaction in taking back at least some of what was rightfully Matt's. But it wasn't enough. "This is all the money Matt's getting back, isn't it?"

Vicki sighed. "I'm afraid so. Three thousand dollars is nothing compared to what Matt lost."

"Yep," Emma said. "Only three percent."

A smile grew on Vicki's face. "And I used to think you were dumb."

"And I used to think you were icy."

Vicki laughed. "Let's keep that our little secret."

Emma laughed with pure relief. She'd cleared her uncle's name, but she wouldn't gloat, even though the truth would knock Matt clear off his feet.

It wasn't until Vicki pulled the Pilot out of the trailer park that the adrenaline started to subside, leaving Emma with a horrible realization. *The truth would knock Matt clear off his feet.*

What kind of a horrible person would even think about gloating? What kind of horrible person would ever tell Matt the truth? It would break his heart. She knew what a broken heart felt like, and she refused to put Matt through that. Matt must never know what kind of a man his father was.

A stone settled at the pit of her stomach. Did this mean she'd have to pulled herself out of Matt's life? The secret would be impossible to keep otherwise. Emma thought she might be sick. She put on her seatbelt and glanced at Vicki. "I won't tell Matt about his dad, and I'm going to give him my share of the house. He can sell it and keep all the money."

Vicki pressed her lips into a hard line. "You have every right to that house, Emma."

"I know, but I'd rather walk away than Matt find out about his dad. It would devastate him."

"Yes, it would." Vicki reached out and wrapped her fingers around Emma's wrist. "You don't know how much I appreciate this, Emma." Her voice cracked. "You just don't know. Those boys worship their father, and even though they're adults, I don't have the heart to destroy their memories or tear apart their happiness." She sniffed, and there might have been a little moisture in her eyes, but it also might have been the glare of the sun against the windshield.

Emma's heart felt as heavy as the iceberg that sank the Titanic. She loved Leonardo DiCaprio but hated that movie. In the end, it only proved that love did not conquer all—that two people who loved each other deeply could be separated by cruel circumstance and there was no happy ending.

There was nothing left for Emma but an aching emptiness.

CHAPTER
SEVENTEEN

M att stood on the edge of insanity, and falling seemed inevitable.

He glanced at Gwen's sunflower clock hanging in the kitchen. Only 7:00 p.m. How long should he wait before he went to bed? And how old was that clock? It looked like an antique, but it just kept ticking. His heart would give out sooner than that clock. At this rate, a lot sooner.

Matt hadn't even bothered to turn on the lights, and he didn't have the heart for an episode of *Gilmore Girls*, so he just sat in the dimness, contemplating what had gone wrong in his life.

He'd give anything to take back the things he'd said to Emma last week. Anything. He should have given her the house—none of this fifty-fifty stuff—just given her the house, no strings attached. He should have swallowed his pride and his anger and pretended that Emma's uncle hadn't stolen his money. What did Matt care about money?

If they could be together, what did he care if Emma lived in denial about her uncle for the rest of her life?

She'd avoided him for five days—that was torture enough —but two days ago, Emma had just disappeared. He'd thought she'd maybe left him for good, but he'd sneaked up to the forbidden second floor and looked in her bedroom which she had left unlocked. Some of her clothes were still there, as were several pairs of shoes. Emma didn't own a pair of boots, but she had enough shoes to last her through the next decade.

Yesterday, Clay had called to inform him that Emma and Mom had gone out of town. Together. If the information hadn't come from Clay, Matt would have dismissed it out of hand. Mom and Emma together on a trip? Had the world gone mad?

How long were they going to be gone? he'd asked Clay. Clay didn't know, but Mellie's birthday party was tomorrow, and Mom wouldn't miss that, would she?

He had to talk to Emma, and she wouldn't allow him near her. Give her time to cool down, Clay had said, but Matt couldn't stand it much longer. Emma was his whole world. If she ever came back from her road trip, he was going to give her the house and ask her to marry him.

Well, maybe he wouldn't ask her to marry him at the same time as giving her the house. She might suspect ulterior motives.

Someone knocked on the door. Matt wasn't in the mood for company, but maybe it was Clay with another bit of information about Mom and Emma. He trudged down the hall, opened the door, and was greeted by a heavenly vision. Emma stood on the porch in Harvey's ridiculously big coat, holding a suitcase in one hand and twirling her ponytail around her fingers with the other. Matt wanted to sweep her into his arms and kiss her until they couldn't breathe anymore, but she hadn't spoken to him for over a week and he couldn't make any assumptions about how she felt about him. "Emma," he said, his voice a quivering jumble of nerves and elation. "You don't have to knock. This is your house."

She sort of smiled, as if he'd told a joke that wasn't really funny but she didn't want to hurt his feelings. "Matt, I just came to tell you..."

"Please, come in. I'll make coffee. I have some of those donuts you like."

She didn't budge. "I'm not hungry."

His heart sank to his toes She wasn't hungry? Emma was always hungry. This was truly an emergency. "I want you to take the house, Emma."

"Me?"

"Of course, you."

She shook her head. "The house rightfully belongs to you. I want you to sell it and keep the money."

"You said we couldn't sell it. I'm not selling it." He mentally kicked himself. It sounded like he was blaming her.

She gave him that polite, unhappy smile again. "You should sell it, Matt. I want you to sell it. I'm going to Johnny's tomorrow and signing the deed over to you. That way it will be yours, free and clear."

"I don't want that, Emma. Don't you understand? I'm giving it to you. Please come in. We need to talk."

She was like a fence post set in cement. "I have good news. Your dad pulled his money out of his account before Uncle Harvey accessed it. Your dad didn't lose any money, so when you sell the house, all the profits will be yours."

"I don't want any of the money, Emma. I just want you." He tried to pull her in for an embrace.

She stepped back. "You are going to live a very happy life. I know how important your family is to you."

His family wasn't nearly as important as the woman standing on his porch. *Her* porch. "Tell me about your road trip." He was grasping at straws now, but he'd do anything to keep her on this porch and in his life.

She frowned. "What do you know about the road trip?"

"I know you went with my mom."

"Oh, well, we…went to visit your dad—so I could get an exact figure on how much Uncle Harvey took from him. That's when he told us he didn't lose a thing. Isn't that wonderful, Matt?"

Matt drew his brows together. "What do you mean? He lost as much as I did."

"It was all a misunderstanding. The transfer didn't go through."

"Oh, that's great." Matt hesitated. Dad hadn't lost any money. That was good news. It didn't make him feel any better now, but in three or four weeks, he'd remember and be over-joyed. He should have been ecstatic. He only felt numb. "Come in and sit for a while. I'll build a fire. Or better yet, you could build a fire."

She barely cracked a smile, but she stepped into the hall. "I apologize, but I have to stay here tonight and then…"

She said she knew how important family was to him. What had she and Mom talked about for twelve hours? "Whose idea was this road trip?"

"Does that matter?"

Matt narrowed his eyes. "What did my mom say to you? Because if she said anything to hurt your feelings or to make you think I don't love you, I will cut her off so fast, her head will spin."

Emma looked confused for a brief minute. "Your mom is a wonderful woman. Strong and kind. And she's loyal. Never take that quality for granted. It's everything. Don't be mad at your mom. She loves you more than life itself." She stepped forward and laid a hand on Matt's arm. He thought he might melt into a puddle. "I want you to be happy. I want you to be so happy."

Her voice cracked, and before he could kiss her, she bolted up the stairs. Even with her suitcase in tow, she went really fast.

"Wait, Emma. Can we talk?"

She paused halfway up. "I'm pretty tired."

"Okay, okay. I understand. Let's talk tomorrow. I'll make cheesecake."

She gave him an affectionate, sad smile. "Since when do you make cheesecake?"

"It's just an expression. Roy Howell will be making the cheesecake. I'll be ordering it from the restaurant."

"Trudy will be glad. She has a thing for you."

Matt tried to hide his frustration. She was being so obtuse. "Well, I don't have a thing for her."

"I know."

Emma climbed the rest of the stairs, and Matt came pretty darn close to following her up there, but she looked exhausted and quite discouraged. "Emma," he called.

"Yeah?"

"Everything is going to be okay."

No response. Maybe she didn't believe him. Maybe he didn't believe it himself. Seething on the inside, he went into the kitchen and brewed himself a pot of strong coffee and poured some into his *Gilmore Girls* mug. Time for a serious and angry conversation with Mom. What had she said to Emma, and how would he ever fix it?

MATT LEFT WORK an hour early so he would be sure to be home when Emma got there. He told her he would bring cheesecake, but nothing less than a fancy dinner at the Hair Museum would do.

He hadn't been able to get a hold of Mom last night. When she hadn't answered her cell, Matt had called Clay, who said she wasn't home and he didn't know where she was. The only thing to do was to apologize to Emma for his mom and his behavior and anything else he could think of and hope she took pity on him. It had only been a week since she'd told him she loved him. Surely his mom hadn't squashed all that love on the road trip. Surely he hadn't killed her love with his stupidity.

This morning, Matt had made bacon and eggs and brewed Emma's favorite hazelnut coffee, but she hadn't stirred from her room before he'd needed to leave for work. Maybe she'd been tired from her trip. Maybe she was just sleeping in. Maybe it was nothing personal against Matt.

Maybe LaVerle Pratt would stop smoking.

Matt pulled his truck into its usual spot in front of the house. Emma's truck was gone. He'd beaten her home. The minute she walked in the door, he was going to throw himself at her feet. Well, not literally. Matt's heart pounded against his rib cage. Did he dare ask her to marry him? If he even breathed the word "marriage," would she start throwing thimbles at him?

Something told him that if it were anything less than a marriage proposal, she wouldn't believe he was sincere. She probably wouldn't believe he was sincere even if he did propose. Even though he'd told her like four times last night, she still thought he wanted the house.

The idea of marriage had taken up residence in his brain last night, and he hadn't been able to get it out. Almost twenty-four hours later, he wanted to marry Emma so badly, he thought he might pass out. He wanted Emma like he'd never wanted anyone before in his life. Wanted her clear down to his bones.

He wanted to wake up next to her every morning, brew her coffee, and start her truck so it was warm when she climbed in to go to work. He wanted to make her laugh by singing Barry Manilow songs while she drank from the Barry Manilow mug. They could make dinner together every night. She could insult his basketball games, and he could make fun of *Gilmore Girls* while they roasted marshmallows by the fire. She could annoy the heck out of him, and he could periodically tick her off. It would be so much fun.

His life would be absolutely pointless without Emma in it. He needed to marry her.

And he needed to change this shirt. Emma hadn't insulted his flannel for weeks, but he wasn't going to take any chances.

Matt walked in the front door and stopped. Something was different, but he couldn't put his finger on what. He set his keys on the hall table and snatched them up again. The table was empty. Where was Gwen's thimble collection? Emma shouldn't move the thimbles. She needed them to protect herself. He strolled into the kitchen. The coffee sat in the pot, and the bacon and eggs were still in the pan where he'd left them this morning. It wasn't like Emma to leave pans unwashed. She couldn't bear to leave for work unless everything was cleaned and put away.

There was a note taped to the television. Something was definitely wrong. Emma had a pet peeve about anything touching the TV, and tape was definitely unacceptable. Matt carefully peeled the tape off the TV and read the note.

I couldn't say it last night, but I'm sorry about what Uncle Harvey did to you. You deserve the whole house. I'll meet with Johnny today and sign the papers. Don't be mad, but I took the thimbles, the mugs, my bedspread, and Zac Efron. And the truck. I need it to transport my lung to the Dandelion Jelly Festival. Then you can have it back, even though you don't like Chevys. Have a good life.

What did she mean, *have a good life?*

He'd promised Emma he wouldn't go up there ever again, but Matt ran upstairs and into her room. The High School Musical bedspread was gone, along with the curtains. She'd forgotten to mention the curtains. The outrageously pink chest of drawers was also missing. He went into the bathroom and opened the drawers. They were empty.

A key sat on the bathroom counter with a small note underneath. *This is the key to the deadbolt on my bedroom door. I bought it because I didn't want you to sneak in and paint it. I've obviously unlocked the door, but I hope you'll honor my last wish and leave my room pink. But, I'll be in Dallas, so I won't even know if the room gets painted. Do what you want.*

Matt stood in the bathroom, paralyzed by his own confusion. His chest felt hollow, like someone had cut it open and ripped out his heart.

Emma had moved out.

But how could she?

He'd told her everything was going to be okay.

CHAPTER

EIGHTEEN

M att sat in the Pioneer Hair Museum auditorium with his elbows propped on his knees and his head cradled in his hands. He had absolutely no interest in Cement Awareness Week, and Max Hooper was the most boring speaker ever to walk the face of the earth. No joke. Insomniacs should hire Max to come to their house at bedtime. There'd be a lot more restful nights in town.

Matt shifted in his chair and folded his arms. Who cared about cement anyway? Cement never cured cancer or performed heart surgery. It never sang a song or made a YouTube video. Not even Emma Dustin cared about cement.

Matt instantly remembered why he'd come. He had hoped that Emma would show, that maybe she was a closet cement enthusiast. He glanced around the room. It seemed there were only seven cement enthusiasts in Dandelion Meadows—really only six because Matt shouldn't count himself. Three of them were asleep.

Frankie had promised she'd tell Matt when Emma left for Dallas. She hadn't left yet, and Matt had grabbed onto the foolish hope that she'd show up for Cement Awareness Week.

Matt hated cement. He hated everything about it. He hated the Pioneer Hair Museum, he hated Gwen Dustin's thimble collection, he hated his mom, and most of all, he hated that house. If it hadn't been for that house, Emma would be sitting next to him right now, maybe with her head on his shoulder because Max Hooper had put her to sleep. Maybe he would have made her coffee this morning, and she would have pulled out the Dustbuster when he put his feet on the coffee table.

But no. He was sitting all alone, listening to the most snooze-worthy presentation in the history of presentations, wishing Emma would call him or text him or even post something on Instagram—anything for some sort of connection.

Frankie said Emma hadn't gone back to Dallas, but it was as if she'd disappeared from the face of the Earth. He'd spent a whole week searching for her and had discovered her truck parked in Max Hooper's barn. He had found the truck but no Emma. Apparently she never drove it anywhere, because Matt had staked out that barn for days and Emma never came.

He had tortured himself by visiting Emma's Etsy page seven or eight times a day, just to see if she had posted anything new. Just to see if she was spending her time drawing pictures instead of going on dates with interesting men like Kyle Strong, even when she couldn't stand outdoorsy types.

He'd ordered a picture of a dog with a bowtie, just to keep some connection to Emma. It had come in the mail just this morning. He'd hung it right next to the TV.

Max finally wound down, and Ladasha stood to congratulate him on an excellent presentation and to remind everyone that next week was Landfill Awareness Week.

Another winner.

Matt helped put the chairs away because he and Ladasha

were the only two people younger than seventy in the entire room. Ladasha sidled close to Matt and pretended to have a hard time getting one of the chairs to fold. "That was the dullest presentation we've had all year. I sure enough wish we had Emma back."

Matt could only nod. There was no speaking past the lump in his throat.

"Although right now, I'd even settle for Teancum Madsen. His delivery is boring, but his stories are always interesting."

Matt put up the last chair and picked up the broom. After sweeping, he was going home to get stinking drunk. He'd bought a bottle of Jack Daniels in Boise this afternoon, and it was sitting in his truck. Alcohol was just about the only thing he hadn't tried to dull this sharp pain in his chest.

"He's in bad shape, isn't he, Ladasha?"

Matt turned toward the door. Mom leaned against the doorjamb with her arms folded and a resigned look on her face. Matt pretended she wasn't in the room and went back to sweeping up the little pile of cement dust Max had dropped during his presentation.

"Worst I've ever seen," Ladasha said. "Why don't he just get over there to Frankie Hiatt's and talk some sense into that girl?"

Matt whirled around as if he'd been blown by a stiff wind. "Emma's at Frankie's?"

Ladasha smirked. "She moves around. It's like she's in the Witness Protection Program."

Matt had seen Frankie just yesterday, and she hadn't said a word about Emma staying with her. That little sneak! Matt thought he might have a heart attack. How long would it take him to get to Frankie's? He left his pile of dust, propped the broom against the wall, and tugged his coat from the hook. "Thanks, Ladasha. I owe you one."

"She won't talk to you." Mom was still standing at the door. Matt tried to walk past her. She blocked his way. For someone so little, she took up a lot of space.

"Mom," Matt said, "I don't care that you don't like Emma. Do you hear me? I don't care. Because I'd choose her over the whole family any day."

Mom nodded smugly. "That's what I thought you'd say."

"She's the best thing that ever happened to me or ever will happen, and I refuse to lose her. I don't know what you said to her, Mom, but if you ruined my chances with her, I'm cutting you out of my life."

Mom seemed unimpressed. Well, if she didn't believe he was serious, that was her mistake.

Ladasha put her hand on her hip and grunted. "It's about time he stood up to you, girl."

Mom pooh-poohed that idea. "You don't know what you're talking about, Ladasha. He stands up to me all the time. I have no control whatsoever. It's quite frustrating."

"Mom, get out of my way. I'm going to get Emma."

"You need to hear what I have to say first."

Matt ran his fingers through his hair. "I won't listen to you. It's your fault she won't talk to me."

Mom dropped her self-assured demeanor, and her eyes reflected a certain vulnerability that Matt had only seen one time before—when she'd sat the boys down and told them she was filing for divorce. "Matt, you have to listen to me. I know how you can get Emma back."

"That's ironic since you're the one who drove her away."

Mom motioned to the folding chairs hanging on the rack. "Can we sit? Give me ten minutes, and I promise Emma will fall into your arms."

Matt narrowed his eyes. "You don't like Emma. Why would you want us to get back together?"

"Of course I like Emma," Mom said, as if she and Emma had always been besties. Matt let her get away with it because he was too puzzled to argue. "I didn't like it when I thought she was trying to steal your house, but I've always liked Emma. You two belong together, and I'm not going to be responsible for keeping you apart." Mom grabbed two chairs from the rack and unfolded them. "Sit, Matt. I have to tell you something, and it's going to be very painful."

"For me?"

"Yes."

Ladasha grabbed another chair and set it next to the others. "Mind if I listen in? As the mayor, I feel responsible for the happiness of all Dandelion Meadows citizens."

Mom cocked an eyebrow. "You just want to hear the gossip."

Ladasha nodded. "For sure. Through my position in the city, I'm privy to a lot of juicy stuff. It's the best part about being mayor."

Mom shrugged. "Might as well join us. The whole town should be warned."

Ladasha's smile bloomed like morning glory. "You mean I can tell people?"

"Yes."

Matt held up his hand. "Wait a minute. I'm not comfortable with everyone knowing my private business." Especially if Emma rejected him. He didn't want Max Hooper or Teancum Madsen or anybody else analyzing his love life.

Ladasha swatted away his objections. "We all know, honey, and it isn't pretty. You're an expert at making a mess of things."

Matt gave Ladasha his most irritated look. "Thanks for reminding me."

Ladasha merely nodded. "You've messed up so many times, we should assign someone to follow you with a shovel like the Kimball boys do in the parade with the horses." She sat back in her chair. "They have manure duty this year."

Matt slumped. "This is proving to be a depressing conversation."

Ladasha's laughter echoed off the walls of the auditorium. "You're not beyond hope, sweetie. Poop happens. You just have to be willing to clean up after yourself."

Matt exhaled a deep, aggravated breath. "Much as I'd like to sit and discuss manure with two old ladies, I need to go to Emma."

He could tell he'd said the wrong thing as soon as it came out of his mouth. Ladasha scrunched her lips together and gave him the stink eye. Mom folded her arms and stiffened like an icicle.

"That's what I mean," Ladasha said. "You have a reputation for making messes."

Mom got that no-nonsense, if-you'd-do-exactly-as-I-say-we'd-all-be-better-off look on her face. She wore it a lot. "I'm trying to help you, Matt. You're not going to gain my cooperation by calling me old."

Matt stood up. "I don't need your cooperation, Mom. I need to talk to Emma."

Mom grabbed his wrist and pulled him to sit. "Believe me, I may be old, but you want to hear what I have to say."

Matt frowned and shut his mouth. If he sat quietly, this would go so much faster.

Hopefully.

He still had the option of leaving at any minute. He'd use it if he had to.

Mom leaned forward and took his hand. "Harvey Dustin did not steal your money."

"You know about that?"

"Emma has a lovely PowerPoint presentation that explains everything."

Ladasha nodded. "Emma is an excellent PowerPointer."

"Mom," Matthew warned.

Mom squeezed Matt's hand. "I'm to blame for all of this. I wanted to protect your memories. I didn't want you to resent your dad. I thought I was doing the right thing."

Ladasha patted Mom's leg. "No regrets, Vicki. No child ever died from being loved too much."

Mom gave Ladasha a weak smile. "Thank you." She looked at Matt. "I can't be responsible for your dad's actions, and I can't let him hurt you boys anymore. This is going to be painful, Matt, but you're an adult. It's better to know the truth."

Matt held his breath. That was how he'd justified telling Emma about her uncle.

"Your dad is addicted to gambling, Matt. It started several years ago, with an occasional trip to Reno or Las Vegas. Then it was every weekend and placing bets over the phone. He lost our life savings then sold the cattle and the equipment."

Matt's chest constricted. "I...thought it was some bad business deals."

Mom nodded. "Your dad took your money, Matt. Emma did a lot of research and found out that your dad had your money funneled into one of his accounts. Harvey set up the investment, but he never touched that money. Your dad stole from his own son, and I will never forgive him for that."

Every word that came out of Mom's mouth was like a smack upside the head with a two-by-four. "Dad has my money?"

"Emma and I went to Reno. He admitted to the whole thing, but he's gambled away all but a few thousand dollars of it. We got three thousand back, but I didn't know how to explain it to you, so it's sitting in my underwear drawer waiting for you."

Matt couldn't breathe. He seriously couldn't breathe. How could Dad do this to his own son?

Ladasha pressed her hand firmly to the back of Matt's head. "Put your head between your legs."

Matt wanted to resist, but Ladasha was pretty strong and he truly felt like he might pass out. He leaned over and took some deep breaths.

Every cell in his body wanted to deny what his dad had done. Emma had been so sure, so stubborn about her uncle. Couldn't Matt be as trusting with his dad? But Matt didn't even question the truth of it. Of course Dad had taken that money. Matt had been foolish, but he hadn't been completely blind. Looking back, he could see the ways Dad had manipulated him, bringing him papers to sign, asking about his account balances, waiting until Harvey was in the hospital to make the transfer. Dad had seemed angry about the theft, but not particularly surprised.

When Matt had visited him in the hospital and Harvey had promised to make it right, he hadn't been confessing. Harvey was hatching a plan to get Matt's money back without having to expose his dad for what Leland really was. Harvey never said a word against Matt's dad. He hadn't wanted Matt to get hurt. The divorce had been hard enough. Harvey knew that more bad news about Dad would be devastating.

Matt's heart broke. All this time he'd been hating Harvey when Harvey had been trying to protect him. So had Mom.

So had Emma.

"Emma decided not to tell me," he whispered.

"Yes," Mom said. "I was grateful."

It all made sense. Emma had been devastated by the news of Harvey's dishonesty. So she wanted to spare Matt those horrible emotions. Matt had told her several times how much he admired his dad. She would rather carry the pain and let Harvey's reputation suffer so Matt would never suspect.

She didn't want him to hurt the way she had hurt.

It was the most unselfish thing he'd ever seen anyone do.

Mom scooted her chair closer to Matt's and wrapped her arm around his shoulders. "Emma doesn't want you to get hurt, but the two of you are hurting worse than anything I could have imagined. I've decided not to let Leland ruin your life."

Matt didn't know if he even dared hope. "Emma didn't want me to know. Do you think maybe she cares about me?"

Ladasha laughed so loud she made Matt flinch. "Well, of course she cares about you. That girl is so in love with you, she's started wearing flannel."

Matt cocked an eyebrow. Emma had started wearing flannel? He didn't believe it for one minute. Ladasha was just trying to make him feel better. It came down to the fact that Emma was exceptionally kind to everyone. When she took the blame for shooting Max Hooper's dog, she did it to help Boone —not because she was in love with him—except in a love-your-fellowman kind of way.

Matt's heart clattered against his chest. Even if she only loved him in a love-your-fellowman kind of way, it was a start. He might be able to talk her into *love* loving him as long as he quit saying stupid things and didn't insist in being right all the time.

One thing was certain. He wasn't going one more minute without seeing her and thanking her for what she'd done for him. He took his mom's hand. "Thank you for wanting to protect me, Mom, but I'm an adult. You've got to trust that I can handle adult problems and adult disappointments."

"I know," Mom said. "But I've never stopped being your mother, even when you've stopped needing one."

"I'll always need you. You know that without my having to say it."

Mom sighed. "I do."

"You're not responsible for my relationship with Dad. You can't spare me pain by withholding the truth. That only prolongs it. If you had told me about Dad two years ago, I would never have agreed to an investment with him."

Mom grimaced. "I guess that's true."

Ladasha patted Mom on the leg. "None of this is your fault." She turned to Matt. "Or yours. Let's put the blame where it belongs."

Yeah. Matt would have to examine *that* pain another time. Right now, nothing mattered but getting to Emma. He shot to his feet. "I have to go now. We can talk about all this later."

Ladasha put her hand on his back and pushed him toward the door. "Go. I'll take care of your mom."

"I'm perfectly capable of taking care of myself," Mom said.

"I'm just giving Matt some reassurance," he heard Ladasha say as he left the auditorium. "He feels guilty for leaving you like this."

"I do not," Matt called back.

He felt Ladasha's displeasure from the parking lot.

CHAPTER

NINETEEN

Emma sat at Frankie's very small table in her very small front room, trying to concentrate on her latest Etsy order even though she couldn't think about anything but Matt and Leland Matthews. Frankie had invited Emma to stay for as long as she wanted, but Frankie's house was so tiny, Emma couldn't lay a sleeping bag in the kitchen without first setting the two chairs on top of the table. It was a rotten way to get a good night sleep, but really, what did it matter? Even if Frankie had a huge house with a luxurious king-size bed, Emma wouldn't have actually gotten any sleep. For the time being, sleep was out of the question.

It would be better when she moved back to Dallas.

But not really.

The light in this room was horrible. It was just as well Emma wasn't going to stay here for any length of time. The lack of good lighting stifled her creativity. Johnny Cleaver had said something like that.

And then there was Frankie's dog, Heber. Emma had never been a dog person—she was just too much of a neat freak—

but Frankie had been nice enough to let Emma stay at her house, so Emma had no right to complain about the dog. It was just that Heber kept trying to eat her artwork, and he licked Emma's face while Emma slept in her sleeping bag. Heber was a huge yellow Labrador with curly fur and paws the size of dessert plates. He was usually an outdoor dog but not during the Idaho winter. Unfortunately, Heber was just too big for Frankie's small shack. When he wagged his tail, the tip almost touched both walls. Heber was cute and friendly and adorable, and Emma just wanted her pink bedroom back.

She should have stayed with Betty a few days longer. The window seat really hadn't been a bad place to sleep.

Emma jumped when Frankie came in the door, bringing a foot of snow with her. The wind had really whipped up in the last hour. It whined through every crack in Frankie's old house. Heber jumped from his rug by the wood stove and barked as if the North Koreans had just invaded the state. That was another thing about Heber. His bark was deafening, like one of the velociraptors on "Jurassic Park."

Frankie stamped the snow off her boots and motioned behind her. "Hey, Emma, look who I brought."

Torie slid into the house and took off her coat. Emma jumped from her chair and gave Torie a big hug. "Nice to see the wind didn't blow you away."

Frankie laughed. "It almost did." She knelt down and gave her dog some love before standing up and peeling her scarf off her neck. "I think a blizzard's coming."

"I kept the fire going," Emma said. Fire building was one thing she knew how to do, thanks to Matt.

"Good for you," Frankie said, smiling at Emma as if trying not to seem concerned. Unfortunately, Torie had that same look on her face.

Emma nibbled on her bottom lip. It seemed she might be in

for something unpleasant. Her friends weren't the type to let her wallow. "How is Cappy's horse?"

Frankie shrugged. "She's fine. When Cappy gets lonely, he calls me to come check on his horse. It's the least I can do for an old man whose family won't even visit him."

"Oh," Emma said. "That's too bad. We should make him some cookies."

Frankie hung her coat and scarf on the hook that served as a coat closet. "Do you know how to make cookies?"

"I know how to look it up on YouTube." A dull ache throbbed at the base of her throat. She wasn't very good with YouTube videos unless Matt interpreted for her. French was like his superpower. And YouTube. And looking handsome.

Emma nodded to herself. Looking handsome was definitely one of his superpowers.

Without warning, Frankie threw up her hands and growled. "Can't you at least call him, Emma?"

Emma winced as if Frankie had shot an air-soft pellet at her chest. "I don't need to call him. Everything is settled between us. I've signed the house over so he can sell it and get his money back."

Torie sat next to Emma at the table. "Frankie and I both think you need to let him apologize."

Emma swallowed hard. "For what?"

Frankie sighed loudly, grabbed a folding chair from against the wall, and sat next to Torie. "For being a jerk. For making you cry. For not being there to help you load your truck."

Emma fiddled with the tip of her pencil. "I really appreciate your brothers' coming over. I hope they know that."

"They were happy to do it," Frankie said. "You only had one thing that needed lifting."

"The mug collection is pretty heavy."

"They didn't mind." Frankie must have been seriously irritated. She was snapping like a turtle.

Emma caught her bottom lip between her teeth. "You don't have to get testy."

Torie traced her finger along a crack in the table. "He hangs out at the Pioneer Hair Museum just for a chance to talk to you."

"I'm taking a leave of absence."

"He drives around town looking for your truck."

Emma pressed her lips together. How nice that almost all of Uncle Harvey's old friends had barns big enough to hide a truck. "I can't face him. You understand, don't you?"

Frankie glanced at Torie and shook her head. "Not really. Why don't you just talk to him?"

"Because of what my uncle did to him." The lie was easier to explain than the truth.

"You're ashamed," Torie said.

Emma nearly choked on her deception. "Yes. I can't face him." That much was true. She didn't want Matt to see anything in her eyes that might give her away.

Frankie studied Emma's face. "That shouldn't keep you apart."

She was hedging. Her friends knew she was hedging. Might as well stop pretending. "I love him." Emma's voice cracked into a million pieces. "Are you satisfied?"

Frankie clapped her hands together. "I knew it."

"It doesn't matter."

Frankie got all agitated again. "Of course it matters. He's going crazy, Emma. He loves you too."

Emma frowned. "I...I think he likes me. He kissed me."

Torie nodded wholeheartedly. "He loves you, Emma."

Frankie and Torie were the best friends Emma could ever ask for, and Emma couldn't bear to deceive them, not when she was already deceiving Matt. She needed some sympathy and maybe a little support. There was no one else to tell. Emma leaned back in her chair and clasped her hands together. "I want to tell you something, but you have to promise not to tell anyone. I mean *anyone*."

Any annoyance Frankie might have been feeling seemed to evaporate at the thought of a secret. She didn't even try to temper her curiosity. "What is it?"

"You have to promise," Emma said.

Torie always took these things very seriously. Her eyes got wide and she nodded slowly. "I promise. Whatever it is, I promise. Unless you killed someone. Then I'd have to turn you in."

Frankie shook her head. "She didn't kill anybody, Torie."

"I know, but I just want to be sure she understands my standards."

Emma didn't have to fake a smile. Torie was honest to a fault. "I didn't murder anyone, but thank you. Neither of you has ever said anything about the dog incident, so I know I can trust you."

Frankie smiled as if a bad photographer had told her to say cheese. "Of course you can trust us." She coughed. She cleared her throat. "Oh, crap."

Torie patted her on the back. "Are you okay?"

Frankie went to the sink and got herself a glass of water. She took several big gulps before sitting down again. "Oh, crap, Emma."

"What's the matter?"

She took another drink. "You really can trust me, but I kind of told Matt about the dog."

This time it was an air-soft pellet to the face—without eye protection. "How did you *kind of* tell Matt?"

The words exploded from Frankie's mouth. "I don't know.

He was so mad at you for not getting out of the house, and he said all sorts of stupid stuff. I had to tell him. He needed to know the kind of person you really are."

Emma's mouth fell open. "Apparently the kind of person who's too trusting of her friends."

"But it was a good thing," Frankie protested. "He started being nice to you. Then he fell in love with you. I'm sorry, Emma, but I don't regret it."

Emma didn't know whether to be ferociously mad or eternally grateful. She had never regretted doing what she had done for Boone, but the town's disapproval had really hurt. Some Dandelion Meadowans still disapproved of her. It was nice Matt knew the truth. But Frankie had given her word. They'd signed it in blood.

Torie frowned. "I have something to confess too. I got home that night and thought I would burst with the secret. I told my cat."

Torie looked miserable. A laugh tripped from Emma's lips. "I guess I can't be mad. I told Uncle Harvey."

It was Frankie's turn to be surprised. "You told Harvey?"

"I couldn't stand to have him think badly of me. I swore him to secrecy. He didn't even tell Aunt Gwen."

"Tell us your secret," Frankie said. "I promise not to tell anyone but Heber."

Heber's ears perked up.

Torie drew her brows together. "Then I'm going to notify my cat."

"You can't tell anyone besides your animals," Emma said. "I mean it. It could cause a lot of pain to a lot of people, especially Matt."

"Okay," Torie said. "As long as you didn't murder anyone."

Frankie shaped her lips into an "O." "This has something to do with Matt's laptop, doesn't it?"

Emma smoothed her hand across her latest drawing, a green frog sitting in the driveway of a Reno trailer park. "Uncle Harvey did not steal Matt's money. Vicki and I went to Reno, and Matt's dad confessed to the whole scam. He took Matt's money and gambled it away."

Torie gasped. "This is too big. Can I tell my mom's cat too?"

Frankie's expression darkened like a looming storm. "You don't want Matt to know what his dad did to him?"

"It would break his heart."

Lightning flashed in Frankie's eyes. "You're letting your uncle Harvey take the blame for Leland's dishonesty so Matt won't get his feelings hurt?"

"Uncle Harvey's dead. What does it matter to him?"

Frankie slapped the table. "It matters very much. You shouldn't let Leland Matthews get away with this, Emma. He'll just do it again, maybe to another son."

"Nevertheless, I *am* letting him get away with it. Matt would be devastated if he knew the truth. I won't do that to him. And I can't look him in the eye every day and lie to him about the house and about his dad. "

"But Emma," Frankie said, "Matt loves you. You can't just walk away. That will break his heart too."

Emma's chest tightened. "I...I don't think that's true, Frankie. I love Matt, and at one time he said he loved me. But he didn't love me enough. Not enough. After everything we've been through, he cares more about that house. He was mad when I refused to sell, so he used Uncle Harvey as a weapon. He knew it would hurt, like a shotgun right to the chest. He wanted to convince me to agree with him—to show me what a rotten person Uncle Harvey was so I'd consent to sell the house."

Frankie shook her head. "You would have handled it differently because sparing people's feelings is incredibly important to you. But, Emma, Matt's not like that. He's honest. He's trustworthy. Maybe lying to you seemed worse than hurting you."

"Well, I won't lie to Matt either. And I don't want to hurt him. So I'm going to keep my mouth shut, move back to Dallas, and let Matt get on with his life. My friend at work says the lawyers are doing all kinds of negotiations."

Frankie fingered an errant strand of yarn on her sweater sleeve. "That doesn't make us feel better."

"We love you," Torie said. "We want you to stay."

"I was kind of hoping the same thing at one point."

Frankie's eyes lit up. "Stay, Emma. You should stay. The Stop Smoking booth won't be the same without your papier-mâché lung. Think of all the kids you could inspire to stay away from tobacco."

"I can make a lung before I leave."

Frankie's brows practically crashed together. "Emma, you hate, *hate*, finance. You never wanted to do retirement planning or watch market trends or help rich people find tax shelters. Be honest. Before you moved here, you hated the trajectory of your life. I could tell in every text you sent."

"It's true," Torie said.

Emma slumped in her chair. "Both my parents were teachers, and they scrimped and saved every penny. I wanted to earn enough that I didn't have to worry about making my rent payment or wonder how I was going to send my daughter to college or take out a home equity loan to fix the water heater."

Torie smiled sympathetically. "That must have been hard on your parents."

Emma had to think about that for a minute. "I don't know. They never complained about money. We couldn't go on all those fancy trips my friends went on, and I seldom got designer clothes, but we were happy. Really happy."

"What about your uncle Harvey? He wasn't a rich man, but he and Gwen always seemed to have more fun than just about anybody."

Emma nodded. "Uncle Harvey always said there were only three things he needed to make him happy: a roof over his head, food in the fridge, and Aunt Gwen. I guess it was four things, because he really loved his truck."

"So where did you get your notions about money? And why in the world did you get an MBA in something you care nothing about?"

"I don't know. I guess it's what every other girl my age was doing—trying to prove myself and get rich. I guess I wanted to make Uncle Harvey proud. He always told me I could do anything. I wanted to prove it to him and everybody else, even though he would have been proud no matter what I'd chosen to do." Emma frowned. "Uncle Harvey was a financial planner because he wanted to help people and he wanted to retire comfortably. Money was just a means to an end for him."

"So stay."

Emma looked at her two best friends. She might as well tell the whole truth. "There's a network of hospitals in the northeast. They've offered me a thirty thousand dollar contract for artwork for three of their children's hospitals."

Torie squealed.

Frankie jumped from her seat. "Thirty thousand dollars? Emma you could live very comfortably in Idaho on thirty thousand dollars."

Emma nodded. "Yes, I could, but if I stayed here, I'd run into Matt. You know I can't have that conversation with him."

A truck crawled down the road in front of the house, illuminating the falling snow in its headlights. It was going slowly. The roads must have been icy.

"Emma, this is your happiness we're talking about. You

can't throw that away because you're scared of Matt Matthews."

"I'm not scared of him."

Frankie looked out the window into the blizzard. "Good because he just pulled up."

Emma nearly jumped out of her skin. "Did you tell him I was here?"

Frankie made a face. "Of course not, but half the town knows where you're staying. It was bound to get out."

"But that's why I moved around," Emma said in disbelief.

"And made a nuisance of yourself."

Emma looked out the window. A truck had indeed stopped in front of the house. "How do you know it's Matt?"

Frankie smiled sheepishly. "He sent me a text about ten minutes ago."

Emma nearly had an aneurism. "And you didn't tell me?"

"He asked me not to." Frankie smiled widened. "I really do try to be trustworthy."

"You stole Matt's computer. You told him about the dog. You pierced your belly button without telling your folks. You're the least trustworthy person I know." Emma grabbed her coat from the hook and sent Torie and Frankie's coats tumbling to the floor. She picked up her pillow and sleeping bag too and threw everything onto Frankie's bed in the other room. This was the last straw. She was definitely moving back to Dallas.

Torie and Frankie mutely sat at the table and watched Emma run around the room like a chicken with her head cut off. She stopped short. "Could the two of you help me?"

"What do you want us to do?" Torie said.

"We need to erase any evidence of my existence so Matt won't suspect I've been here."

Frankie played with a lock of her hair as if she had nothing better to do. "You are one of my best friends, Emma, and I love you, but it's time you faced your demons."

"Face my demons? I'm just trying to tidy up a little." Emma growled softly. She was going to get no help from her friends. Thank goodness there was a blizzard outside. It would take Matt at least an extra minute to get to the door.

Three, *three* of Aunt Gwen's mugs sat upside down on the drying rack next to the sink. Emma grabbed them in one swift motion. Unfortunately, the knock at the door startled her, and she dropped the one that said, "I love my Dallas." Was this a sign or just an unfortunate accident? She didn't have time to find out because Frankie practically sprinted for the door. Some friend she was turning out to be.

With the two surviving mugs in hand, Emma hurtled herself into Frankie's room. Her haste sent her sprawling onto Frankie's bed head first. She grunted as she fell on the mugs and they dug into her ribcage. Frankie liked a firm mattress.

She heard the door open and Matt's silky voice standing on the porch. Well, Matt's voice wasn't standing on the porch, but Matt was, and her heart ran its own race inside her chest.

Torie poked her head into Frankie's room. "It's Matt," she whispered, as if no one had guessed who had come for a visit.

"Get rid of him," Emma whispered back with her face buried in Frankie's bedspread and her arm slung over her sleeping bag. She released her grip on the mugs and pushed herself to a sitting position. "Tell him I'm unavailable."

Torie pressed her lips together. "I'm not going to lie."

"It isn't a lie. I *am* unavailable. I'm busy packing for Dallas."

Torie disappeared, and for one tense moment, Emma couldn't hear one thing in the next room. No talking, no muted whispers, no doors slamming, or face slapping. Not even Heber had anything to say about a stranger at his door. Wasn't this the perfect moment for him to bark like a dinosaur and scare

Matt away? Emma held her breath. What were they doing in there? Practicing their sign language?

She squealed like a chicken when Matt appeared at the bedroom door, as if Frankie had told him he was welcome to search the entire house. Of course, searching Frankie's entire house didn't take very long.

"Frankie said it was okay to come in," Matt said.

It wasn't fair. Matt was even better looking in person than in that picture she'd used in her PowerPoint presentation. How could she be expected to keep her wits and have a reasonable conversation? She grabbed her sleeping bag and wrapped her arms around it. It made a pretty good shield. "I was just packing up some stuff."

He stepped into the room and closed the door behind him. If Emma tried to make a run for the bathroom, he'd be able to ambush her before she even set foot on the floor. She opted to stay on the bed. It was like a game of Lava Monster. If her feet never touched the floor, she'd be safe.

She had a sneaking suspicion that Lava Monster game wasn't real.

"I need to go sweep the floor," she said.

He cocked his perfectly shaped eyebrow.

"I broke a mug. I should sweep it up before someone cuts their foot," she said.

A muffled voice came through the crack under the door. "I'll do it."

Emma gave Matt a weak smile. "Thanks, Frankie." She was out of excuses, and she was going to short-sheet Frankie's bed every day for a month.

He stared at her for what seemed like three days. "We missed you at Cement Awareness Week tonight."

"Oh, that. Well. Max Cooper practiced his presentation for me when I stayed at his house. I gave him some pointers."

323

Matt curled one side of his mouth. "He didn't use them."

"I was afraid he wouldn't. He takes his cement very seriously."

Matt stared at Emma as if he was memorizing her face. "How have you been?"

She didn't need the torture. "Look, Matt, I know...your sense of honor and all that, but I really want you to have the house. I don't want to talk about it anymore. I don't want you to feel like you have to give me half. Uncle Harvey owed it to you. I want you to have it. No hard feelings."

He attempted a carefree smile, but he was very bad at pretending. "I know about the dog."

Emma drew in a breath. Really? He wanted to talk about the dog? "Look, Matt, your sense of honor and all that...just let it go. We don't have to bring that up ever again." She'd never be bringing it up because she was going back to Dallas and never expected to speak to him again.

"You did a very unselfish thing for Boone. I can't just let it go."

Emma blew an imaginary strand of hair from her eyes. "Frankie swore with a blood oath she wouldn't tell. If you don't forget what you know, she'll probably be in a car accident or get a paper cut every day for the rest of her life."

Now his smile was more natural, less forced. "I was so wrong about you in the beginning. I thought you were shallow and high maintenance."

Emma squeezed the sleeping bag closer. "I am high maintenance. And snotty."

She didn't convince him to lose that smile. "You took the blame for shooting the dog. I can't even begin to understand why you would do such a thing for someone you didn't know that well."

"Boone was already in trouble up to his eyeballs. I couldn't stand by and watch him drown."

"You're one of the few people who would have done something like that." His words were like sticky, warm chocolate. "I have never known anyone with such a good heart."

"It was an accident, and Boone might have gone to jail. Hob wouldn't have locked me up. I was his best friend's niece and an out-of-towner. And it was my first offense. I knew I could handle the town's anger. They wouldn't have been kind to Boone."

Matt frowned. "As I remember, we were all pretty mean, but you took the blame anyway. You cared more about Boone than yourself." He frowned as if he wanted to scold her. "It seems to be a pattern with you."

"It was a one-time event, and everybody's past it. You've got to let these things go, Matt."

Matt sat on the edge of the bed and laid a warm hand over her bare foot. She shivered just a little. "Emma, I know about my dad."

"What about him?"

"I know he stole my money. I accused Harvey unjustly, and I'm sorry."

A lump lodged in Emma's throat. She wasn't good at playing dumb, but how could he know? Was he just faking it to get her to confess? "What...what are you talking about?"

He rubbed his thumb across the top of her foot. She had no idea what a sensitive part of her body that was until just now. "My mom told me about the road trip and the PowerPoint presentation. She said Dad owned up to everything."

Emma held perfectly still. "Why would she do that?"

"She finally decided to treat me like an adult."

Emma lowered her eyes and stared at her foot. Matt's hand was still there. It was a strong hand, with long, thin fingers. "I can't believe she told you. Are you okay? I'm so sorry, Matt. We didn't want you to find out."

"Mom changed her mind. She could see it was killing me not being with you." He wrapped his fingers around her arch, apparently not caring she'd been walking around barefoot all day. Who knew what diseases were lurking on the bottom of her foot? "I'm not going to lie. I feel terrible about my dad, but I feel even worse that you thought carrying this secret would keep me from getting hurt. I didn't ask you to do that, and I didn't want it. My dad hasn't really been a part of my life for years. I can let him go, but it would crush me if I lost you. Do you understand? *It would crush me.*"

Emma wanted to believe that so badly it hurt. "It would?"

Matt scooted closer to her on the bed, moving a mug out of the way to sit next to her. He paused to examine the mug before setting it aside. "What is this?"

"It's the entire Declaration of Independence on a mug. Uncle Harvey liked to read it occasionally."

"Look, Emma. Nothing is more important...okay...I'm always saying the wrong thing." He crossed his legs and turned to face her. She was still sitting with her legs out in front of her, wishing he'd touch her feet again, so he was sort of talking to the side of her head. "Will you just listen, and if I say the wrong thing, can you just pretend I said the right thing?"

With breathtaking clarity, she realized she'd give Matt every chance he asked for. A thousand chances. A million chances. Even if he said the wrong thing every time he opened his mouth—which he usually did. "You said you'd be crushed."

He nodded. "Nothing and no one is more important to me than you are. I can't live without you, and that is the honest truth."

"Honest and truth are redundant."

"Yes, they are." He took her hand, and that felt even better than when he'd caressed her foot. "Emma, I'm sorry about all those things I said about the house and your uncle and you. Please let me take them back. I want you to have the house—I should have offered it to you weeks ago. It's rightfully yours, and it's done nothing but come between us."

"It's not the house's fault."

"No. It's my fault. I've been stubborn and angry and really stupid."

"And pigheaded," Emma added.

"Pigheaded and stubborn are synonyms," Matt said, his eyes dancing with amusement.

"I was using it for emphasis." Emma's heart galloped around her chest like a spooked horse. She'd made some very unfair assumptions about Matt when she met him. Just because a guy wore flannel didn't mean he didn't know what a synonym was. Just because a guy drove a Ford truck didn't mean she couldn't fall in love with him.

He caressed her hand with his calloused fingers. It was a pleasant, scratchy sensation. "Can you ever forgive me, Emma? Can you ever love me? Because I love you down to my bones, and I will shrivel up and die if you don't love me back."

Emma crossed her legs and turned to face him. The mug between the bed and her bottom didn't even bother her. She leaned closer and put a hand on either side of his face. He relaxed like putty at her touch. "I have a confession to make. I love you more than I ever loved Zac Efron or Orlando Bloom. I love you more than bunny slippers, thimbles, and the color pink."

His lips twitched. "More than an entire color?"

"I love you more than blue and purple and Bronco orange —especially Bronco orange. And, Matt," she paused for maximum emphasis, "I love you more than Luke loves Lorelai Gilmore. Way more. Will you marry me?"

Matt smiled wide enough to show all his teeth. He didn't have one cavity. He wrapped his arms around her and pulled her in for a kiss. They were both flexible enough to bend forward with their legs crossed and their knees touching and still manage to get their lips to meet.

The kiss was glorious and uncomfortable at the same time, especially with that mug digging into her gluteus maximus. Matt had the good sense to pull her off the bed and onto her feet, where he promptly got very close and kissed her until she couldn't think straight. She floated off the ground, and not even the lava monsters could get her.

Matt pulled his lips away from hers. "Yes," he said, before kissing her again and making her forget all the other guys she had ever known, including that one guy in that one movie about a high school musical.

Wait.

Matt had said yes. What was the question?

She tightened her grip around his neck, practically strangling him in the process. Did he really want to marry her? Because she really wanted to marry him. Really. Really. Bad.

She had to know for sure. Separating her lips from his, she kept her vice grip around his neck, just in case she had to apply a chokehold in the near future. "Were you just caught up in the heat of the moment, or did you really just say yes to my marriage proposal?"

His laughter was deep and spontaneous. "Emma, I've wanted to propose for weeks. Of course I want to marry you."

Emma squealed in delight. She heard Frankie and Torie's muffled squealing in the other room as well. There was also a lot of jumping up and down going on out there. It was either her two best friends or Heber doing a doggy dance. Somebody needed a lecture on the evils of eavesdropping, but Emma wasn't the one to give it. She'd done her fair share of eavesdropping in the last three months.

Matt kissed her swiftly on the lips. "We can drive down to Vegas and get married in the morning. Doesn't that sound fun?"

"My mom and dad will totally freak out if I don't invite them to my wedding. Then they'd take the first plane up here and kill me."

Matt slumped his shoulders. "They could meet us in Las Vegas."

"Are you kidding? I'm an only child. This is the moment my parents have been dreaming of since my first day of kindergarten."

"We want to come too," Torie called from the next room.

"See?" Emma said. "We've got to plan invitations, bridesmaids' dresses, finger sandwiches, and a color scheme."

Matt furrowed his brow. "How long will that take?"

"Months," Frankie said from the other side of the door.

Matt looked more than a little distressed. "How long will it be if we cut out the finger sandwiches?"

Emma giggled. "Any wedding planner worth her salt could do it in twenty weeks."

"I volunteer!" Torie yelled.

Matt stepped toward the door. "That's getting really annoying, you two." Without warning, he opened the door, and Frankie and Torie toppled into the room. They'd been pressing their ears firmly to the door. "Have you no shame?" he said.

"You can hear better if you lie on the floor and listen at the crack," Emma said. "But your cheek gets dusty."

Torie made a face. "I tried that, but Heber kept licking me." She gave Emma a hug. "This is the best day ever."

Frankie smiled as if she had no choice. "I had a feeling about you two."

Emma couldn't stand to be away from Matt for long. She slid next to him and grabbed his hand. "He wants to marry me."

Matt smiled down at her and squeezed her fingers. She almost fainted she was so happy. "So, how soon can we get married?" he said.

Emma looked at Torie. "How fast can you plan a wedding?"

Torie caught her bottom lips between her teeth. "How fancy do you want it? I can't do uber-fancy in less than ten weeks. 'Casual and low-key' I can do in six."

Matt nodded vigorously. "I like casual and low key."

"Do you want fancy or casual, Emma?"

Emma gave Matt a pained expression. "I really want fancy."

Matt groaned.

"And," Emma said, "I've always dreamed of an outdoor wedding with baby's breath and little white lights in the trees."

"It's not warm enough for an outdoor wedding in Idaho until at least June." Torie looked at the ceiling and counted something in her head. "That's fourteen weeks. Better say fifteen to be safe."

Matt groaned again.

Torie got more excited as Matt seemed more discouraged. "I can plan as fancy a wedding as you want in fifteen weeks. Little white lights and lace everywhere. I'll ask Lucille to help. She's amazing. Your wedding could be exactly like Bella's in *Twilight*." Torie glanced at Matt. "But without the vampires."

Emma didn't want to disappoint Matt, but it sounded like exactly what she wanted. "That would be perfect."

Matt perked up considerably. "It's warm in Dallas. We could fly down there and get married outdoors next week."

Torie shook her head. "I can't plan even a casual wedding out of state in less than ten weeks."

"I don't want to get married in Dallas," Emma said. "Hardly any of my Dandelion Meadows friends would be able to come. Teancum gave me his hair. Max let me hide my truck in his barn. Lucille helped me design the Desert Storm display. I'm inviting all of them."

Matt slid his arm around Emma and pulled her close. "I guess I'd better get busy finding a job in Dallas. The good news is there are several oil companies down there that will hire a geologist."

Emma felt as if her heart would burst like a balloon. She gave Matt a big kiss. "You're not moving to Dallas. I'm staying in Dandelion Meadows."

"Absolutely not. You're not giving up your career for me. I can be a geologist anywhere."

How could she not love Matt Matthews? He was kind and thoughtful and willing to give it all up for her. "I'm not going back to Dallas," she said, though she'd made the decision only about a minute ago. "I want to be here with you."

Matt frowned. "Are you sure?"

"I was meant to be an artist, not a financial planner. As long as I have a sturdy table and paper and pencil, it doesn't matter where I live." She couldn't resist kissing that concerned look off his face. "I want to live in Dandelion Meadows. Then you can keep panning for gold, or whatever it is you do all day."

He laughed, and the pure happiness of the sound left Emma breathless. "Yep. Panning for gold is going to pay off big time."

CHAPTER

TWENTY

M att pounded the "For Sale" sign into the ground with a very large mallet. The ground was still frozen, and nothing but brute force would anchor that sign firmly in place. Emma stood back and enjoyed the sight of Matt's biceps straining under his red flannel shirt.

Matt pressed his hand against the sign and tried to wiggle it back and forth. It held strong. "It's in there pretty good."

"We'll have to pull it out with your truck and a sturdy chain." Emma smiled at the prospect of Matt tearing that sign out of the ground with his bare hands. Maybe she could convince him to do it without a shirt on.

They had decided to sell Uncle Harvey's house. Well, *Emma* had made the decision. Matt had insisted it was her house and her decision. Emma rested her elbow on the "For Sale" sign and gazed at Uncle Harvey's blue house surrounded by acres of snow. She loved this house. It held a thousand good memories for her, but she and Matt needed to make a fresh start somewhere else. She didn't want Matt to feel like a guest in his own house, and neither of them wanted to repaint the whole thing, minus the pink bedroom.

It was a win-win.

Matt put his coat back on and wrapped his arms around Emma, but there wasn't much closeness going on between Matt's thick coat and Uncle Harvey's oversized one. Matt sighed. "The day after we're married, I'm buying you a new coat."

She settled into his embrace as if he was her missing piece. They fit so nicely together. "We're getting married in June. I won't need a coat by then."

"There'll be a lot of good sales."

They both looked east as an old maroon Cadillac inched down the road. Johnny Cleaver was a very cautious driver, and he never seemed to be in a hurry to go anywhere.

"Are there more papers we need to sign?" Matt said, watching the boat of a car come closer.

Emma shook her head. "I don't think so."

Johnny pulled up next to the "For Sale" sign, turned off the car, and slid out from behind the steering wheel. He shut his door behind him then locked his car manually with the key. Why anyone in Dandelion Meadows locked their car was a mystery. Even Emma had stopped locking things. Maybe Johnny had seen too much as an attorney on the mean streets of Dandelion Meadows.

Johnny gave the "For Sale" sign a stiff pat, testing it to see if it was good and tight. "Good morning, Emma. Good morning, Matt. You finally put the house up."

"Yeah," Matt said, tightening his arms around Emma, as if to make sure it was still what she wanted to do.

Emma smiled up at him. "We're thinking of building at the end of Ktunaxa Street. Althea Mills said she'd sell us a piece of her pasture, and then we'll be close to the park and the museum."

"Marian can set you up with a mortgage," Johnny said. "It's one of her new services. And crocheting. She crochets dishrags, two for ten dollars."

Matt smiled. "We'll keep that in mind."

Johnny pulled an envelope out of his pocket and handed it to Emma. "This is for you."

"For me?"

"I felt real bad about not being able to win the house for you."

Emma drew her brows together. "It was a hard case, but it's all settled now. There's nothing for you to feel bad about."

Johnny nodded. "Be that as it may, I still felt bad about it. A good lawyer should win cases, and I let you down. I should have won the house for you. Matt didn't even have a lawyer."

"Levi was giving me legal advice." Matt sounded a little defensive.

Emma nearly laughed out loud. For some reason, having no lawyer had been a sore spot for Matt.

Johnny pointed to the envelope. "I felt so guilty, I decided to help you in another way. Open it carefully. You don't want to rip anything."

Emma dragged her fingernail along the top of the envelope then pulled out the contents. It was a check. "Johnny, you don't need to give me any money."

"I didn't," Johnny said.

Emma looked, really looked, at the check, and her eyes nearly popped out of her head. "But...this is..." The check was written out to her in the amount of $126,000 payable from her financial planning firm in Dallas. Her heart started kicking her ribs. "I don't understand." She showed the check to Matt. He gasped.

Johnny smiled as if he was very pleased with himself. "Marian told me what happened at your job. It all sounded pretty fishy, so I flew down there to find out for myself."

"You went to Dallas?" Yes, he had. He had told Emma he'd seen the JFK Memorial.

Johnny pulled his scarf tighter around his neck. "They underestimated me. They always underestimate us hayseeds. But that was good. They tend to ignore you when they think you're stupid."

Matt smoothed the check in his fingers. "But how did you get this money?"

"Emma's boss was setting up fake accounts to get the big commissions. He was also signing documents without client authorization. When the SEC started snooping around, he blamed it on Emma and fired her."

Emma huffed out a breath. "He framed me?"

Johnny nodded. "I told your company I was going to sue for lost wages and damaged reputation. Of course they settled. I hope you don't mind, but I took five thousand dollars as my fee. It paid for my plane tickets and hotels, and I took Marian to the Mansion Restaurant. It's beyond fancy. A waiter hovers around your table the whole meal in case you need a straw or something."

Emma pressed her fist to her heart, just in case it tried to burst out of her chest. Was she dreaming? "I know what the customary attorney fees are for something like this. You'll be getting a lot more from me as soon as I deposit this check."

Johnny swatted away her suggestion. "It was my pleasure. I got to take Marian on an early anniversary trip."

"Johnny, I can't thank you enough. This is...this is more than I could ever have hoped for." Emma gave Matt a warm smile. "Now we can help your brothers with the ranch."

Matt gave her the check. "I won't take your money."

Emma got on her tiptoes and gave him a peck on the cheek. "Once we're married, it's *our* money. Clay and Holt will be just as much my family as they are yours, and I want to help."

"But, Emma, people will think I married you for your money."

"I'm a witness," Johnny said. "You were engaged before you knew anything about the money."

Emma squeezed Matt's arm. "See?"

Johnny adjusted the hat on his head. "Although people will still say you married her for the house. It's a real good house."

Matt smiled in spite of himself. "It *is* a real good house."

Emma slid the check into Matt's coat pocket. "Take the money. It's given with all my love."

His lips twitched upward. "How can I refuse?" He leaned down and kissed her on the lips right in front of Johnny Cleaver, town barber and crackerjack attorney.

Johnny reached into his pocket and retrieved his keys. "Much as I'd like to stand out here in the cold for another three hours, I've got a haircut in fifteen minutes. Don't spend all that money in one place. I recommend putting it in a REIT. Harvey always said that was a good return on your investment."

Emma and Matt met eyes and laughed nervously. They weren't likely to invest in a REIT any time soon. Holding onto each other tightly, they watched Johnny drive away. "We didn't need that money," Matt said.

"I know."

"I am perfectly, wildly happy without it."

Emma snuggled her face into his great-smelling coat and smiled. "But it doesn't make things worse."

Matt chuckled. "We don't need it to be happy, but I'm not giving it back."

A Chevy Suburban came down the road toward them going a lot faster than Johnny Cleaver ever drove.

"It must be visiting day," Emma said.

"I didn't get the memo."

LaVerle Pratt's Suburban was old, like almost every other vehicle in Dandelion Meadows. People around here thought you were pretentious if you bought a new car, especially when the old one still ran just fine.

LaVerle's vehicle was one of five Suburbans still in existence on the streets of Dandelion Meadows. Everybody liked Suburbans. They guzzled gas, but they could hold eight people and three bales of hay at the same time. And who didn't need more room for hay?

LaVerle parked his Suburban and jumped out as if he'd been called in on an emergency. He practically ran at Emma and Matt then seemed to think better of his haste. He folded his arms and strolled forward, as if trying to perfect the art of appearing casual. But his agitation was plainly written across his face, and the long hair of his comb-over sat plastered across his forehead. A cigarette dangled from his mouth. He pulled it from between his lips and tossed it into the snow.

What would happen when the snow melted and someone found a cigarette butt in Emma's yard? Would they think she was a hypocrite? She was, after all, in charge of the Stop Smoking booth for the Dandelion Jelly Festival.

She'd have to come out later and collect it—with gloves and a hazmat suit, just to be safe.

"How ya doing, Emma?"

"I'm fine, LaVerle. How are you?" She asked the question as a courtesy, because it was obvious how LaVerle was. He looked like a muskrat stuck in a trap, nervous and agitated.

Nervous and *agitated* were synonyms.

Oh, well. There was no better way to describe LaVerle at this moment. Nervous and agitated, with his lungs full of smoke and in sore need of a haircut.

LaVerle wore those thick, fur-lined boots that made it hard to drive but kept your feet warm down to a hundred below zero. He shifted from one foot to the other. "Well, you see. Well, you see, there's a problem." He tapped the "For Sale" sign with the palm of his hand.

Still nice and sturdy.

"You see, I see you put the house up for sell. Well, you see, here's the thing. You can't sell it."

Emma glanced at Matt. "Why not?"

LaVerle shuffled his boots in the snow. "Here's the thing." He lowered his voice and leaned in, obviously about to tell them a great secret. Emma didn't know if she could handle another great secret in her lifetime. "You see, Harvey told me that he told you not to sell the house."

"That's true," Emma said, "but we decided it would be all right. Under the circumstances, I think it's what Uncle Harvey would have wanted."

LaVerle shook his head so adamantly, the long hair plastered to his forehead came loose and fell over his eyes. He pushed it back onto the top of his head. "No." He glanced behind him, just in case someone had decided to sneak up on them and listen in on their strange conversation. "You see, Harvey couldn't bear the thought of Gwen being all the way across town at that cemetery. He asked me to help him bury her here."

Emma was momentarily speechless. What in the world?

Fortunately, Matt recovered more quickly than she did. "You say Gwen is buried here?" He pointed to the ground at his feet.

LaVerle clasped his hands together. "Well, not right here. About thirty feet behind the house. Then when Harvey died, I buried him next to Gwen."

Emma thought her throat might close off. "You...you buried my aunt and uncle in the backyard?"

LaVerle swiped his hand across his mouth. "It was Harvey's last wish."

"But why?"

"He was always a good friend to me," LaVerle said, as if that explained everything. "He served as my campaign manager three times, and we won twice. I think he always felt kind of bad he couldn't win it for me the last time."

Matt's puzzlement was chiseled into his face. "So there are two dead bodies in the backyard?"

LaVerle wiped the sweat from his forehead, upsetting the balance of his hair. It flopped over his ear. "I'm telling you this because Harvey was a good friend. The thing is, in Dandelion Meadows it's illegal to bury a body in your yard."

"So who's breaking the law? You or us?" Matt said.

LaVerle pushed his glasses up his nose. "Yes."

Matt thought about that for a minute. With a pained look on his face, he turned to Emma. "I've always liked this house."

Emma swallowed hard. "It has cherrywood doors."

"And a pink bedroom."

"And seventeen garden gnomes."

And two bodies buried in the backyard.

Maybe they should put *that* in the sales flyer.

GET YOUR FREE BOOK

Get your free ebook copy of *Dandelion Meadows Christmas Kisses!*

To download ***Dandelion Meadows Christmas Kisses***, visit jenniferbeckstrand.com

TO MY READERS

Thank you for reading! If you loved *Dandelion Meadows*, could you help spread the word about it? Reviews on **Amazon**, **Goodreads**, and **Bookbub** not only help us authors but help other readers find our books. And please, tell your friends if you liked my book. Word of mouth is invaluable!

For updates on new releases, giveaways, and my other books, please sign up for my email newsletter on my website. You'll get a free copy of ***Dandelion Meadows Christmas Kisses*** just for signing up! Don't miss the latest adventures of LaVerle, Ladasha, and a guy named Jack with a brand new truck.

Be sure to join my Facebook group, where I interview a sweet or inspirational romance fiction author every other Wednesday night. You might just discover a new favorite book.

Be sure to stop by my Facebook page and check out all the news and posts there. I have a great group of readers, and we have a lot of fun!

Thank you for being such amazing readers and fans. I wouldn't be where I am without you!

Jennifer Beckstrand

ABOUT THE AUTHOR

Jennifer Beckstrand is the USA Today and #1 Amazon bestselling romance author of *The Matchmakers of Huckleberry Hill* series, *The Honeybee Sisters* series, *The Petersheim Brothers* series and *The Amish Quiltmaker* series for Kensington Books. *Huckleberry Summer* and *Home on Huckleberry Hill* were both nominated for the RITA® Award from Romance Writers of America.

Dandelion Meadows is her first sweet small-town romance, set in a charming community in Idaho filled with quirky characters and fresh mountain air.

Jennifer has written thirty-eight Amish romances, three sweet romantic Westerns, two sweet contemporaries, and the nonfiction book *Big Ideas*. Jennifer is a member of ACFW, FHL

Christian Writers, and is represented by Nicole Resciniti of the Seymour Agency.

She and her husband have been married forty years, and she has six children and eleven adorable grandchildren, whom she spoils rotten.

ALSO BY JENNIFER BECKSTRAND

Cowboys of the Butterfly Ranch

Rachel and Riley

Maggie and Max

Jessie and James

Anson and Abigail (coming 2025)

Dandelion Meadows

Dandelion Meadows

Dandelion Meadows Christmas Kisses (part of *Six Kisses for Christmas*)

Larkspur Ranch (coming 2025)

Apple Lake Amish

Kate's Song

Rebecca's Rose

Miriam's Quilt

The Matchmakers of Huckleberry Hill

Huckleberry Hill

Huckleberry Summer

Huckleberry Christmas

Huckleberry Spring

Huckleberry Harvest

Huckleberry Hearts

Return to Huckleberry Hill

Courtship on Huckleberry Hill

Home on Huckleberry Hill

First Christmas on Huckleberry Hill

A Peanut Butter Christmas (A Petersheim Brothers Romance) in *Amish Christmas Miracles*

Huckleberry Hill Secret Santa (A Huckleberry Hill Romance) in *More Amish Christmas Miracles*

Ivy's New Beginning (An Amish Quiltmaker Romance) in *Amish Spring Romance*

Peanut Butter Christmas Cookies (A Petersheim Brothers Romance) in *Amish Christmas Cookie Tour*

Nonfiction

Big Ideas

To download a free ebook copy of *Dandelion Meadows Christmas Kisses*, visit JenniferBeckstrand.com.